D0563336

Also by Bethenny Frankel

A Place of Yes
The Skinnygirl Dish
Naturally Thin

skinnydipping

BETHENNY FRANKEL

with Eve Adamson

A TOUCHSTONE BOOK

Published by Simon & Schuster

New York London Toronto Sydney New Delhi

Touchstone
A Division of Simon & Schuster, Inc.
1230 Avenue of the Americas
New York, NY 10020

This book is a work of fiction. Names, characters, places, and incidents either
are products of the author's imagination or are used fictitiously. Any resemblance
to actual events or locales or persons, living or dead, is entirely coincidental.

Copyright © 2012 by BB Endeavors, LLC

All rights reserved, including the right to reproduce this book or
portions thereof in any form whatsoever. For information address
Touchstone Subsidiary Rights Department,
1230 Avenue of the Americas, New York, NY 10020.

First Touchstone trade paperback edition December 2012

TOUCHSTONE and colophon are registered trademarks of Simon & Schuster, Inc.

For information about special discounts for bulk purchases,
please contact Simon & Schuster Special Sales at
1-866-506-1949 or business@simonandschuster.com.

The Simon & Schuster Speakers Bureau can bring authors to your live event.
For more information or to book an event contact the
Simon & Schuster Speakers Bureau at 1-866-248-3049
or visit our website at www.simonspeakers.com.

Designed by Joy O'Meara

Manufactured in the United States of America

1   3   5   7   9   10   8   6   4   2

The Library of Congress has cataloged the hardcover edition as follows:
Frankel, Bethenny.
Skinnydipping : a novel / Bethenny Frankel ;
with Eve Adamson. — 1st Touchstone hardcover ed.
    p.   cm.
"A Touchstone book."
I. Adamson, Eve.   II. Title.
PS3606.R3856S58 2012
813'.6—dc23
2012005941

ISBN 978-1-4516-6737-0
ISBN 978-1-4516-6738-7 (pbk)
ISBN 978-1-4516-6743-1 (ebook)

This book is dedicated to our imagination. Without it, we wouldn't be able to travel to places we never thought we could go, to dream about things that we never thought we could do, and to feel the feeling of pure freedom. Let your imagination run wild. It may take you somewhere so incredible that you can hardly believe it is true.

skinnydipping

prologue

"Where are the stilt walkers? *Has anybody seen the stilt walkers?*"

I'm calm, but I can hear the shrillness creeping into my voice as I picture the absolute disaster that will result if Andy doesn't show up soon with the damn stilts and the people to put on top of them. The stilt walkers are essential—the dramatic cherry on top of the charity carnival. The finale of *Domestic Goddess,* and the deciding factor in the rest of my life. And isn't that typical? You raise $80,000 for charity, you erect a forty-foot tent practically single-handedly, you hire and coordinate seventy-five employees, and you produce the whole goddamn spectacle, and then your life hangs in the balance because of a couple of clowns on sticks. Meanwhile, the cameras are rolling and America is watching. My failure would make just as good TV as my success, so nobody cares whether I win or not. Nobody but me. And this is just what Sybil Hunter expects. I *have* to make this work.

Somebody runs past pushing a popcorn cart that dribbles grease along the floor. The amplifier blares circus music, then cuts out with a crackling pop. A chunky, squinting boy in thick glasses grabs my arm—Jerome, the facility manager's assistant I roped into helping me. He looks barely twelve years old. "The sno-cone machine is broken, one of the ponies is sick, and somebody left the banner on the floor and it got trampled," he says, pushing up his glasses nervously.

Easy, Faith. Easy. You've done this before. I'd handled events bigger than this, and disasters bigger than this, too. My eyes are fixed on the wide double doors standing open across the warehouse space, where Sybil Hunter stands, backlit, imposing, the evil overlord ready to reign terror and destruction on the final challenge of what has come to be, in my mind, a sell-your-soul-to-the-devil concept: reality television. I imagine her smirk, her lust for my failure. I'm barely noticing the cameras rotating around in front of us, though part of me recognizes that my alarm is being recorded for national consumption. Tears are welling up, but I bite my lip hard, reminding myself what Sybil told me during the middle of the season, when my team lost a challenge and turned on me, the team leader. "A woman who shows weakness in this business won't last long."

Suck it up, Faith. This is it. Keep your eye on the prize. With a last glance at Sybil's Hitchcockian outline, I turn to the pimply kid waiting for instructions. They come out of me like machine-gun fire: "Call the vendor and demand another sno-cone maker within forty-five minutes. Get the sick pony out of here, call a vet, call the rodeo, whatever it takes. Repair the banner—just make it look good. And for God's sake, get Andy and Jodi Sue over here *now*! I need my fucking team."

He nods and runs off. I stare at my clipboard. The list of unchecked items is three times longer than the list of checked items. I persuade a man with a mop to clean up the grease that's trailing the popcorn machine. My eyes dart over the list, trying to prioritize at warp speed. Suddenly, Jodi Sue, eliminated contestant and disgruntled team member, is in front of me.

"I can't find Andy," she says in her squeaky voice, her cleavage even more evident and elevated than usual in a bright yellow wrap dress with a plunged neckline. "I finished the caramel apples, the cotton candy machine looks great with the neon, and the programs were just delivered and they're perfect."

"Show me," I demand. She holds out one and I grab it. The glossy, oversized program has saturated carnival colors, balloons, clowns, and a Ferris wheel on the cover. Good, very good.

"But Andy's still MIA," she adds, shrugging.

"Where the hell is he? What could he possibly be doing with five stilt walkers in the middle of Manhattan?"

"I really don't know," she says, shrugging again. "He won't answer his cell phone."

"This is great. Just great. This is Shari Jacobs's lucky day," I mutter. I could just imagine Sybil Hunter fawning over my ex-BFF/archenemy and fellow finalist, as she pulled off her final challenge with typical high-rent perfection. I get a carnival, and she gets a baby shower for Sybil's pregnant cousin. *A fucking baby shower.* I can just see the fondant baby bootie cupcakes and sterling silver rattle party favors and pink champagne. They'll all act like best friends, trying to impress each other with how rich their husbands are.

And here I am, sweating it out, pits soaked, with swamp crotch, trying not to have an anxiety attack, and running on fumes both on this warped excuse for a television show and in my life, with just eighty-seven dollars in my bank account and a team that hates me. Everything depends on an out-of-control carnival about to go horribly wrong. I'm so damn close to winning, and I need that prize more than anything, more than anyone else on the show. I just can't bear going back to my so-called normal life.

Now I'm sweating blood to make this event happen, and I can't even get some paid extras on poles to show up—hell, I can't even get my whole *team* to show up.

I look around: total chaos. A group of union guys tries to unroll artificial turf into the same spot where another group is trying to set up the Ferris wheel. A speaker on the sound stage wobbles and topples over with a crash, nearly crushing the woman trying to secure it to the stand. I look at Jodi Sue in despair.

"How are we going to do this?" I say. "How is this even possible?"

"Search me," she says. "It's your challenge. I was eliminated weeks ago, thanks to you, and I wouldn't be here helping you if it wasn't in my contract, because I think you're a bitch." She smiles sweetly.

I'm in this alone. It's a zero-sum game.

"OK, Jodi Sue," I say. "Why don't you just go sit on your ass out of the way and get your cleavage ready for the stilt walkers. They're going to have a great view." Her mouth drops open as I spin away and set off to track down Andy. Because if I don't find those clowns in the next fifteen minutes, I might as well not even show up at the finale. As I storm past Sybil—she stands silently, critically in the doorway with her arms crossed—I can't help myself. "What do you think, Sybil?" I ask. "Are you entertained? Is it everything you hoped to see from me? Because you haven't seen anything yet."

PART ONE

chapter one

W ho do I have to sleep with to get a drink on this plane?"

I called out the request randomly, hopefully, as passengers pushed down the aisle into coach, their suitcases bumping my arm. Some of them raised their eyebrows at me, but I'm used to that. I'm rarely what you would call "appropriate," although what these people around me didn't seem to realize was that tequila is *always* appropriate. I just smiled at them.

Besides, I couldn't contain myself. Just minutes before, I had been sitting at the gate in Kennedy, devastated, trying with every inner resource I had not to break down into tears in front of everyone, and dreading how I would tell my father I'd missed the flight. Getting onto this flight meant everything to me. *Everything.* I'd skipped college graduation to catch this flight, but last night I'd stayed out until four club-hopping with friends I hoped never to see again, celebrating the end of my four-year imprisonment at NYU. I'd gone home with some handsome dark-haired Wall Street trader whom I'd then wrangled into driving me to my apartment, double-parking out front while I ran up-stairs to grab my bag (and pull off last night's sequined halter top and mini skirt in favor of a black jersey dress that didn't wrinkle too badly), then driving me to the airport. Heading toward JFK, I lectured him about how fast to drive and which route to take. He'd dropped me off in front of the terminal, not sure what to do about my tears and hysteria about missing the plane. What was his name again?

Anyway, I'd been too late—or so they'd told me, until the woman at the desk called my name.

"Faith Brightstone, please come to the ticket counter." I was sitting right in front of her, for God's sake. Did she have to use the little microphone?

"Yes? What! I'm here," I said, jumping up and clutching my carry-on with suddenly renewed optimism.

"There's one seat left. Hurry!" She pointed to the door. I sprinted down the jetway, nearly toppling off my sample sale Manolos with the four-inch heels, the ones that had finally tipped my credit card over its $30,000 limit. I rushed breathlessly into the first-class cabin, where a flight attendant with her hair severely restrained in a blonde bun looked me in the eye, and there was that moment when we both knew I didn't really belong in first class. I wondered, self-consciously, if I still smelled like champagne and sex. I pursed my lips to contain any telltale alcohol fumes and hoped the spray of Chanel No. 5 to the crotch had taken care of the rest.

She surveyed me with undisguised condescension, her gaze traveling over my unwashed hair, my slightly puffy face and probably bloodshot eyes, and my rumpled dress, and fixing on my red leather carry-on, the one I'd purchased because I knew it would absolutely meet any airline's carry-on standard. And because it was red, and stood out from the others. "You're going to have to check that, *dear*," she said, smugly.

"What? But it's small! We can squeeze it in, I know we can. Please!" Frantically, I unzipped the front pocket and pulled out the tangle of bras and underwear I'd packed, and stuffed them into my purse. "There. Just let me try to make it fit."

She sighed, barely able to keep from rolling her eyes. "I suppose we could move *this*, and *this*." She spit out the words as she rearranged two other bags in the compartment above that one beautiful empty seat that was about to be mine. She took the carry-on from my hands and jammed it unceremoniously between a silver hardshell Tumi carry-on and a Louis Vuitton tote the color of browned butter. Then she actually wiped her hands on her skirt, as if my bag was covered in cooties. I almost laughed—with relief, because of a slight sense of hysteria I'd been nurturing since I woke up in a panic, and because she was just so mean that it was funny. She turned primly and walked away. Bitch.

One day, I vowed, I would belong in first class, and people would wonder who I was. She'd be kissing my fully-paid-for Manolos.

I threw myself into the seat and sighed with deep contentment. I made it! And now, at last, I could relax. I looked at the man sitting next to me—schlubby, middle-aged, with a thick rectangular mustache. An almost–Tom-Selleck type. He wore an expensive suit and had a pile of scripts on his tray table. I noticed a very nice briefcase under the seat in front of him. I smiled to myself. I was intrigued. It wasn't the standard reading material I usually noticed on planes. I was really on my way to Los Angeles.

So, in that spirit, where was my drink? Wasn't that the whole point of first class?

The woman with the blonde bun walked by, brusquely checking that everyone was following the rules for takeoff. She stopped at our row and told Almost–Tom-Selleck, "Sir, please put your tray table up for takeoff." He moved the scripts to his lap, as if he'd done this a thousand times before. Although I didn't like my odds considering our previous encounter, I decided it couldn't hurt to ask again: "So . . . when do we get those drinks?" I asked her, trying out my best Hollywood smile.

"We'll be serving the drinks momentarily, Miss," she said icily. "Please try to be patient."

I sat back, closed my eyes, and imagined a serious-faced man in some sort of flowing university regalia reading my name in a monotone: "Faith Brightstone." He'd move on to the next name on the list when I didn't appear. And why would I? I'd escaped that place like I'd just broken out of prison, and besides, I had no patience for sitting through the pointless ritual, even if my mother had begged me to attend. "Darling, I just want to see it happen," she'd said over the phone, her words a-slur with her third highball of the afternoon. "Because who would be-leeeve it?"

Nobody thought I would actually graduate, much less on time, but I had surprised them all. I'd always been good at getting by—I could memorize well enough to ace the tests, and I was an expert grade finagler. Plus I had a knack for briefly dating the T.A.s until after the tests were graded. I hadn't exactly been a model student. Once I made it into NYU, I quickly became more interested in partying than studying. I smiled, imagining my college roommate, Samantha, seeing me right now. I know what she'd say. "Faith, only you would avert certain disaster and end up in first class." I would miss her . . . and her fabulous shoe collection.

But I couldn't get out of Manhattan soon enough. I was L.A.-bound, baby. My star was rising. I could feel it. I had fame to chase. Success to score. Moguls to meet, whom I would allow to seduce me. And who knows what else? Movies to make? Sitcoms? High-profile commercials? I was going to take Hollywood by storm, damn it. I would show my mother what to *be-leeeve.*

All I'd ever really wanted out of life was success in my chosen career, and perfect, passionate, eternal love with a hot and preferably independently wealthy soul mate. As I waited, *patiently,* for the drink the airline owed me, I decided I wasn't asking too much of life. I'd been dealt a fairly shitty hand so far, all things considered. Now, it was my turn to cash in. I'd certainly paid on the front end.

The flight attendant reappeared at my elbow with two glasses of something bubbly. Obviously, she'd failed to find any loopholes that would allow her to deny me this simple pleasure. I sipped gratefully. In a sudden impulse of solidarity, I held up my glass to toast my seatmate. He gave me a wry smile and clinked my glass with his. "Hair of the dog," I said. I could feel a killer headache coming on, and I hoped the cheap sparkling wine might head it off. Of course, there was a fifty-fifty chance it would just make it worse.

I held out my hand. "Faith Brightstone. What do you do?"

He smiled a surprisingly attractive, genuine smile and took my hand. He had a firm handshake. But so do I.

"And?" he said.

I paused, confused. "And?" I repeated.

"Aren't you going to ask what I drive?"

"Should I have?"

He laughed. "No. No, you should not have. And I'm Larry Todd. I'm a producer."

"Really? Wow. That is such a coincidence," I said.

"Let me guess. You're an actress?"

"Not yet," I admitted, suddenly embarrassed. I didn't want to sound like just another MAW—the acronym I'd heard for a Model-Actress-Whatever. I didn't want him to discount me as somebody who wasn't anybody. I wanted to sound more intellectual, more *significant* than that. "I'm fresh out of NYU and headed to L.A.," I said, trying to sound smart. "I'm going to give it a try."

"Courageous," he said. "But let me give you some advice, New York. And this is just because you're not from L.A."

"What's that?" I said, my interest piqued. I was ready to learn whatever Larry Todd, producer, had to teach me.

"Every gold digger in L.A. asks 'What do you do?' and the follow-up question, 'What do you drive?' Avoid those two questions and you'll separate from the pack."

I blushed. "That wasn't what I was trying—"

He interrupted me with a laugh and raised his hand. "It's fine. Now you know." He paused, then added, "And as long as I'm dispensing advice, don't *ever* ask anybody's sign. That's just annoying. I hope you never become *that* comfortable in California! There's definitely something to be said for being from somewhere else."

"Thanks, I really appreciate the advice, and I'll take it. I learn fast," I said.

"I'll bet you do." He smiled. "So, an actress. Do you have any experience?"

I couldn't help cringing at the way he said *actress*. It sounded wrong. I didn't feel like I could call myself that yet because I hadn't earned it, but I wanted so badly to claim the title. I was salivating for it.

"I did a little theater in college. But frankly, I couldn't wait to get out. College wasn't really my thing." I paused, wondering if I should continue. "I'm too impatient."

"You want success and you want it now," he said.

"That's so true," I said. "When I was just a high school freshman, I was cast as the understudy for Maria in our school production of *West Side Story,* and I turned it down because I wanted to be the lead, not the understudy."

He smiled in a fatherly way. "Sometimes you have to pay your dues first."

As the plane backed out of the gate and headed toward the runway, I thought about my father. He was probably a little bit older than Larry Todd, but I hadn't seen him in fourteen years, and I'd spoken to him only a handful of times. Ever since my mother left him, taking me to New York with her to marry one of my father's friends and rivals, I felt responsible, like I had left him, too. I'd been four years old.

My mother used to tell me he blamed us both for leaving him. I believed her. I'd spent the last eighteen years trying to make it up to him, but he was a hard-bitten, unforgiving man who hardly ever made himself available to me. When I'd called my father and told him I was moving to L.A., I asked if I could stay with him for a little while, just until I found a place. He'd reluctantly said yes. I'd expected a no, but I had the impression that someone in the background was telling him to let me visit. Probably his latest girlfriend. As far as I knew, he'd had a long string of them, always girls from the racetrack, horse trainers or exercise riders, girls who would be impressed with his reputation as one of the best thoroughbred horse trainers in the business, girls not much older than me. But even if he hadn't exactly said he was going to throw me a welcome party, I still held out hope—maybe he was ready to have a relationship with me. Maybe he had wanted to be convinced. Maybe he had just needed me to come to *him.*

I glanced at Larry. He was handsome, in his way. Maybe a six. Out of habit, I immediately looked for a wedding ring. He wore a thick gold band. He was wealthy, powerful, influential. Married. Money intrigued and excited me, and fame was a dream.

"So, Larry Todd, what exactly do you produce?"

He had been flipping through another script, looking bored and distracted. He tossed it onto his tray table and turned to me. "Have you ever seen *Hollywood & Highland*?"

My eyes widened. "Shut up. You produce that? I watch that every week." He'd suddenly gone from a six to an eight. *Hollywood & Highland* was one of the hottest new primetime soap operas. Everybody I knew watched it. The show followed the personal lives of a group of beautiful people who worked in the sprawling Hollywood & Highland complex of theaters, clubs, restaurants, and the hotel on the corner of Hollywood Boulevard and Highland Avenue in Hollywood, California—right where I was headed. When something big was about to happen on the show, viewers would call in sick from work, skip studying for tests, even cancel dates.

"I'm glad you're a fan," he said.

"You could say that." I said it lightly, shrugging. The wheels were already turning. I wanted in. I belonged in that world. I would fondle Larry Todd's balls in the airplane bathroom right now if it would get me on that show. I'd been with worse-looking men for less compelling reasons than this. This was *Hollywood & Highland*! I felt like I already knew the characters. Brighton, the core character, was a gorgeous, sexy power blonde who ran the hotel. Ethan was the hot bartender at Glo, a trendy Hollywood restaurant. Chloe was the waitress who was always getting into trouble. Isabel booked acts for Dark Side, the nightclub, and Jayden was her philandering husband. I *loved* that show. *OK, Faith. Don't fawn. Don't be a groupie. Connect.* I groped desperately for words. "It's a well-done show. It really is."

"Where are you staying in L.A.?" he asked. I wondered if it was a proposition.

"My father lives there. I'm staying with him until I can afford my own place. He's a horse trainer," I added, hoping he might ask for my father's name so I could impress him. Just for a moment, I imagined sharing my fantasy that we were close, that I was proud of his success, that I somehow had something to do with it. *Faith Brightstone, loving daughter of legendary horse trainer Frank Brightstone, stands behind her father as he is once again honored as Trainer of the Year. Camera bulbs flashing . . .*

"Not Frank Brightstone—is he your father?"

Ah. He knew. "Yep. Dear old dad." It made me feel low, knowing my father didn't give a damn about me. I hadn't done anything for him to be proud of . . . nothing spectacular . . . not yet.

He raised his eyebrows at the edge in my voice, but didn't comment. "I don't know him personally, but I know of him. He trains a horse owned by a friend of mine."

"I'm not surprised," I said. "He knows people." *Not that I'm one of them,* I wanted to say, but bit my tongue. I smiled, brightly. "I haven't seen him in a few years, so it will be a reunion of sorts, I suppose." I suddenly felt the urge to change the subject. "But what about you? Are you coming home from a trip?"

"I have to go to New York every so often. It's usually boring. This has been the most interesting part of my weekend."

I elbowed him lightly, flirtatiously. "Flattery will get you everywhere." *Don't go too far, Faith,* I lectured myself. *Stay on the right side of the line. Don't blow it.*

"You know, you impress me," Larry Todd said, again with that warm genuine smile. "I have a daughter about your age, and I send her money all the time but she never wants to spend any time with me. I don't see too many young women who want to chat with the old guy in the seat next to them."

"You certainly are not old," I said, wondering why my father didn't long for a relationship with me the way Larry Todd wished for more time with his daughter.

He laughed. "I appreciate it. And you'll be just fine in L.A. I can see you've got energy, and dare I say, ambition?" Was I that obvious?

Larry Todd continued, "I'm actually in need of a production assistant right now." He looked me over, thoughtfully, non-lecherously, as if sizing up my potential self, rather than my current self. "It's an entry-level position. You'd be getting coffee and faxing and running messages, but maybe you'd like a chance to see the show from the inside?"

I played it cool. Very cool. "Sounds interesting," I said, taking the magazine out of the seat pocket in front of me, not looking at him so he couldn't see that my head was about to explode just considering the enormity of this opportunity. I wasn't even in the air over California yet, and I'd already scored a job? I was afraid to say anything more, lest I end up groveling on the floor and kissing his black Ferragamo loafers, so I waited a beat, then carefully, nonchalantly, said, "That might be just the sort of thing I'm looking for."

"It isn't acting," he said, looking at me with amusement. Could he tell I was about to burst out of my skin? "But it's a beginning. You would meet a lot of people. Put in the time and the effort, and maybe you'll get a break."

I looked him in the eye and smiled. "I would love the opportunity," I said evenly. A master of self-control. Hell, I'd be the best damn coffee-fetching, faxing, message-running production assistant they'd ever encountered.

He reached into his jacket pocket and pulled out a cream-colored card with his name and phone number in embossed tobacco-brown script—elegant but masculine. "Give me a call, and have my assistant set up an interview. Her name is Mia."

"Thank you," I said. Mental note: Find excellent, affordable gift to send to Mia. "Really. Thank you so much." I touched his shoulder lightly, meaningfully. *"Thank you."*

The hours passed. We chatted, drank, flirted benignly, drank some more, debated about the relative worthlessness of the products in the catalog. Another drink? Why not? He never mentioned his wife, and I never asked. Finally, I closed my eyes and drifted off. My headache began to melt away. The last thing I remember thinking was: *Am I really taking a nap? Me, the insomniac? Auspicious . . .*

When the plane jerked with the release of the landing gear, I bolted awake and looked around, momentarily confused. "I think we're descending," Larry said, orienting me. I looked past him, out the oval window, as the plane dropped lightly through the clouds. Below, I could see the sprawl, and the yellow-gray haze that hung over most of the Southern California coastline.

Together, Larry and I watched the city rise up to meet the wheels of our plane, and I felt like my new life was ascending to meet me. I had arrived, and I was going to make the most of every second.

"Can I get your bag for you?" he asked, as we rose stiffly from our seats. I blushed, realizing he'd certainly watched the flight attendant's treatment of me at the beginning of the flight.

"No, I've got it," I said quickly, yanking the handle to unwedge my bag from between its more aristocratic brethren. I noticed a scratch in the red leather. I would show that flight attendant. When I'm famous someday, she'll be groveling. "I like to travel light."

"To move here? Surely you've got more than this."

"I didn't want to bring anything with me," I said. "I'm starting over. Underwear and a toothbrush." I paused. "Not that I'll need the underwear," I said, giving him a wink.

He laughed. "A toothbrush and a whole new life, then."

We filed out of the plane, and as the crowd jostled us apart, I called out to him. "Good-bye, Larry! It was great to meet you! I'll give Mia a call on Monday!"

"Off to the races," he called, raising his hand in farewell.

chapter two

It wasn't that I expected him to be there to pick me up. We had arranged that I would come to the house, but I still scanned the line of drivers holding up signs, a tiny part of me hoping that one of them would say my name, that maybe he would even surprise me and meet me here. I was always living in a TV movie, hoping for a happy ending. I wasn't going to get one today. Would I ever learn?

I gripped my bag tighter, for courage, and marched resolutely past baggage claim and out to the taxi line. Normally, I would have taken whatever was cheapest—the shuttle, the bus—but this was my big debut in L.A. I wanted a cab.

As I waited my turn, I looked at the palm trees across the road, lined up in front of a white parking garage, and I couldn't help but smile. California. I climbed into the cab. "4191 Alta Drive, Santa Monica," I said in the brusque New York way I always spoke to cab drivers. The driver turned to look at me. He was ancient.

"Yes, Miss. Why in such a hurry? You are in California now. No more New York. You can relax now."

I laughed. "Is my accent so obvious? OK, I'll relax now. I'll enjoy this beautiful day." I leaned back against the seat and looked out the window. Sunny, and not a cloud in the sky. I could get used to this.

"That is very good. People always want to be in a hurry. They want to control everything around them. Even the weather. They say, 'What is the weather today?' The only thing they don't control is themselves, when that is the only thing they *can* control."

"Ha, that's true. I come to L.A. and I get a guru for a cab driver."

He chuckled. He sure was friendly.

"I think the weather here is perfect," I said. "I won't ever try to change it."

"Nothing wrong with the weather. And nothing wrong with you." He nodded firmly, then guided the taxi onto the freeway.

I was definitely not in New York anymore.

The cab merged onto Pacific Coast Highway, then turned into my father's neighborhood. The nearer we were, the more I began to panic.

The cab slowed, creeping along a beautiful residential street with ridiculously large houses, then stopped in front of a gorgeous two-story Spanish-style home with a red-tile roof, balconies in front of the windows, and a set of coral-colored granite steps leading up to the front door, which was hidden behind flowering trees. Classy and private, just like my father.

I paid the cab driver with the last of my cash and stepped out onto the little strip of grass along the curb. I took a deep breath, summoned all the confidence I had left in me, and climbed up the stairs to the front door. I knocked, my heart pounding in my chest. People always used to say I looked just like him when I was a child. I was hoping I still did, so I could feel some kind of ownership, or at least some kind of connection—some biological evidence that I really was his daughter. I knocked again, then tried the handle. The door opened. Cautiously, I peeked inside and called out. "Hello? It's Faith! Is anybody here?"

"Come in!" A deep voice resonated through the atrium from somewhere upstairs. I assumed it was him. He wasn't coming down to meet me? I couldn't help but feel disappointed as I stepped inside, but disappointment quickly turned to awe.

The entryway was covered in a rich, gleaming, honey-colored tile.

An elaborate brass-and-crystal chandelier hung from the cathedral ceiling, which rose to a dramatic peak above the second floor. To my left, an intricately carved dark walnut table held three of the biggest white irises I'd ever seen, surrounding a silver bowl full of white roses.

A marble staircase with an elaborate wrought-iron rail spiraled up to the second level. Beautiful, dark, brooding paintings hung on many of the walls. In front of me, a door led to what looked like a sitting room with a two-story wall of windows looking out over a swimming pool. Behind the staircase, I could just glimpse a long, carved dining room table and another chandelier. I'd never been more impressed in my life. I pretended it belonged to me—that I was home.

My heart fluttered again as I heard someone coming down the spiral stairs. I felt foolish, standing there in my messy cheap traveling dress, and I self-consciously smoothed it over my now-concave stomach, which growled lightly in response. I hadn't eaten since yesterday. I tapped my toe nervously on the tile, and froze when the sound echoed. I looked expectantly at the stairs, waiting for him to appear.

But he didn't appear. Instead, a girl about my age came down the stairs, her face eager. She had long blonde hair pulled back in a high ponytail and she wore pink lip gloss the exact color of her pink satin track shorts, a tight, capped-sleeved white T-shirt cropped short to show her midriff, and white running shoes. She was deeply tanned with muscular legs, great curves, firm arms, and a stomach as concave but a lot more ripped than mine. My hand brushed against my own stomach again, for reassurance. *You could look like that,* I thought, doubting that it was true. I was probably fifteen pounds heavier than she was, and I hated that I immediately put myself in competition with whoever this was. She looked like the type who probably went running every morning at six, before she freshly squeezed her own juice and got her B_{12} shot. I wondered for just a second if my father had some other daughter I didn't know about. It took only a few more seconds for me to recognize that this was, of course, *not* his daughter.

"I'm Brooke," she said, extending a perfectly manicured hand.

"Faith," I said, extending my unmanicured one. Note to self: get manicure *before seeing even one more human being!*

"I'm so happy to meet you finally!" she said, then pulled me into a California embrace. Her silky ponytail brushed my cheek. She smelled like jasmine. Is this how they make girls in California?

"Right!" I said, as if I'd already heard all about her and had anticipated our meeting with her same level of exuberance. "Brooke. So nice to meet you."

"Frank will be down in a bit. We were . . . right in the middle of something." She smiled slyly and winked at me. I felt the urge to retch. "Can I get you something to drink? Iced tea? Perrier? Chardonnay?"

"Chardonnay," I answered, too quickly. But it was urgent. Medicinal.

She laughed. "Like father, like daughter." Her voice sounded like pretty little chiming bells. Was this chick for real? "We just brought home a case from this beautiful little vineyard we visited last weekend."

My father visited vineyards? I remembered him as overweight and never wanting to do anything fun or laid-back. I had heard, though, through the extensive network of people I still knew at the track, that he was now into health and fitness and that he skied. It was hard for me to reconcile this version of my father with the one I remembered and the one so often and so vividly described by my mother. I looked at Brooke. I suppose if he wanted to keep up with girls like this. . . .

"I think you're going to love this wine," she said. She handed me a glass and took a sip out of hers.

I tried not to gulp mine. The wine really was good—buttery with a rich fruity flavor. "Mmmm."

She smiled with relief. "I'm glad you like it!" she said. It amused me to realize that she might actually be trying to impress *me*. I straightened up a bit, wanting to earn her envy. "Your father has quite a collection," she added.

I looked around, noting the streamlined sculptures out by the pool. So this is what he was doing with his money instead of paying child support all those years? Buying wine and art and supporting girls the age of his daughter, but with perfect bodies and blonde hair and un-challenging personalities?

Someone cleared his throat in the doorway and Brooke's pony-tail swung around, narrowly avoiding whipping me in the corneas. I turned slowly, almost afraid, almost overeager. Brooke skipped over to my father and threw her arms around his neck. He sized me up, and I squared my shoulders and gave it to him right back.

"Faith," he said.

"Frank."

My father wore a pale gold silk sports jacket and ivory slacks. He had the olive skin and wide mouth I remembered, but his hairline was receding slightly and the temples were gray. He looked older, more weathered.

I wondered which one of us would speak next. Brooke looked back and forth, as if realizing for the first time that I wasn't going to call him Daddy and he wasn't going to call me Kitten. She turned out to be the one who couldn't take the silence.

"Well!" she said, bouncing nervously into the space between us. "What should we do this afternoon?"

He ignored her and addressed me directly for the first time. "If you're going to live out here, you should probably get outside more," he said, looking me up and down. He walked over to the counter and poured himself a glass of wine. "People are fit out here." He glanced at Brooke, as if she was the proof. Which, I suppose, she was. "And don't wear black. This isn't New York."

I couldn't even respond.

Brooke laughed nervously. "I know, why don't we all go out and have a drink by the pool."

"I'm going to the track," my father said, not looking at either of us. "I'll meet you at the restaurant."

I wanted to say something. I wanted to say, *Did you seriously just call me pale, fat, and badly dressed?* I wanted to say, *Don't you want to sit down and get reacquainted? Show me around the city? Show me around your own house? Ask me why I'm here? Ask me what I've been doing for the past fourteen years? Don't you want to know me at all?*

Instead, I said nothing. I just stared at him, hoping to catch his eye for some kind of connection. Hoping for some sign that he was glad I had come, that we were even related, that he had ever loved me at all. I knew then that this was how it would be. It would only get worse. Startled, Brooke looked at me, then back at my father. "OK, sweetie," she said to my father—an endearment I found almost humorously misapplied to this sullen, sour-faced man. "At seven o'clock?"

"Eight," he said, then turned back toward the stairs. With his back to me, he said, in a monotone, "See you later, Faith."

Brooke and I stood alone in what had seemed, five minutes earlier, like a dream kitchen. Now it seemed more like a mausoleum. I felt like I'd been hit by a bus. That was it? He hadn't seen me in fourteen years, and it was "You're too fat for L.A." and "See you later, Faith"? At least he'd said my name. I hung on to that one little scrap, the only sign that he cared, that he even knew who I was. I felt dizzy.

Brooke must have noticed. She guided me over to the table by the window that viewed the pool. Lowering her voice, she said, "Before you came, you were all he could talk about. He was really excited. He kept telling me how smart you are, how you just graduated from NYU, how he hadn't seen you in so long, and how much he missed you. He was looking at a picture of you just the other day, and he said, 'She has great taste, just like her mother.'"

I looked at her suspiciously. "Really?" I tried to look like I didn't believe her, but I clung to the words, like they were a lifeline.

"Yes, really!" she said, grabbing my forearm. "I was so nervous to meet you! You're Frank Brightstone's *daughter*! I'm so intimidated by you!"

I smiled gratefully, thankful for her efforts, even if I didn't really believe her. At least *she* acknowledged that I was his daughter, even if she was a gold-digging bimbo. I wondered if, when she met my father, she had asked him what he drove.

"Do you want to go out?" she continued, clearly trying to cheer me up. "We could go shopping, and then I know this little bar down by the beach." She paused. "You look like you could use some sun," she said, confidentially. "And maybe a strong drink."

I laughed. She was probably no more than three years older than me, and my father was sleeping with her, and she was so gorgeous that she would outshine me in any public place, but she was the one with my father's credit card and car keys and sympathy. If I ever wanted my father to acknowledge me, I was probably going to have to go through Brooke. Besides, she was my only friend in L.A.

"Brooke, you are absolutely right. I do need some sun. And a strong drink."

"Cool!" she said. "We'll take the convertible."

I was beginning to feel better already.

chapter three

I had a headache that no amount of aspirin was going to fix, but I couldn't lie in bed any longer. I needed to call Larry Todd's office again. Try to get an answer. Try to get my life moving.

I'd been at my father's place three weeks now, and I could tell I was overstaying my welcome. Every morning, I came downstairs to make breakfast, and my father would be sitting at the table. He'd give me that "Are you still here?" look. My mere presence irritated him. When he was home, I was walking on eggshells, but cooking was my consolation. I kept my favorite cookbook of all time, the well-loved, much-used *Domestic Goddess* cookbook by Sybil Hunter and the one actual possession I'd brought with me from New York, in the beautiful kitchen.

Every morning, I swam laps in the pool, trying desperately to work off the extra pounds my father so obviously disapproved of. Every afternoon, Brooke and I had cocktails, and my father made up some excuse not to join us.

I'd enrolled in a week-long bartending class, putting the tuition on a new credit card. I figured, if all else failed, I could be the cool bartender making drinks in a hot club and raking in $500 a night. I could do that. Mixing drinks was fun, and so was bartending school. Every afternoon, I offered to make my father some of the new drinks I'd learned to prepare. He always said no. Scotch and soda or wine were all he would drink.

Still, I'd found a kind of equilibrium, if not a fragile peace, as I adjusted to L.A. and my father's house.

But this weekend . . . oh no. This weekend had been bad. I'd really screwed up, and I had the headache to prove it.

I was going to stay home on Friday night. I really was. I hadn't slept much the night before because I'd been anxious about why Larry Todd hadn't called me back. I kept making up excuses for him. He was traveling. He was in back-to-back meetings. He was trying to find the perfect position for me before he called. And I kept wondering whether I should call again. I didn't want to seem obnoxious or needy, but what if my message had been lost?

Just as I was thinking of crawling into bed to watch bad TV, or maybe try to sleep, Brooke called. She was in a club and I could barely hear her, except for the part when she yelled, "You have to come! Great prospects! Roxbury!"

Although I was dead tired and stressed, I had a hard time saying no to Brooke. To me, she represented the glitz and glamour of Hollywood. She'd once dated one of the band members in Guns N' Roses, and she seemed to know everybody in town. Brooke was the beginning of my journey, the key to my father's heart, and my insider secret to Hollywood's potential.

I had an even harder time saying no to the fantasy of a potential soul mate. She knew she could get me with the lure of "great prospects." I sighed.

"How do I get down there?" I yelled back, even though the house was quiet and I was the only one there. I didn't know where my father was.

"Take the Mercedes!" she yelled back at me through the phone, club music thumping in the background. "The keys are on the hook!"

My father has always had a Mercedes, and he kept his current vintage convertible sitting, protected, in the garage. I never saw him drive it, although it was the only extra car they had. Drive that car down Hollywood Boulevard? Don't mind if I do. But if I was going to the Roxbury, I was going to have to look hot or I wouldn't get in. I dragged myself off the couch and into my room, and looked in the mirror. Hot rollers, lip gloss, red dress, my highest heels. Maybe that would do the trick.

As I dressed and worked on my hair, I thought about the so-called great prospects that might be at the club. Would I connect with the perfect guy? Would he be hot, rich, successful, maybe even famous? I knew Brooke wouldn't steer me toward someone ugly or destitute—you can't even get into the Roxbury if you're ugly or destitute. But would she be able to help me find *the one*? I knew he was out there somewhere. And I was on my way to find him—in a vintage Mercedes convertible.

Feeling flush with sex and power, I stepped into the club, which pulsed with blue light and a thumping bass. The chick DJ high up in the booth over the dance floor looked like she'd just finished her shoot for *Penthouse,* and the dance floor was crowded with cleavage and high heels, and guys dressed in fitted shirts that showed their chests and weight-lifter arms.

I looked around, hoping to see Brooke, but the room was so crowded, I couldn't see anyone beyond the people right in front of me. I pushed my way to the bar and caught the bartender's eye. He asked me what I wanted. "Vodka and soda with a twist," I shouted over the noise and music. He winked at me and grabbed a bottle of Stoli. I really wanted a margarita, but I knew where that would lead—I'd be fatter tomorrow. Maybe this time I could be good. I knew my pattern. I would start with the virtuous drinks, but the drunker I got, the more I'd lose my resolve, until I was swilling cosmopolitans and apple martinis and margaritas with sugar on the rim.

I turned and surveyed the room. All the round booths were full of people, and people on people—women sitting on laps or lounging behind and draped over the men. In one dark corner, a thin, dark-haired rocker type chopped a mound of cocaine on the glass table, then handed a rolled-up bill to the girl beside him. Another girl with long blonde hair, tanned skin, and great legs had her shirt off and was dancing on top of a table in her bra. Then I saw them—Chloe and Isabel from *Hollywood & Highland*! Maybe this was a sign from the universe that Larry Todd was getting ready to call me back.

The bartender handed me my vodka soda, and I squeezed over closer to Chloe and Isabel—their real names, of course, were not Chloe and Isabel—what an embarrassment if I actually called them the names of their TV characters! *Susan Terence and Donna Shannon,* I reminded myself. *Their names are Susan and Donna.*

I was almost able to get myself next to them and in hearing distance of their conversation. Chloe/Susan was rail thin with platinum blonde hair and big brown eyes. Her red lip gloss was slightly smeared at the side of her mouth and she had a silky, wispy little lavender dress that hung on her skeletal shoulders. Isabel/Donna was raven haired with full pouty lips, jet-black eyeliner, a sprinkle of girl-next-door freckles, and curves to die for. She wore high-heeled patent-leather stilettos and a tight black dress with a scoop neck that showed off the efforts of her push-up bra.

I cleared my throat. I would befriend them by telling them I was waiting for a callback from Larry Todd about a job. Or maybe I should say I'm a friend of Larry Todd's. Or something more casual? "Excuse me," I said as loudly as I could without sounding like I was yelling. Neither of them turned.

"Excuse me, Susan?" I tried again. "I thought you might want to know your lipstick is a little smeared there in the corner." I smiled in a friendly, confidential, girlfriend way, but the bitch didn't even look at me. She did, however, daintily wipe the corner of her mouth.

Maybe Donna would be more receptive. I moved in closer. "Excuse me, Donna?"

Donna did turn to look at me, but her eyes were like ice. She checked me out, up and down, exactly the way the flight attendant had evaluated my human worth with a cursory glance on my way to L.A. She began to turn away again, so I reached out and lightly touched her forearm. "No, wait! I don't mean to bother you, but I just wanted to say hello because I'm a friend of Larry Todd's, and . . ."

"Did you just touch me?"

"What?" I was taken aback by her tone and the way she recoiled from me, like I was some venomous creature she wanted to crush with her spike heel.

She looked at me with pure disdain. "I said, did you just touch me? Don't you ever touch me again. What's wrong with you?"

She didn't wait for an answer, but turned her back to me. Out of nowhere, a huge, muscle-bound man in a tight black T-shirt stepped between us and crossed his arms. Susan giggled and rolled her eyes, and they resumed their conversation.

I was humiliated. I felt ridiculous standing there in my cheap red dress with some lame TV star's personal bodyguard staring me down. I turned away and plunged into the crowd. This was going to ruin my entire week. I'd been smacked down and I wanted to get as far away from those two bitches as possible. And yet something inside me bucked against this treatment. I'd show them who was worthy. I'd get a job on their show, and soon, they'd know exactly who I was, and they would be sorry they ever treated me that way. They had the chance to befriend me on my way up, and they blew it. Screw them both.

Just as I was considering turning around and going right back home, Brooke appeared in front of me. "There you are!" She was breathless, and had obviously been dancing. Her blonde hair was mussed in a sexy way and her cheeks were pink. A lusty-looking man with sandy, feathered hair and a beautiful face stood behind her, his hands lingering around her waist.

"Is that Rob Lowe?" I whispered.

"Who, him?" she said, looking behind her. "Nah, that's Brett Jones. He's an actor. I told him I'm not interested, but he's following me around like a puppy." She laughed. Surely Brett Jones had heard her, but he didn't seem deterred. "We've been friends for ages. Where have you been?" I wondered if she was cheating on my father. I almost hoped she was. He was probably cheating on her, if the stories my mother told me were true, and I couldn't help wanting him to be punished for being such a crappy father.

"Getting dissed by Donna Shannon at the bar," I said. "I can't believe what an asshole she is. Susan Terence, too. I'm so embarrassed. And pissed off!"

"Fuck her, who even watches that show," Brooke said loyally. "C'mon, you've got to meet this guy, he's your perfect match. He's just an actor, but I think you'll like him." Just an actor! I couldn't help being impressed by actors, even though Brooke kept telling me to go for the producers. Brooke had access to an older, wealthier, more powerful crowd, and she understood who had the real power, but she also knew me and she knew what I liked. Once, when we saw Christian Slater in a bar, I was drooling over him. "Christian Slater would probably love to be sitting next to someone like your friend Larry Todd," she told me. "It's the producers who have all the power, you know. It's not the actors." But I still found it hard to believe. The actors were so beautiful and glamorous.

Brooke grabbed my hand and pulled me through the crowd, around the edge of the dance floor and over to one of the booths, next to the one where the shirtless girl was now sitting, eyes closed, cross-legged, as if to meditate.

She pushed me into the booth next to a tall man with wavy hair cut like a young Elvis. He had dark eyes, great facial structure, a prominent nose, and the body of an athlete—not muscle-bound, but broad and tight. Brooke slid in next to me and leaned over. "Tony, this is my friend Faith. Faith, this is Tony. He's an actor, and . . . he's from New York!" She sat back and crossed her arms, obviously pleased with herself.

I smiled my best movie-star smile. He was handsome in a rugged, Italian sort of way, a little rough around the edges, probably a character actor and not a leading man. No Rob Lowe, but still. I held out my hand. *Don't tell him you want to be an actress*, I schooled myself. *Be mysterious, don't be lame.*

"Nice to meet you, Tony."

"Hello." He smiled and shook my hand, but he didn't seem particularly thrilled to meet me. I was going to have to win him over. My looks were OK, not great, so that wasn't going to seal the deal. But my attitude was a ten.

"So, you're a New Yorker, too," I said. "Do you ever just hate the fucking sun and pray for snow and cold?"

That got him to laugh. "I know what you mean. I'm shooting a movie in New York next month and I can't wait to get back, even though it will be August when that beautiful garbage aroma wafts over the city."

"I miss that smell!!" I said, longingly, still in that bitter phase so many transplants from New York linger in, where we all say how much we hate L.A. and long for New York, even though we've obviously chosen to live in L.A.

Brooke leaned in. "Faith, you've been here for three weeks."

"I know, but I haven't met any other New Yorkers here yet. It makes me nostalgic!"

"I know," Brooke said. "That's why I found Tony for you!"

Tony leaned in toward me. "How about some X?" He held out his hand confidentially to reveal two brown pills with the word LOVE stamped on them.

"OK," I said. Let's get the party started. I swallowed them with the last of my drink, hoping I wouldn't regret it.

"Do you want to dance?" Tony asked me.

"Sure. Why not?"

He grabbed my hand and led me to the dance floor and we started to dance, shoulder to shoulder with all the beautiful people. I liked that he wasn't so perfect looking. I felt like we matched. We danced close, moving apart and back together. He began to brush his crotch against my hip. I could feel the beat of the music in my chest. I felt the intense need for another drink.

The lights swirled around me and the whole club looked like a beautiful kaleidoscope. I grabbed on to Tony, feeling a little dizzy.

I couldn't stop smiling. I felt like I'd known him all my life and he was my best friend.

He grinned at me. "Let's get another drink."

"I need some water."

He nodded and guided me through the crowd. I felt like I was with the best man in the whole club. I wondered how successful of an actor he really was. At the bar, he raised his hand for the bartender. He was so tall, his arm extended above the crowd. "Two vodka martinis," he said.

Brooke slid beside me again and motioned for another sex on the beach. "How's it going? Do you like him?" she stage-whispered.

"We're rolling," I said.

"Cool," she said.

Tony and I danced and drank all night. We were feeling passionate and thirsty and rubbing all over each other and making out to the waves of euphoria. Occasionally we collapsed in a booth and talked and made out a little. It felt casual and friendly. Then we'd talk some more, telling each other all our stories. He was smart and curious and articulate, in spite of the alcohol and drugs. It was a turn-on. There was also something inaccessible about him, which I took as a challenge. We definitely had sexual chemistry. I told him all about Susan and Donna, and how angry and embarrassed they'd made me. "You're getting upset about what two immature little Hollywood soap opera actresses think about you? What kind of New Yorker are you, anyway?" he asked.

"Good point," I admitted.

"Tomorrow they'll be yesterday's news. Longevity is the key. Once you hit it, never let it get away. That's what I plan to do. It's a rocket you hang on to, and I can guarantee *those* two don't have a clue," he said. "Besides, haven't you noticed how wildly superficial everybody is in L.A.? They're all big-timers and they're all fronting. It means nothing."

"I guess so," I said. "But they still made me feel like a piece of shit."

"Come here, I have an idea," he said. He pulled me out of the booth and led me over to the bar, straight toward Susan and Donna.

"No, no, no, no . . ." I protested, panicking.

"Stop," he said. "Trust me. Just pretend you don't even notice them at all."

"OK," I said doubtfully. I was starting to come down off the Ecstasy high and suddenly, everything wasn't coming up roses anymore.

He put his arm around me, then pretended to bump into Donna accidentally. He looked at her with complete disinterest. "Oh. Sorry. Whiskey soda and a cosmopolitan!" He called out the drinks to the bartender, who immediately stopped what he was doing to start making them.

Donna Shannon turned, and the annoyance on her face melted away as soon as she saw who had bumped into her. Then she looked at me, and then at him again. Her eyes widened.

"Oh," she said, trying to sound cool. "Hi, Tony."

Tony ignored her. Her face turned just one shade pinker. She nudged Susan, who turned around and froze when she saw Tony. Who *was* this guy?

Susan looked at me with alarm. I smiled and looked away. "Thanks, honey," I said to Tony when he handed me my cosmo. Payback was sweet. We took our drinks back to the table, and I could feel Donna's and Susan's eyes on us the whole way.

"Who are you, anyway?" I said as we sat back down.

"Just an actor," he said, laughing.

"But what are you in?"

"I love that you're only just asking me that," he said. "Most girls would have led with that question."

"I was more interested in your status as a New Yorker," I said. "But obviously your mere presence impressed the bitches. Why?"

"I'm on a Showtime series called *American Money*."

"The one about Wall Street?"

"That's right."

"Oh my God. I don't have Showtime but I've heard of it. I thought you looked vaguely familiar."

"Vaguely, huh?"

"Yes, vaguely. *Only* vaguely."

"That's actually very refreshing," he said.

The more famous I realized he was, the cuter he got. At one thirty a.m., the bartender announced last call and I hadn't had a drink in a while because I knew I had to drive home. Tony said, "I know where there's a great afterparty. Do you want to go?"

"We'll go," said a voice from behind Tony. He turned around. Donna Shannon and Susan Terence were there looking hopeful. "We'd love to go. Do you have room for us?" Donna asked, somewhat sheepishly.

Oh, this was too good.

Tony looked at me: my call. This forced Donna and Susan to look at me, too. "I don't know," I said. "We've got to fit Brooke and Brett and you and I, and that convertible only seats four." I looked doubtful. Donna and Susan looked desperate.

Just then, Brooke came bouncing up behind me with her pseudo-boyfriend Brett in tow. "Do you want to go to a party?" I asked Brooke.

"I drove my car, so I'll take Brett," Brooke said helpfully, with a half smile. "You take those two," she said, as if she had no idea who they were. "We'll meet you there."

Tony gave her the address, then turned to Donna and Susan with a pained look. "Shall we?"

I loved that Donna and Susan followed *me* out of the club. When the valet brought "my" car back around, Donna's mouth practically fell open. As they climbed into the back, it was with a newfound respect. *This* is what I'd been looking for all along, even if I hadn't really earned it yet. They obviously thought I was some rich trust fund chick. If only they knew the truth—that I hadn't even been able to afford my own apartment. That I wasn't getting any money from Daddy at all. I was, nevertheless, someone to contend with.

chapter four

Tony pointed west down Hollywood Boulevard, toward the Hollywood Hills, and I was feeling powerful and sexy again, like I could do anything, absolutely anything, not the least of which was to steal my father's vintage Mercedes and drive a minor celebrity to an afterparty in the Hollywood Hills. I sped down the road, marveling that this was me, that any of this was happening. Tony's hand rubbed my inner thigh as I drove. The night was clear and cool and perfect.

After a couple of miles, Tony directed me to pull up along the curb in front of a huge, white and red-trimmed, multistoried Mediterranean-style home in Beachwood Canyon. The front gate stood open and people milled around on the wide, sloped driveway with drinks in their hands. The four of us walked past and into the house, which had vaulted ceilings and gleaming white floors with expensive Persian rugs in every room I could see. The black granite kitchen counters held at least forty different bottles of liquor and mixers, and Tony went over to make us more drinks.

I was immediately drawn to the liquor bottles. "I'll do it," I told Tony. I began inventing. I loved creating new cocktails, and I was always searching for that one perfect cocktail. Let's see. I looked in the refrigerator and grabbed a pitcher of lemonade and a bowl of fresh mint. Only in L.A. would you find fresh mint in the refrigerator. I added a splash of cranberry juice to the lemonade to make it pink, then put it with ice, white rum, and mint in a cocktail shaker. I muddled it, shook it, and poured it over ice, topped it with club soda, garnished it with a lemon and a lime, and handed it to Tony.

"Here you go," I said. "It's a pink lemonade mojito."

He took a drink. "Hey, this is really good," he said.

"Thanks," I said. "I just made it up."

"That looks great, what is that?" asked Susan. I had been so absorbed in mixing that I hadn't heard her come up behind me.

"It's a pink lemonade mojito," I said, cooly. "Do you want one?" Secretly, I was thrilled that she wanted something I was making— something I'd invented.

"Sure," she said. "Thanks."

I made her one, then started making another one.

"This is really good," she said. "It's not too sweet. Perfect. Donna, come here!"

Before I knew it, I was making the drink for everyone, and I loved that they loved my invention. People filled up the kitchen. When Brooke came over, I handed her one, too. "Wow, this is great," she said. "They should be paying you."

"Nobody's tipped me yet," I complained.

"They should! Here," she said, pulling a $20 bill out of her purse.

"Ha ha." But I took it. I was totally broke.

Brett came up behind her. She looked at me, embarrassed, and slapped his hand away. "Stop it, I told you I'm *with someone*," she said, but she couldn't help giggling. I decided not to mention to her handsome but thwarted suitor that "someone" was my father, just in case Brooke's resolve was actually foreplay.

Brooke turned away, arguing with Brett about something (probably her honor, or lack thereof), and for the first time in almost an hour, nobody was asking me for a drink, so I slipped out of the kitchen and wandered around the dazzling house. Then an arm holding a drink appeared from behind me. I turned and took the vodka martini from Tony.

"I see you're admiring the house," he said. "One of my former producers lives here. We met on the set of *Murder, Inc.*"

I did a double take. "You were in *Murder, Inc.*?" It wasn't the greatest movie ever made, but I'd actually seen it, and suddenly I realized
I'd seen him in it, too. "Oh my god! Now I know who you are. No
wonder those girls were impressed with you."

He shrugged. "Are you a professional bartender or do you just play
one on TV?"

"So now you're going to ask me what I do for a living?"

"I didn't ask before because I just assumed actress, and I was hoping you weren't one. I get so tired of actresses."

"I happen to be getting a job on *Hollywood & Highland*," I said,
with more confidence than I felt. "And it's not an acting job." I said it
with pride.

"Network TV, huh?" he said. "Yeah, TV's OK. So, do you want to
check out the upstairs?"

"I guess." I had no intention of sleeping with him, no matter how
much I drank or how much X I did. I'd intentionally not shaved and
worn hideous granny panties to ensure that. My bikini line was a chia
pet. And I wasn't about to give up that much power this soon. Still,
I wanted to see the bedrooms. We climbed the polished wooden staircase and peeked into the spacious rooms with windows overlooking
the canyon. Everything was so perfect, I found it hard to believe anybody actually lived here. It looked like a magazine home. Of course,
they would have a team of housekeepers.

A few of the bedrooms had people in them, but we found an
empty one. I walked over to the window and looked out. "Nice pool,"
I said. I turned around and Tony was pulling out a bag of coke.

"Want some?" he said.

"Um . . . OK," I said. What the hell. The Ecstasy had worn off and
I could use another boost. I didn't even like the coke high. God knows
I didn't need anymore nervous energy. But I did like the danger, the
intrigue, the ceremony of it, and the tingling sensation in my mouth.
More important, it was an appetite suppressant.

Tony portioned out the lines and I snorted one line. That was enough, and I wanted to stay in control. He inhaled the rest. He leaned back on the bed, his arms behind his head, and looked at me. "You're cool," he said. "I like you." He patted the space on the mattress next to him. I crawled over, trying to show my cleavage to best advantage. He put his arm around me. "And you're so much hotter than my wife."

"Your wife?" I was angry for about a second. We'd shared so much about our lives in the bar all night, but he'd left out this one minor detail. Then, somehow, I wasn't surprised.

He looked guilty. "Yeah. She's back in Brooklyn with my daughter. I really miss them. But I like you. You're smart. Not like most of the women I meet at clubs. I can actually talk to you."

"Um . . . thanks?" I said.

"You'd probably really like my wife."

I leaned back against the headboard and looked at him. "Yep. I probably would." We smiled at each other. And another potential soul mate bites the dust.

This confession and my tacit acceptance of it seemed to open a door for him. He told me all about his family, how he had met his wife, how he felt when his daughter was born. He wanted to talk all night. He wanted me to be his shrink. "You're probably too young to get what it feels like to have that responsibility, but it's a lot of pressure. It's great, but it's also hard. When I'm away from them and I go out like this . . . it's just really nice to flirt with someone young and pretty like you. You know what I mean?"

"Not really," I said.

"I just love talking to you!" he said.

"Tony, I think you're a sweet guy," I said. "Handsome and charming and obviously very successful. Your wife is a lucky woman. But you should set a better example for your daughter," I said, noticing the coke residue under his nose.

"Yeah, I know." He sniffled a little. Oh God, was he going to cry? "I'm sorry. I didn't mean to lead you on. I *am* an asshole. You should see my daughter. She's beautiful." He looked up at me hopefully. "We could still fool around?"

"No," I said, patting his leg maternally. "We could not." I got the impression he wasn't really the cheating kind. He could probably have been persuaded. But maybe he liked me because he sensed I wouldn't go there.

I left him alone, staring into space.

I went back downstairs to find Brooke. She was talking to a group of women seated in a circle on the floor. "He's married," I said.

"What?" she said, alarmed. "Married?"

"Yep."

"Oh no, I'm sorry. I really didn't think he seemed like the type. Isn't he too young?"

"Apparently not. He's even got a kid." Defeated, I threw myself onto a sofa. I felt like I had a motor running in my chest. My heart was beating fast but my body was exhausted.

One of the girls sitting on the floor leaned back against my knees. She had long wavy blonde hair and a perfect tan. "Have another drink, honey," she said. "Then come talk to us."

"I'll get it!" Brooke said, eager to do penance for introducing me to a married man.

"I'm Sandra," said the blonde. "And you are adorable." She had a lilting British accent.

I didn't feel adorable. I could see my stomach pushing against the tight fabric of my dress—and I hadn't even eaten anything.

"I'm Faith," I said. "I thought I was getting lucky tonight, but apparently not."

Sandra laughed. "Men. They're hardly worth it unless they're disgustingly rich. And actors hardly ever are."

"Hm," I said, nodding as if I already knew this. Which I didn't.

Another one of the girls, who had long reddish-brown hair and bangs and the body of a supermodel, crossed her long legs and held out her hand to me. She wore a cocktail ring with the biggest emerald

I'd ever seen. I had a feeling it was real. "Come, sit with us," she said, in an accent I guessed might be French.

I sat down on the floor with them, shifting to keep my knees together in my mini dress. The French girl eased my heels off and rubbed the bottoms of my feet. I was surprised—but it felt really good. Brooke put a pink lemonade mojito in my hand and I sipped it gratefully. "I hope I made this the right way," she said. "I'm so, so sorry about Tony. I should have done more research."

"It's OK," I said. "How would you know? I did like him. He's actually a pretty decent guy."

Brooke sat down next to me and put her head on my shoulder. She was really drunk. I could smell the fumes rising off her. Or maybe it was me.

"You're so nice," she said. "I wish Frank was as nice as you are."

"I'm really not that nice," I assured her. "Like father, like daughter."

"Yes, you are!" she said, leaning back away from me and looking at me earnestly. "I feel like we're sisters!"

"No, I'm not nice, and we're not sisters. I hate to even try to dissect the bizarre idea of us being sisters and what that would mean you were doing with my father. And I'm not nice because I'm going to tell you that you shouldn't be putting up with him. He's a jerk to you. You deserve better."

She looked miserable.

"Tell me you don't think you deserve better."

"Your father is . . . he's everything!" she protested. "He's a legend. Everyone knows him. Everyone admires him. Worships him!"

"Everyone on the track worships him, I know that," I said. "But he's just lonely. He just wants someone around. He's wasting your time. The world is a lot bigger than the racetrack, you know. You could do anything. You could have anyone."

She didn't answer. I could tell she didn't believe she could do anything.

The coke was really starting to click. I couldn't shut up now if my life depended on it, and as long as I'd opened this can of worms, I figured I might as well say what I'd wanted to say to her since the first day I met her. "Look, Frank Brightstone is a coldhearted man who doesn't know how to love anyone. You'll always be disappointed. The only thing he really wants to do when he's not with his horses is sit in that leather chair all day. There's a stain where the back of his head rests, he's such a fixture there. He's boring. He never goes out, and he doesn't like you going out, either. What does he expect you to do all day? You're young and beautiful and you're giving him the best years of your life, and you're not going to get them back. You'll never get what you want out of him. He's not going to marry you. You should cut yourself loose and move on to someone who can appreciate you. He just wants you because you worship him. Wouldn't you rather be the one who's worshipped?"

I could tell I was talking too fast. This always happened. I'd hold it all in, then as soon as I drank too much or did any drugs, it would all come spewing out—diarrhea of the mouth. It was a chronic problem.

She started to cry.

"Oh God, don't do that," I said. "I just feel like somebody has to say this to you."

"How do you know he's not going to marry me?" she sobbed.

I just shook my head. We both deserved better. My father deserved my mother, and she deserved him, and I wished they would have stayed together and spared everyone else from their mutual dysfunction. Brooke, on the other hand, had been nice to me, and although I never would have picked her out as a friend, she was in my life now. I felt like we would probably remain friends, even if she and my father really did break up. I felt obligated to tell her the truth.

"He's not a total jerk to me," she said, swallowing. "No, Faith, really he's not. He acts differently when you're around. I think you're projecting your own feelings onto me. I don't feel like that about him," she sobbed. "And he talks about you all the time. He thinks you're wonderful—he thinks you're a much better person than I am."

Brooke stopped crying and got very quiet. I put my arm around her. "It's OK," I said. "It's OK. You'll figure it out. Don't listen to me, what do I know? I'm just an angry, deprived daughter with a long list of grievances. I'm hardly unbiased. Let's change the subject."

I turned to the group of women on the floor with us, looking for a way to redirect the conversation. Every single one of them was beyond stunning. "So, what do you all do? Are you with some Gorgeous Women of the World Club?" I asked.

Sandra laughed. "In a way," she said. "We run a . . . well, sort of a talent agency."

My ears perked up. "Talent agency? For what kind of talent?"

A creamy-skinned Japanese woman answered: "We hire beautiful girls to attend events."

I looked around at them all, with their expensive clothes and alien glamour. "Events . . . involving your vagina?" I asked, suspiciously. Everyone laughed.

"It's a social group," Sandra said. "A very exclusive social group."

"You should come out with us sometime. We have a *very* good time," said the French woman. Everyone laughed again.

Sandra handed me a personal business card. "Call me if you'd like to go out some night." I couldn't really figure out what the game was, but whatever it was, it sounded fun.

"Sure," I said, taking the card.

The party was getting more crowded. So what? I didn't have anywhere to be. I looked at my watch: four a.m. We heard shouting out on the back patio, so Brooke and I went to see what was going on. Two men were shoving each other and bellowing. A girl in the swimming pool looked up at them. She was topless, and probably bottomless, I couldn't quite tell. In what was probably a burst of drug-fueled energy, the smaller man shoved the larger one backward into the pool. The girl shrieked and jumped to the side. Yep, bottomless.

Suddenly, people all around us started peeling off clothing and jumping into the pool. I looked at Brooke. "Don't you dare," she said. Of course, that's all I needed to hear. I pulled my dress up over my head, tossed it to her, and jumped into the pool in my granny panties.

The shock of the water felt enlivening, but didn't sober me up at all. My head spun a bit as I dove under the water and came up right in front of Brett. He really did look like Rob Lowe.

"Hey, beautiful," he said. "Where's your movie star man?"

"Upstairs in the bedroom, being married," I said.

"Ah. Well, I'm not married at all," he said.

"Not even a little?"

"Not in the slightest." Underwater, his hand slid down over my hip and under the panties. Had he noticed how lame they were?

"You've got a lot of balls. Is that an actor thing?" I asked.

"I have a feeling yours are bigger than mine."

"Oh, they are," I said. "I can guarantee it."

"Let me feel," he said, groping at my underwear.

I pushed his hand away. "Creep."

"Sure I am, in the best way," he said, moving closer. I felt dizzy. He was really hot. When he leaned in to kiss me, I thought, *This is nice.* Then I remembered who and what he was—Brooke's sloppy seconds. I pulled away and looked up. Brooke was still standing at the edge of the pool, staring at us. Her face was red. She turned and ran into the house.

"Shit, I've got to go," I said.

"Wait," Brett said, grabbing my arm. "Just wait. She'll be OK. She was never going to let me get anywhere anyway."

"And you think I will?"

"I just got more from you than I ever got from her," he said.

"That's because she lives with my father, you jerk," I said.

"Your father?"

"Yes. Her boyfriend is my *father,* idiot! I've gotta go."

I climbed out of the pool, found my dress lying on the pool deck, and slid it back on.

I had to get out of here. It was all going bad. "Brooke!" I called as I ran into the house. I didn't see her. People were passed out everywhere. That looked so nice. I wished I could fall asleep in one of the well-furnished corners, but I had to find Brooke. She was too upset and drunk to be driving, and my dad would never forgive me if anything happened to her.

I opened the front door and ran out into the driveway. Then I saw Brooke's Jaguar pulling out. She was leaving me here. "Brooke! Wait!" I yelled and waved my arms. "Don't be so sensitive! He's a creep! I told you I wasn't nice!"

The car sped off. I threw my purse into the passenger seat of the Mercedes, jumped in, and gunned it down the street. I couldn't see the Jaguar anymore, but I thought I'd just meet her at home and work it out there. I felt incredibly guilty, and also angry. What was her problem? What did she care if I was making out with some actor jerk when she had my father's house to live in and his car to drive and his money to spend and his fucking *love*? I followed the road down out of the Hills and somehow missed Hollywood Boulevard. When I saw Sunset Boulevard, I turned right and began to follow it as fast as I could. I hit the gas harder when I passed Chateau Marmont. Near the Los Angeles Country Club, the road started to wind around and the last thought that crossed my mind was that maybe I should slow down. Then everything vanished.

I woke up in the hospital. Brooke was there, asleep in a chair. When I groaned, her eyes sprang open and she stood up. "Are you OK? Oh God! Are you OK? Were you following me? I'm so sorry I left you there! This is all my fault."

"Where am I?" I looked around. Oh shit. "Is the car alive?" It was the first thing I thought of—I hoped it was still intact. I might have to be living in the thing because this was going to get me kicked out of my father's house for sure. I felt my head. There was a bandage on the right side of my forehead.

"The doctor said you were really, really lucky. Amazingly lucky. Somehow, you just have a concussion and a cut on your forehead where you hit the steering wheel."

"But what about the car?" I didn't care if my face looked like a burned pepperoni pizza. Was the car OK?

She cleared her throat. "The car is . . . a crumpled ball of tinfoil."

"Fuck."

"But at least you're OK!" she said, encouragingly.

"He's going to *kill me*. What time is it? Is my face OK?"

She reached in her purse and handed me a mirror. A little fearfully, I held it up to my face. I looked hung over and a little pale, but even the forehead bruise didn't look very bad. "It's ten thirty," she said.

"Morning or evening?"

"Morning," she said. "You've only been here for a few hours. Someone saw your car go off the road and called the police right away. You were brought in here at four thirty a.m."

I didn't want to know the answer, but I had to ask: "Does he know yet?"

"Actually, he was really terrified that you'd killed yourself," she said. "When the police called, I answered the phone, and as soon as he heard it was about you, he made us come right down here. He was here by five."

"Where is he now?"

"He . . . had to go to the track. But he was scared to death for you, he didn't even care about the car!"

"I believe he's at the track. I *don't* believe he doesn't care about the car," I said, rubbing my face, trying to get the feeling back. God, my head hurt. "He loves that car."

"He loves *you*."

"Uh-huh." I had to face her. "Brooke, look, I'm really sorry."

"I know." She looked down at her feet. "I'm not mad at you. I shouldn't have been involved with him anyway. I was just trying to get revenge. I was so mad at Frank about . . . oh, nothing. Never mind."

I didn't have to ask. He was cheating. My father had a reputation.

And so, here I was, on Monday morning, the sun pouring in the windows, dialing Larry Todd. Following up. Because it was high time I got out of here and got on with my life. The phone rang three times and a young woman answered.

"Larry Todd's office."

"Hi, is this Mia?"

"Yes."

"Hi, Mia. This is Faith Brightstone. I'm just following up—I called a few weeks ago for Larry Todd."

"Faith, of course!" she answered brightly. "Larry just got back from Vegas—he's been at a conference, but he told me he wanted to speak with you. Hold on, I'll put you right through."

chapter five

I stared into my closet. I had nothing to wear. Nothing. It was my first day of work on the set of *Hollywood & Highland,* and my stomach was turning over on itself, I was so nervous. I envisioned me, hanging out with the actors, laughing and talking, being one of them. Even Donna Shannon and I would soon gain mutual respect and go out drinking together. The boys would flirt with me, I'd be clever and make jokes that would have everyone in hysterics . . . and then, a part would open up on the show. . . .

When I finally went for the interview, it was nothing like what I'd overplayed in my head. Larry Todd was gracious and incredibly friendly. Normally, he told me, one of his assistants would do the interview, but he had come into the office just for me. He put me at ease right away, giving me a big hug and asking about how I was ad-justing to Los Angeles. He explained that the position was a temporary one—I would be a production assistant on the set during the summer, when the cast of *Hollywood & Highland* was doing a series of episodes at a beach house in Santa Monica. He explained that the job wouldn't be glamorous, but I read into his words that it would be whatever I would make it. Ever since, I'd been picturing how it would go. When

Larry offered me the position, I accepted with a friendly handshake, and I felt like my life was beginning.

He introduced me to Mia, then told me he had to go to a meeting. Mia was tiny and slender and blonde, and one of those few people who can pull off the pixie cut and look sexy. She thanked me for the tin of cookies I'd sent her, and told me how much she and her nieces had enjoyed them. I liked her right away. She wore a cheerful yellow tank top, white jeans rolled up at the cuff, and gold sandals, and she told me that casual dress was appropriate on the set. "You'll mostly be running around, sometimes on the beach because we're about to film a resort segment, so you want to be comfortable. T-shirts, shorts, whatever," she'd said.

"So a thong bikini is fine, then? With heels or flats?"

She laughed. "Definitely flats," she said. "I'll need you to be on the set at five every morning, but you'll be off by three p.m."

Holy shit balls. Five a.m.? The last time I saw that hour, I hadn't been to bed yet.

"Here's the address where you'll need to be," she said, then brought out some paperwork for me to sign.

"This is five minutes from where I live!"

"Lucky you! It's the beach club. See you there!" I stood up to leave. "Oh, and a word of advice," she said to me as I reached for my purse. "Whatever they ask you to do, do it like it's the most important job in the world, no matter how trivial it seems. Everything's your business. That's how you'll go far around here."

"I'm all over it," I said.

I told my father about the job a few days later and said I'd be out as soon as I got my first paycheck and could afford to pay a deposit on an apartment. He took another one of the raspberry–chocolate chip muffins I'd made that morning and didn't even look at me. I was even more fired up to please him now that I'd wrecked his Mercedes and told his girlfriend she deserved better, but he made it very clear that he could care less about the job, or anything I did. I told myself that his nonresponse to the news meant he didn't want me to leave, that he loved my cooking and thought of me as family, but that was just my fantasy talking. I had to get out of there, and I knew it.

A few days after the accident, he'd actually initiated one of our few conversations. He knocked firmly on my bedroom door, then opened it and stood in the doorway, and although he didn't really yell, he definitely turned up the volume: "You need to learn not to talk about things you know nothing about. My life is none of your business, and your life is none of my business, but you are a bad influence on Brooke, and that I cannot tolerate."

"None of my business?" I couldn't help yelling back. "Your life is none of my business? I'm your *daughter*. I should be part of your business. What do I have to do to get into the inner circle? *You're* the bad influence. She's too good for you."

He looked at me for a minute, then said, in a lower, more frightening voice, "Destroying my cars and my relationships isn't going to work for you." Then he closed my door.

"I'll be out of here as soon as I can, so don't worry about having to put up with me too much longer!" I'd shrieked at my closed door, hating myself for losing my temper when he'd stayed so cool. I felt like a rebellious teenager. I needed to learn to keep my emotions on ice like he did.

So here I was, on the cusp of a whole new stage of my life—and I couldn't figure out what to wear! I had bought some inexpensive clothes at Rampage that seemed appropriate for the California weather, figuring I could make them look good with the right accessories, but I just wasn't sure what Mia meant by "comfortable." Being from New York, I couldn't quite imagine showing up on my first day of work at a new job wearing a T-shirt and shorts. It just seemed so . . . disrespectful. Still, I didn't want to look stodgy and overdressed.

Finally, I decided on a fitted, light cotton sundress and wedge sandals. I looked at the clock. Four-thirty. Kill me now. I had thirty minutes to get there. At least I wouldn't have to worry about traffic. The set where they wanted me was literally just down the street, in a vacated beach club. I could have walked—but I'd already learned that the rumors were true—nobody walks in L.A.

On the way out the door, I grabbed a light sweater. I'd imagined L.A. would be hot, but it was June Gloom—the time of year when mornings are clammy and chilly and the haze doesn't burn off until about one p.m. In the morning, it feels like it could snow. By the late afternoon, it's blazing hot.

I went out to the driveway and got in my car. After the accident, my father said he would get me my own car, so I wouldn't wreck any more of his. He took me to a used car lot and bought me a blue Ford Escort. I tried to be grateful, but I kept thinking, *An Escort? You're rich, and you're going to buy your only daughter a used Ford Escort?* I dreaded pulling into the beach club parking lot in that thing, but what choice did I have?

As I got out of the car, I could see craft services unloading the daily spread, and I panicked. Big tubs of candy, cookies, pretzels . . . I knew I wasn't going to be able to resist that stuff. Of course, I hadn't eaten any breakfast. I could see it now: I'd start shoving pretzels and Red Vines into my mouth at five a.m., I'd be ready for lunch by mid-morning, and by the end of the day, I'd have managed to fit in seven meals. I couldn't start eating this early. I just *couldn't*! On that fateful day when they suddenly needed an extra for a beach scene because someone didn't show up, they'd point at me, and hand me a bikini, and I wouldn't be able to fit into it. Then they'd say, "Sorry, Faith, we thought you wanted this," and they'd choose someone else—someone thinner, with more willpower.

Pull yourself together, Faith. Get your mind on business. I took a deep breath and headed toward the building. I could see Mia through a window talking with a tall bearded man.

"Faith! I'm glad you're here," she said as I came in the door. "I need you to run these scripts over to the Burbank office. Make six copies of this one, five copies of this one, and six copies of this one," she said, piling scripts into my arms. Each script had a Post-it note with a number on it. "Then get this form signed by a man named Vince Beck. He's one of our associate producers. The receptionist will tell you where to find him. Don't leave it for him; actually watch him sign it. Fax it to this number, and also to me at this number, and then bring it back here with the photocopies of the script." She paused. "Are you writing this down?" Obviously I wasn't.

"I'll remember," I said with confidence, repeating the items to myself, and thinking about what she had told me about doing everything to the best of my ability.

"There's more. Take this card so you can get onto the lot. *Don't* lose it, it's your pass. Otherwise, you won't get in. Take *this* card and bring me back a blended nonfat mocha from the Bean. Got it?"

"The what?"

"The Bean. On Sunset Boulevard."

"Oh. OK, absolutely!" A company credit card! I'd never been given one of those before. I could do this. I was great at this kind of high-speed multitasking. I turned to go.

"Oh, and Faith?" Mia called after me. "Get yourself a coffee, too."

I found the NBC studio lot and parked my car, then gathered the scripts and papers and cards into my arms and headed for the gate. I loved the thrill of showing my card and being admitted. I might have been a grunt, but I *belonged here*.

I took the pile of scripts to the *Hollywood & Highland* office, just down the hall from the main set, and asked the receptionist where the copy machine was. "And I need to speak to Vince Beck."

"He's occupied right now, can I take a message," she said, as if it wasn't even a question. She was a bored, enviably skinny brunette. Are they all frickin' clones out here? Are there *any* chubby girls, or do they detain them at the city limits?

"Mia said I had to speak with him personally."

She sighed and picked up the phone.

"It'll be just a minute," she said with a yawn.

I took the scripts to the massive industrial copy machine, lifted the Post-it note off the first stack, and put the script facedown in the slot on the lid. After I pressed a series of buttons—six, collate, copy—I turned and the receptionist said, "You can go back there now."

"Can I leave my copies running?"

"Sure."

She pointed at a door down a hallway. I picked up the folder with the form in it and nervously approached the door. I peeked in and saw him reading a script at his desk. Shit. He was really hot.

I instantly regretted my outfit. I backed up and quickly pulled my hair out of its ponytail and ran my fingers through it. I fumbled for the lip gloss in my pocket and slicked it on. Note to self: *When getting dressed,* never *assume you're not going to meet a hot guy.* Let's try this again.

I stepped back into the doorway.

"Excuse me," I said, trying to appear both sexy and businesslike.

Vince Beck looked up at me. He had shaggy, swept-back gold hair, deep green eyes, the tan of a surfer, and a smile that made me go weak in the knees. This was an associate producer? I hadn't yet seen any producers that looked like this guy. He looked more like a musician. Or a major mistake waiting to happen.

"Hey there, darling. What can I do for you?" he said, his eyes twinkling. He had an Australian accent. Just show me to his bedroom, right now.

I cleared my throat and steadied myself. Why was everyone in California so goddamned hot? "Mia asked me to get you to sign this," I said, holding out the folder. I did my standard check: no wedding ring.

"Well then, why don't you come on inside?" he said. I put the folder on his desk, but he didn't look at it. He just kept looking at me. "Are you the new production assistant?"

"The one and only. Or . . . not the one and only, if they hired more than one . . ." I stuttered. So much for being at ease.

"Relax, darling, you *are* the one and only!" He gazed at me for a long moment, winked, then looked down at the folder and opened it. "Ah, yes. Well." He reached for a gold pen and signed, then held the folder out to me. When I leaned in to take it, he pulled it away, just out of reach.

"Not so fast. First, why don't you tell me a bit about you?"

I smiled. I knew this game.

"What do you want to know?" I said coyly, subtly tossing my hair back behind my shoulder.

"For one thing, what's a pretty New Yorker like you doing in a place like this?"

"How do you know I'm from New York?"

He shrugged. "Accents don't lie, sweetheart."

I blushed, in spite of myself. I did *not* want to seem taken in by someone so obvious. "Then I have to ask what an Aussie is doing in a place like this?"

He laughed. "Touché. So let me guess. We're an *actress,* are we?" He enunciated the word *actress* in a tone I was sure was condescending. I hated the sound of it, but decided I could play along.

"I don't know about *you* . . . but *I'm* trying to be an actress."

He laughed. "And a bit of a smart ass, eh?"

"That I can cop to," I said.

"Well then, here's your form, Miss Brightstone. You can tell Mia I approve." Holy shit, did he mean he approved of me?

"How do you know my name?" I asked, flattered. He really was cute. A player, obviously, but definitely cute. And obviously doing well financially. I made a mental note *never* to ask him what he drives. If I was lucky, I'd see for myself.

"I make it my business," he said, inscrutably.

"Hmm," I said flirtatiously. "What will you find out next?" I turned and walked out the door, conscious of my posture. Proud of myself for handling the interaction without coming off like a complete idiot, I strutted to the copy machine. The receptionist watched me.

"Careful with that one," she said.

"Yeah, I can spot them," I said conspiratorially. She gave me a second look, like maybe I wasn't clueless. "Can I fax this?" I asked.

She held out her hand. "I can do it for you."

The beach club was a much different place than it had been at five a.m. Inside and out back, it was crowded with cameras, lights, big boxes of equipment, cords running everywhere, dollies loaded with props, and people—tech guys and directors and producers and actors, beautiful actors.

Linda Heath, who played Brighton, the powerful business-savvy blonde who ran the hotel, lounged in a wicker loveseat next to Chris Thomas, the dark, devil-may-care actor who played Jayden, the philandering husband of Isabel, aka Donna Shannon. A leggy teenager with long blonde hair who played Bliss, Brighton's illegitimate teenage daughter, sat on the floor with her legs crossed, wearing a bikini. A woman who looked like her mother hovered nearby on the periphery.

I looked around for Donna Shannon—there she was, standing by the wide French doors that opened onto the beach, staring out at the water. Too good to talk to anyone.

"There you are!" Mia startled me, coming up from behind. "Thanks for the coffee. And the scripts. And the fax." She took things out of my arms, one at a time. "Ogling the cast? Who wouldn't? Such pretty people."

She winked at me, and somehow I didn't think she was all that impressed with any of them.

But I was. I soaked it all in. I watched plain-looking people go into the makeup trailer and come out looking fabulous. I watched the set go from dark and shadowy to perfectly lit, the cameras sliding by on their dollies, and most of all, I watched the actors.

They were living the dream. Sexy, exciting, beautiful, rich. And here I was—making photocopies and getting coffee. I had to catch up; I felt a sense of urgency, my career clock ticking. I turned to Mia. "What now? What would you like me to do next?"

"I need you to call craft services and confirm the vegetarian order, which we didn't receive yesterday. Here's the number. Ask for Martha.

Use the phone over in that room. I'll meet you in there in fifteen minutes. I've got some more errands for you to run."

"OK, I'm on it."

"What did you think of Vince Beck?" Mia asked, while looking over one of the scripts.

"He's a man," I said lightly.

"Yes he is." She laughed. "I'm sure he was quite interested in you."

"No more than any other twenty-something girl who walks by his office, I imagine," I said, although I couldn't help being flattered yet again.

"He'll probably hound you for a while, just so you know. It's his pattern."

"I'll consider myself warned," I said.

But I couldn't help looking forward to it. I was getting to know all about L.A. power guys from Brooke. They never commit . . . until they do. It was mogul roulette. When they stop spinning, if the ball goes into your number, you're the one they marry. They don't go out looking for gorgeous, amazing women. They have plenty to choose from, and they marry the one who happens to be there when the time is right. When they're ready, and it's good for their careers, they get themselves trophy wives. If you happen to be the number it stops on, there you are. It usually isn't the best-looking girl. It's rarely the hot model they've been dating for years. It could be an assistant, another producer, someone totally unexpected. Maybe it was going to be Vince Beck's time, and I would be there. Brooke once told me, "You might have a shot if you're the girl who's slept with the fewest of their friends." Well, Vince Beck . . . here I am. New in town. I don't even *know* your friends.

The next few weeks flew by quickly, and it didn't take me long to realize that I wouldn't be interacting with the cast members, like I had imagined. I was too busy running errands for the crew. At the main studio, I was more often in the office making photocopies or in the commissary getting coffee or food than anywhere near the set, although I often peeked in and watched for a few minutes when I passed by and they happened to be filming.

I watched Donna and Susan in particular with jealousy, but tried to get past it. Time would be my ally, I told myself. My day would come. I caught Donna looking at me sometimes, and I tried to ignore her, but sometimes I couldn't help holding her stare with a cold stare of my own. She always looked away first—one of my small victories.

I quickly developed a routine. At three, I headed back home. I tried to nap until six, which sometimes worked and sometimes didn't. In either case, I was chronically sleep deprived. Then I would get up, shower, have some dinner in or out, flip through the trades looking for auditions, circle anything promising, then go out to the clubs.

Most often I went with Brooke. We would go to bars or go dancing, and she was always trying to find me the perfect guy. She also advised me on the L.A. dating scene. For instance, she told me to watch out for what she called "trick guys."

"They look pretty plain," she warned me, "like they wouldn't be an obvious catch. But that's the trick. They tend to be short, maybe balding, maybe Jewish or maybe not, but clever and articulate. They have a lot of money and power, and they're charming, but because they aren't flashy or obviously handsome, you think you've found a diamond in the rough, someone that no other girl has noticed. You think you've got the secret winner, disguised as a guy without any flash."

"How is that a trick?" I was thinking about a guy I'd met the night before who almost perfectly fit her description. His name was Joshua Levin. He was about five foot seven, had a receding hairline, and a great sense of humor. I'd talked to him all night, thinking I was doing him a favor, and I was surprised at how charming he turned out to be. When he'd asked for my number, he'd been so embarrassed that I gave it to him, and had actually been hoping he'd call me.

"Because the whole ugly duckling thing is a lie. *All* the girls are after him for the same reason you are, and he knows it. He lets you think that he's this great undiscovered guy, that he so appreciates that you've lowered yourself to date him when you're so beautiful, but he's secretly a player, ready to screw you and dump you for the next oblivious girl who comes along. He's the guy who was a nerd in high school, and who now resents all the women who will have sex with him now but wouldn't then. He hates women and he doesn't respect them because he thinks they are only after his wallet."

"Wow," I said. "Duly noted."

Occasionally, I went out with the irrepressible and mysterious Sandra and Babette and some of their friends, the gorgeous women from the party with all the expensive jewelry. They apparently continued to find me amusing and often introduced me to some of the richest men I'd ever met. I had high hopes of becoming a gold digger, especially of Sandra's caliber, but I just couldn't ever quite get myself to flirt seriously with the paunchy, balding, misogynist men, many of them foreign, whom they introduced me to, no matter how rich. I envied the girls' Versace dresses and Gucci bags and Bulgari jewelry, but not enough to go to the lengths I suspected they went to get that stuff. I never asked the specifics, and they never offered.

I also kept auditioning, although not as often as I probably should have. It was so frustrating because I was always just one of hundreds of hopefuls trying for some small part in a television commercial or indie film. I never seemed to be able to crack the code. Nobody ever called, and I never quite felt like I knew what I was doing. Still, I kept trying. I wanted it so badly . . . even though I still wasn't entirely sure what *it* was. Fame? Money? Recognition? Validation?

Once I had my first paycheck, I got the required actress headshots taken. Everybody told me that a headshot is your business card in L.A., so I spent $500 on a big stack of 8x10s of me with my hair and makeup done, smiling like I thought an actress was supposed to smile. I sent them out with a carefully constructed cover letter to a list of a hundred agents. Nothing. No response at all.

"This was a huge waste of money," I complained to Brooke one day, after checking the mail.

"Just get your face out there," Brooke told me. But what did she know? Her life was at the racetrack, not trying to get in front of the camera. I wasn't comfortable being alone and was always looking for Mr. Right . . . or at least Mr. Right Now. Although living with my father kept me from ever bringing any of my dates home, I occasionally went home with them. Older married men seemed to be particularly attracted to me, and they always wanted to talk, talk, talk about their problems, dumping them all on me, maybe because I didn't look or act like the typical Hollywood bimbo. Maybe my opinionated attitude was off-putting, so they didn't know what else to do with me but talk. I wasn't "wife" material. That was obvious.

There was one older guy whose mother had produced a popular series of spy movies from the 1960s, so he'd had early success as a director, specializing in cheesy sci-fi movies. I met him at a VIP reception for the network executives. We struck up a conversation. It turned out he knew my father, so we talked about the racetrack all evening. Then I went back to his place and we made out, but it never went further than that. I found out later he was married. Typical.

Then there was Ian McGinnis. Ian was the editor of one of the largest entertainment magazines in the country. After meeting him at the gym where I liked to work out, I'd hung out with him a few times. He was that uniquely L.A. personality: an over-fifty bachelor who drank excessively, was addicted to fitness, and was also completely unable to fathom the meaning of the word *intimacy*. But Ian was a sweet man and I enjoyed his company. He liked to buy me things, and he sometimes invited me to sleep over in his guest room and use his home gym in the morning. He loved to talk to me, but beyond a fatherly peck, nothing ever happened. He was nice, although I'd been relieved when he eventually stopped calling. He was much too old for me, and his proximity in age to my father made me uncomfortable.

Sometimes I went out with casting directors I liked, telling myself that this would be a good way to find out about the really great acting jobs, but then I could never get myself to admit to them that I was an actress. It just sounded so cliché. The few times I did mention it were to the wrong people—the lecherous ones whose eyes lit up the second they heard the word *actress*. One of them was even blatant enough to tell me he could get me a starring role in his new film if I would be his girlfriend. I admit, I gave it a few seconds of thought, but I just couldn't get past the big fleshy mole wedged between his nose and upper lip.

Men my own age weren't completely blind to me. One afternoon, after Brooke and I had been roller skating in Venice Beach, we went into a bar because they had a sign outside that said "Nickel Beers." This cute surfer guy came over to join us. He was tan with sun-streaked hair and he wore a muscle shirt that said *Hang Ten*. He said his name was Tim. He started drinking with us, and I started flirting. After about an hour, Brooke told me she was going home, and I waved her on. She gave me a look, but I ignored it. I was having fun. "I'll meet you at home later," I told her.

"Your friend's kind of uptight," he said, finishing his beer and waving at the bartender for another one.

"She's my mother-in-law," I told him, with a straight face. He didn't even blink. I was so flattered that he had chosen me over Brooke that I liked him even more. The beer goggles helped, too.

After about seven beers and a Long Island iced tea, I had to pee. I'd been putting it off for as long as possible. The room spun around me, but I stayed on my skates. I looked all the way across the bar to the bathroom, then I looked back at Tim.

"Are you gonna make it?" he said, looking very serious.

"I think you better give me a push."

He stood up and made a big deal out of giving me a shove toward the bathroom. I rolled about five feet past the bar, then had to roll and clomp and maneuver my way into the bathroom and the tiny stall.

It was a long squat down to the toilet—the skates made me taller than I really was. When I bumped my way out of the tiny stall to the mirror, I was horrified at what I saw. I looked down at myself. I was sweaty, rumpled, and my ugly white sports bra was showing under my once-cute, once-fresh pink tank top. My eyebrows looked like two caterpillars and I realized with even further horror that I hadn't shaved my legs in a couple of days. When I'd left the house, I'd planned on getting a workout, never thinking I would meet someone. *When will you learn?* I scolded myself. *Always dress like you might meet a hot guy.* What did this guy *see* in me? Gross. I ran my fingers through my flattened sweaty hair, trying to at least give it a little lift at the roots. I splashed water on my face and pinched my cheeks, trying to bring back some color. There wasn't anything I could do about the eyebrows. Or the sports bra. I don't have the type of boobs that can fly free, unless I want to risk an indecency charge.

"OK," I said out loud, to the empty bathroom stall. "I'm going back out."

I rolled out of the bathroom and through the bar, and I felt like everybody was staring at my skates. Or maybe it was the hairy legs. Tim was talking to another girl, but as soon as I came back, he turned his back on her and pulled out my bar stool for me. "Nickel beers are over," he said. "Do you want another Long Island iced tea?"

"Why the hell not?" I said. The more he drank, the better I would look.

Sometime after dark, we both stumbled out of the bar, with me still on my skates. He pulled me down the street for a while, and then I pulled him for a while, skating backward and giggling a lot. He was staggering and we were hanging all over each other. At one point, I think I remember boasting to anyone on the street who would listen, "I can skate better than I can walk!" I think that's when I did the round-off. On skates. A few people walked by and clapped. Somehow, I didn't break my neck.

Back at his building, he pointed up the stairs. "I'm on the third floor." He looked down at my feet. "Are you gonna take those off?"

"No way! That would take waaaayyy too long. I can *do* this!" I said with alcohol-fueled optimism.

Clomp, clomp, clomp, clomp—up I went, two floors on my roller skates, Tim nervously following me, ready to catch me if I suddenly pitched backward, but I held on to the rail and made it. Out of breath and even sweatier than I had been before, I fell into his apartment and onto the bed, and the room was spinning faster than my skate wheels. I'm pretty sure I gave him a blow job, although I don't exactly remember the experience. After fooling around for a while, we both passed out.

Bright sun through the thin mini blinds woke me up the next morning to a searing headache and a wave of nausea. I looked over at Tim. He was cute, in a rugged way, but for the first time, I noticed his thinning hair and the spare tire under the Hang Ten muscle shirt. In horror, I noticed that his pants were around his knees. What was I thinking?

I scrambled out of bed, trying to be as quiet as possible, my skates still firmly attached to my feet. I adjusted my clothes, smoothed my hair, rolled over to the door, and opened it. Just as I was about to make a clean getaway, he stirred and groaned. I froze. He opened his eyes and looked at me.

"Hey," he said, grinning woozily. "Where are you going?"

"I was . . . I have to get home."

He looked disappointed. "Can I get your number?"

I sighed. "Really? You want the number of the hairy wildebeest in the bad sports bra that you picked up in a bar last night? Who's still wearing roller skates?"

"Sure," he said.

"Let's just play it like we're now dreaming, and I didn't actually blow you on the Starlight Express." As if my whole life and so-called career weren't degrading enough . . .

I shut the door behind me, then carefully, treacherously, painfully worked my way back down two flights of stairs, on wheels, excruciatingly hung over, clutching the railing like my life depended on it. It probably did.

Then a first: the long roll of shame home.

Larry Todd was in and out of my life, but more in the role of father figure than flirtation. Once, he took me out for lunch. We laughed and talked and I asked about his daughter, and he seemed a little sad. At the end of our lunch, he put his hand over mine on the table and looked me in the eye. "You know you can always talk to me about anything that's going on, at work or in your life," he said. "Consider me your friend."

"Thanks, Larry. I really appreciate it. You're . . ." I almost said "like a father to me," but I didn't want to insult him or make him feel old. "Your support means everything to me. I think I'm almost ready to move out of my father's house and get my own place."

"That's great," he said, finally removing his hand. "Do you know where you'll live?"

"Not yet. Somewhere not too far from work."

"A friend of mine owns a building in West Hollywood. Do you want me to ask him about vacancies?"

"You would do that for me? That would be great," I said.

"Of course."

"How about a roommate? Can you conjure one of those up, too?"

"Let me ask around," he said kindly. "Mia might know someone." He looked at me wistfully. "This is an exciting time for you. Are you out there auditioning?"

"A little. Not as much as I should be," I admitted. "I've been too busy working for you."

"Of course. We don't want to lose you! But keep your eye on your own career path. Don't get so caught up in the daily grind that you forget where you're going. You didn't come to L.A. to make photocopies for me all day."

"Thanks, Larry," I said again. And, oh, what the hell. "I really feel like you're a father to me."

He didn't seem offended at all.

chapter six

The day that Vince Beck finally asked me out was the day Mia told me she had a friend who needed a roommate. "Her name's Perry Kaufman. She's an actress. She's really more the thespian type so I don't know how much she works, but I think she's done a few television commercials and some theater." Mia handed me a piece of paper with a phone number. "I think you'll like her. Give her a call—her lease ends soon and she's kind of desperate."

I had just received my fourth paycheck, and I was ready to get out. My father certainly didn't want me around. Whatever fantasies I'd had about our reunion had faded. Poor Brooke obviously felt caught between us, and I was tired of watching out for her feelings. She was one of those girls who needed a man to take care of her, no matter how he treated her, and I cringed watching her fawn all over my father and watching him spurn her affection. She maintained her story, that he was different when they were alone, but I was tired of hearing about that, too.

That afternoon after work, I called Perry Kaufman and left her a message. Almost as soon as I hung up, the phone rang.

"Hello?"

"Hello darling. Vince Beck here. How are you doing this after-noon?"

My heart skipped. Was he really calling me? *Be cool, Faith. This could be big. Don't screw it up.* "Oh, hey, Vince. I'm just getting home. How are you?" I tried to sound casual . . . and open to suggestions.

"Resting up after a long hard day at work, are we?"

"Well, I don't know about *you* . . ." It had become our little joke. He laughed.

"Listen, I've got a thing tonight, a kind of industry party. My date's canceled on me at the last minute—apparently she's down with the flu. You immediately sprang to mind. Shall we make a night of it?"

Ouch. There's nothing sexier than being a seat filler. On the other hand, all hail the flu virus! "Let me see . . ." I said, as if I was paging through some imaginary appointment book filled with opportunities and options. *Don't sound eager, Faith. Don't sound desperate.* "I do have a thing at seven," I lied, "but I could meet you at nine."

"Nine's perfect, darling. I'll pick you up at your place. Good-bye then."

I immediately began to rethink. Normally, when a guy takes you out at nine, he has no interest in feeding you dinner. He just wants to get in your pants. Should I have waited to see what he was going to propose first? But if he had invited me to dinner, then I'd have to deal with eating in front of him. I wasn't ready for that yet. Not that I was so opposed to the idea of rolling around with Vince Beck. I'd sug-gested nine o'clock, not him. I rationalized that this brilliant sugges-tion made me sound like I wasn't desperate. Like maybe I actually was busy. I liked that. Then again, he'd jumped right on it. I started to feel anxious. Did I make a mistake? Did I send the wrong message? *Calm down, Faith. You're obsessing again.* But I couldn't stop.

I couldn't help wondering how he knew where I lived. He said he would pick me up. And what the hell was I going to wear? Maybe I could borrow something from Brooke. I didn't own a single piece of clothing that was actually expensive.

Just then, the phone rang again. It was Perry. She sounded nice, sensible and articulate, and her voice had a certain theatrical tenor that I liked. Since I'd said I had a thing at seven, I decided to try to make it come true. "Do you want to meet up at seven for a cup of coffee?" I thought we should probably see whether we actually thought we could stand each other. I paused. "I've got something at nine."

"Perry?"

"Faith." She held out her hand. She had a beakish nose and a high forehead, the face of a character actress, and a rail-thin figure. Her best feature was her long, shiny, dark-gold hair. She was taller than me with narrow shoulders and great posture. I liked her calm manner, and as we sat and talked, she seemed to like my sense of humor. That was a good sign—not everybody gets me in the beginning. I also liked that I felt I could tell her I wanted to be an actress, and not feel demeaned by it. She was legit—a real actress. She didn't seem to approach acting like I did at all. For her, it was a passion. I was beginning to suspect I wanted it for the wrong reasons—for the attention and love I never got as a child. But I hated to admit I was so textbook.

"Are you auditioning?" she asked seriously, sipping her black coffee.

I hesitated, then nervously began tearing open packets of artificial sweetener to stir into my coffee. "A little. Not with any success. I feel like I really don't know what I'm doing. I could probably be doing it more, but I have a job on the set of a TV show, and that's been taking all my time."

"What show?"

"*Hollywood & Highland.*"

She thought about this for a minute. "I think I've heard of it. But I don't actually have a TV."

I loved that she didn't know about the show, and that she took acting so seriously. Maybe living with her would inspire me to get out there. "It's not even an acting job, but at least I'm learning how TV works. Anyway, I might have a line on a place in West Hollywood. Would that work for you?"

"Sure," she said, sipping her coffee. "I just need to find somewhere soon. Somewhere halfway decent and not too far away from things. I can afford about five hundred a month. Frankly, I'm more into theater than film, and that doesn't really fly in L.A. I should probably go to New York, but . . . I don't know. I was born here. I don't think I'd survive the climate change."

"That sounds about like my budget, too," I said. "And theater is cool." As if I knew. "But Mia said you've done some commercials?"

"A few little things—just not anything that's going to allow me to quit my day job as a waitress. I don't know." She sighed. "I may end up working for an agency or something like that. But for now, I'm going to keep trying."

"Yeah. I feel like I threw away five hundred dollars on headshots because I haven't gotten a single call."

"A headshot's a place to put your phone number. It's for when someone needs to remember who you are, but if you send it out blindly, it doesn't really do you any good, unless you're extraordinarily good-looking." She stopped. "No offense," she added.

"None taken." I knew what I looked like.

"It's a necessary evil," she said, "and extraordinary acting talent helps, too, but none of it is as important as who you know."

"I just wish it would come to *something,* so I wouldn't feel like I wasted my money."

"It will," she said. "You seem ambitious."

She picked up the tab (much to my relief—I realized halfway through my cup of coffee that I didn't have any cash and I suspected my ATM balance was negative), and we agreed to talk the next day.

I rushed home, took a quick shower, and stared at Brooke's closet. Now, on to Vince Beck. I wondered what "a kind of industry party" really meant. I thought about calling Mia, but I didn't want her, or anyone else at the studio, to know I had actually agreed to go out with

Vince Beck—at least not just yet. It just felt embarrassing. I didn't want to be some obvious notch in his belt, one of a thousand cards in his Rolodex. I already had a reputation for being fast on the job. I didn't need a reputation for being fast in general. Although I suppose anybody at the party would see us together and would clock the information for later.

I decided I couldn't go wrong with a tight black Versace dress that showed plenty of cleavage and heels that showed off my legs. I got dressed, unrolled my hair and tossed it around a little, then considered what to do about makeup. I never really wore much because I never quite felt confident that I knew how to put it on. I swiped on some red lipstick and some blush, then put some extra blush on my eyelids, thinking that might look sexy. I looked at myself in the mirror. Not bad, but . . . I reached down the front of my dress and aligned my nipples. I had my real boobs, but they drooped, since I'd been heavy in high school and my weight fluctuated so much. There, that was better. I was good to go.

I spent the next twenty-five minutes pacing and looking in the mirror every thirty seconds. When the doorbell rang, I jumped. I walked slowly, steadily, on my high heels, trying not to look too eager. For a moment, I wondered if my father would come downstairs to see who it was, and I hoped Vince Beck would be there, and I would have a moment of pride about the house and my father. But it was only the driver standing at the door. Brooke told me nobody has drivers in L.A., so I wondered what that was about. I peered over his shoulder and saw a black Town Car with tinted windows waiting at the curb. I looked back toward the stairs. No sign of life. My father didn't care what I was doing.

I followed the driver to the car. He opened the back door, and I slid in next to Vince.

"You look fantastic, sweetheart," he said, looking me up and down. "Absolutely hot. But what's with this black, then? Are you going to a funeral? You should try some color, darling. Brighten up your pretty face. What about red? You're dazzling in red." I remembered what my father had told me the first day I arrived: "Don't wear black. This isn't New York."

I blushed. "In New York, a black dress is like a white shirt—it's what you wear," I admitted. "But I do what I want, no matter where I am. And what's with the driver?"

"Ah yes." Vince Beck smiled. "A little run-in with the law. It seems they frown on drinking and driving. So I've got Carl here, to take me around," he said, gesturing to the driver.

"I see," I said, embarrassed that I'd asked. "Well, you don't look so bad yourself." I looked him up and down. He looked hot. Motorcycle boots, tight black jeans, and a fitted shirt unbuttoned just one button too far . . . at least, one button too far for New York. Apparently, it was fine for L.A. Sleeves rolled up, a gold Rolex Daytona. "So where is it we're going?"

"Just a party, darling. I'm required to go—producers, investors, some directors. Maybe you'll meet your *dream man*," he teased. "Maybe you'll get your *big break*." He leaned in close when he said it, whispering in my ear and pressing his chest against my arm.

I looked at him, trying to decide whether he was being condescending. My sleaze monitor was going off. This guy was coming out of the gate at 150 miles per hour. He began rubbing my shoulders and grinning at me. I was conscious of my uncomfortable thong riding up, but resisted the urge to yank it back into place. Can someone please tell me why we spend our entire childhoods trying to dig our underwear out of our asses, and our entire adulthood trying to put it back in there? "You mean *you're* not my dream man?"

"I could be for tonight."

He grinned even wider. "You're much juicier than the girl I was going to be seeing tonight," he said. It broke my heart a little that he wasn't even trying to fool me into thinking he was my dream man. He wasn't even pretending not to be a player. I wished he wouldn't be so transparent about it, so I could have my illusions for a while.

"We'll see how you stack up to the competition," I countered. He leaned back and smiled, seeming to appreciate the notion of a contest.

"I'm a fan of your father's, you know," he said.

Oh God. A racetrack guy. Did I have a death wish? Why did I always go for these types? "Are you a racing fan or a gambler?"

"Aren't all racing fans gamblers?"

"All the ones I know," I said, thinking back to my childhood, growing up on the racetrack. It wasn't an appropriate environment for a little girl, but I learned a lot about human nature. And people like Vince Beck. On the sleaze meter, he was an eight.

The driver turned onto Sunset Boulevard and pulled up in front of a small dark club. "What club is this?" I said.

"It's new. The top floor's private," Vince said, as he got out of the car.

I loved learning about cool new places on someone else's dime, places I could never afford to go on my own. Vince came around to my side of the car, opened my door, and helped me out, which was actually necessary because of the combination of the height of my heels and the brevity of my dress. I swear when I left the house, this dress was just above the knee. Now it had my crotch in its sights. Maybe that was why I had never seen Brooke wear it. I yanked it down as I tried to get out of the car with some modicum of grace.

The elevator opened to a lush room with giant windows on all sides looking out over the city—a stunning panoramic view of sparkling L.A. There were only about fifty people in the room, some sitting against the piles of pillows on the modular couches or perched on ottomans holding elegant drinks in martini glasses with fresh flower garnishes.

"I'll get us a drink," he said.

He didn't ask me what I wanted, so I wondered what he would bring me, but I was more interested in getting my underwear straightened out and my dress yanked back down to its proper location. Very classy. There's nothing like your ass crack hanging out when you're trying to be taken seriously. I was starting to believe I was trying to pass off as a dress what was meant to be a shirt. I looked around for a bathroom. I didn't see any obvious sign of one. Self-consciously, I backed into a darkish corner filled with potted palms and rearranged myself, praying nobody was watching me.

I had a good view of everyone from my dark corner—it was an older crowd for sure, a few younger glam girls, probably actresses. I didn't know who the big players were, but I tried to guess. I recognized an actress from a movie I'd seen last year, but I couldn't remember her name—and wait, was that Jennifer Aniston over by the window? Everyone must have been someone—not that I would know.

"There you are, darling. Not being a wallflower, are we? Because that's certainly not *you.*" Vince handed me a cosmopolitan in a generously sized martini glass. He lifted his bourbon on the rocks and we toasted. "To your career," he said.

"To my career." I took a sip. "Do you see me as ambitious?" I asked, genuinely wanting to know.

"Of course, darling. Isn't everyone in this town?"

"But I mean, do I seem *particularly* ambitious to you?"

He looked me straight in the eye. "Yes, actually."

"OK, then." I took a sip of my drink. "So, what do you think I should be doing about my career?"

"Oh, baby, the things I could do to your"—he winked—"*career.*"

I realized I wasn't going to get any serious advice out of this one. But maybe he had influence.

He clinked my glass again and drained his bourbon. "Off for another," he said. "Are you ready?"

I quickly drained my drink and nodded.

He started to go off, then paused. "Come with me, darling. I'll introduce you around. This is the crème de la crème. Perfect for your *career.* I've got some business, but I can insert you into a conversation somewhere."

I winced. I was annoyed at first that he had abandoned me, even for a moment, but I also hated the idea of being shuttled around and introduced to people like I was arm candy. I wondered if being with him was a cliché. Was I making people's eyes roll? Was I the new flavor of the month? I decided I'd rather navigate on my own terms, even if I was with Vince Beck.

"No, you go on. I'll mingle a little. I'll be fine," I assured him.

He looked relieved, then promptly deserted me.

I wandered around the room holding my empty glass and wishing I hadn't gulped it down. Finally I was rescued. A handsome young guy with a perfect jawline stood up from a nearby chair and came over.

"I like your dress," he said.

"Thanks," I said. "I'll let you know when it's finished. I'm expecting more fabric to arrive any minute."

"I refuse to believe you're here by yourself," he said.

I looked around. Vince was on the other side of the room, talking to a group of girls with plunging necklines and short skirts. He was holding two drinks, one of which I assumed must be meant for me.

"Oh, my date's around here somewhere, conducting business. By which I mean, hunting for vagina."

"Ah. I came here with my agent, and I haven't seen him all night. He's probably doing exactly the same thing." He held out his hand. "Jake Mandell, actor." He had a cute southern accent.

I shook it. "Faith Brightstone." I paused. "Actress." My voice sounded falsely confident.

"Oh no, we're doomed from the start!" he said in mock alarm, flashing a megawatt smile. He had perfect teeth. I wondered how much they cost.

"I'm also a production assistant," I added, for good measure. "Where are you from? I love your southern accent."

"South Carolina," he said proudly. "Born and raised. And let me guess: You're a New Yorker."

"Guilty," I said. "So, who do you know around here?"

"Hey, Jake-ster!" a voice said from behind me. I turned around. Oh shit. It was Brett Jones, of the ill-fated swimming-pool granny-panty groping session. What a small town this really was. I prayed that none of them had seen me rearranging the relationship between my thong and my crack behind the potted plants.

"Hey, Buddy," Jake said.

"How's Jessica?" Brett asked.

Jake blushed. "I wouldn't know."

"He used to live with Jessica O'Conner," Brett told me.

"Oh really?" I asked, looking at him with new respect. He'd dated America's Sweetheart, star of dozens of romantic comedies?

"That was a long time ago," Jake said.

"Still," said Brett. "*Hot.*" He turned back to me and held out his hand. "I'm Brett," he said.

"Seriously?" I said, ignoring his hand. "You're seriously going to pretend you don't know who I am?"

"Um . . ." he stammered. "Oh, right. You're . . . Brooke's friend, right? I'm sorry, I can't remember your name."

I couldn't tell if he really couldn't remember, or if he was just trying to assert his superior social position.

"That's OK," I said breezily. "I'd prefer you *didn't* remember my name."

"How do the two of you know each other?" Jake asked.

I shrugged. "Let's see. Hmm. If memory serves, weren't you the one trying to finger me in a swimming pool? Were there roofies involved? It's all a little dim for me as well," I said.

"You weren't acting very passed out, as I recall," Brett said, leering at me. Creep.

I spent most of the evening talking to Jake, hardly ever seeing Vince Beck, although he checked in with me now and then. Toward the end of the evening, I met the president of our network, who stopped in at the party for fifteen minutes. Jake pointed him out, and minutes later, Vince swept into our conversation and whisked me away for an introduction: "Lyle Williams, this is Faith Brightstone, one of our most promising young assistants," he said. The president shook my hand. I was as thrilled as I would have been if he'd been president of the United States.

"Nice to meet you, boss," I said. He laughed, and it wasn't a condescending laugh at all.

I was feeling really good. In one day, I'd scored a roommate, an apartment, and a hot producer for a date, and I'd flirted and bantered with real actors and real directors and a television network president. I was getting this L.A. thing down. This was the kind of career advancement I could understand. This made sense to me—much more sense than stumbling my way through random auditions or putting photographs of myself in the mail to agents I'd never met. I felt like I could do anything, like the road ahead was wide open and I really was going to be a star.

The lights came on around three a.m. and I felt Vince's arm around my waist. "Let's go, sweetheart," he said. I waved good-bye to everyone and Vince took me back downstairs, where the car was waiting.

He was obviously very drunk, and so was I. As soon as I slid in beside him, his hand was on my thigh and he leaned in to kiss me. Oh, what the hell. I kissed him back and we made out for a good ten minutes while the driver sat in the front seat, waiting. Vince was a practiced groper. He'd obviously been to this rodeo before. He expertly unhooked me and unzipped me and was all over the inside of my clothes without actually disturbing much from the outside. I still looked almost completely put together. "You've been driving me crazy all night," he murmured in my ear. "The hottest girl in the room." I knew it wasn't true, but I certainly didn't mind hearing it.

Finally he stopped and turned to the driver. "Go," he said.

The driver pulled out onto Sunset Boulevard, and we rode around L.A. for an hour, doing just about everything except actual sex. He kept trying to coax my hand to his zipper, but I resisted. I'd never been much for giving hand jobs, and I knew better than to give a blow job in a moving car—I could hardly afford to bite off a television executive's penis at this early point in my career.

As consolation, I let him dry-hump my thigh, probably the low point in his dating career, and the high point in mine. I had to brace against him, my foot pressed so hard against the car door that I got a cramp.

"Ow!" I shrieked, pulling away and tearing off my shoe to bend my foot back and ease the cramp.

"What is it, darling?" he said, straightening himself out and running his fingers through his hair to get it back out of his face.

"Sorry," I said. "Foot cramp."

"Ah, I see. Well then, let's have a look."

Oh no! Anything but my unpedicured toes! The second one looks like E.T.'s finger, and that's being kind. I cringed.

He took my foot into his hands and began to massage it. Then he started sucking on my toes, which tickled so badly that I could hardly stand it. At least he couldn't see them if they were in his mouth. I instantly regretted that I hadn't gotten the pedicure, or waxed—but I hadn't, just to avoid this exact situation. As if that would be a deterrent after a few drinks. My sober self was so unrealistic.

I distracted him by putting my hand on his thigh and sliding it up and back inside his fly, which he'd finally unzipped himself. "Oh, baby, that's it," he said. So cheesy, and yet, it turned me on. We started kissing again, and I wondered if I could taste my toes on his tongue. Thank God for small favors . . . and long toes.

After a while, I could tell Vince was losing steam. He was probably one of those hot and heavy guys who had trouble actually sealing the deal—especially with that much alcohol in him. This made him seem vulnerable and sweet to me, like an overeager puppy who burned himself out and needed a nap. And at least I wouldn't have to worry about trying not to sleep with him on our first date.

I feared his sudden fatigue might make him self-conscious later and that he wouldn't call me back, but he didn't seem embarrassed at all. I leaned into him, resting my head against his arm. He told the driver to take me home. Even though he'd obviously cooled off, he stretched his arm around my shoulders and it felt incredibly safe. I snuggled into him.

"You know, darling," he murmured. "*Hollywood & Highland* is planning a spin-off. It's very hush-hush, so don't let on you know," he said, his words slurring together as if he was about to fall asleep. I felt like we were in bed together, cuddling, having pillow talk after a night of passion.

"Really?" I said. "And they need a new star?"

"Actually, yes . . ." he said, his voice getting softer. "Brighton's going to buy an apartment complex in Santa Monica—we'll fill it up with juicy young professionals with *drama* in their lives." He waved his hand vaguely as he said the word "drama." "And we're auditioning for the new cast next month."

That got my attention. I looked up at him, suddenly feeling very sober and alert. My temporary position was ending soon, and I'd been wondering if they would offer to keep me on or if I was going to have to find something else. Maybe this was the answer. "Really?"

"I think you'd be great for it, darling." He patted my head, encouraging me to rest it back against his shoulder, and he snuggled me in closer, but the lovely drowsiness I'd been feeling had evaporated.

A spin-off! This could be just what I was waiting for—exactly the reason I'd taken this job. It sounded perfect—I could skip all the degrading auditions and low-rent theater productions and cheesy local commercials and go straight to network television. I'd be Donna Shannon's equal. "And . . . you think I should audition?"

The thought made my stomach lurch. *Steady, Faith,* I warned myself. *Freak out or handle Vince Beck the wrong way, and you could destroy your chance.*

"Sure, darling. Why not?" His eyes were closed.

I shook him a little until he opened his eyes and looked at me. "No, really. Do you think I have a chance?" This could be different than all those cattle call auditions. I knew someone. It was the thing Perry had said was the most important. Maybe this was it.

"I don't know. Do *you* think you have a chance?" Vince smiled at me, fondly, and then his hands were on the move again, like I'd reminded him I was actually here, a warm body in an insistently short skirt. His hand crept up my thigh again.

"Yes." I felt like I was saying yes to more than the audition, but I didn't care. Let him take me! Vince Beck could be the one. Rich, successful, ambitious, inappropriate, a party boy—like me, but with more money and an established career and the motivation to send me straight to the top. He was probably thirty-five, so he was definitely older than me, but not *old* old, not needing hand-holding like most of the men out here who I seemed to attract like a magnet. Vince Beck didn't need to be saved. And he wasn't interested in saving anyone else, either. He just wanted to have a good time, and he needed someone who could keep up with him. We'd be a power couple. Me, the TV star. Him, the producer. We'd get married in a small ceremony, barefoot on the beach.

"Does this new show have a name?" I asked.

As he stuck his tongue in my ear, he murmured, "*Ocean Avenue.*"

"I like it."

"I like *you*," he said, nuzzling my neck.

Suddenly I noticed the car had stopped and we were in front of my father's house.

"I guess we're here," I said. "I'm sorry I can't ask you in."

"That's OK, darling. I've got to be up early," he said. "Until next time." He gave me a long, slow, sloppy kiss, then told the driver to open my door. I wondered what the driver must think. Oh hell, he probably saw this kind of thing all the time. I got out, then looked back into the car. Vince seemed to be passed out already. But that was fine. I'd gotten a real audition.

chapter seven

I might as well have been naked.

Standing in front of the director and the small group of strangers responsible for casting *Ocean Avenue,* I was so self-conscious, I could feel my face getting red. Suddenly, I didn't know what to do with my hands.

"Your name please?" The director sounded bored, like he was doing some family favor—not a good sign. I smiled, rolled back my shoulders, and tried to look more confident than I felt.

"Faith Brightstone." I enunciated the words the way Perry had advised me to. We had moved into a small apartment in West Hollywood just a week before, and she had stayed up with me the past few nights helping me memorize the audition script, or in Hollywood speak, "the sides." I knew it wasn't necessary to memorize it, that the director just wanted to see how well I could act, but I wasn't confident about the acting part. I thought I would make a better impression if I showed them I could memorize anything.

"Just act natural," said the director, who was short and balding with glasses and a bland face. I was pretty sure I'd never seen him on the set. They must have hired someone new for the *Hollywood & Highland* spin-off. "Whenever you're ready."

I cleared my throat, and then I panicked. For a moment, I forgot everything. How do I not have this? I read those sides a million times. *Breathe, Faith. Breathe.* Then I remembered my first line. I shifted my weight and threw my hair back over my shoulder, trying to remember what Perry told me: *Just find yourself in the character. Relate to the character. Make it real.* I wasn't exactly sure what she'd meant by that—I had no idea how the character was feeling, but at least I'd figured out what I thought she would wear. That had taken me another few hours of contemplation, until I'd decided I had to go shopping and buy a new dress. And shoes. And get a facial. And have my hair done. Because aren't those the things that get you the really good roles?

"I don't know, Drake," I said, in my best California voice. It sounded too loud. I cleared my throat again, then lowered my voice a little. "I just don't believe you. You've lied to me too many times before."

"I'm not lying, Claire." The director read the line back to me in a monotone. "Nothing happened, I swear to you. I would never do anything to hurt you."

I wanted to laugh at his deadpan delivery, and also at the clichéd script, but I tried to stay in character, whatever that means, as the jilted lover, constantly deceived by her no-good boyfriend. "Oh, Drake," I said, trying to convey some kind of passion. "I want to believe you. I do. After all we've been through, you're everything to me. I can't imagine my life without you." Gag. "But . . . but I've got to go. I've got to find myself. I've got to start my life over, somewhere far away from here."

At least I could relate to that line. I gave the director a meaningful look. *I'm relating to the character,* I tried to convey, wordlessly. *I'm starting my life over, too.* But I knew I was bombing. I could feel it. Bombing. I was talking too fast, but I didn't know how to stop myself.

"No, Claire," the director said, with a little more feeling. "Please don't leave me. I'll do anything." You know you're in trouble when the casting director is a better actor than you are. *Get out of your head, Faith!*

"No you wouldn't, Drake. You wouldn't do anything." I gestured dramatically, then second-guessed myself, dropping my arms to my sides. "I'm going to walk out that door, and you're not going to do anything at all. I know you, Drake. I know you all too well." Dramatic pause. I eyed the director, to see if he was buying it. "You're going to be just fine without me."

Who the hell would actually say any of this stuff? I turned, as the script directed, and took two steps stage right. Then I turned back, snapping back to myself, expectantly searching the faces of the director and the others for a reaction. Nothing.

"Thank you, Paige. Next!"

"It's Faith. And . . . is that it?" I was surprised it could be over so quickly. "Is there anything else I can show you?"

The director looked at me as if he'd already forgotten who I was. "That's it. Thanks for coming in. We'll be in touch." Oh no. Kiss of death. It was the don't-call-us-we-won't-call-you routine. He turned away from me, toward the next girl, who was just coming into the room. A taller, blonder, tanner, thinner girl. A *real* California girl.

"Thanks." I tried to catch his eye and give him one last great smile, but he obviously wasn't interested. Yeah, thanks for nothing.

Defeated, I walked toward the door, but turned when I heard the next girl's voice.

"I don't know, Drake," she said. She looked at the director like her heart was breaking. "I just don't believe you. You've lied to me too many times before." Her voice caught, like she was actually going to cry. I watched, enraptured. She wasn't reading from the script. She didn't even look like she was aware of any script. She was just *feeling* it.

"I'm not lying, Claire," the director said, grinning broadly. "Nothing happened, I swear to you. I would never do anything to hurt you."

The girl looked like she wanted to believe, wanted so desperately to believe. Her lips trembled and her eyes filled with tears. "Oh, Drake," she said. I'd seen enough. I ducked out and closed the door quietly behind me to the sound of the director saying, "Beautiful! That was gorgeous. Now, the second scene."

Second scene?

I sighed and headed back across the lot to the commissary, bought a cup of black coffee, and sat at one of the small tables.

So that was it. That was my big audition. I'd invested hundreds of dollars in looking the part, and I couldn't act my way out of a sack. I'd missed nights of sleep memorizing those stupid unrealistic lines. All for five minutes with a director who obviously wasn't buying what I was selling. What a waste.

Mia walked in and I waved to her.

"I just auditioned," I told her, putting my head in my hands. "I totally sucked."

She patted me on the back. "Oh, honey, it's OK."

"No, it's not OK!" I whined. "This was my big chance. I feel like I disappointed Larry, and you, and *myself*. I wish I could have another chance. The girl who auditioned after me just blew me away." I didn't mention that I also felt humiliated about letting down Vince Beck. I didn't want her to know Vince was the one who told me about the audition. Thank God he wasn't one of the people watching my ridiculous performance!

Mia sat down. "Faith, look. I'm going to be honest with you because I like you and I think you deserve to hear the truth. They were never going to give that part to you. You have no experience, you're not a draw, you've never done any acting work except in high school and a couple of scenes in college. They just let you audition because you're a friend of Larry's."

"What?" I felt betrayed. "Why didn't you tell me? I just humiliated myself in front of—"

"In front of who, five or six people you don't even know? Listen, Faith, consider it a good experience. If you want to do this acting thing, you're going to have to get used to rejection. It's most of the business. Even the best actors blow plenty of auditions. And even if you were great, that girl after you has guest starred on a dozen different-prime-time shows, and before that, she was Binny Pines."

"The child star?"

She nodded. I felt a little better, but also a little angrier. I'll take righteous indignation over humiliation any day.

"How can I compete against Binny Pines?"

"You can't," Mia said. She looked at me sympathetically. "But that's OK, because every audition, every screen test, every contact can teach you something," she said. "Take what you can from it and keep going. Whatever you do, make something out of it. Learn something. The more you know, the more you'll be able to find your truth, and where you fit in to this crazy business. You're one of the quickest-thinking, wittiest people I know. You'll get there. You just have to be patient, and never assume anybody is better or smarter than you. Whoever gets that role was just more experienced, and experience comes with time."

I wondered if Vince Beck had set me up. "Vince told me about it," I confessed.

Mia sighed. "I know." She knew? "But it's not Vince's fault. He has no influence over casting this show. He probably really was trying to steer you in the right direction. But it's not the right direction for you yet."

"Thanks," I said. "Still, I wished I would have known I wasn't really going to get it. Then I wouldn't have practically peed my pants in there."

Mia laughed. "Even if you had, I'm sure they've seen it all."

"I think I need to take some acting classes."

"Then go take some acting classes," she said, standing up again. "But before you do, could you make ten copies of this script?" She handed it to me. "See you back at the office."

After work, I couldn't wait to get home to our little two-bedroom apartment. Although it was Spartan compared to my father's house, it was such a relief to be on my own. I missed Brooke in some ways, but it was also nice to get a break from her. Here, I could breathe.

I liked Perry. She was a good support system, and she kept to herself. She encouraged me to go out with her to auditions, and she had just the body I wanted—tall and superslim. She was obsessed with dieting and she was militant about what she ate. Since moving in with her, I'd already lost two pounds.

When I walked in, she was sitting on the floor flipping through *Casting Call.* She looked at me.

"Well? How did it go?"

I covered my face. "Let's just say I sucked."

"That bad?"

"Ugh, don't ask for details, *please*. They won't be calling me."

"You never know," she said, encouragingly.

"Yes, I know." Still, I knew I would bounce back. I always did. There had to be a reason it happened like this. Something better would come along.

"Well . . . maybe you're more of a business person. You love your job. You rock that job." Perry patted my shoulder sympathetically as I collapsed on the couch behind her.

"No, that's not it!" I knew in my heart I was an in-front-of-the-camera person, but acting still didn't feel quite right. It didn't feel like me. Saying those lines had felt false and strange. A voice inside of me protested whenever I pretended to be someone else. "I wish I could just be myself up there. I don't know how to be someone else."

"Maybe you just need to figure out how to find yourself in the characters," Perry said.

"I don't know. I think I just need more training. I've wanted this for so long. My job is ending soon, and I thought this was my big break."

"Then maybe you should take it a little more seriously," Perry said. "You don't ever want to go *see* any plays. You hardly ever go to movies. You haven't invested in acting lessons. Acting isn't easy, you know. You don't just automatically know how to be good at it. It's a craft. It takes a lot of training and skill and tal—" She stopped herself.

"Were you going to say 'talent'?" I asked.

"No. I was going to say . . . I was going to say . . . OK, I was going to say talent, but I'm not saying you don't have it. It's just . . . undeveloped. You've still got a lot to learn."

"I don't see you starring in any movies lately," I said, meanly.

She looked hurt, but didn't take the bait. "It takes a while, Faith. We both have to keep trying. Why don't you join Meisenburg with me?"

Perry had recently enrolled in the part-time six-week program at the Meisenburg Theatre & Film Institute, and it was all she talked about.

"I can't afford that. And I don't have time, I have to work."

"It's part time, you can do just two classes a week, and that's cheaper anyway," she said. "Ask your dad to pay."

"That's hilarious. I guess you're going to be a comedian now instead of an actress?"

"Do it with me! You keep saying you think you need to take acting classes. Where better?"

Maybe she was right. I considered. Maybe it was time for a change. My job was ending anyway, and that had largely kept me distracted from really trying to make it. I thought about what Larry Todd had said: I had to focus on progressing in my career, not just on a job that wasn't taking me anywhere. Obviously, I needed to be doing something differently. Maybe the acting classes could open doors, show my commitment to learning the craft. Give me the credibility I needed to own what I was trying to do.

"Maybe . . ." I conceded, "maybe I could put it on my credit card. But if I do that, then you have to go to a party with me tonight. After today's disaster, I need a night out."

"Sure," she agreed. "That sounds fun."

Gorgeous Sandra and her expensively bejeweled posse had just told me about a pajama party that night in Beverly Hills, and I thought it would be a perfect tame outing with Perry, who wasn't fond of my wild lifestyle and didn't drink much or do any drugs. I imagined us meeting some cute guys wearing boxers and T-shirts, and playing truth-or-dare. Or spin the bottle. I had just the pair of cute new flannel cow pajamas and fuzzy slippers.

We parked outside the house and walked through the damp grass to the front door, me in my new PJs with a big teddy bear, and Perry in a modest silk robe. Perry stepped back and let me go first, since she didn't know anyone at the party. I opened the door, peeked inside . . . and immediately slammed it shut again.

"Shit."

"What!" Perry stared at me. "What's wrong?"

"Take off your clothes!"

"What?" she looked alarmed.

"It's not . . . exactly the kind of party I thought it was going to be." I'd been picturing PJs and nighties. What I'd seen were thongs and bras and teddies and pasties. This wasn't going to be about spin the bottle. This looked more like spin the penis. I should have known. Sandra wasn't exactly the flannel-pajama type.

I dragged Perry back to the car, tossed the teddy bear I was carrying in the backseat, and pulled off my pajama pants and slippers. Thank God I had a pair of high heels in the backseat for emergencies. "Quick, switch bras with me!" I demanded, as Perry hesitantly disrobed.

"What? Why? What did you see in there?" she squeaked.

"Everybody's in their underwear," I hissed. *"I cannot possibly wear this bra, do you understand? My jugs are hanging out like a porn queen."*

I hadn't planned on showing anybody my bra, so I'd worn an old one that was too small and made me look giant and saggy. Would I ever learn? I knew Perry would be wearing something more modest, and her perky little bumblebee breasts would look just fine in the skimpy sling I thought of as my beater bra.

"Are you kidding me?" she said.

"I'm deadly serious."

Perry looked like she might be sick, but she did it. She handed me her cute black lacy bra, and I put my arms through and hooked it in front. I was still busting out of it, but it was definitely better than the one I had been wearing. Mine looked cute on her—pink and strappy and skimpy, almost angelic.

"But I'm wearing black underwear!" she said.

"We're not trading thongs—that's where I draw the line," I told her.

She rolled her eyes. "At least you have standards."

"If we're both wearing pink and black, we'll match each other. It'll be cute," I reassured her, slipping on my heels. She was already wearing sandals, and they worked with her long legs. "OK, let's try this again."

Self-consciously, we walked back across the lawn in our underwear. "I can't *believe* you're making me do this," Perry said. "I thought you said this was going to be fun."

"You'll thank me later," I said. "I saw some really hot guys in there."

But it wasn't fun. As soon as we walked into the crowded room, I was conscious of how thin and fit everybody was compared to me. And I thought I'd been doing so well, starving myself and haunting the gym. I was going to have to try harder. I sucked in my stomach and looked around for the liquor. A bartender in a black thong and a bow tie was making drinks in one corner of the spacious great room. I dragged Perry with me and ordered two margaritas.

"I want a glass of wine," Perry said.

"Fine, then. One margarita and one glass of white wine."

"Certainly, ladies," he said, professionally. I tried not to stare at the silky black tube of fabric encasing his sizable package.

We took our drinks. The ice in mine was shaped like little penises and boobs. Cute. I looked around for Sandra. I could only imagine how perfect she looked. All I could see around me were firm tan butt cheeks and perfectly shaped, artificial breasts and a lot of sleek muscles. One table had a tray of cupcakes with fondant nipples on them, and another tray offered a selection of dildos and a bowl of cock rings and anal beads. Was it someone's birthday? Were these party favors? I picked up a dildo and examined it. Veins and everything. Very realistic. Then I wondered if it might have been used, and quickly put it down. "This party gives new meaning to the word *cock-tail*," I whispered to Perry. She giggled nervously.

Then I saw Babette, wearing red lace and little else, fitting in perfectly, looking so comfortable. She waved at us and came over. She looked Perry up and down dismissively, and I wondered what made me so special that they didn't all look at me that way. "Faith, I've got someone you must meet," she said in her cute French accent.

Perry looked awestruck. She stared at me and mouthed the words "Who *is* that?"

We followed Babette over to a small group of men with dark skin and jet-black hair, wearing what looked like Speedos. They were definitely hairier than most of the other people in the room. "These guys look pretty excited to be here . . . if you know what I mean," I whispered to Perry, who was obviously trying not to notice that one of them was getting visibly hard in his Speedo. She sucked her lips in, trying not to laugh. "Maybe they have a full-figured-woman fetish," I said, glancing down at my stomach.

Sandra stood with the men, and had one of them by the arm. She was laughing and absolutely stunning. She seemed to be completely at ease in a room full of nakedness. She smiled when she saw me. "Faith! So good to see you. I want you to meet Azwan and Erick." She gestured to the man whose arm she held and to the man standing next to him.

"Nice to meet you," I said, extremely conscious of their eager eyes on my barely contained breasts. They all nodded and smiled.

"We're flying to Singapore tomorrow for a vacation. Would you like to come?" Sandra asked lightly, raising her eyebrows. She always asked. I always declined.

"Who, me?" I said.

"We would love to have a beautiful woman like yourself to join us," said the one I think was Erick, in some sort of accent.

I could sense Perry behind me, holding her breath. "Singapore, huh? Wow. Thanks so much, it sounds amazing, but I've got to work tomorrow."

"A woman like you shouldn't have to work," said Azwan.

"Well, tell that to my landlord," I said.

Relieved, Perry left me to find us a couple of stronger drinks. I knew I was going to need one. I turned to check out the crowd and see if I recognized anyone else. A woman in a champagne-colored slip holding a martini came up to me. "Are you one of Farrah's girls?" she asked.

"Whose girls?"

"Farrah's. One of them," she said, gesturing toward Sandra and Babette.

"They're friends of mine, if that's what you mean, but I don't know who Farrah is," I said.

"Farrah," the girl said, gesticulating impatiently with her martini glass. "You know. *The* Farrah?"

"Wait," I said, suddenly thinking of a news story from a few years back. "You mean . . ." I looked around to be sure I was out of hearing range from Sandra and the other girls. "The *madam*?" I whispered. "The *Hollywood* madam?"

"Of course," she said. "You aren't . . ."

Now it was all beginning to make sense. Farrah Hughes was notorious—Hollywood insiders were serviced by her girls. The "talent agency." The expensive clothes and jewelry. The luxury apartments where they all lived. Sandra and Babette and their friends were the highest of high-end call girls. Somehow, I realized I'd known it all along. It's why I'd always kept just enough distance.

"Well, I appreciate your mistake," I said. "But I'm not one of them."

"Oh. Whoops! Sorry," she said, just as Perry came back with the drinks. The woman spun around on her heels and walked away quickly.

"What was that all about?" Perry asked me.

"I have *no* idea," I said, not wanting to sully my friends in Perry's eyes. But I could almost see myself doing it. The money. The beautiful stuff. I was up for a lot, but I just didn't think I could pull off a life like that. I couldn't sleep with someone I didn't genuinely like. It just wasn't my style.

Neither were some of the other things going on at that party. We saw people with needles shooting up in dark corners, people smoking things with odors we didn't recognize, people who looked like zombies—beautiful, perfect zombies.

Perry and I didn't stay much longer. We talked to a few cute guys, but the ones we liked were as embarrassed to be there as we were, and it was just so obvious that everybody was trying not to stare at everybody else's junk. I was feeling a little sick and freaked out. It was a darker side of L.A. I realized I didn't actually want to know any more about.

The next morning, I left a letter for Larry with Mia, thanking him for my first break in L.A. and telling him about acting school. I would finish out my last few weeks on the set, but when the show moved back to the main studio, I would move on. I decided not to say goodbye to Vince. If he wanted to find me, he'd find me.

chapter eight

D‍o you have hostess experience?" he asked in a thick Italian accent.

I nodded, bending the truth a bit. "I was a hostess at a bistro in New York." Actually, I was a coat check girl for about two minutes. I quit when one of the waiters slapped my ass. Close enough.

The manager looked at me doubtfully. "We need someone. But I haven't advertised the position yet."

Score.

"You don't need to advertise it," I pleaded. "Just give me a chance. Here I am, coincidentally walking into your restaurant right when you need me. It's fate," I said. "You have nothing to lose, and a lot to gain." I gave him a winning smile. "You won't regret it. I promise."

He looked at the current hostess, then across the room at an older, heavy-set waitress glaring at us. "At least I find someone, before you leave me high and dry," he said to the hostess. She shrugged. "Give me two references and tell me you can start tomorrow," he said.

"Yes sir to both," I said, and reached out to shake his hand.

Was it really going to be that easy?

Finding a new job was exactly that easy. The next day, I began as a hostess at La Fenice, a pretty little Italian bistro that was currently the hot spot for Hollywood to lunch and talk business. Nobody would have known I'd never been a hostess before. I took to the job immediately. I handled the lunch shift and was responsible for greeting and seating people, taking care of special requests, and supporting the waitstaff.

I got to know many of the regulars and where they liked to sit, who needed what accommodations, and how to juggle tables and customers so everybody ended up happy. It was like a complicated puzzle, fitting everyone in just right, taking care of everyone with perfect timing. I loved it.

After a week, I felt like I'd worked at La Fenice for years. It was great to be back in an environment that was comfortable and familiar. I was happy around food, and since my mother never cooked, I'd grown up eating in restaurants. Restaurants felt like home. I also loved the busy, intense work ethic of the restaurant environment. The money was OK but regular. I didn't usually get tipped, but once in a while, someone would hand me a ten or even a twenty when I got them the table they wanted or otherwise accommodated them, and it was a very big deal to me. I loved meeting and greeting the Hollywood power elite and being the one to show the who's who of Hollywood to their lunch tables. Movie and music producers, directors, entertainment lawyers, plastic surgeons—it seemed like everybody who was anybody in Hollywood came to La Fenice for lunch. It certainly was different from being a cocktail waitress in college, serving sex on the beach shots to hoards of drunk frat guys.

I was too busy to think about *Hollywood & Highland,* but I did think about Vince Beck, and I always hoped the next person through the door would be him. Why wouldn't he come here for lunch? Our interactions hadn't been that meaningful—not to disrespect dry-humping and toe-sucking—but more than anything I was addicted to the feeling I had when I was around him. I couldn't resist our chemistry, and I missed our office banter. As much as I thought about him, however, I decided never to call him. I'd let him pursue me. I liked thinking that he was out there, somewhere, knowing exactly where I was.

Meanwhile, acting school wasn't going so well. On the first day, Perry and I showed up clad in tights and legwarmers and big sweatshirts, our hair tied back, ready to work. Perry was so excited, but I was skeptical. Yes, I wanted to get better at acting, but was it something you could really learn in a school? I was having buyer's remorse, but Perry said yes, I had to do it, so I agreed to give it a try, even though I couldn't help being anxious about the money I'd spent. At least the banks still had faith in me, though I'd almost hoped they wouldn't give me another card. Then I would have had an excuse to tell Perry no.

"Welcome, welcome, young actors!" bellowed Frances Crane, the distinguished acting teacher who would be revealing the mysteries of the craft to us over the next six weeks.

With fifteen other students, Perry and I sat on the wood floor in a big warehouse-type room that looked like it might once have been a dance studio. "I welcome you here to find what lies inside you—to find your own transformative power—to find your *character*!" She sent that last word off with a dramatic flourish of voice and hand, then eyed us all, suspiciously. "Do you *know* what character is?" she asked us.

Nobody said anything. I looked over at Perry. She was obviously buying this spiel. "Character is what fills you—you, the empty vessel. To be an actor, you must empty yourself of your own personality and fill it with your character." Her voice rang out through the huge space. The old crone certainly could project. "When you become your character, with every ounce of your being, you will understand what acting is."

The room was silent. I looked around to see if anybody else was taking this as seriously as Perry. Apparently, they all were. I tried not to roll my eyes. An empty vessel? Seriously? Why would I want to get rid of my own personality? That was just bizarre. I liked my personality. Wasn't acting just *pretending* to be someone else? What was so hard about that? *Just listen, Faith. Keep an open mind.*

Frances Crane went on, making the whole thing sound like a surgical procedure, or some sci-fi personality transfer experiment. "Pour yourself out, and pour the character in. Infuse yourself with the character, and you will transform into someone else!" she crowed.

Maybe that's why so many actors get divorced, I thought. You would never know who you were going to be married to, if personalities had to change with every role. I began to rethink my big ideas about dating actors. What if you couldn't stand the person your spouse had to become for every movie? What if you couldn't stand the person *you* had to become?

After telling us that she knew what she was talking about because she was on Broadway three decades earlier, had supporting roles in a few movies, and won an Emmy for her role in a major television drama, and after giving us a lengthy speech on why Ashley Judd (her former student) was the quintessential actor alive today, she had us get up and warm up our bodies with some strange stretches and some jumping around. I felt silly doing it, but I played along, trying to look serious and committed.

When we warmed up our voices by making vowel sounds at different pitches and saying tongue twisters, I had a hard time not laughing. After twenty minutes of OH-YE-OH-YEs and AH-ZAH-AH-ZAH-AH-ZAHs—we sounded like the teacher from those *Peanuts* cartoons—finally, the teacher had her assistants bring out chairs for everyone.

"Now, I want each of you to sit in a chair. Sit, sit, everyone." We all scrambled to secure a chair. I settled into the molded plastic and tried to give Perry a "here we go" look, but she was clearly drinking the Kool-Aid. "Close your eyes, everyone. Now. First, I want you to breathe deeply. Breeeeeathe deeply . . ."

I tried to breathe deeply.

"Now, listen to my voice. Let my voice be the only thing you hear. Feel your body sitting in the chair. Feel it! Imagine you are a beautiful bowl, and imagine tipping, tipping, draining your contents."

Whatever.

"Now. Breathe. And listen." She cleared her throat. "You are eight years old," she said. "Feel what it feels like to be eight years old. How do you see the world? What do you think about? Feel it." She paused.

I flashed back to being eight and asking my mother if I could be an actress and go to acting school. I remembered her telling me not to bother trying, that it would be too hard, and the angry feeling I had when she said that, and the feeling of wanting to do it even more. Eight years old: the age of big dreams and the complete inability to achieve them. And now, here I was, ridiculing what I'd longed for so desperately. *Pay attention, Faith. Get your money's worth. Stop being so cynical. Live your dream, stupid! And while you're at it, could you please get the hell out of your head?*

I felt preposterous. I opened my eyes again and looked around, and I was astounded to see people's contorted expressions. One girl held her knee and wept. One guy rocked back and forth, cradling himself, and tears streamed down his cheeks. Perry's whole face was scrunched tight with genuine pain. Give me a break.

I wasn't getting this. I looked down at my hands. I really needed a manicure. I peered at my toes. A pedicure, too. I thought about when I could fit this into my schedule, and whether I could justify the expense. Actors need to be well groomed, right? So it could be a tax write-off. I thought about my bank balance.

"Goood!" said Frances Crane, then she looked directly at me, my eyes disobediently open. I forgot to close my eyes! We stared at each other for a moment, and then she slowly raised her clawed hand and pointed at me. "Feeeeel it," she whispered. I closed my eyes and tried to look like the other students—like I was *feeling* it. "Good!" she repeated. She thought I was doing it. *I'm acting like I'm acting,* I thought. *Maybe I've found my calling.* I wondered if there was a market for that.

It was always such a relief to get home after class. Perry liked to hang around and talk to the other students, while I tapped my foot impatiently. I just wanted to fall onto the couch, or get into the kitchen and cook. These days, I was thinking more about food than about acting. I felt guilty about this, but it didn't keep me from thumbing through my Sybil Hunter cookbooks for inspiration. I now owned all five of them. Pretty soon, I was adapting her recipes, and then creating dishes entirely based on my own ideas. Some weekends, I spent almost a whole day in the kitchen.

The savory smells from the kitchen upset Perry, who watched her diet so scrupulously that I wondered whether she'd ever actually enjoyed eating. That didn't stop me. During the first month of acting classes, I perfected a roast chicken with crispy skin. I tweaked my scrambled egg recipe until it was no-fail. I baked muffins, cupcakes, and cookies, and I experimented with lowering the fat and sugar content, so Perry and I could eat them guilt-free.

At least when Perry was around, I exhibited great self-control, but sometimes, the food I cooked was so tasty, it was hard to eat just a little. Perry began to act nervous whenever I opened up a cookbook. When she got too tempted, she would go into her bedroom and practice the Meisenburg breathing technique we learned in class. When I got too tempted, usually by cookies or muffins, I'd stack them up on a paper plate, wrap them in foil, and take them immediately next door. Our neighbors loved us.

I understood Perry's anxiety, but I had my own problems, and food was my therapy, my consolation, and my favorite routine. I'd cook, I'd eat, I'd feel guilty, I'd vow never to do it again, I'd starve myself, I'd lose a few pounds, and then I'd do it all over again, despite my vow. It was all a great excuse to avoid what wasn't actually happening in my life, but I didn't want to think about that. I would rather just cook.

chapter nine

F aith. Get up!" Perry shook me awake. "Come on. I have the perfect audition for us. No one else knows about it yet."

I was sleeping off a lasagna, garlic bread, and cookie dough binge. It was worse than a tequila hangover. The guilt combined with the bloat made me want to hide underneath the covers for a week. My eyes were swollen and I knew I had days of juicing and repentant starvation ahead of me. I vowed not to step on a scale today. I couldn't take what I might see. It was going to be a baggy-sweatpants day. An audition was the last thing I could face.

But Perry was insistent. Ever since she had taken a part-time job at an agency, she was privy to the breakdowns from a service that listed all the good auditions regular people without agents never heard about. "It's for a major studio, and Matt Dillon is the lead, and they've got most of the cast but they're still looking for Matt Dillon's love interest, and they want an unknown!" She composed herself. "At least, that's what I heard. So get up! I want to talk about it!"

I opened my eyes, which was no easy feat, considering how puffy they were. Matt Dillon? I could see myself being Matt Dillon's love interest. Why not? I might have the exact look they want. God knows

I had a ton of headshots left. I'd been using them as place mats. Wall paper. Toilet paper. I groaned.

"Let's go for it!" Perry urged me.

"What's the point?" I said, feeling fatalistic—and nauseated. As if a food hangover wasn't humiliating enough, Perry wanted to subject me to the ultimate humiliation of another audition? Perry gave me her best pleading face.

"When is it? Because I'm definitely not leaving the apartment today."

"It's not for two days. Please! Say you'll go with me! We both have a real chance. It's not a cattle call!"

I sighed, deeply and cynically. But how could I say no to her? She looked so hopeful. "OK," I relented. "But I'm juice-fasting until then."

"Yay!" She jumped up and hugged me. I smiled weakly, still queasy and full of self-loathing. "I'll get us the sides."

Two days later, I was feeling debloated, confident, and mostly back to normal. The juice fast had definitely helped me feel in control of myself again, and my stomach was back to its preferred state: flat. And Perry was right—it wasn't a cattle call. This was a more select group than usual, and I actually recognized a few of the girls, although I couldn't say from where. Maybe television commercials or small parts in small movies.

And this time, I felt like I could actually measure up. The audition went better than I'd expected. Maybe acting school had taught me something after all—I actually felt like I knew what I was doing. After I read my lines, the director looked at me with some interest. I could tell I'd nailed it. I'd used every trick I'd learned from school, and I was motivated because I was doing it for Matt Dillon. Because c'mon! I was perfect for him. I was sexy and flirty and funny, and I couldn't believe the director wasn't going to be at least somewhat intrigued.

But something was wrong. I could see it on his face.

"I liked it," he said. "But . . . well, can I give you a little bit of advice?"

"Of course." I lowered my script and stepped forward. I assumed he was going to critique my delivery. I imagined him praising my sex appeal and humor, maybe suggesting I try the scene again in some other way.

"Look, you were OK. It was actually pretty good. But frankly, you're a little too heavy. If you could lose twenty pounds, we might consider you, but I'm just going to tell you right now that as is, we've got to pass."

What? It was everything I could do to keep my mouth from dropping open. "You . . . you think I need to lose twenty pounds?"

"I do. Consider it a valuable tip for the future. This is L.A. Thanks for coming in."

He looked away from me to the assistant at the door, signaling her to admit the next girl, and I could tell I'd been dismissed. Doubly dismissed.

I was stunned. I knew I'd been cooking too much lately, but twenty pounds? I thought I'd been doing pretty well, depriving myself on a daily basis.

In a daze, I walked back out to the waiting area. Perry gave me a "How did it go?" look, and I just shook my head. I walked outside to get some air.

Was I really that fat? I was five foot seven and I weighed 135 pounds. Wasn't that . . . relatively normal? I was going to have to be harder on myself. Every ounce counted. I sat down on the step in front of the building and put my head in my hands. I was so embarrassed, I wanted to die. I would never eat again. Ever. I would find a better diet plan. I would go to the gym twice a day. I'd eat breakfast and nothing else. Something. I had to do something!

A few minutes later, Perry came out and sat down next to me.

"What happened?" she asked.

"Nothing."

"No really. What happened?"

I couldn't look at her. "The director said I was too fat."

"What? He said that?" She stared at me in disbelief. Then she looked down at her own stomach and put a hand on it. "I wonder if that's why they didn't like my audition." She looked at me with resolve. "OK, we just both need to lose some more weight. We can do this. No more cooking. No more baking. No more eating out. You are banned from that damn Sybil Hunter cookbook, do you understand me? No more fat for us. Got it? *No more fat.*"

Somehow, this made me feel a little bit better. It seemed proactive. And appropriately punishing.

"Agreed," I said. We shook on it. "Let's skip dinner tonight."

"OK," she said. "I've got a bottle of wine. We can just drink."

I was definitely ready for a drink.

The next week, I felt better than I had in years. I'd lost five pounds and Perry had lost three. I was more tired and wired, especially from the herbal diet pills I was taking. They got me wound up and feeling a little bit high, but they killed my appetite. I felt thinner and more free because I was so much more in control of what I was eating (which was, essentially, nothing). I was a new woman—strict, disciplined, in control. My new confidence prompted me to end it with Meisenburg, too. It just wasn't me. I'd learned what I needed to know.

Amazingly, the school bought my fictitious sob story about my father being in the hospital—proof that I really *had* learned to act— and I was able to get half my tuition refunded. That was a huge relief. I probably should have paid it right back to the credit card, but instead, I went shopping. If I was going to be twenty pounds lighter, I was going to need a new wardrobe. Every day, I spent the time I would have been in acting school obsessively pedaling on the exercise bike at the gym and visiting the Diet Center for weigh-ins—and not following their meal plans because I thought they had too many calories.

Then, on a random Wednesday afternoon, at the peak of the lunch shift, it finally happened: Vince Beck walked into La Fenice with a big group of corporate suits. He looked even more handsome than I remembered, and I got a little hot and prickly seeing him.

He was talking with an older man as they came in the door. I didn't recognize any of them, but they could have been from the network. Vince broke out into a big grin when he spotted me.

"Darling!" he said, leaving the man he'd been talking to, midsentence. He gave me an L.A. hug and a kiss on the cheek. "What are you doing here? I've missed your"—he looked me up and down—"your presence in the office. You look *fantastic*."

"This is my new job," I said. I waved at the room, a little embarrassed.

"Sweetheart, we have to go out again!" he said, and he sounded sincere. For the thousandth time, I wondered if he really was the one. There was just something about him. "Here, call me when you're free, will you?" He handed me his card. As if I didn't already have his number on speed dial.

"Sure, Vince," I said, a little sarcastically. "I'll call *you*."

"That's my girl!" he said, and kissed my hand. "Got to go. But seriously, darling. Call me!" As he walked away, he turned and yelled over his shoulder, "I'm at your disposal!"

"Who was that?" asked one of the waitresses walking by. "He's hot."

"Yes he is," I agreed. "He certainly is."

Through the rest of my shift, I couldn't help looking over at him, posing, trying to catch his eye. It worked two or three times. He winked at me, but never called me over. When he left, he didn't look back.

About a week later, a bone-thin, high-strung movie director's assistant came into the restaurant to book a screening party. She said she worked for Josh Kameron, one of Hollywood's biggest directors and screenwriters, behind multiple major box office smashes, and she was freaking out because the date she wanted was booked.

"Let me see what I can do," I said. "If you want the smaller private room, you can have it at eleven a.m. You could market it as a screening brunch."

"What a great idea," she said. "I'll take it. I think it's the last thing on my list. Oh my God, if I get through this without losing my mind, I might actually make it to Paris."

"You're going to Paris?" I said, envious.

"Yes, an opportunity I can't pass up. Now, all I have to do is find my replacement . . . since the Kamerons don't even know I'm leaving yet. They're going to murder me, I swear to God."

"What does your job involve?" I asked, trying to sound neutral.

"Why? Do you want it? Oh God, tell me you want this job." She looked at me, practically wild-eyed with hope. "A La Fenice hostess is *exactly* the kind of person Carol would want to be her assistant."

"You work for Carol? Josh's wife?" That sounded a little bit less intimidating than working for Josh Kameron himself. "I might be interested." My lunch shift at La Fenice definitely wasn't covering the bills, and I needed something else to do—some other excuse to avoid auditioning.

"Basically, you do everything Carol tells you to do, which could be picking up her dry-cleaning or planning her parties or walking her dog or making reservations like this one or just listening to her throw a fit about something and nodding and smiling. It's never boring. Are you good at multitasking?"

I wrote down my phone number and gave it to her. "I am *very* good at multitasking," I said.

"Great. You might have just saved my life." She dashed off and my mind started racing. Me, personal assistant to Carol Kameron? Who might I meet doing a job like that? This could be exactly the opportunity I'd been searching for all along, the one I thought my *Hollywood & Highland* job would provide. I let myself feel the familiar but always exciting sensation of change. I loved nothing more than casting aside the old and embracing the next big thing.

As I obsessed, I gazed out the window and noticed a small shaggy dog sitting next to the door outside the restaurant, peering in through the glass. She didn't seem to have a collar on, and she looked hungry. And she was looking at *me*.

chapter ten

Hey, little muffin," I said.

The dog had shaggy gray and white fur and soulful brown eyes. She wagged her tail and barked at me. I knelt down and petted her. She wasn't wearing a collar and her fur was dirty and matted, like she'd been on the street for a while. "What are you doing here?" I asked. "Where did you come from?" I stood up and looked around. Nobody seemed to notice her. "Dogs aren't allowed in my apartment," I explained, as if she could understand. She cocked her head at me. "Hmmm. How quiet can you be?"

She wagged her tail and didn't make a sound, as if to prove she could do it. I wondered what Perry would think if I brought home a dog. I walked down the street to my car, and she followed me, right at my heels. I opened the passenger side and looked at her. She paused. "Well? Are you coming?" I asked.

She jumped right into the car. That's when I knew she was going to be my dog.

She was such a little muffin, so that's what I named her: Muffin. After a good bath and a bowl of dog food she gobbled up hungrily, she settled right in, as if she'd been living with me all along. Perry told me I'd better put up posters to find her owner, but I couldn't believe she had one, and if she did, I didn't like the way they'd been treating her. She was jumpy and skittish and she'd obviously been neglected. I tried not to think about whether she'd been abused. Still, I made a halfhearted attempt, in case she really was just lost. I called a few local animal shelters and described her, asking if anyone had reported a missing dog like her. I even put up one sign on a post by the restaurant, but nobody called.

Muffin seemed to know to be quiet. She barked one time when someone came to the door, but not enough to annoy anyone. Unlike a typical small dog, she wasn't yappy at all. She was protective, though. She didn't like people coming near me, and while she stopped growling at Perry after the first few days, any visitors had to watch out.

My landlord was hardly ever around, and my neighbors were so eager to get more of my baked goods that they didn't report me. When I told Muffin someone was OK, she condescended to let them pet her. She stuck to my side most of the time when I was at home, and every morning I took her on a walk around the neighborhood. Sometimes we drove over to Runyon Canyon, where everybody else walked their dogs.

Neither of us questioned that we belonged to each other. There was something about the way she looked at me that made me feel like everything was OK in the world.

"That dog sure likes you," said Perry one evening, her feet on the coffee table, a glass of white wine in her hand. Muffin was half on the couch next to me and half on my lap with her chin resting on my thigh. "It's kind of weird."

"No it's not," I protested. "That's what dogs do. They bond to someone." I stroked her head. "She's my girl."

About a week after I found Muffin, the phone rang.

"Faith, it's Mara Callahan . . . Carol Kameron's assistant? Carol would like to meet you." Muffin was starting to feel like my good-luck charm.

The Kamerons, it was no surprise, lived in posh Benedict Canyon, near so many other movie stars, directors, and producers. The interview went well. Carol had a crisp British accent and kept a fastidious house. She was dressed in the tastefully understated way of the very rich, and she seemed impressed with my style and efficiency. I was proud of myself for coming across as the person I really felt I was—practical and quick-witted and down-to-business. It was a side I couldn't show in auditions, where they expected you to be creative and emotional and arty, and a side I couldn't show enough at La Fenice, where my shift was only a couple of hours long and my duties were limited.

On my first day working for Carol, she introduced me to her other assistant, Chad, who looked mildly threatened by my presence in the office. Carol said he had to leave most days by three, and I would take over where he left off. First I had to go with the driver to pick up her twin daughters at school and take them ice skating. That was actually pretty fun. Heidi and Hannah, both gorgeous blonde nine-year-olds with high cheekbones and long legs, were interested in me and asked many questions: Was I married? Did I have a boyfriend? Did I want to be an actress? Was my house as big as their house? Did I think Scott Baio was cute? When they saw I could skate backward, they were particularly impressed. I taught them both how to do it.

On day three, I sat down in the office and waited for Carol, who was nowhere to be found. Was there something I could straighten? Nope. The office was far beyond my organizational skills, and I'm pretty OCD when it comes to cleaning. Everything was perfect. Were all the pencils in the pencil jar white, with white erasers, and perfectly sharpened? Yes, they were. I made sure they were all aligned. All the papers were filed, or precisely stacked. The carpet was vacuumed. The room smelled faintly of disinfectant. After about thirty minutes of doing nothing, I was about to burst. I came back out of the office and looked around. I didn't see anybody but the maid. I walked into the kitchen, where she was cleaning.

"Excuse me, Flora?" Carol had introduced me to all the household staff on my first day. "Do you know where Mrs. Kameron is?"

"Mrs. Kameron's still sleeping," she whispered, not looking at me, intent on wiping the counters.

"Oh . . ." I wondered if she remembered I was supposed to come today. "OK, thanks." I went back into the office and sat back down. Then the phone rang. Thank God, something to do.

"Kameron residence," I said in my most businesslike voice.

"Carol, please. This is Trish Copeland."

Trish Copeland! She had starred in Josh's most successful TV show and had been on the cover of every entertainment magazine ever published. "Oh, hello Trish," I said, thrilled that I was calling her by her first name. "I'm sure Carol would love to speak with you, but she's still sleeping."

As soon as I said it, a little part of me wondered: *Should I have said that?* But Trish just laughed. "You're new, right? I suppose you're not comfortable enough yet to go tell her to get her lazy ass out of bed."

"No, not really," I admitted.

"Good answer—no employee should ever be *that* comfortable!" She laughed again, a boisterous laugh that wasn't entirely benevolent. "Just tell her I called, honey. And good luck!"

About an hour later, after I'd resorted to alphabetizing the mail, Carol came down, fully dressed and looking like she'd been up for hours.

"Hi, Carol," I said, "I didn't want to wake you, so I've been organizing the office. I hope that's OK."

Her smile faded and her eyes narrowed. "What do you mean you didn't want to wake me? What gave you the impression I was asleep?" Uh oh.

"Flora told me," I said. "And Trish Copeland called for you." I was eager to change the subject. Then I thought: *Shit. I'm a dirty rat. Now Flora's going to get it.*

"Trish Copeland? What did you tell her?" she demanded.

"I told her you were . . ." Suddenly I had a bad feeling. "I told her you were still asleep. . . ." I confessed.

Her face turned pink. "You told her *what*?" she screamed. "No. No, don't you *ever, ever* tell *anyone* that I'm ever still asleep. Oh my God." She threw up her hands. "I absolutely hate new employees. Look, as far as you're concerned, I never sleep. I'm a fucking vampire. Do you understand me? I was not in bed. I was upstairs meditating, not that it's any of your business. And now that bitch Trish thinks I was sleeping all day." She looked flustered. "Oh, this is a disaster. I can only imagine what *she's* going to do with *that* information."

I couldn't help thinking that if *my* husband had directed twenty-five blockbuster movies and I had a billion dollars in my bank account, my assistant could tell anybody anything she wanted. *I'm sorry, ma'am, but Ms. Brightstone is currently involved in a three-way with two Calvin Klein models in the hot tub. Can she get back to you?* What the hell did she have to hide?

"I'm really sorry," I said. "I didn't think it would—"

"You obviously didn't think at all!" she said, pointing a finger at me. "That was just stupid. Really, really stupid. If you make another mistake like that, you're gone."

"Yes, I understand. I'm very sorry, Mrs. Kameron. It won't happen again." Suddenly, it didn't seem appropriate to call her Carol.

The next day, she seemed to have forgotten all about it, but I'd learned my lesson.

And so the job went. Every day, I worked the lunch shift at La Fenice, then showed up at the Kamerons' house at three. I would pick up Heidi and Hannah from school, spend time with them, then take a few hours of abuse from Carol. Afterward, I'd come back home, eat some brown rice or a fat-free frozen yogurt, go to the gym and burn it off, then go out for the night, drink vodka with club soda or a white wine, and look for my soul mate. Sometime in the early morning, I'd fall into bed, alone or not, before waking up to do it all over again.

It wasn't my ideal life, but at least it was a regular schedule. And at least I was skinny.

chapter eleven

How attached are you to your current living situation?" Carol asked me. I'd just come in and she met me at the door.

"Not very. Why?" I said, following her into the office.

"We own a beach house in Malibu Colony, and we are having it remodeled. We need someone to live in it while it's being worked on. Keep the lights on and make sure nothing gets stolen. What do you think? You could even drive our car, if you need it." Did she mean the Range Rover?

I couldn't believe my luck. Vince Beck still hadn't called me. I still didn't have enough money to quite cover my bills. I wasn't yet cast in a blockbuster movie, and I still hadn't found my soul mate. In the meantime, as a consolation, could I tolerate living in a gorgeous Kameron beach home in Malibu?

"I think that would work," I said, feigning indifference. "Could my roommate move in with me? She's very responsible." I figured I wouldn't mention the dog.

"Yes, but no parties," said Carol. "The more often someone's home to let the workers in and make sure they don't steal anything, the better."

"No problem," I said. Well, except for the part about the beer-swilling, shot-guzzling, tassled-titties, celebrity-packed parties I intended to throw. I'd just have to be sure Carol never heard about them.

"We'd like you there as soon as possible, so feel free to make any calls you need to make today so this can happen." She paused. "Oh, and Faith? Don't screw this up."

"Of course not, Carol. Never. I will be a model citizen." With any luck, the citizens at my parties would be models, too—male models, who would be required to lounge naked in the hot tub.

"And another thing. I need you to plan a party for me. I'm going to be out of town until the day before."

I swallowed. Carol had always been incredibly fastidious about her parties—about everything, but especially her parties. She was notorious for planning every detail herself, and torturing everyone else involved. She wouldn't say she exactly liked throwing parties, but I would say she was addicted to throwing parties. I'd helped her plan several already, and I'd been on the receiving end of some of her rants, yet hadn't suffered like the caterers, decorators, and entertainers who had really been the focus of her wrath. Carol's niece and my new friend, Jeannie Klein, who came by the house occasionally and whom I'd befriended because I liked her wicked sense of humor, had filled me in on the horror stories about some of Carol's most notorious past parties. And she wanted me to be in charge?

"Sure, Carol," I said. "I can do that." I said it with confidence I didn't feel, but it also sounded like an opportunity. I had a good idea of what needed to be done, and if Carol was going to be out of town, maybe I'd be able to do it with a minimum of abuse.

"The party is for the opening of Josh's new movie—it's a sweeping, epic sort of fairytale thing he dedicated to the girls," she said, waving her hands as if to dismiss the entire project. The rumor around town was that it cost nearly $300 million to make. Carol continued, "I want it to be big, impressive, memorable. I'll need a venue, catering, music, all of it. Think princesses and kings and dragons and that sort of thing." She waved her hand again. "I just don't have time to do it. It's in eight weeks, so get started."

Eight weeks?

I spent the next eight weeks in a frenzy.

At home, Perry and I got ready to move into the beach house, but all I thought about was party planning. Carol was very specific about one thing: the party would have to be dramatic. The studio was throwing a party, too, but this was the private event, and Carol wanted it to be more memorable than the studio's event—even though that opening was going to be at Disneyland. "I don't care if they have it at the fucking Buckingham Palace, I want my party to be the one they talk about," she said.

Whenever Carol had more than thirty seconds to sit and think about the party, my marching orders changed—a revised guest list every few days, a revised menu every weekend, and constantly evolving opinions on the entertainment. I spent almost two weeks negotiating with top-40 rock bands about playing the party, and when I finally found one who would agree to our price, Carol tore up the contract because she wanted her nephew's band to play. She finally agreed to locate her nephew's band in the lobby, and "my" band in the garden. Her obsessiveness and perfectionism were battling with my own, and I wanted to take her by her scrawny shoulders and shake her, saying, "Carol! Just let me do it!" But I knew better. That would be exactly the way to lose this job.

Fighting her at every step, I had to arrange for everything—the Hearst Castle was booked for the weekend we wanted, but I coaxed and cajoled and name-dropped until I got them to switch things around and give us the entire lobby, patio, and garden. I sent out the invitations in waves, to accommodate Carol's constant additions. I hired a special-effects company to handle the lights and sound, working in conjunction with a designer who would turn the lobby into a facsimile of one of the movie's most fantastic sets, complete with an animatronic dragon, and a garden transformed into a magical fairyland.

I found a caterer who could accommodate both vegans and children, and whose food Carol actually approved of. I hired a company
to handle the bar, and when Carol finally left town two weeks before
the party, I could really ramp up my efforts without her interference.
To get inspiration, I watched Josh's movie on videotape almost every
night.

"I can't watch that again. This party is going to be the death of
you," Perry said, leaving the living room when I inserted the movie yet
again.

"No it's not," I said, grabbing my binder to write down a new
idea—fairy-wing cocktail stirrers. "I'm rocking it. I love doing this!"

"Well, I don't love you doing this," she said from her bedroom.

"Careful or I'm uninviting you!" I said.

"As if Carol Kameron would let me come!" she yelled.

Eight weeks later and three hours before the party, I arrived at the
castle feeling like Cinderella in a pink dress with frothy tulle wrapped
around the waist and acrylic heels I'd found at a consignment store.
Everything looked amazing—better than I could have hoped. Tiny
lights twinkled in rows of potted trees that formed a walkway leading into the lobby. The special-effects team had created an artificial
drawbridge, and the animatronic dragon in the center of the lobby
breathed steam and had flashing eyes. On one side of the lobby, a
medieval-style groaning board was set with rough-hewn wooden
plates, ready to be filled with the fairytale food, and every fifty feet,
there was a portable bar. The bartenders were dressed like knights.

Outside, the entire garden was webbed and woven with lights
and exotic flowers, and tiny fairy figurines with buzzing electric wings
hung from the trees. I checked with everyone on my list to make sure
they all had what they needed. Apart from a few small disasters—
a temporary delay on the delivery of the princess cake, a permit that
had been misplaced that I needed to refax—the event was running
like a well-oiled machine.

Then Carol arrived. It was four, and I was feeling pretty good about what I'd done. I'd followed through on all her wishes, and added a good dose of my own creativity. Serving wenches were dressed and ready to wander through the room with trays of champagne and hors d'oeuvres, the bands were tuning up and sounded great, and on the patio, I'd arranged a children's costume station, where the youngest guests could temporarily don beautiful princess dresses that easily slipped over regular clothes, or knight's chain-mail vests made from sequined fabric, with scabbards for plastic dragon-slaying swords.

"What the hell is this?" Carol said, as soon as she found me on the patio.

"Hi, Carol," I said, cautiously. "How was your trip?"

"Don't ask me about my trip. Explain to me what the hell this is."

"What the hell *what* is?" I said, unable to conceal my annoyance, and crestfallen that she hadn't immediately been pleased with the impact of walking into the castle and straight into wonderland.

She waved her hands around vaguely. "This? All this? Oh my God, this is a disaster. My friends are coming to see *this*? What's that ridiculous green monster? And swords? Toy swords? Were these a quarter a piece at the Salvation Army? Tacky, tacky, tacky," she said. "This won't do. We're going to have to change everything."

"Carol, the guests are coming in less than two hours."

"I don't care when they're coming," she said. "I trusted you to put on a fantastic event, and this is what you give me?"

I knew better than to say I thought it looked great.

"Carol, you wanted the dragon," I said.

"I wanted a *real* dragon!" she said, hysterically. "Not some fake plastic dragon with googly eyes!"

I knew better than to mention that there were no such things as real dragons. Or to suggest that perhaps *she* was the real dragon.

"Let me see what I can do," I said.

"Good! Yes! Go fix it. I'm going to go change," she said. "When I come back, I want this to be a *real* party."

She disappeared in a puff of green smoke—or so it seemed to me.

Carol was crazy. Everything looked fabulous. It was fun and whimsical and beautiful. The caterers were just setting out the food, and it looked perfect—like a banquet hall in a medieval castle. The staff all looked like they came straight out of Josh's movie. I'd even arranged for the star, a young actress who played the princess, to make an appearance in the first hour. *Stay calm, Faith,* I reminded myself. *She's just being Carol. She's upset right now because she's nervous. The guests are about to come. Keep your head, and everything will be fine. You know you've done a great job, so just keep going the way you're going.*

I walked back into the lobby and stared at the dragon. What else could I possibly do to make him look more real? I found the special-effects guy and pulled him aside. "Carol wants the dragon to look more real," I said.

He rolled his eyes, but found some green-and-gold netting that he cut to fit over the dragon's glowing eyes and draped it around the rest of the dragon to emphasize the moving parts. It looked even better.

Guests started to arrive shortly after, wandering in and ooh-ing and aah-ing at the dragon and the bridge, the lights and the costumes. They loved it! I felt vindicated and unusually calm. No matter what Carol would dish out, I would handle it. I had this. Perry walked in, and as soon as she saw me, she ran up to me. "Faith, this is *amazing*! I can't believe you did all this! Thank you so much for getting me an invitation!"

Good old Perry, I could always depend on her to make me feel better.

"Go get a drink," I said. "I have to get back to work."

Carol came back down at six thirty with her two daughters, who were already decked out in their own handmade silk princess outfits, with ruffled crinolines and glittering shoes and tiaras. Carol warmly welcomed her guests, directing them to all the features of the party, as if she'd done it herself. She hugged and double-kissed everyone, smiling her perfect smile, not a pale blonde hair out of place, her legs perfect beneath her white pencil skirt, in her silver high heels.

Josh showed up about an hour later, already drunk, with a group of his friends. He never drank when he was filming a movie, but as soon as the movie premiered, he would always celebrate pretty intensely. Jeannie, Carol's niece, was there, and as people poured in, I recognized several people from the L.A. club scene—the TV actress Tammy Moore, a party girl named Katie Swindell who was known for taking off her top in bars and dancing on tables, rock stars, and there was Tony Magnelli, the married actor I'd spent the evening with the night of my car crash, with his beautiful wife and daughter, who must have been visiting from New York. He nodded to me, and I smiled, then directed his daughter to the costume corner. Jake Mandell, the cute actor I met at the industry party with Vince, waved at me across the room, then came over with a pretty girl on his arm. "I thought you were a production assistant. What are you doing here?"

"Now I'm a Kameron assistant," I said. "I put this party together for Carol Kameron."

"Wow, great job!" he said, impressed. "This must be fun." He didn't introduce me to the girl, who looked mildly annoyed.

"Hardly," I said. "It's pretty intense, and everything has to be perfect, so it's not like I really get to talk to anybody or meet anybody. Speaking of which, I really have to get back to work."

A little later in the evening, Ian McGinnis, the older producer I used to see, tapped me on the shoulder. I turned and gave him a hug and he asked me how I'd been. "We had some good times," he said. "I miss you."

"I miss you, too, Ian." I wondered how old he was. Surely nearing sixty, if not already there. His nose was even redder than when I last saw him—probably from the large amount of Scotch he drank every night after working out. "It's great to see you, too," I said. "But I'm afraid I have to go, I'm working for Carol Kameron."

"Of course, my dear, off you go. Off to work!"

When the bands started to play, I heard a commotion in the bar area I'd set up and roped off. I was on duty, so I was constantly making the rounds, never spending too much time talking to anyone, always making sure the party was progressing as it should. I walked quickly into the bar area and saw Josh on the floor, fighting with another man. Carol stood over them, shrieking: "Stop it! Stop it right now! Stop it this instant!" As soon as she saw me, she turned on me. "You! Faith! What have you done? I told you not to open the bar until eight, when the children left. What were you thinking?"

"Carol, I don't recall anything about—"

"I don't need your excuses. The party is ruined. I'm the laughing-stock," she said, turning red. I noticed one stray hair working its way out of her perfect up-do. I couldn't help watching it wave back and forth on top of her head as she screamed at me. "Fix this, do you understand me? Fix this! We've got food spilled on the floor and children trying to climb that horrible dragon and . . . and . . . and drunkenness! I've got to find the girls and make sure they don't see what their father has become!" She stormed out of the room.

I looked at Josh, who by now was lying on his back, laughing, as the man he'd been fighting scrambled to his feet. It was Josh's business partner, Peter Jarrell. He and Peter had cowritten several big projects, including several successful television series and something like fifteen movies. Peter was known to be brilliantly creative, a genius at fixing scripts, but he was also one of those middle-aged Hollywood extremists. He was the kind of guy who would stay up for days at a time, madly writing, then after he finished, he would go on infamous drug/alcohol/sex benders. He came to the house a lot, so I'd seen him, but I'd never actually spoken to him.

"OK, boys, time to pull it together," I said, good-naturedly. I whispered to Peter, "Hey, do me a favor—keep an eye on that girl by the bar, will you? She's trouble." I winked. Peter Jarrell sidled over to the bar, where party girl Katie Swindell was lounging, her hip jutted out, her midriff and most of her upper thighs exposed.

"Sorry about that, Faith," said Josh, as Carol's other assistant, Chad, came dashing into the bar. Obviously, he'd just been screamed at, too. "Got a little carried away."

"No problem," I said, astounded and flattered that Josh Kameron actually knew my name. "Just trying to keep things running smoothly."

"I'm glad someone knows how to keep her head on," he said. "Bartender, another shot for me, and one for the lady here."

"No, no, it's all right, thanks, I've still got lots to do," I said. I could just imagine what Carol would say if she walked in and saw me doing shots with her husband—tempting as it sounded. "Gotta keep the head on," I said, tapping my temple. Josh grinned and tapped his temple, then drank his shot. I turned to Chad. "It's all under control," I said.

"She hates the band!" he said.

"Her nephew's band?" I said.

He nodded, looking miserable.

"I'll take care of it," I said.

And I did. I took care of everything. I'd planned for this. I told the nephew's band that we only needed them for one set, and drinks were on the house. I had a DJ service on reserve, so they stepped in immediately.

All night, I kept an eye out for Vince Beck, but he never showed up. I regretted not sending him a quick note, or giving him a quick call, mentioning I'd seen his name on the guest list, and telling him I looked forward to seeing him. But it was too late. And I was too busy, distributing the gift bags the movie studio had provided, keeping the caterers informed when plates were less than half full, and soothing Carol. Every thirty minutes or so, I'd walk by her and whisper something reassuring in her ear. "It's going so well, everyone is raving," or "Your daughters are the belles of the ball," or "I keep overhearing people talking about how fabulous you look." It was a shallow, obvious ploy, but it worked. Carol slowly calmed down, unwrinkled her brow, and smiled. After a few hours and a few bottles of wine, she was as raucous as her husband, all the children had gone to bed, and half the remaining guests were in the swimming pool, including Carol.

Watching the party unfold, from a rated-G fairytale to a rated-R boozefest, was supremely satisfying. At the end of the night, Perry found me and gave me a big hug. "You did it," she whispered. "Was it worth all the work?"

"It's the best time I've had since I've been in this city," I said.

chapter twelve

Carol was so pleased with the party that the next morning, she actually told me I'd done a good job. A first. That night, to celebrate my success, and our new fancy beach house that I was finally going to get to enjoy now that I could stop obsessing about planning Carol's party, Perry and I went for after-hours cocktails at The Cathouse. We dressed up in our skimpiest clothes and highest heels, congratulating each other on even more weight loss, and drove over to Hollywood. The club was packed and sweaty. We heard that somebody cool was going to show up for a surprise show, but nobody seemed to know who it was. Perry and I pushed through the crowd to the bar.

"Are you stalking me?" I heard a voice behind me. I turned and it was Jake Mandell, the handsome actor I'd just seen again at Carol's party.

"That's what all the stalkers say to shift the suspicion," I said.

"Are you still seeing that producer guy?" he asked me, leaning toward my ear so I could hear him.

"Nope, I haven't heard from him in a while. I don't work at that job anymore," I said with a pang.

"If he hasn't called you, he's an idiot," he said. "Do you want to dance?"

"Sure!"

Just then, the lights on the stage went dark. A guitar began to wail, and then the lights went up. "No way!" Jake yelled, raising a fist. "Rock on!" It was Guns N' Roses!

The crowd went crazy as the sound of Slash's guitar vibrated through the room and Axl Rose joined in with that long scream that kicks off "Welcome to the Jungle." When the drums joined in, we all started jumping up and down to the beat. After the first few songs, we were drenched in sweat and ready for another drink. Perry was dancing with someone she'd just met, so Jake and I went back to the bar.

"I see you on TV all the time now!" I yelled over the music.

He shrugged. "It's a living," he said. "But what about you? Have you been in anything?"

"No," I admitted. "I'm working a lot—hostessing at La Fenice and working for the Kamerons."

"Wow, that's cool," he said. "Maybe you'll get into one of Josh's movies."

"Yeah, right. That's the problem with being an assistant in Hollywood. They always see you as an assistant." This I'd realized after only a few weeks working for the Kamerons. "Note to self: Don't take any more assistant jobs!"

Jake laughed. "Good advice." I found his southern accent even more charming than I had the first time I met him.

He had such a handsome, boyish manner about him that I couldn't help flirting. He went for the kiss and it was soft and exciting. He brushed his fingers along my jawline.

"I've been wanting to do that ever since I met you," he said.

"I've been waiting for you to do it, too." It wasn't totally true, but somehow in retrospect it seemed true.

We danced all night, and drank, and danced more, and drank more. When the bar closed, we all piled into Jake's car for either a very late or very early party in Hollywood. It was at a humongous loft owned by a middle-aged gay couple, a costume designer and a very wealthy producer. At the door, a spectacularly tall drag queen in heavy makeup and a blonde wig greeted everyone. "Hi, honey," she said as I walked in. "Welcome to the headquarters of the gay mafia. We run Hollywood, and don't you forget it!"

"Thanks," I said, laughing. "But I thought the Jews ran Hollywood."

"The Jewish *gays* run Hollywood, honey," she said loudly. "There's more crossover than you think!"

Inside, Jake and I got a drink from the huge polished wood bar along the edge of the sunken living room, then snuck out to the back porch. He pulled out a joint. "You want to share?"

"Absolutely."

We smoked in amiable silence and I started to feel dizzy in a really nice way. I leaned into him and he put his arm around me. "Hey," he said, looking down at me. "You know what? I really want you to come home with me tonight. But I'm not going to ask you. Instead, I'm going to ask you if you want to have breakfast with me tomorrow."

Some part of me was swept away by this romantic move. He didn't want me to be a one-night stand. Another part of me wondered if he was powerful enough, rich enough. He felt more like friend material than potential husband material. Is this what I was going for? Jake struck me as the kind of guy who would live on a girl's couch while she went to work and paid the bills. He was young and handsome enough to get his way. Then again, he was pretty hot right now, the actor of the moment. This could be the start of a long and successful and illustrious career, and I could be the woman who was there with him, right from the start. A true Hollywood romance.

"Breakfast sounds great," I said, kissing him again.

True to his word, Jake called first thing in the morning to invite me over. "I make great pancakes," he said to lure me in. "Come over and play."

He opened the door to his apartment on Venice Beach, wearing a frilly apron over jeans and a tight T-shirt. He had very nice shoulders.

His eyes were a little red and his hair was mussed up, like he hadn't looked in the mirror yet. Also charming.

"Cool apron."

"I know, isn't it?" he said, laughing. "I wore it just for you. You said you like to cook." His southern drawl was even more adorable in the light of day.

"I did? Well, it's true, although I haven't cooked in ages."

He waved a spatula at me. "Come on in! Welcome to my humble abode," he said. It wasn't exactly humble. It was about twice the size of my apartment, decorated in bachelor-pad style, but hardly the starving-artist version. He had a huge stereo system, wood paneling on the walls, a leather sectional with a lot of furry pillows, and wood floors that looked new.

I sat down at the table and he began piling pancakes on a plate. I panicked. "Um . . . just one is all I can probably eat. Oddly, I'm not that hungry."

"No way, you can't eat just one pancake," he said. He put a plate in front of me. Three pancakes, all dripping with butter, surrounded by bacon. I was like a deer in the headlights. It looked delicious, but there was no way I could eat it. "Do you want orange juice? Coffee? Cold pizza?" he said, opening the refrigerator door and surveying its contents.

"Coffee's fine."

"Cream and sugar?"

"Just black," I said, fearfully eyeing the bottle of syrup on the table. I turned it around and looked at the back. The label said 80 calories in two tablespoons, so if I had only one teaspoon, that would be, let's see . . . about 15 calories.

He handed me a mug and sat down, his own plate piled with a stack of pancakes and a pile of bacon. He dug in. I looked nervously at my plate.

"Are you gonna eat?" he said, pausing with his mouth full to look at my untouched plate.

"Of course!" I assured him. I picked up my fork.

Careful. Careful. Don't trip the binge switch. I cut off a tiny piece of pancake. Jake stopped chewing and watched me. I speared the little piece of pancake with my fork and brought it halfway to my mouth. Jake stared at me.

"What?" I said, self-consciously.

"I'm just waiting to see what you think. I'm not sure whether I know how to make pancakes or not. I want a review. Here, you forgot this," he said, handing me the syrup.

I put my fork down and drizzled a little bit of syrup over my pancakes. No more than a teaspoon. Maybe less. Then I picked the fork back up and took a bite.

The pancake was tender, warm, cakey, just slightly crisp on the outside. The butter and the tiny drop of syrup added just a tantalizing flirtation of rich sweetness. Perfect.

"You definitely know how to make pancakes," I told him, sincerely.

He grinned and went back to wolfing down his food, satisfied with his pancake prowess. With his attention elsewhere, I was able to cut a few more pieces into smaller pieces and eat one more magnificent delectable bite before putting down my fork.

"Wow, I'm so full," I said dramatically, holding my stomach, which felt more bloated already.

"Are you gonna eat that bacon?"

"No, I'm . . . not much of a bacon eater." Lies! My loins would quiver at the taste of just one bite of crusty bacon. Oh, the naughty things I could do to a piece of bacon. But I knew what the salt and fat would do to me.

"Cool," he said, grabbing it off my plate. "You want to go to the beach?"

"That sounds great. But I didn't bring a bathing suit."

"I probably have one you can borrow," he said.

"You're not a cross-dresser, are you?"

He laughed and went into the bedroom. He came back out with a little pink bikini. "Will this fit you?"

"Are you kidding me? I'm not wearing somebody else's cooch,"

I said. "If you want to go swimming, you're going to have to buy me a virgin bikini."

Jake and I spent the afternoon at the beach, lying in the sun or cooling off in the surf. It felt natural and easy. When we got back to his place that afternoon, we fell right into bed. He was gentle and sweet and romantic and passionate, and I felt like we were locked away in a private little world.

In the middle of the night when I got up to get a glass of water, I opened the medicine cabinet and saw a tube of mascara and a bottle of Clinique eye makeup remover. The sticker on it said $24.95. Who in God's name spends $25 for eye makeup remover? Give me a jar of Vaseline and a few baby wipes and I'm good to go. I leaned over to peer out the bathroom door at Jake, asleep in the bedroom. Who else was he sleeping with? I found a cotton ball and took off my mascara. I had to admit, the fancy stuff worked really well. Then I went back to bed.

Over the next few weeks, Jake and I went out a lot, and I was becoming a serious beach bum between his place and my new (though temporary) home in Malibu. I really liked him, and I loved the recognition he got wherever we went out together. It made me feel like I was important. One night, lying in bed, I asked him the question I'd been thinking about for a few weeks.

"Jake, who's the owner of the bottle of eye makeup remover in your medicine cabinet? I don't care, I'm just curious."

He blushed, but acted cavalier. "Oh, you know—some chick I used to date. She's no you."

"No really, it doesn't bother me. I'm just curious." I realized as I said it that it really didn't bother me. I liked Jake, but I wasn't threatened by his romantic past, and I certainly hadn't stopped looking for Mr. Perfect.

chapter thirteen

My L.A. days were quickly passing into months. I'd wake up just in time to get to La Fenice for the lunch rush, then run to the Kameron house and put in my time as Carol's slave laborer. I was probably netting $10 an hour total, but to me, it was a fortune. I was paying the few bills I had on time, chipping away at my credit card debt, and continuing to starve myself successfully on most days, so I felt totally in control.

Sometimes, in weaker moments, I'd pull out the Sybil cookbook and flip through the pages, longingly gazing at beautiful photographs of cupcakes and roast turkeys and potato gratins. *Someday I'll cook again, when I'm married and settled and I have a beautiful kitchen, and it doesn't matter if I'm fat,* I thought to myself, although I didn't really believe that day would ever come—the getting married part, the beautiful kitchen part, or the part where it wouldn't matter if I was fat.

One afternoon at La Fenice, Carol's niece Jeannie Klein came in to see me. It wasn't unusual to see her at the restaurant, because she worked in the neighborhood and liked to drop by to say hello and share the latest gossip over lunch if she hadn't been to the Kameron's house for a while. I could tell she hadn't come in to eat. "Faith, guess what?" she said, with a twinkle in her eye.

"What?" Jeannie always had the best gossip about Hollywood. I figured she had something especially juicy. Maybe something on Josh or Carol.

"That guy you're dating, Jake?" This took me by surprise.

"Yes?"

"He's the guy I was dating last month."

I couldn't help sitting down. I stared at her. She looked at me, pleased with herself, as if she'd figured out the answer to a puzzle that had been driving me crazy. In fact, she had.

"No. Way."

"Yep, I finally got it out of him," she said. "I knew he was seeing someone else, and frankly, I'm *so glad* it's you! He had no idea we even knew each other. Hilarious, right? We have to get together to compare notes sometime."

I burst out laughing. "I'm so glad it's *you!*" I said. "But shouldn't we hate each other now?"

"Are you kidding? Jake's nice and cute and stacked and all, but girlfriends are forever. Besides, I broke up with him."

"You're so enlightened. Oh, shit, wait a minute. Was that *your* pink bikini?"

"I think I still have one over there. Why?" she said.

"You have no idea how intimate you and I almost were. We practically had a three-way."

"Sounds fun," she said with a laugh.

"Hey, I've got to go, but wait . . . first . . . you just have to answer one question for me. This is the thing that's been bugging me ever since I first spent the night at Jake's."

"Do tell."

"Why, Jeannie, why on earth would you spend twenty-five dollars on a bottle of eye makeup remover?"

"*That's* what's been bugging you most? Faith, you crack me up."

The next day, during the five minutes I was home between La Fenice and the Kamerons', the thing I'd been waiting for months on end, even while I was dating Jake, finally happened. The phone rang and I heard the voice I remembered so well and missed so much. "Darling!"

Vince Beck. My heart started pounding. I didn't know why he had this effect on me. I couldn't let on. But to hear his voice, after all this time . . . *play it cool, Faith.*

"Who is this?" I said.

"It's Vince, sweetheart. I've missed you! Why haven't you been in my life?"

"I don't know, Vince. I guess you'd be the one to answer that question," I said, matter-of-factly.

"To tell you the truth, sweetheart, I've been out of commission. I'm afraid I'd slipped into a bit of a binge, a bit too much of the hard stuff, and I've been . . . clearing things out, shall we say." Clearing things out? What did that mean? Was he a drug addict?

"Do you mean you were in rehab?" I said.

"I was at the spa, darling, at Canyon Ranch."

That was so L.A. Go to a spa and pretend it's rehab.

"And you didn't take me?" I laughed, trying to make it sound like a joke, rather than a bitter nag.

He ignored my question. "You know what the funniest thing is about people in California?"

"No, Vince. What's the funniest thing about people in California?"

"They say they're vegans, but they chain smoke. They go out jogging every morning like it's a religion, and then they go home and do heroin."

"Is that what you do?" I asked.

"No, no, dear. I never go out jogging." He laughed.

My mind reeled. No wonder he hadn't called me. He'd been detoxing! I was simultaneously filled with sympathy for him and anger that he hadn't told me or called me in so long. Was he a junkie? Or was he kidding? Not that he had any obligation to tell me anything, or call me ever again, but I'd felt a connection between us, and I was sure he felt it, too. There was something so sweet and appealing and sexy about him. How could he be an addict?

"Well, Vince, I've been pretty busy working. I'm sure it was nice at Canyon Ranch."

"Oh, it was, darling. It reminded me of Australia out there. We must go sometime."

"Sure," I said. "I won't hold my breath."

He finally seemed to figure out I was pissed off. "Darling!" he said with surprise. "Sweetheart! Are we angry?"

I smiled. Damn his charm! "I don't know about *you* . . ."

"Don't be angry with me! I was going to call you right after that day I saw you at the restaurant. You were so gorgeous and confident in your little dress. But then I was . . . waylaid. I meant to congratulate you on your new job with Josh!"

"How did you know about that?" I said.

"Oh, Josh and I go way back," he said. "And I keep tabs on you, darling. You know that."

"I see," I said, wanting to believe it. "And why are you calling me now?"

"*Now* . . ." He paused dramatically. "I'm calling to see if you would do me the honor, Faith Brightstone, of having dinner with me on Friday night."

"That was a very gentlemanly invitation."

"Spoken by an aspiring gentleman," he said.

I paused, not wanting to sound too enthusiastic, but desperate to accept. He could tell me all about his troubles, his struggles to get sober. He'd confide in me, like he'd never confided in any other woman. He'd look deep into my eyes and he'd fall in love with me.

"Sure, Vince," I conceded. "I'll have dinner with you."

chapter fourteen

As I lay in the giant bed in the Kamerons' beach house with Jake early on Friday morning, I couldn't stop thinking about Vince. Jake and I always had fun, but the more I got to know him, the more I realized that, famous or not, I probably was never going to take him too seriously.

Acting was everything to Jake, and it was all he really talked about. That, and his own biceps. He was a nice guy, but not particularly quick or witty. In some ways, he reminded me of what I'd learned at Meisenburg—he was like an empty shell that he could fill up with any character he wanted, but when he wasn't being a character, there wasn't that much to him. Maybe that meant he'd be a superstar—but it didn't bode well for our relationship, such as it was.

Vince was different. Unlike the other men I'd met in Hollywood so far, he wasn't needy, he wasn't stupid, he wasn't using me for anything. He was invested in his own career, but not at the expense of having a personality or the ability to actually listen when someone else was talking. And he just seemed genuinely to like me. Maybe that was the biggest turn-on of all.

Jake stirred and rolled over, draping his arm around my waist. "Hey, babe. What's up?"

"It feels like you are," I said, as his erection poked the back of my thigh. "But I've got to get to work."

"Yeah, me, too," he said, sadly. "Sorry, fella." He liked to call his penis "fella." I no longer found it cute. "But hey, I've got something to tell you."

"Uh-oh," I said. "Lay it on me."

He rolled over onto me. "I'll lay it on you," he said, and kissed my forehead.

"Ha ha."

"No, but really . . . I'm leaving town for a couple of months. Don't be sad!"

I tried to look a little sad.

"I got a part in a movie that's filming in Texas, and my parents moved there a few years ago, so I'm going to spend some time with them. I could even be gone through the end of the year, depending on how it goes. Are you gonna miss me?"

"Sure I am," I said. And I would. A little. But I couldn't help thinking that Jake leaving would open the door for me to start officially dating Vince Beck. The timing was kind of perfect. "But that's great that you got another movie! You're headed straight to the top." I kissed him, just in case it would be for the last time.

Friday finally arrived—my date with Vince. I was nervous. I hadn't seen him in so long, and now that he'd been to rehab or detox or whatever it was, would he be different? Would he still drink? If he was off any drugs he might have been on, that was great. But was *I* allowed to drink? I had a feeling I was going to need a drink.

Once again, I found myself staring into my closet in desolation. I remembered Vince's comment on our first date about the black dress. I needed something more colorful. He'd said I looked good in red. I took out my strapless red mini dress and looked at it. I brushed it off and smelled it. It still smelled faintly of smoke, from the last time I wore it out to a club. Why hadn't I gotten it dry-cleaned? I was annoyed with myself. I sprayed it with Chanel No. 5 and hung it up outside to air it out.

I was starving, but there was no way I was eating anything until tonight, when I would have to eat food like a normal person in front of Vince. To take my mind off food and calm my nerves, I decided to go ride the exercise bike at the gym for an hour, to burn off as many calories as I could before tonight.

After a long steam and a shower, during which I obsessed about Vince and how to make him fall madly in love with me, I plastered foundation over the dark circles under my eyes. I put on three coats of mascara, brushed just a little bit of glittery blush on my cheekbones, and decided to go with lip gloss instead of red lipstick this time. But then my face looked too shiny. I rethought the glitter and tried to wipe it away with a tissue but it wouldn't come off. I didn't want to start all over again. I rubbed off the lip gloss and went with a matte red lipstick that matched the dress.

I thought my black strappy stilettos might look best, but then again, I couldn't forget Vince's comment about going to a funeral. Did that apply to shoes? And even if it did, would I look weak for not wearing what I wanted to wear just because he'd made a comment? Like he'd ever remember he said it—but I remembered. I decided to go with the black shoes. Red dress, black shoes—a compromise. I can take constructive criticism, but I'm still my own person. I looked at myself in the mirror. "You look good," I said out loud.

"You look *hot*," said Perry from behind me.

I turned. "You think?" I posed for her.

"Oh, yeah. Who's the lucky guy?"

"Oh, nobody . . . just a certain *Vince Beck*."

"No way. He finally called you? That's awesome!" she said, clapping her hands.

"I can't believe I forgot to tell you. And I'm *so* glad you're home, I've just spent the whole afternoon totally obsessing about our impending marriage and children and my future career as an NBC executive."

"Of course you have," she said. "That's how you roll. Now, what are you going to wear for a wrap?"

A wrap! I hadn't thought of that! A sweater? A shawl? A scarf? I didn't have anything that matched. "Oh no! I don't know!" I shrieked. "Is it too cool outside for this dress without one?"

"It's getting that way," she said. "But don't panic. I think I have something."

She went into her room and brought out a gorgeous light woolen scarf, incredibly soft, like cashmere, in an exotic pattern of reds, golds, and greens. "This is beautiful!" I said. "What is it? I've never seen anything like it!"

"Supposedly it's called a pashmina," she said. "It's made out of some rare type of cashmere. It was really expensive, but I saw it at Bloomingdale's last week and I had to buy it, now that I'm gainfully employed."

I rubbed the pashmina between my fingers. "I'm in love with this," I said. "I can't believe everybody's not wearing them." Perry and I sat out on the veranda watching the waves and she helped me obsess some more, until Vince walked around the house and surprised us. He gave Perry a winning smile. "Good evening, darling!" he said. "You must be Faith's lovely roommate."

Perry gave me the "OK, this guy is good" look.

And he looked great. He had more color in his face than I'd ever seen, and he was a little slimmer. He'd always looked like a heavy drinker before, with that characteristic puffiness. Now he looked more like the outdoorsy type. "Arizona agreed with you."

"That it did, darling, that it did," he said, as he came over and kissed me on the cheek.

"Would you like a glass of wine or . . ." Perry looked stricken, suddenly remembering that I'd told her Vince had been in detox—or whatever. "Or . . . water?" she finished lamely.

"I think we should get going," I said, glaring at her.

"At your service, Miss," Vince said, offering me his arm. "Good-bye, dear!" he said to Perry. I realized I hadn't introduced them, but we were already halfway out the door, so it seemed too late.

I recognized the black Town Car, although the driver standing by the back door was different. I guess Vince must not have his driver's license back yet. The driver opened the door for us and we climbed in. "I wondered if you knew I moved out of my father's house," I said.

He took my hand and kissed it. "Darling, I always know where you are."

That could be creepy. Or flattering. I decided to go with flattering. "So . . . now that you're all detoxed . . . do you feel different?"

He turned to look at me. "Interesting question, dear. Actually, yes, I'd say so."

"And . . . in a good way?"

"Most definitely in a good way. Let's say I can"—he brushed his fingers along my thigh—"*feel* things more sensitively. Probably all the yoga they made me do. And the meditation . . . ommmmm . . ." He put his hands palm up on his knees, thumbs and index fingers together, and closed his eyes.

"Mmm, well that sounds nice," I said. But I had to get to the burning question, at least for me. "And . . . do you still drink?"

"Now and again," he said. "If I feel like it. Why, darling? Were you afraid I was on the wagon? It was just a spa."

He pulled me in closer and kissed the top of my head. "We'll have a drink together tonight, darling," he said. "I can promise you that."

"Maybe even two," I said.

A few minutes later, the driver pulled up in front of Boa Steakhouse and let us out. We walked under the arched entrance and into the restaurant. It was spacious with cream walls, dark wood, white tablecloths, and globe lamps casting a soft glow over the black leather booths.

"Good evening, Mr. Beck," said the well-dressed hostess. "We have your table ready. Right this way, please." It felt funny to be seated by the hostess, instead of being the hostess. But I could certainly get used to it.

I surveyed the menu with both interest and trepidation. Oysters? Crab cakes? Shrimp cocktail? My mouth watered at the thought of the New York strip, but I didn't dare eat something that rich. Cobb salad? No way. I couldn't eat all that bacon and egg and avocado. I was starting to get more and more nervous, until the waitress arrived with vodka martinis. Then Vince said to her, "We'd both like the shrimp cocktail, then the New York strip, two green salads with the house dressing, and let's see, darling, what kind of vegetables do you like on the side? Spinach? Mushrooms? Asparagus?"

"Mushrooms and asparagus, please," I said, relieved that he'd ordered, and delighted that somehow, he'd known exactly what I wanted, even better than I did.

"Mushrooms and asparagus it is, then," he said.

We talked and laughed and drank our martinis and ordered another round and a bottle of wine. I told him about my two jobs and the crazy things Carol Kameron made me do—a complete breach of the confidentiality agreement I'd signed with her, but after a couple of drinks, I managed to forget I'd ever signed it. Vince regaled me with hilarious stories about the network and *Hollywood & Highland,* and why the pilot for *Ocean Avenue* didn't get picked up.

My steak was huge, and delicious, and I could eat only about a third of it, so I had the waitress wrap up the rest to take home. Muffin could have a little treat in her dinner. Vince held my hand under the table and occasionally rubbed my thigh teasingly; throughout dinner he edged closer and closer to me in the leather booth until we were shoulder to shoulder and leaning into each other like honeymooners. The martinis had definitely gone to my head—I was eating mushrooms like they were French fries, and when Vince ordered a slice of New York cheesecake for us to split, I inhaled almost the whole thing while he watched in amusement. "I like a girl with a good appetite," he said. "It bodes well for her appetite in . . . other areas." I just smiled. With Vince, being a big eater seemed like a source of pride.

After dinner, Vince took me to a little out-of-the-way bar he said he liked. He ordered a port and I ordered a Sambuca over ice, and we flirted furiously until finally we had to get out of there. We ended up making out in the backseat of his Town Car again, but this time, he didn't show any sign of losing steam, or asking the driver to take me home. Whatever they'd done to him at that spa, I liked it.

"Darling," he whispered in my ear, after kissing my neck. "Do you want to come over to my place? I've got a bottle of champagne with your name on it."

Like I was going to say no to that.

Vince's driver took me home the next day, late morning. Perry was at the kitchen table drinking coffee when I walked in. She looked at me, in my red dress and smudged mascara and mussed-up hair, humming happily. "You've got to be kidding me," she said.

I just smiled.

"So, are we going down this road again?" she said.

"I don't know," I said. And I really didn't. But I did know we'd had amazing sex, and he'd been sweet and attentive and generous and gentle, and then I'd fallen asleep in his arms. "But I think this is it. It feels different this time."

Perry rolled her eyes but couldn't help smiling. "Here we go," she said.

chapter fifteen

With about thirty other girls, Perry and I sat together in a long row of chairs against a wall outside the audition room in a studio space in Burbank. I was nervous, but Perry wasn't auditioning, so for her, the pressure was off. Her job was going so well, she'd decided to take a break from acting, or maybe even quit. She was just there for moral support.

"Stop fidgeting," she whispered. "You'll be fine."

It was our policy never to show weakness in front of the other candidates at an audition.

The girl next to Perry looked at her anxiously, then looked at me, then turned away. She was fidgeting, too.

I clutched the sides in my hand and looked them over again and again. I'd at least learned by now that I didn't need to memorize them. I did need to practice them, and most of all, *feel* them. *Be* the character. I thought I'd gotten a lot better. Even the little bit I'd absorbed from Meisenburg before quitting had probably helped, as had the number of auditions I'd done. I was so much more experienced now than when I'd first started auditioning.

"This part is perfect for me," I whispered in Perry's ear, trying to convince myself more than her. "It's the perfect role to break into film.

It's a small part, but it's really interesting, and smart, and potentially memorable. It could be one of those 'steal the film' kinds of parts, don't you think?"

Perry just shrugged. "Whatever." She was clearly past all this.

An older woman with a clipboard came out of the audition room and called a name. The girl next to Perry jumped up. I noticed her hands were shaking slightly. She steadied herself and went into the lion's den.

I practiced the lines in my head. The sides suggested a script that was a lot more intelligent and well written than the script I'd auditioned with for *Ocean Avenue,* not to mention a thousand other TV shows and indie films I'd seen. This was a part I wouldn't be embarrassed about. I wanted it so badly, I could taste it. Now that I was officially seeing Vince Beck—or at least, it felt official—I wanted to do something more significant. I *had* to get this part. I wanted to deserve him.

The girl who had been sitting next to Perry came out, and everyone looked up, to see whether she looked elated, or disappointed, or anything else that would give us a clue, but she wasn't giving anything away. I stared at the lines again. The words were beginning to blur. *Focus, Faith. This is important. Call up every tool you've got inside. Be this girl. You can do it. Reel it in. Be the classiest version of yourself. Make it count, before your faith runs out.*

The woman with the clipboard came out again. My heart started beating faster. "Faith Brightstone," she said. She looked around, then looked at Perry. "I don't have you on my list. Did you want to audition, too?"

"Oh no," Perry said, "I'm just here for moral support."

The woman looked at Perry for a moment. "You can come in with your friend," she said.

"Come in with me!" I said. The idea of having Perry in there made the whole audition seem less intimidating, since I'd spent the last few nights reading the lines with her already.

Perry shrugged. "I guess so," she said.

"Here goes everything," I said. Perry patted my shoulder and I stood up. We followed the woman into the room, where two middle-aged men and a younger woman sat in chairs. The director smiled at me.

"What we're looking for here is a smart, sarcastic, highly educated girl—a painter who cares more about her art than her commercial success. Sarah is self-directed. She sees how scattered her best friend, the lead, can be, and she sees the bad decisions she makes, and provides somewhat of a cynical yet compassionate running commentary about it throughout the film—her opinions are always there in the background, but nobody ever takes her advice."

"Got it," I said. "Sounds familiar." I smiled, hoping to win them over, although the part of the lead sounded more like me. *Just pretend you're your own best friend, giving yourself advice,* I thought. But maybe they'd hear me read, and they'd give me the lead instead of the supporting role! Maybe I'd be even better for the part than whatever starlet they'd already cast. I could dream.

"Hey, you know what? You're closer in age to the other character than I am," said one of the women holding a script to Perry. "Why don't you go ahead and read the other part?"

"I guess I could," Perry said. The woman handed her a script. It seemed strange to me, but I shrugged it off. Perry and I already had a rhythm going, reading these lines together. I'd been making her help me with it all weekend. I'd be better with her reading the lines.

"Are you ready?" the director said to me.

"Sure." I cleared my throat, straightened my shoulders, and tried to channel "intellectual girl." "Art girl." "Smart girl." The director motioned to Perry to begin.

"I don't know what I'm going to do," Perry said. "I feel like I'm everywhere at once, and I want to connect with people but it's like they don't even see me. It's like I'm standing right there in front of people, and they look right through me, and I want to scream, 'Hey, I'm right here!' "

"What do you see when you look in the mirror?" I said.

"I see . . . nothing," Perry said.

"They see what you see," I said. "If you can't find yourself in your own mirror, you can't expect anybody else to find you. I don't think this is the time to get involved in another relationship. Why don't you take some time to figure out who you are, on your own terms? Stop trying to be what everybody else wants. What do *you* want?"

As I read the lines, I began to feel it—I began to understand what it meant to become the character. The words came out of me so naturally, but I wasn't watching myself, the way I usually did, stuck in my head. I was right there. I *was* Sarah.

"I don't know what I want!" Perry said. "I don't know what I want from myself, but I do know that I want him."

"You're not going to find your answers from him," I said, shaking my head, thinking instantly of Vince Beck. "He's no savior. He's a man-child and he just wants to play with you."

"But I love him!" Perry whined.

"You're going to do what you're going to do anyway," I said. "I don't know why you're asking me for advice. Go ahead. Fall in love again. You're just running around the same track you've been around a hundred times before, but what do I know? I don't even have a boyfriend."

"Thank you," said the director. "That was very good. But, do you mind switching parts? I'd like to see how it sounds the other way."

I'd nailed it. I could feel it. And now they wanted to hear more. Maybe they really were considering me for the lead! "Sure," I said. "I'd love to give it a try."

In the car on the way home, neither of us said anything. We were both occupied with our own thoughts, but I was feeling hopeful and excited. Something had happened to me in there. Something had shifted in my mind. I kept hearing the words from the audition, the words I'd said to myself: *If you can't find yourself in your own mirror, you can't expect anybody else to find you.* And, *you're just running around the same track you've been around a hundred times before.*

When we got home, the answering machine light was flashing. Perry pushed the button. "Hi, Faith? This is John Wallace, you auditioned for us today at Studio Z." My heart leapt.

"This is a bit awkward, but we're actually trying to track down your friend Perry," the voice continued. "We understand she wasn't really auditioning today, officially, but we really felt like she *was* Sarah. We liked your audition, too, but we just didn't think you were quite right for the part. You're very talented, obviously. But we were hoping you could put us in touch with Perry? We would really appreciate it. Just have her call us at this number."

The director left the number, and the message clicked off.

Perry and I stared at each other for a moment. Then she burst into tears.

"Hey!" I said, feeling like I should comfort her, and trying to swallow my anger and disappointment. "Hey, don't cry, this is great news! I mean, not for *me*, but . . ."

"I'm sorry!" she sobbed. "I know *you* wanted it, and I didn't even want it. And now . . ." She began to cry harder. "Now I *want it*."

"Maybe that's why you got it," I said, patting her on the back. "Isn't that the way it always goes? When you want it, you don't get it. When you don't want it, you get it. Scared money never wins." But I hadn't been scared. I'd been *good*. That's what was really beginning to sour me on this whole business. Even when you nail it, you might not get it, and that sucked.

She hiccuped. "I still love acting," she said, miserably.

"Of course you do," I said, trying to hide my devastation. "This is happy! You did it! You're going to be in a real movie!"

"If I can work it out with my job," she said, through her tears. "But I just feel so . . . awful for"—she gulped and sniffled—"for *you*."

"Oh, don't worry about me," I said, with resignation. "I'll be just fine. I'm a survivor."

I could see the police cars from two blocks away. Three of them were parked in front of the Kamerons' house, lights flashing. I parked on the street in front of the neighbor's house and walked up the drive.

I wondered if they would stop me, but nobody did. I knocked on the door, and the maid answered.

"What's going on?" I whispered.

She looked behind her, then leaned toward me. "It was Josh's writing partner," she whispered.

"Peter Jarrell?" I whispered back. The last time I'd seen him, he'd been rolling around on the floor at Carol's big party. "Yes," she hissed back. "He and Josh were doing a marathon writing session all weekend. This morning, they found him . . . dead . . . in the Kamerons' pool!"

"Oh my God! Are you serious?" I said.

She nodded vigorously, then let me in. I walked cautiously into Carol's office. It was empty. I peered out into the kitchen. Carol was talking to a police officer. I could see the pool through the glass doors. It looked empty. Then I saw the stretcher and the body bag. I shivered. Carol looked up as she saw me. "Faith, come here," she demanded.

I went into the kitchen. Carol looked pale and visibly shaken. "This is a nightmare, just a nightmare; what are the papers going to say?" she said. I'd seen her overreact to a million stupid little things, but this one finally seemed worthy of her hysteria. She was standing right next to the refrigerator with a glass in her hand, but she didn't seem to know where she was. I took the glass from her and poured her some orange juice, which she used to swallow a handful of pills she had in her other hand. "We're going to have to go away for a while. I just don't see any other option. Sandy's prepared a statement and faxed it to everyone," she said. She seemed to be talking to herself. Sandy was Carol's publicist.

"OK, Carol," I said.

"Oh, and Faith—I'm sorry, but with all of . . . this . . ." She waved her hand toward the pool. "I'm really going to have to leave town. I can't be here in this house now. So I won't be needing your services anymore. Tomorrow can be your last day. Also I will need you out of the Malibu house by the end of the month."

I didn't know what to say. I was numb. I hated the job and knew the house was only temporary, but it was all too much too fast. I just nodded and walked back down the hall to the office.

Jeannie found me before I left. "Can you believe it?" she whispered. "They're going to have to drain the pool. Vomit and shit. He let everything out when he croaked. And now they're leaving. Well, all for the best," she said, looking into the kitchen and shaking her head. "Carol's gearing up for a major anxiety attack, and neither one of us wants to be here to see it."

"Maybe you don't," I said. "But now I'm out of a job *and* out of a house!"

"Shit, that sucks," said Jeannie. "Well, I guess you better start looking. I'm out of here. I paid my respects but this is too much for me."

Propped up with big feather pillows in Vince Beck's bed, I scanned the classifieds. We'd been together for a month now, and we'd progressed from dating a few times a week to staying overnight more often than not, settling into a sort of weird domesticity that I didn't quite understand, but was trying not to overthink. Were we rehearsing for the real thing? I didn't dare ask, but I imagined what it would be like to be Mrs. Vince Beck.

"Maybe I should sign up with a temp agency," I said. "At least the jobs would keep changing." Part of me was hoping Vince would offer to support me, or let me move in, but so far he hadn't, and another part of me knew it was for the best, if I was ever going to make it on my own. I had to figure this one out for myself.

"That sounds fine, dear," he said, vaguely.

"I could always sign on as a top-shelf call girl. I have an in with Farrah Hughes," I said. "That would probably be the most profitable option."

"Lovely, darling," he said.

I punched him in the arm. He was absorbed in an exposé in *People* magazine about the gory details of Peter Jarrell's final binge. The reporters had dug up all kinds of witnesses willing to offer up their quotes. "It sounds like he'd just finished a script," he said, more to himself than to me. "I wonder if old Josh's got it, or if someone else has it."

"Josh's probably got it. They were working on something all night," I said. I was sure every director and producer in Hollywood would be mad to get ahold of it, no matter what it was. Peter Jarrell's final opus.

"I wonder if I could get hold of it," Vince said, murmuring to himself.

The first temp agency I called took me on, and I began working jobs before and after my La Fenice shifts. Receptionist, file clerk, envelope stuffer, telephone operator.

For the past week I'd been working as a receptionist for a booking agency. I was mostly responsible for answering phones and alerting agents when clients arrived. One of the agents who worked for the owner seemed to be particularly interested in me. His name was Henry Davis, and while he had an annoying habit of talking to my breasts, he kept telling me I should be an actress. I didn't bother to tell him that I was already trying to be one.

"You've got what it takes," he would tell me, over and over. "You've got something special. There's just something about you."

One day, about an hour into my shift, he came into the reception area and sat on the edge of my desk. "Can I help you?" I asked him, slightly annoyed. I was trying to file a stack of client folders, and had been surreptitiously looking for clues as to how I might convince one of the agents to take me on as a client.

"I'm waiting for a client," he said, looking toward the door. The parking lot outside was empty. "And"—he leaned over toward me— "I also wanted to ask you something."

I prayed he wasn't going to ask me out. While I had to admit that Vince and I had maybe fallen into a bit of a rut, and had started to argue a lot about stupid things that made me hate myself—like why he hadn't called or why he'd forgotten I had to work and made reservations for us, or why he left his clothes on the floor (what did I care, it wasn't even my house?)—I was still crazy about him. When we argued, I always waited until he left to cry my eyes out, so he wouldn't know how weak and smitten I was. My knees still felt wobbly whenever he smiled at me.

"What?" I said, suspiciously.

"Well"—he raised his eyebrows as if he was about to imply something more than his words—"I'm involved in helping a promising little studio cast a new movie. They told me about the storyline, and the first person I thought of was you."

"Really?" I put down the file in my hand and turned my chair toward him. "I'm listening," I said.

"Oh yeah," he said, "I think you would be the perfect person for one of the characters. The script practically describes you."

I hesitated. "I'm . . . always looking for something worthwhile."

"On the make. I like it," he said, leering at me. It occurred to me that the number of leering men was disproportionately high in L.A. "OK, so listen. Here's the number." He took one of his cards out of the card holder on the front of my desk, where all the agents kept a stack, and wrote a phone number on the back. "Call this number. Tell them Henry Davis sent you."

"OK . . . thanks," I said.

"If it goes well, I'll even sign you," he said. He pointed to the stack of client folders. "One of those folders could have your name on it."

I looked at the folders, and then I looked at Henry Davis, and I thought, *What the hell.* I really hoped this would come to something. I was so sick of false leads. Last week, I'd gone to an audition I'd seen advertised for a "high-profile media event." It was in a gorgeous mansion with a strange vibe. When I got there, a man introduced himself to me as an auditor and said he had to test whether I would be right for the position. He sat me down next to a machine with dials and gauges and told me to hold two cylinders with electrodes in them, and began asking me all these questions. He said the machine would register my thoughts. That scared the shit out of me. Was he trying to turn me into a brainwashed zombie? When he asked me if I knew what Scientology was, I realized it wasn't an audition at all. I told him I had to go to the bathroom, and then I bolted out of there as fast as I could.

"Sure," I said to Henry Davis. "Thanks. I'll call."

chapter sixteen

Vince hadn't called in two days, which was unusual. I started to obsess about where he could be, who he was with, what he was doing. Then I felt Henry Davis's card in my pocket. I took it out and looked at it. *Forget Vince Beck,* I thought. *You've got a career to manage.* I dialed the number.

"Rocket Productions," said the woman who answered the phone. She had a sexy, husky voice.

"Hi," I said nervously. "My name is Faith Brightstone, and Henry Davis asked me to call about a part in a movie."

"Of course," she said, in a matter-of-fact manner. "Can you come to the studio on Wednesday at four to meet with the producers?"

I'd have to get off work, but I thought I could make an excuse. She gave me an address downtown. That night, Perry and I went out and I didn't tell her about the audition. I'm not sure why, but I felt like I should keep it to myself. Instead, we talked about why Vince hadn't called me. I knew Perry had never been Vince's biggest supporter. She was suspicious of his motives, no matter how much I defended him.

"You can't be objective about a guy you're that ga-ga about. Sorry," Perry said. "I just see you losing your common sense around him."

"But he could be ideal husband material," I said, pleading.

"In what way?" she said.

"In the way that he's . . . funny and charming and cute . . . and rich and successful. And he really likes me. We have great chemistry."

"Has he said he loves you?"

"No," I admitted.

"I just don't want to see you compromise yourself for him. Granted, I don't know him all that well, but Vince Beck seems to me like a man who needs a lot of attention. I just don't see you as the woman standing behind the successful man. You're too ambitious. You need someone who can stand alongside you, and be your support and rock. You're not exactly the type to be someone's rock."

I sighed. She couldn't possibly understand.

I put on a simple blue cotton dress and sandals, lip gloss and blush, and clear polish on my nails. I curled my hair and shook it upside-down to give it some volume, spraying the roots with hairspray.

It took me a while to find the building, but finally I saw it—a run-down-looking studio that needed new paint, with a makeshift sign over the door that said "Rocket Productions." The girl at the front desk had platinum-blonde hair in a bad perm and lipstick much too bright for day. She wore a tight, scoop-necked pink T-shirt that showed her impressive cleavage.

"Faith Brightstone, here for a meeting with the director," I said to her, realizing I didn't even know the name of the movie.

"Hi, Faith," she said with a familiarity I didn't quite like. "Have a seat. He'll be with you in a moment."

A few minutes later, a broad-shouldered man with thick, side-parted brown hair and a wide walrus mustache emerged from behind a black curtain. "You must be Faith," he said. I stood up as he reached out to shake my hand. "I'm Rick Burton, the director. Henry speaks very highly of your abilities," he said.

I wasn't sure what Henry knew of my abilities, or what abilities he was talking about, but I smiled.

He held up the black curtain for me and I walked into a large unfinished space with a cement floor. On the other side of the space, five men and two women sat in chairs in a circle. They were all holding scripts and talking. It seemed legitimate. I thought maybe this was the way low-budget indie films go.

He brought me over. "Everyone, this is Faith Brightstone. Henry's sent her over. He thinks she's the Tanya we've been looking for."

Everyone looked up at me and smiled. The men all looked like late thirties, and the women all looked like early twenties. "Hi, Faith," some of them said.

"Yes, welcome, welcome," said Rick Burton. "We were all just going over the script." He handed me one. "OK, is everybody ready? Let's try Scene Three, on page forty-six."

I got the part, although it all seemed too easy, considering what I'd been through in the past year. I cheerfully told Perry I'd gotten cast in a movie, too, and we went out to celebrate, but somehow I couldn't drum up the same level of excitement about my so-called movie as she obviously had about hers.

We began filming the following week, at a house in the Valley that the director said belonged to a friend of his wife's. The script wasn't the worst I'd ever read, but it certainly wasn't going to win any Oscars. It also involved me taking off my shirt and kissing another girl, but I was beyond caring. Even if it went straight to video, they were paying me $500. And that was $500 more than I had in the bank. Nobody would ever see it, and what did I care if they did? I had to pay my rent.

I arrived on the set and while the blonde receptionist, Celeste, who was also apparently the makeup person, powdered my nose and arranged my hair, the director told me we would film the whole movie in four days. Being in the makeup chair made me feel cool and professional and glamorous, and I began to feel more positive about the movie. Maybe it would be OK. Maybe it would even become a cult classic. It had that strange, offbeat, indie-film feel to it. Either that or it would be just another cheesy B-movie.

"OK, girls," the director instructed. "First scene. You're on the bed together, watching TV. You're best friends, and there's always been a certain chemistry between you. April is boy crazy, and Tanya, you're the one who's more mature and interested in experimenting."

We climbed onto the bed. I tried not to show my nerves.

"Ready and . . . action."

"This show sucks," April said, pressing the fake remote. "Is there anything else on? When are the boys getting here?"

"Not for at least a half hour," I said. "I think we're going to have to think of something else to do."

"Like what?" she said, all Midwestern innocence.

"Have you ever kissed a girl?" I said it in my best teasing voice.

"What?" April giggled her lines. "Of course not! Have you?"

"No . . . but I'd like to try." The script said that I slipped my arm around her waist as we both lay on the bed. "Maybe we should try it. Just to see what it's like. As long as there's nothing on TV . . ."

"OK," April said it with a little thrill in her voice.

"Wait a minute," I said, breaking character. I was feeling very uncomfortable. "Hold on. This is all feeling a little soft-core porn to me." I wasn't even sure what that meant, but something just felt wrong.

"What? No, no!" said Rick, in a booming voice, as if the very notion disgusted him. "It's an art film. No, not soft-core porn, nothing like that."

"OK," I said, hesitating.

"It's going to be classy and cool. I can guarantee it," he said.

I looked at April. She smiled at me.

"Action!" Rick said.

I leaned on my elbows and tried to look slyly at April. "So, April," I said. "Have you ever kissed a girl?" I could feel my face turning red, and willed myself to stay calm.

"Cut!" Rick yelled. He walked over to us.

"Just relax, Faith," he said. "It's film, not stage. You don't have to be so loud. Think soft. Think *sexy.*"

"OK," I said. *It's acting,* I told myself. *Pretend you like kissing girls! You've never even kissed one before, so how do you know you* won't *like it?*

"Hold on," said Celeste. She ran up to me and powdered my nose again, and arranged my hair around my shoulders. "You have such a great body," she said. "I love your shoulders."

"Thanks," I said, feeling creepy.

Celeste and Rick stepped back. "Action!" Rick called.

I regrouped. *Come on, Faith. You can do this. You need the money. It's not so bad.*

"So . . . Have you ever kissed a girl?" The words came out with surprising ease this time. I looked at her flirtatiously.

She stared at me, shocked. "What?" She blushed. "Of course not. Have . . . have you?"

She was actually pretty good, I thought. I tried to match her level of believability. *You're the seductress, Faith. So horny, you'll kiss anything.*

"No . . . but I'd like to try." I slipped my arm around her waist and then started rubbing her back. It felt strange, alien, to touch a girl like that. "Maybe we should try it. Just to see what it's like."

"OK," she said, shyly but eagerly. We leaned in toward each other. I tried not to cringe. Was I really going to do it? Was I really going to kiss a girl? On camera?

Our lips met, and we kissed. I tried to make my lips do what they did when I kissed a man, but it felt so foreign. She seemed really into it. She started to make little moaning noises, and then her tongue touched my upper teeth. When she slipped her hand down the front of my dress, I pulled away suddenly, out of surprise, but fortunately, it was just when the boys came through the door, so it didn't look like I was pulling away out of disgust. April was flushed and grinned at me. I suddenly became preoccupied with whether or not this counted as an actual girl kiss.

"Hey," said one of the boys. "What are you guys doing?"

"Oh, nothing," I said. My ears were ringing and I felt a little dizzy and sick, like I knew I'd done something wrong.

"Nothing at all," April giggled. "We were just talking about you guys."

"Yeah, I'll bet. Hey, we brought more beer and sandwiches, and this is Rita! She was just knocking off work and she wants to party with us."

Rita, the character played by the other girl, slithered into the room with all the charm of a reptile.

"Hi, Rita," said April. "Hand me a beer, will ya?"

"Cut!" Rick called. "Excellent, that was excellent work everyone. Great take. We'll probably do it a few more times, but I'm loving what I'm seeing."

I wasn't. In fact, I wasn't loving any of this. I wasn't loving the kiss, or April, or Rick, or Celeste, or the sleazy studio, or the grungy set in the strangely abandoned house, or the meaningless script. If this wasn't soft porn, I didn't know what was. I wasn't loving Henry for getting me into this, or the temp agency for sending me to a place that agented films like this. In fact, at this moment, I wasn't loving La Fenice or my new apartment or Perry or Jake Mandell or even Vince Beck. Most of all, I wasn't loving *me*.

You've got to finish, I told myself. *Follow through.*

So I did. I finished out the week. I kissed April probably a hundred times. And the girl who played Rita. And both the boys. I took my shirt off, and nobody would know I wasn't enjoying every minute of it. The director loved me. He said I was a natural, and I realized with increasing horror, as the week rolled on, how easy it would be to keep doing movies like this, and how it could slip into something even darker, until I was swallowed up in a black hole. Until I would be able to call Sandra and say, sure, sign me up, I can be a call girl; it'll be a step up from what I'm doing now. Until I'd be willing to do anything.

At the end of the week, we wrapped. I got paid. As I walked out of the studio, April called after me, "Call me, Faith!"

Faith. I thought about my name. The word echoed in my ears.

I went home to my empty apartment that Perry and I hoped would be a new beginning, but felt stale already.

There were two messages on the machine when I got home. The first was from the restaurant: "Faith, this is Givanni, from La Fenice. I'm sorry, my dear, but the restaurant is going through a slow period. We're going to have to lay you off. I'm so sorry, you've done a good job for us. Come in for a drink though, on me. We'll get you back here when we can." Lovely. Perfect.

The second message was a woman's voice I didn't recognize. "This message is for Faith. This is Trina Beck. Vince Beck's wife." Her voice was filled with poison. "Look, I don't know who you think you are, but I want you to stay away from my husband, you little slut. Just because we're separated doesn't give you the right to steal him away from me. We're working it out now, and he told me everything, and if I ever see you again, I won't be responsible for what I might do. You bitch."

I felt incredibly stupid, and incredibly free. So that was it for me and Vince. The coward never even had the guts to tell me himself. I would never again have to agonize over whether or not he was the one. He was *not* the one, and I was never going to be Mrs. Vince Beck, because there already was one. My heart was torn in two, but I also felt cool and calm. I'd been released—from my obsession, from this path I was on. And I realized I'd had enough, not just of auditions, not just of acting, but of L.A. itself. Suddenly, I missed New York like I'd never missed anything before.

I took a deep breath and calmly packed up all my essentials into a suitcase and a carry-on. Perry could either throw out the rest of my stuff or send it to me. I wrote her an apologetic note. I put Muffin in the car and drove straight to the airport. New York on the red-eye. I was going home.

PART TWO

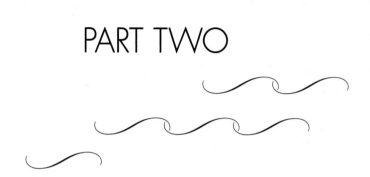

chapter seventeen

Five years later . . .

just need a week. *Please.* Can you give me a week?"

The woman from the charge card company paused, as if consulting the script in front of her, looking for the part that tells you what to say when the in-default charge card customer starts begging. "Your payment is already three months late," she says finally, without an ounce of emotion or empathy.

"I know. I do. *I am trying,*" I said, "but ever since I moved back to New York from L.A., nothing has worked according to plan. I am not trying to get out of paying, and I am not making excuses. Really. Just give me a minute to explain. I think things are finally about to turn around."

"Ma'am, I sympathize, but we need your payment or I'm going to have to refer your account to collections."

I snorted. Collections. Collections and I go way back. Still, if I could avoid it . . .

"If you can look in my records, you'll see how regular my payments have always been," I said, hoping she couldn't really look back and see that they weren't very regular at all. "I've been through a lot but I almost always make my payments on time."

"That doesn't mean you can stop making them now," she said.

I sighed. "Can you tell me your name?"

She hesitated. "Gloria Murphy."

"Gloria, I'm Faith."

They say you're supposed to humanize yourself to violent criminals, so they don't hurt you. I figured it might work with creditors, too.

"I know your name, ma'am," she said. This wasn't going to be easy.

"Look, Gloria. Maybe we can work something out. Membership has its privileges, right?"

"Yes, and we're about to revoke yours," she said.

"Oh c'mon now, don't you think that's a little harsh? Just let me explain. Will you let me explain?"

Gloria sighed loudly. "All right," she said. "But don't take too long, I've got a lot more calls to make. And this better be good."

I stood up and started pacing across my tiny apartment on the Upper East Side, the apartment I was barely managing to afford, trying to find a new angle that might possibly buy me a little more time.

"O.K. the short version. When I moved back to New York with nothing but the clothes on my back and my dog, I started working for a high-end event-planning business in the evenings. But it still wasn't enough money to get by. So I tried to figure out what else I could do. I'm a huge fan of eBay. You know eBay, right?"

"Mm-hm," said Gloria, as if I were trying to sell her a used car.

"So I got this idea that I could open up one of those little storefronts that sells people's stuff on eBay. I thought it would be really fun, and I'd be great at it because I buy everything on eBay. I'm an eBay expert at this point. In fact, you should see the Michael Kors skirt I just got . . ." I paused. Oh Jesus, maybe I shouldn't be telling her about my recent purchases.

"Anyway. I was seeing this guy at the time, Saul D'Angelo. He was an Italian mobster wannabe, who happened to have gone to the best private schools, so the gangster persona didn't really fly. You know the type?"

"Not really," Gloria said.

"Well, he wasn't the nicest guy. He'd tell me I was frigid whenever I had a headache. He'd tell me my boobs were saggy, or he'd make fun of me for being old, because I was two years older than him."

"I know *that* type," Gloria said. Did I detect a hint of sympathy? I jumped on it.

"An asshole, right?"

"Mm-hm," Gloria said. Now she sounded more like she was in church. I was preaching to the choir.

"And I knew it, but I couldn't get away from him because just after he was at his meanest, he'd tell me how sorry he was and how much he loved me, and I couldn't resist him. There was just something about him. I kind of bought his tough-guy bullshit. And I thought I was in love with him, when I was really just trying to forget someone else I'd been in love with before."

"I hear that," Gloria said. "But ma'am, remind me what this has to do with your inability to pay this bill."

"I'm getting there, I swear!" I said. "So, I wanted to open this eBay store. I saved up money, but I wasn't making very much so it was taking forever. When I finally told Saul about it, he told me he could get me a storefront, and if I put the year's rent on my credit card, he would pay the monthly payments."

"And you fell for that?" Gloria said.

"He seemed like he really wanted to help me," I said. "In my defense, we'd paid for things like that before. Saul had a ton of money but really bad credit."

"Mm-hm," Gloria said. I could see she wasn't won over just yet.

"So, he finds me this great place on the Upper East Side, not too far from my apartment, and I put the whole year's rent on my card. So then he tells me he can get me a huge amount of inventory to sell, because he knows people. I probably should have been suspicious, but he said I just needed to make a deposit on the stuff, and then I'd get double the money back when I sold it."

"Honey, you're too trusting," she said. "Tell me this didn't turn out badly."

Gloria was very perceptive.

"It was all so much fun for the first couple of weeks. I got the coolest stuff—antiques, beautiful designer clothes, a Vera Wang wedding gown, a couple of Rolexes, and this beautiful five-carat diamond engagement ring. I would pretend it was all mine, and then I started taking photos and listing everything."

"So what happened?" Gloria said.

"Within two weeks, the police were at the door. Everything had been stolen. It was all hot. *Everything.* Jewelry, designer clothes, antique china, electronics. The list of sellers I'd been given to forward the money to were all fake, it was all going to the people who stole it in the first place—apparently it was some Russian crime ring. The cops took everything into evidence. And that was the end of my business."

"Did you make him pay up?" Gloria said.

"Um . . ." I said. "Well, actually, that's when I found out Saul had been cheating on me the whole time with an eighteen-year-old waitress."

"Mm-hm," Gloria said.

"So I dumped him. I had to. My self-respect was at risk! But then he refused to pay the rent on the place. I had to close down. I couldn't afford to sue him for it, and I didn't even know if I would win. I didn't have any merchandise, but there I was, stuck with a year's worth of rent and a big deposit on all the stolen stuff, and nobody to help me pay for it."

"And that's what's on this credit card? Because I'm not hearing the good news."

"But wait, there *is* good news!" I insisted.

"Ms. Brightstone, please get to the point," she said. At least "Ms. Brightstone" was a step up from "ma'am."

"I just wanted to explain to you how the balance on the card got so high. And let me tell you, I certainly learned to be a lot more careful about selecting business partners. Anyway, so here I am, with this huge balance, and an empty storefront on my hands for the next year. I needed money, and I'm a really good baker, so I got a job at a vegan bakery to help pay the bills, while doing the event planning at night. But I still wasn't making enough. So then I got an idea."

"Does this one involve any boyfriends?" Gloria said.

"No, and that's exactly why I think it's going to work!" I said. "I developed a lot of great muffin recipes while working for this vegan bakery, and people started asking specifically for the muffins I made. So, our event-planning company had these portable stoves. And I had this empty shop space. So, I sort of borrowed one of the stoves and brought it over to the shop space, and I bought a bunch of the baking supplies for cost down in Chinatown, and I started baking my own vegan muffins."

"Vegan muffins?" said Gloria.

"Yes!" I said. "They're so good. I wish you could try one right now, you'd totally see the opportunity. Give me your address, and I'll send you a package."

"Is that supposed to be a bribe?" Gloria asked.

"No!" I said. "Of course not! I just want you to understand how much potential they have."

"Mm-hm," Gloria said, back to playing the cynic. "And this is going to make you some money how, exactly?"

She was killing me! But I was determined to finish my story.

"There I was, perfecting my recipes and trying them out on all my friends, and they're all saying, 'Faith, you have to start a business!' So, I start talking to one of my ex-boyfriends, Stefan, who used to work for a bakery corporation as an executive, and I convinced him to invest."

" 'Invest' is the first promising word I've heard out of you so far," she said. "But I thought you said this didn't involve a boyfriend."

"Ex-boyfriend," I corrected her. "And I told you the good news was coming," I said. "So, Stefan told me about the Fancy Food Show, this major trade show here in New York where a lot of gourmet food businesses debut, and he signed me up. We're going to introduce Have

Faith Muffins at the show. We've even hired a bakery assistant and a small temp staff to get us ready, and transformed my old eBay shop space into a little bakery."

"Thanks to the ex-boyfriend."

"Well, true, but Gloria, you should taste these muffins. They're fantastic. They're going to be huge. They can't fail. Who wouldn't want to eat Have Faith Muffins?"

"Cute name," she admitted.

"So you see, I predict a big influx of cash in the very near future. Please, tell me you can give me just a little more time. I can probably pay off the whole balance at once, after the show."

"Mm-hm," said Gloria.

"Come on, just give me a chance. Things are going to change for me, I can feel it."

"Well . . ." said Gloria, pausing. I waited in hopeful silence. Finally, she said, "Let me see if I can get the eBay merchandise charges removed, since that was for stolen merchandise. Do you have any proof, like a police report?"

"Yes!" I said. This was great news. I didn't even know that was possible.

"Fax it to me. And as for the rest of it, the year's lease, I can give you until the end of the month. But at that time, the remaining balance needs to be paid *in full*. Do you understand?"

"Yes, I do, thank you so, so much Gloria!" I said, feeling a huge sense of relief. "I won't disappoint you."

"And honey? Do it on your own next time. Don't rely on a man."

"That sounds like very good advice. Thanks, Gloria," I said.

I hung up the phone and collapsed on the couch. Convincing strangers that my luck was about to change was exhausting. Now all I had to do was convince myself.

I had a feeling I was going to need some insurance, just in case the Fancy Food Show didn't go as I hoped it would. I went into my bedroom and stared into my closet at the rows of expensive shoes and designer handbags. I didn't want to do it, but I realized I had no choice. I was going to have to sell something.

I took a red Marc Jacobs hobo bag off of a hook. I loved it. Could I bear to part with it? Maybe that and the Gucci tote. I picked up a pink Fendi baguette and put the Marc Jacobs bag back on the hook. I eyed the Van Cleef & Arpels necklace that my former fiancé had given me. No, maybe I would keep those in reserve. I didn't want to think about him right now. I'd process that later. I put the two handbags into a shopping bag, and headed out the door.

"Faith! You brighten my day whenever you come into my modest little shop."

"Sure, Gus . . . modest," I said, looking at the black leather thigh-high Jimmy Choo boots he was repairing. Gus's Shoe Repair Shop was a tiny, old-fashioned storefront just a few blocks from my apartment, where Gus reheeled and repaired some of the most amazing shoes I'd ever seen. He also sold shoes and handbags on consignment, originals and knockoffs, and had a case of jewelry and watches. I'd first discovered him when I broke a heel off my favorite pair of red pointy-toed Manolos. "Can you sell these for me?"

Gus was an unusually short, wrinkled little German man with a head of thick, lush wavy gray hair and a big grin that showed off his dazzling false teeth. "For you? Of course!" He held out his thick, stubby hands and I handed him the Gucci and Fendi bags. He looked them over. "Nice. Very nice."

"As soon as possible—I need the money yesterday," I said, trying not to think about the fact that I was selling handbags to pay a bill that I'd racked up in part by buying handbags. And shoes. I hadn't mentioned to Gloria the fashion purchases that had further elevated my already bloated bill. I picked up a pair of black patent-leather Louboutin platform pumps with red soles, on consignment for just $300, less than half of what they cost new. "These are gorgeous."

Gus raised his eyebrows at me, and I put them back down. "You're going the wrong way," he said.

"I know. I know!" I said.

He wagged a finger at me. "Now you be good!" he lectured. "And I'll have some money for you soon."

I walked out of his store and down Madison, past bistros and spas, wine bars and the pet salon where I had Muffin groomed. I passed one of those euro-cafés on Madison that I can never afford unless someone takes me there, where I'd heard that the high-class prostitutes get a 40 percent discount. I was still annoyed that I couldn't get the hooker discount. But I'd passed on that opportunity back in L.A.

Although I hadn't burdened Gloria with the details, I'd just broken off an engagement to a man who loved me, who was nice and handsome and wealthy and had actually offered to pay off every penny of my debt if I married him and moved to Westchester. And I'd just said no. I needed my friend Bronwyn to remind me why.

She was the only mostly happily married friend I had, though she was never one to push the institution on me. Instead, she'd obsess about all the details of my single life, the good and the horrific, living vicariously through me. She dieted obsessively and went on and on about how I could eat whatever I wanted and still be skinny, no matter how many times I told her how much I'd struggled to get over all of that. I waved to her. She was already sitting at a table outside.

"What's wrong with me?" I said, as I pulled out the chair. "I practically left him at the altar. Am I insane?"

"Orin was a really nice guy, but he wasn't right for you," said Bronwyn. She waved at a waiter. "Iced tea and . . ." she looked at me.

"A pint glass of vodka?" I suggested.

"Two iced teas!" she said.

"I have creditors about to knock down my door. He was going to pay off everything."

"And you're not some whore looking for a payoff," she said.

"That's a matter of opinion," I said.

"Look, he's a catch. On paper. He's a big Wall Street trader, he's rich, he's handsome, he's nice to you. He wants to rescue you and whisk you off to suburbia to live in a big house with a white picket fence and have his babies. Come on, he's so not your type."

"Why isn't that my type again?" I said.

"You want to make it on your own."

"Well, I'm doing a bang-up job so far," I said, cynically.

"Three words: Fancy Food Show."

"You're right," I said. "You're right."

It was a warm beautiful day and suddenly I was full of hope. Bronwyn was just telling me what I already knew, which is exactly what I needed. I couldn't have married any of the men I'd been with before, and although I got the closest with Orin, had even accepted his proposal, I'd had to break it off. I realized I wouldn't have been happy. None of those men were the right men at the right time. Maybe I would never get married. Did it really matter?

"I don't care if I ever get married," I said, trying out the idea.

"Good for you," said Bronwyn. "That's the spirit. Go for yours!"

After lunch, I took a cab over to the Jacob Javits Convention Center to help set up for the Fancy Food Show, which would open the next day. Alanna, the bakery assistant I had hired, and my ex-boyfriend and current investor, Stefan, were meeting me there. We had a lot to do, but Alanna and I had spent two weeks perfecting three different recipes for the show: Cranberry Almond, Maple Pecan, and Banana Oatmeal Chocolate Chip. We'd mixed and sifted and baked and tasted for hours each day, almost always agreeing about which ones were good and which ones we should scrap, until they were perfectly irresistible. We needed fifteen hundred mini muffins to hand out, and we'd spent the last forty-eight hours baking them.

When I arrived at the convention center, Alanna was already there. Although she was just barely five feet tall, she was excellent at barking orders and managing the temp baking staff, and she already had everything under control. She'd grown up in a bakery in Mexico City that her parents owned, so she wasn't intimidated by large orders, and at just twenty years old, she was extremely efficient and practical, and had an excellent palate. She had been on the kitchen staff during a party I'd planned for the opening of a Zen Spa in Chelsea, when I was still working as an event planner. I'd spotted her immediately. She was fast, efficient, and no-nonsense. I knew I would hire her someday, and here she was.

"How's it going?" I said.

"I've got everything unpacked," she said. "We just have to set it all up."

I'd bought tall, narrow glass pasta jars and filled them with muffin ingredients, to decorate the display: almonds, cranberries, chocolate chips, oats, pecans, lemons. I had red aprons designed with my Have Faith logo, which we would all wear. I hung them on a hook along the back of the booth. I had my order book, my calculator, my cash box, and the table we would use to write orders. We hung the sign and set out the brochures and order forms. After covering the booth, I went home to figure out what to wear.

That night, I lay in bed, obsessing. I had no idea what to expect from the Fancy Food Show, but whatever it would be, I decided I was *definitely* ready. I was poised for success. *Now sleep, Faith. At least just close your eyes. You want to look your best when your ship finally comes in.*

chapter eighteen

On Sunday morning, I couldn't believe the convention hall was the same space that we'd labored in the day before.

The place was packed with major national food companies taking up the equivalent of ten booths, whose products are in every supermarket, to the tiniest of start-ups, like me. Although the show didn't open until ten a.m., the hall was already full of people at seven a.m. Exhibitors milled around checking out one another's displays. There was an air of high tension in the building—everybody desperate or hopeful or a little of both. It was also a room full of dreams, brilliant ideas, aspirations. Row after row of The Little Product That Could wedged in between the food industry giants. Would it be a good year? How many orders would we all write?

Victoria, my often-late-night partner in crime and good friend, was already helping Alanna put the last touches on the booth. She gave me a big smile and a hug.

Victoria was a hairdresser, not a baker, but she was always helping me out. She worked on models, but celebrities sometimes called her to come to their homes to do their hair before a big event. I met her when a former boyfriend brought me backstage at a show during Fashion Week because he had to interview Gisele Bündchen. While he was talking to Gisele, I was standing back against a wall, waiting, feeling out of place and slightly intimidated by the frenetic activity all around me, when this girl with black hair in a high ponytail and Betty Page bangs yelled at me. "Hey, you, girl against the wall, could you hand me that case?" She had a model's hair piled into one hand and couldn't quite reach the metal box full of bobby pins and scissors and hairspray. "You know . . . as long as you're not *doing anything.*"

I'd been so grateful to have something to do that I volunteered to be her unofficial gofer for the next hour. She was funny and cynical and a fast talker like me, so when my date was ready to go, we exchanged numbers and had kept in touch ever since. Victoria was also a foodie, so whenever I wanted to try a new restaurant or test a recipe, she was my girl. I knew she'd love the Fancy Food Show.

We had a good booth space—Stefan had pulled strings, and we were just down one row from the entrance, near the new product showcase. Alanna set the muffins out on silver trays. They looked adorable—cute little buttons of oats and chocolate chips, pecans, cranberries and almonds, in bright red muffin wrappers. I obsessively straightened the stack of brochures, the table skirts, the signage. Then I stepped back. The booth looked good. Inviting. Delicious. I picked up a brochure. There I was, right on the front, in my red apron, smiling, holding a tray of muffins, my hair wavy and perfectly arranged around my shoulders (Victoria had done it), and in an arc over my head were the words "Have Faith: A Bakery You Can Believe In," with a white dove forming the H, and then in smaller letters below, "Always vegan, always whole grain, wheat-, egg-, and dairy-free!"

At ten, the buyers filed into the hall. The first few people walked past us, and I began to panic, but then a young woman in Birkenstocks stopped. "Vegan?" she said. Victoria and I both nodded eagerly. "Nobody died to make these muffins," I assured her. And before I knew what had hit me, people were asking questions, sampling muffins, grabbing brochures—and I was writing orders. I had a line.

I put Alanna on order-writing duty, and I took a tray of muffins and stood in front of the booth, calling out to the crowd:

"Saving the world, one muffin at a time!"

"Excuse me, sir—would you like to try a muffin?"

"Muffins! They're not just for breakfast anymore!"

"Miss, did you know that nothing goes better with your afternoon martini than a Have Faith Muffin?" That last one didn't even make sense, but I was on a roll, and I found it hilarious.

People turned, smiled, came toward me, laughed, sampled a muffin, mmm-ed and ooh-ed and asked for more. We were a hit! "We've got this, boss," Alanna said.

I began to worry we'd run out of samples. Could we bake another fifteen hundred for tomorrow? I didn't have time to think about it. I kept answering questions, sending people to Alanna's table to fill out orders, and smiling, smiling, smiling. "Saving the world!" I called out some more. "Nothing goes better with a martini than a muffin!" I was riding high.

After an initial hour-and-a-half flurry of activity, we had a brief lull and a chance to regroup. Alanna looked hopelessly at the savaged trays of muffins, then tried to arrange them and fill in the gaps with fresh product. "Is this really working?" I asked her. "Are we really doing something big here?"

"I just hope we can fill all those orders," she said, grinning.

"I'm going to go forage," said Victoria.

"Keep the apron on—you can be our walking advertisement," I said.

I looked at the stack of orders. A local vegan café put in one order for fifty muffins to be delivered weekly for six weeks. Two delis wanted onetime deliveries of twenty-five muffins. There were a handful of other orders from health food stores, and several individuals who wanted to sign up for regular deliveries to their homes. A vegan café in New Jersey wanted a hundred for a party, and a vegan catalog wanted to set up an as-needed account, if we could guarantee we could ship frozen. I said we could. Another store asked if we could do vegan birthday cakes. I said sure. I was agreeing to everything, and just hoping I wouldn't promise something I couldn't deliver. I could always figure it out after the show.

We'd also had eight or nine people who said they would come back to order, five people who complimented me on the name of the company, even though they didn't order anything, and one guy who said I was prettier in person than I was on the brochure. Flattering, of course, but he obviously wasn't going to order anything.

"That was pretty amazing for less than two hours. Is the rest of the day going to keep going like this?" I asked Alanna.

She shrugged. "Search me. But I hope so!"

Just then, Stefan came up to the booth. "How's it going, girls?" he asked.

"We've already got orders!" I said, waving the stack of order forms at him. "A lot of them. We're a success!"

"I knew you would be, kid," he said.

A few more people began to gather around the muffin trays. "Have Faith and help yourselves," I encouraged them. "We're saving the world, one muffin at a time!"

Just then I noticed a group of people standing across the aisle, watching me. I smiled and waved them over. "Come on over. Try a muffin. Is it happy hour yet? Muffin happy hour? We should be serving these with tequila shots." I was getting giddier and sillier by the minute.

The three men and two women came across the aisle and one of the men reached out and shook my hand. "We've been watching you for a while," he said. "Are you Faith?"

"I am," I said, handing them a brochure. "Proprietor of Have Faith Muffins. Always vegan, always whole grain, always wheat-, egg-, and dairy-free!"

"Is this your business partner?" the man said, gesturing to Stefan.

"Oh no, this is just an investor I used to sleep with," I said breezily. Everyone laughed, including Stefan.

"So you're the sole owner?"

"She's the sole owner all right," Stefan offered, smiling. "No room for anybody else at the top of this organization!"

They all looked at each other. "Tell us about your business," said one of the women.

I wondered if they were investors. "It's called Have Faith Bakery," I said, hopefully. "The product is absolutely fantastic. I've got major interest. In the first hour of the show alone, we wrote over fifty large orders." A slight exaggeration, but close enough. "My only limit has been in having the backing to really take it to the next level. Frankly, I've got the drive, and I think the health-conscious community as well as the vegan community will go wild for my products. They're that good." I straightened my shoulders and tried to look confident. Whatever they were interested in, it looked like they had a lot of money behind it.

I turned to the muffin trays and was relieved to see that Alanna was finished restocking them, so I invited them all to sample the muffins. They all nibbled and smiled and nodded.

"I'm vegan," said one of the women, "and I can't believe these are dairy- and egg-free. They taste delicious."

"Vegan baking is the next frontier," I told her. "I truly believe that. And these mini muffins are only fifty calories each. I think every deli in the city should be carrying them. And every organic café and vegan market and anybody else offering health-conscious food. I want to democratize health, bringing it to the people. It shouldn't be so elitist. You shouldn't have to be rich to be healthy . . . and God knows I've tried to be both!"

"Excellent. Just excellent. Faith, my name is Darren Donlon, and these are my colleagues, Max Weidenbach, Priscilla Higgs, and Marissa Poland. We produce a television show and we think you might be right for a role."

I stared at them, momentarily speechless. I'd imagined they owned a health food store, or maybe a restaurant chain. "Wow. OK. Well,

I . . . gave up acting, actually," I said. "As you can see." I motioned to my booth.

"No no, it's not a show that requires acting. It's a reality show."

I had no idea what he was talking about, but I smiled. I wasn't sure what to say. Finally I looked at Stefan, and then back at the group. "What's a reality show?"

They all laughed. The woman Darren had introduced as Priscilla said, "Faith, we are with Tidal Media Group, and we represent a show that's going to be on television next season. It's a kind of contest, and we're looking for people to compete for a hundred-thousand-dollar prize and the opportunity to launch their own business."

"Wow," I said, still not imagining what any of this could have to do with me. But I definitely liked the sound of $100,000. That could really take me to the next level. And I always loved a contest. "That sounds great. What kind of a contest?"

"A group of contestants will be pitted against each other to complete certain tasks having to do with cooking, baking, decorating, gardening, and fund-raising. For each task, there's a winner, and then a loser who gets eliminated from the competition."

"What do you mean 'eliminated'?" I said.

"You must not watch much television," said Priscilla.

"Actually, I don't even have a television right now," I admitted.

"That's good! That's very good," said Marissa, a warm, friendly-looking woman in her mid-thirties. "We want somebody fresh. Somebody who doesn't have preconceived notions."

"Oh, I have plenty of preconceived notions; they just don't have anything to do with television."

Everyone laughed.

"Do you mean a show on . . . *national* television? Or is this a local thing?"

"No no, this is national. Well, cable. We've signed with Ovation TV," said Max.

That I'd heard of. Ovation TV was known for its wildly popular and addictive celebrity-driven shows. I felt a flutter of excitement in my stomach, but I tried to stay calm.

"Faith, would you be interested in coming in for an audition? We'd like to take the next step to consider you for a contestant on the show."

"Really?" My knees felt a little weak. The word *audition* sent up red flags, but this sounded a lot different from any of the auditions I'd ever done back in L.A. It also sounded too good to be true. "Sure, I could come in," I said. "I'd like to hear more about it. But I should warn you, if this is a contest, I don't pull my punches."

"Are you *sure* you've never heard of reality TV? Because frankly you seem like you're made for it," Darren chuckled.

Just then, Victoria walked up to the booth, her mouth full of cheese. She looked at me, and the producers, and raised her eyebrows. Marissa said to me, "We think you're just the right kind of character for the show. We want you to be exactly who you are."

"I'm very good at being exactly who I am, just not so good at being anybody else," I said. "And if this show is about cooking, well, let me just tell you that I can cook better, faster, and with a healthier result than anybody I know. You get everything you ask for and more with me."

"It's true," said Victoria, swallowing and leaning in. "She's larger than life. *Perfect* for TV." She winked at me.

"There's one other thing you need to know about the show," Darren added. "The contest will be run by a celebrity, a domestic icon in fact, who will be a personal mentor and judge for the contestants, so much of your time on the show will be about dealing with her or doing what she tells you. Each week, she will present the contestants with a challenge, which they will try to complete. Afterward, she will name a winner, who will get some kind of prize, and each week she will also name a loser, who will be eliminated from the show, until only one remains. At the end, she will crown the next Domestic Goddess, essentially naming a successor."

Suddenly, the flutter in my stomach turned into a slam dance. The name *Domestic Goddess* was more than familiar to me. Could there really be a connection between this random group of producers at a trade show where I was peddling my muffins and the beloved cookbooks that I'd kept with me all of my adult life? My eyes widened. I stared at the producers. I tried not to let my jaw go slack.

Darren smiled. "Perhaps you've heard of Sybil Hunter?"

chapter nineteen

Roxanne Howard, executive producer for the show and the woman who almost single-handedly invented reality TV (I'd Googled "reality television" the second I'd come home after the Fancy Food Show), crossed her arms and nodded. Darren, Max, Priscilla, Marissa, and three representatives from Ovation TV were all grinning from ear to ear. Max was still chuckling. "I think we found our girl," Darren whispered.

I had nailed it. This time, I had no doubt, as I sat there in the red Missoni sheath dress I'd picked up on eBay, swinging a Dolce & Gabbana leopard-skin sling-back shoe from my pedicured toe. The other potential contestants looked like they didn't know what had just hit them. I'd been clever and more than a little snarky. When they asked me what I thought of one contestant, I said, "If you're going to carry a knockoff Chanel bag, it should be a better one than that." I rolled my eyes when the so-called chef said she would win because she was exactly like Sybil Hunter, and, when asked who in the room I thought I'd be friends with, looked around and said, "I don't have time for friends. I'm too busy creating a muffin empire."

No audition I'd ever attempted in Los Angeles had ever gone anything like the *Domestic Goddess* simulation. There were no scripts, there was no memorization, there was no anxiety about trying to channel somebody else's personality. This was all me, and I hadn't been nervous at all. I'd been confident, articulate, and, frankly, funny at all the right moments.

I was a renewed Faith—a Faith who knew exactly what she wanted: to be herself, to be strong, to be entertaining, and brash, and bold. A Faith who knew that if Sybil Hunter was doing a show, she was not only destined to be on it but destined to *win it*. It wasn't a matter of wanting. This was a done deal. You can't argue with destiny.

"Will you all excuse us for a minute?" said Priscilla. "If you don't mind . . ." She gestured to the door.

"Of course," I said, standing up. I walked out of that room with a little swagger, followed by the other contestants. We sat in the outer waiting room, in chairs along the back wall. The woman with the knockoff Chanel sat fuming and casting me evil looks. The Sybil Hunter wannabe said, "We're already cast, you know. We're just here to help them find the final cast member. This is about whether *you're* good enough, not us." I shrugged and smiled. I'd been good enough, and I knew it. It took them only five minutes to call me back in.

Roxanne Howard shook my hand and offered me a seat. I'd heard how arrogant and pompous she was, so I looked with amusement at her cheesy striped pant suit. "Faith, we liked what you did in here. We think you're just the person to shake up our cast. You're a ballbuster, like Sybil herself, but you're also an original. We'd like to offer you a spot on the show."

"Holy shit balls," I said.

I knew I'd get it, but somehow, this sudden offer seemed so final. I was about to lease a real space for the muffin bakery. I'd had several offers for TV interviews since the Fancy Food Show. Stefan told me he thought I might even be able to get a spokesperson job. But he'd also advised me to do the show if I got it. "Those TV people are scum," he'd told me. "Bottom feeders. But you never know what this could turn into. It could be a major opportunity. How often do you get a chance to be on television?"

Bronwyn and her husband weren't as onboard. I had their words playing over and over in my head: *Do you want to derail everything you've been working so hard to achieve? What if you fail? I've seen the women on those shows. Train wrecks. Do you want to be a train wreck?*

Roxanne continued. "Now, normally the process wouldn't happen this quickly or easily. Everyone else has been sequestered for a few weeks, getting ready for the show. But the fact is, we need one more person—someone who might actually be able to stand up to Sybil Hunter. Someone exciting, who can add energy. Ovation won't proceed with filming until we find her. We believe it's you."

"I'm . . . flattered," I said, hesitantly. I kept hearing the words *train wreck* in my head.

"You should be flattered," Roxanne said, matter-of-factly. "And we need to move on this. We start filming on Monday, so you'd have to be ready to go in less than a week. We'll be shooting twelve episodes in two months, during which everybody is sequestered. Then we've got an October 15 air date, and afterward, we'll need a couple of months of availability for publicity, and then of course your participation in the live finale in January."

My head was spinning. "Sequestered?" I asked.

"Yes," said Darren. "In a competition reality show, we can't have any information leaked. All the contestants will live together in a loft in the city, at an undisclosed location. When contestants get eliminated, they move to a different apartment, but they can't go home because we can't let anybody know who's been eliminated. After the show begins airing, we still need to keep things under wraps until the live finale. You'll all sign a nondisclosure agreement."

"So, I wouldn't be living at home, or running my business, for how long?"

"Two months. You'd have to make arrangements for other people to take care of those things. Then you go home, but you'll need to be able to leave again whenever we need you."

I thought about my dog, Muffin. I wondered which one of my friends might be willing to take her. Could Alanna handle the muffin business in my absence with all those orders? And how could I possibly say no to something like this? It was everything I'd never realized I wanted.

On the other hand, what if my cautious friends were right? What if this would foil my new career right when it was just getting started?

"Can I think about it?" I said. Roxanne Howard looked taken aback, as if nobody had ever said no to her before.

"We can't give you more than forty-eight hours. We need to move on this. There's a lot to do."

"OK. Forty-eight hours."

"Maximum," she said.

I practically skipped out of the Ovation Network offices in Times Square. They wanted me. If I wanted it, I could have it. But did I want it? I had this feeling that if I didn't do it, I might regret it for the rest of my life. I didn't want to make a decision out of fear, but when in doubt, I always tended to err on the side of saying yes.

The best part was that I would have the chance, not just to meet my idol, but to have a working relationship with her. It was a dream come true. How could I say no to Sybil Hunter? As soon as I was out on the street, I called Victoria.

"Don't even think about not coming out with me tonight," I told her.

"Why? Wait . . . *did you get it?*"

"Oh, I got it. The question is, do I want it?"

She shrieked so loudly, I had to hold the phone away from my ear. "Girl, you are on the way. Don't be ridiculous, of course you want it. This is *it*. Have you signed anything?"

"Not yet. I have to decide!"

"I'm canceling all other plans," she said. "I'm calling everyone."

"Fine, but don't call *everyone* everyone. I'm not actually allowed to tell anyone I'm doing this. If I do it. So you are sworn to secrecy! But

I do want to celebrate," I said. "Let's have dinner at Pastis, then go dancing at Spring Seven."

"I am so in," Victoria said. "You totally rock! I always knew you were poised for bigger and better things."

"You know, so did I," I said.

Victoria called our friends, but promised not to tell them what we were celebrating. We didn't have any trouble getting a table for six at Pastis. "See, they already know you're somebody," Victoria whispered, as the hostess showed us to a patio table underneath the restaurant's red awning. I had a quick flashback to the days when I worked as a hostess in L.A., and Victoria was right—you do sense when somebody is important. I was feeling pretty damn important. Or maybe it was that, even at my most financially insolvent, I always tipped the hostess $10 for a good table, and she remembered.

It was a warm June evening and flowers bloomed in the restaurant's window boxes. Victoria ordered a bottle of champagne. She was always in charge of ordering the wine. I was in charge of ordering the food. "Any preferences?" I said. After too many dinners where everybody bitched about not ordering what I'd ordered, nobody ever even bothered to look at the menus anymore when we all went out together. The waiter brought the champagne and poured us each a glass. It tasted perfect—rich and fruity.

"Ladies, are you ready to order?" he asked.

"Yes," I said, perusing the menu. "We'll have one arugula salad, one roasted beet salad, and one order of calamari with the harissa mayo. We'd also like the goat cheese tart with the leeks, one order of mussels, one order of the bar steak with the butter, and one order of the steak frites with béarnaise." I looked around. "Does that sound like enough for everyone?" They all nodded eagerly. I handed the menu back to the waiter. "Thanks! And please don't bring the bread basket."

"Oh my God, my mouth is watering. I'm starving," said my friend

Jennifer, putting her napkin in her lap in anticipation. "So, what's the occasion?"

Victoria looked at me. "Tell them!" she said.

"Let's drink our champagne first," I said mysteriously.

"Victoria knows?" said Jennifer. "Then why don't we know?"

"I haven't decided about something yet," I said. "Can we talk about something else?"

"No!" they said. They all looked at me expectantly. Victoria looked like she would burst.

"OK, listen, this is totally confidential and you can't tell *anyone*," I said at last, leaning in. "It's just that I've been offered a role on a new television show . . . a reality show . . . starring . . . Sybil Hunter," I said.

"No. Way." Jennifer stared at me. "I love her morning show! I watch it every day when I'm getting ready for work!" Ovation was Jennifer's favorite network. She was the only reason I'd ever heard anything about the channel. "Wait . . . I read an article in her magazine about a reality show she was developing. You're going to be on . . . *Domestic Goddess?!*"

"Well . . . I haven't exactly said yes yet. But I think I will."

Samantha, my old college roommate I'd reconnected with, rolled her eyes. "Really, Faith? Have you ever seen those shows? They're horrible!" she said.

"No, they're not, they're awesome!" Jennifer said.

"But the people on them . . . do you want Faith to be one of those people?"

"I think she can handle herself," Jennifer said. "And what great exposure! Sybil Hunter is everywhere." She imitated the announcer's voice: "You love her recipes. You love her products. You envy the way she can throw a party. Nobody knows how to celebrate a holiday or create an empire like she does. Sybil will make your day better—you can count on it!"

"I know, they play that constantly," said Victoria, who had a TV in her salon. "I love all the shots of Sybil. Sybil beating cake batter by hand, Sybil kneading dough, Sybil decorating cookies, Sybil arranging flowers, Sybil in her craft studio, Sybil picking heirloom tomatoes, Sybil feeding her rare chickens, Sybil grooming her lovable Newfoundland." Victoria stuck her finger in her mouth, a simulated gagging.

"Don't mock my idol!" I demanded. "That's not fair. Feeding chickens is the least of what she does. Sybil Hunter is an icon. She makes the best products I've ever used. Her recipes are perfect. She's one of the first female self-made billionaires in this country. No woman has ever done what she's done, in business or for the domestic arts!"

"Did you just say 'domestic arts'? Who are you?" said Jennifer.

"She's a muffin baker, of course she loves Sybil Hunter," said Victoria.

"And I'm not ashamed!" I proclaimed. "She *is* a domestic goddess, *and* a mogul. And I'm going to be one, too."

"Whatever, Faith. You live in a closet on the Upper East Side. Where are you going to put your chickens?" Victoria said. "Where are you going to keep your collection of antique rolling pins? Are you going to wear those heels when you weed your heirloom tomatoes?"

"Shut up," I said, laughing. "Just you wait and see. Sybil's as much if not more of a businesswoman than anything. She can cook and arrange flowers but she can also run a board meeting, design a killer ad campaign, and build a billion-dollar company."

"Does that mean you're actually going to say yes to this?" asked Samantha, looking horrified. "You're actually going to be on a reality TV show? Are you sure you want to do that?"

"You know . . ." I said, thoughtfully. "I just might."

"Well, if you do it, then don't lose yourself," Samantha advised. "They want you because of who you are. Don't become one of those reality TV clones. Separate from the pack."

"First muffins, then the world!" Victoria said, holding up her champagne glass. We all toasted. "By the way," she said, after taking a sip, "did you end up having any leftovers from the show? I fucking *love* those muffins."

"We ran out before the end of the show. We were definitely a crowd favorite," I said with pride.

When the food came, we devoured it like any respectable group of famished and champagne-fueled women would, leaving only a pile of mussel shells and a couple of fries. "We are *not* getting dessert," Victoria decided. "We've got to go dance this off."

"Agreed," I said. "But first, let's have a game plan. I'm thinking that getting this show is a sign."

Victoria rolled her eyes. "Here we go," she said.

"I'm serious. None of you would describe my love life as particularly, well . . ."

"Lucky?" Samantha suggested.

"Functional?" offered Jennifer.

"Sane?" said Victoria.

"Successful," I decided.

They all nodded.

"Well, I think what's been going on with me is that I keep looking for a man to save me. But Sybil Hunter definitely does *not* have a man, right?"

"Not anymore," said Victoria. "Not since her husband died."

"And she had her greatest success after that happened," I said, "the point being that I think my getting this show is a sign that I need to stop looking for men to save me. I need to save myself."

"Why not?" Victoria said. "You always end up dumping the men who want you anyway. Maybe you should give it a rest."

"Exactly. So, I'm just proclaiming to you that I am *not* going to this club tonight to look for a man. I'm through with them. Through!"

"Where have I heard this before?" Jennifer said.

"No, I'm serious this time!" I said. "We're going to Spring Seven, to see and be seen, to dance, to have girls' night. No boys allowed. Are you with me?"

"Sure," said Victoria.

"I'm in," said Jennifer. "Unless I meet somebody."

Everybody else nodded their assent, with varying degrees of enthusiasm. We split the bill—I chipped in the very last of my cash—and after a stop in the restroom to refresh lipstick and arrange hair and check wardrobe, we all maneuvered in our heels over the cobble-stones on Little West Twelfth Street to the club. Spring Seven was just around the corner from Pastis, in the heart of the meatpacking district. I wasn't worried whether we'd get in. Victoria used to date the bouncer, and we all looked hot, even if we were older than the average crowd there. We walked to the front of the line and the bouncer winked at Victoria and let us in.

The club was packed for a Tuesday, full of its usual beautiful people. My friends voraciously and blatantly eyed every good-looking guy we passed on the way in, but I didn't. I was so over that. I certainly didn't have time to invest in another good-looking guy with too much money and no personality, or vice versa. It was time to focus on *me*.

"Let's get a drink!" I yelled over the booming music, and pointed to the bar. We all moved through the crowd up to the bar. I paused. I really wanted something sweet and girly and fun, but I decided to be good. I ordered a raspberry vodka with a lime wedge. We toasted Sybil Hunter and then we all headed out to the dance floor.

When girls dance together in a little cluster on the dance floor of a hot club, men are going to try to get in on the action. Within thirty seconds, half our group was bumping and grinding with whoever had moved in on them. Victoria was trying to choose between two arty-looking guys vying for her attention. I shut my eyes. I didn't even want to see who might be trying to dance with me. I just wanted to dance, by myself, to release this beautiful surge of energy I was feeling—a surge of my own power. Then I backed into somebody.

I turned around and found myself face to face with a tall, athletic-looking man with wavy hair and blue eyes that seemed to look right into my soul. I swallowed, then in the haughtiest voice I could summon, I said, "*Excuse me*. Trying to dance here."

He grinned. I couldn't help noticing his adorable dimples. "Wow. Cold. It's like a meat locker in here. Can I get you a sweater? A parka? Mukluks?"

I smiled, in spite of myself. "I won't be cold much longer if you keep sweating me," I said. Was I already flirting with someone? I was beyond help.

"Pardon me, ma'am." He tipped an imaginary hat and backed off, but he didn't stop looking at me with that funny little grin and those blue eyes. I had to admit, I was intrigued. Guiltily, I remembered my resolve. *You're not interested,* I reminded myself.

I looked around. Jennifer was draped over the guy she'd been dancing with, and Victoria had obviously picked the more punk-rock of her two suitors. I felt my resolve weakening. He was still looking at me. I started subtly grooving toward him, and he quickly cut the distance between us. We were both smiling, and it was the strangest feeling—almost a recognition. "Do I know you?" I said.

"I don't think so," he said. "What's your name?"

"Faith."

He put his hand over his heart. "I love that name. And I have it."

"You have what?"

"Faith," he said.

"Really. Well, you don't have me."

"Not yet," he said, moving in rhythm to the music with his eyes locked onto mine. I could feel the heat between us.

"What's your name?" I said.

"Harris."

"Nice to meet you, Harris," I said, holding out my hand, and looking him up and down. "You're pretty cute."

"I'm glad you think so," he said, taking my hand in his, then twirling me around, probably so he could get a better look at me.

I waited for him to return the compliment. He didn't. I was even more intrigued. We really started dancing, moving together in a perfect rhythm. It felt disconcertingly natural, sexy, harmonious. Our faces were inches apart as the song ended.

"Harris!" We both moved quickly away from each other at the sound of his name, like teenagers caught making out in a car. Over his shoulder, I saw an indignant-looking girl with long blonde hair and a teeny black dress. "What are you doing? I've been looking all over for you!"

I raised my eyebrows at him. He looked embarrassed. "I've been out here the whole time," he said to the girl, obviously irritated. He looked back and forth between her and me, as if he were comparing us. I think I held up pretty well, although her skirt was at least three inches shorter than mine. She grabbed his arm. "C'mon, let's go over here," she said, giving me a dark look. As she pulled him away, he looked back over his shoulder at me, grinned, and shrugged.

"Player," I muttered. I joined my friends at the bar, ordered another raspberry vodka, and distractedly listened to Victoria and my other friends point out cute guys in the club. But I was replaying the dance with Harris in my head, trying to figure out what just happened. Then I felt a hand on my shoulder. "Hey." It was him. And his grin. And his beautiful eyes.

"Hey, yourself," I said.

"Would you like to finish our dance?"

I looked over his shoulder. "Are you allowed?" I said. "Or will your babysitter tell you it's time to go home?"

He rolled his eyes. "That girl? I just met her tonight. I was working that angle—until I found a more interesting one." He gave me a sly, suggestive look. He was irresistible, player or not. I checked my sleaze meter. Nothing.

"Well . . . since we never finished the dance . . ."

He took my hand and led me away. I looked back at my friends, a silent apology for breaking my vow so easily.

We danced without stopping for the next hour, until we were both sweating. "I need another drink," I said. We went to the bar and he ordered me a raspberry vodka. "How did you know what I was drinking?" I said.

"Actually, I noticed you before, when you came in. I saw that's what you ordered. I was standing right next to you at the bar."

"Really?" What was wrong with my radar, that I hadn't immediately picked up on him? "Well, now what I really want is a margarita."

I was buzzed enough that I'd stopped caring about my waistline. "I'm through being virtuous."

"Your mother would be proud," he said.

"Oh no she wouldn't," I said. "And don't get me started on my mother."

"I won't get you started on yours if you don't get me started on mine," he said.

"Agreed," I said. "So what do you do?"

"I'm one of those despicable lawyers."

"I won't hold it against you," I said.

"I appreciate it," he said. "Hey, you want to go sit down?"

We ducked into a dark booth with our drinks, and he put his arm around me, as if we'd been together for years. Our intimacy was instant. I told him all about my muffin business, and he told me about the firm where he worked. He was an only child, and so was I. Beyond that, we didn't talk about our families—I didn't want to go there, and apparently neither did he. "I'm so tired of this scene," he told me. "I hardly ever go to clubs anymore. I just came tonight for a friend's birthday."

"I know what you mean," I said. "I don't do it much anymore, either. It's not like you ever meet anybody good at a club."

He leaned in and kissed me right then. A long, slow kiss that made my toes tingle.

"Hey, you're pretty good at that," I whispered. "Practice much?"

"It's a matter of finding the right lips," he whispered back.

Suddenly I felt like I was being sucked down a black hole. I could fall for this guy. And it scared me.

"Let's dance some more," I said, grabbing his hand and pulling him out of the booth, trying to break the spell.

We dove back onto the dance floor just as the strobe light hit and the DJ began projecting images of body silhouettes onto the walls. The music throbbed.

I hadn't had this much fun in months. His arm felt good around my waist, strong but not muscle-bound. It felt like the arm of a basketball player or a swimmer—firm and sure. As we danced, we looked each other square in the eyes, and then he leaned in and kissed me again, the longest, slowest, sexiest kiss I ever remembered experiencing. I pulled away at last and looked at him in surprise. He looked surprised, too. What was going on? For a moment, I forgot where I was.

He looked stunned, as if all his bravado had dissolved in the wake of that kiss.

Just then, Victoria and Jennifer came up behind me. "Whoa there, girl," Jennifer said.

"Let's get her out of here before she gets engaged again!" Victoria said, pulling at my arm.

"Stop!" I said, irritated that they were grabbing at me. "Just one second. OK?"

"Geez, whatever," said Victoria, backing off. I turned back to Harris. He was gone.

"Where did he go?"

I pushed through the crowd, looking for him. Then I saw the bathroom. *Pull yourself together, Faith.* I went inside and took a few deep breaths. I stared at myself in the mirror. *What the hell are you doing? This is no time to start obsessing over some guy in a club. Snap out of it! Are you going to be on the show or not? Don't say no because you think you have some chance with another guy. You've been down this road before. Insanity is doing the same thing over and over, and expecting different results. It's time to do something different.*

I took a deep breath, splashed water on my face, then stepped back out onto the dance floor. I would find him, tell him he was great, but that I had more important things to do with my life right now. And then I saw him—with her. The blonde girl in the short skirt. She had both arms around his neck, and she was kissing his cheek, and he had an arm around her waist. They were talking to each other, leaning in toward each other, and then she stumbled and he caught her, tenderly, and then led her out the door. He was leaving? *He was leaving with her?*

Just as they walked out of the bar, Victoria came up to me. I just stood there, staring after him. She followed my gaze.

"What the hell?" she said.

I just shook my head. What kind of man was he? I'm out of his sight for two minutes, and he goes home with another girl? I didn't care that I was about to tell him I couldn't see him. How dare he act like that with me, kiss me like that, talk to me like that, hold me in his arms like that, make me believe we had a real connection, and then leave with another girl?

"Get me out of here," I said.

Victoria took my arm. "You broke your own rule," she said, as we walked back up the street to catch a cab. "See what happens? Stay away from them."

I thought about him all night, and the more I thought about him, the angrier I got, until he began to represent all men to me—every man who had ever disappointed me, betrayed me, or left me. Had I learned *nothing* from my time in L.A., and from the last five years in New York? It seemed like we connected, but I guess my sleaze meter was off. Screw him. The next morning, I picked up the phone and called the number on the card Roxanne Howard had given me.

"I'm in."

Over the next week, I was so busy that I didn't have too much time to dwell on what might have been. I shook it off. All the other contestants had been undergoing a complex evaluation process for several weeks, but because I'd been cast so late in the game, I had to squeeze into a few days what the rest of them had been doing for the past few weeks: interviews with the network producers, meetings with lawyers, and even meetings with psychologists and doctors, to be sure I was mentally and physically fit. I'd never been able to afford therapy. "I'm getting free therapy!" I'd proclaimed to Victoria on the phone.

"And you're excited about this?" she said. "You're so bizarre."

"These people you'll be living with will be competitive with one another, and with you," the psychologist had advised me. "This can be very stressful, especially since you won't be able to have a break or go back to your normal life until the show is over. You'll feel alone, unsupported. Do you think you can handle this?"

"Doc, I've handled much worse than that," I said.

"What do you mean?" he asked.

"Do you really want to know?"

I spent the next hour spilling out my guts: my father, my mother, the divorce, my failure in L.A., and the disaster that was Vince Beck. I'd just read in an entertainment magazine that Peter Jarrell's last script was coming to the big screen, and the executive producer was Vince Beck. I felt betrayed. Then I told the psychologist about the string of men I'd dated in New York, even the guy I'd just met in the bar, Harris. And finally, did I want to get married, or have a career? I explained to him that I'd decided to choose the career, which is why I agreed to do the show. "I'm through with men," I told him.

The therapist nodded and listened and finally told me our time was up. He had to see all the other contestants. I don't think he quite knew what to make of me. All I knew was that it felt great to talk to someone without an agenda about all of it. And for free!

On Sunday night, I packed my bag for two months, as minimally as possible. I would be efficient, low maintenance, distraction-proof. No little reminders of my regular life. A clean break. As I packed, I realized how relieved I was that I had something to do for the summer. I didn't have to try to figure out how to finagle my way to the Hamptons, which I could never afford, and it was always so depressing to be stranded in the city every weekend all summer, when everyone was hanging out at the beach or having pool parties. None of that mattered because I had a job to do.

After I was packed, I put my old red suitcase by the front door and sat down on the couch. The apartment seemed cold and dark and lonely without Muffin, who was already at Bronwyn's.

What would it be like to have cameras filming me all the time? I hoped I'd get to do a lot of cooking, especially baking. I imagined

Sybil trying one of my muffins, her face lighting up, the way she would say, "Mmm, Faith, these are *excellent*. Could I get the recipe to use in my next cookbook?"

And the money . . . oh, the money. Every contestant was being paid $750 per week to film the show, up until they were eliminated, and that was just one more reason to hold on as long as possible. But I needed to win that prize. I could last for years on $100,000. I couldn't even imagine what a relief it would be, not to have to worry about money for a while.

Then I imagined myself being crowned Sybil Hunter's successor—Domestic Goddess, *the next generation*. I smiled, sitting there all alone in my dark apartment with the summer heat rising from the concrete, the moonlight casting its silver light over the buildings outside my window. This was happening, and tomorrow, my new life would begin. I wished Perry was here. I still missed my old roommate, and I knew she'd have such encouraging words for me. I thought about calling Victoria or Bronwyn, but decided I could handle it on my own. I didn't want to have to explain this intense mix of fear and hope. I was going into a bubble, and I wanted to be ready. No more ties. Finally, exhausted, I folded myself into the covers of my own bed for the last time in what would be months. Just before I fell asleep, I saw Harris's face. I hoped he would remember me. I hoped he'd see me on TV and be filled with regret for what he'd almost had.

chapter twenty

Stay right here for a moment, miss," the driver said. He got out, said a few words to the camera crew, then got back in. "Now, when you get out of the car, they're going to be filming you, so do not look at the cameras." It must have been the twentieth time someone had told me that, but I was glad he reminded me. I didn't realize it would be happening before I even knew where I was or what I was doing. I guess that was the point. I felt a surge of panic. I took a deep breath. "Does my hair look OK?" I said, smoothing it down. I grabbed lip gloss out of my purse and slicked it on.

The driver smiled. "You look beautiful, dear," he said kindly. I stepped out of the car, and the first thing I did was look directly at the camera. *Idiot! What are you doing? What's wrong with you?* I scolded myself. *You can't do that. They're filming. They saw that.* I quickly looked away.

I tried to regain my composure as I stepped into the building. The cameras followed my every move, and it felt strange trying to pretend they weren't there. Behind the camera, a girl in a production T-shirt directed me to an elevator. "Go to the twenty-third floor," she said. "Someone there will tell you where to go next." The camera lens stayed on me until the elevator door closed. When it opened again, more cameras hovered. I couldn't imagine ever getting used to that.

"Right this way," called another production girl, directing me toward a cameraman.

"Can I mike you?" he said. Without waiting for a reply, he had his hand up my shirt, attaching a wire with a microphone to my bra, right over the cleavage, with sticky tape. Then he was attaching a mike pack to the back of my bra strap. It was like a hot brick on my back. "Now, you are never to take off this microphone unless you are given express permission, do you understand? I don't care if you're getting up to get a glass of juice in the middle of the night. I don't care if you're in the bathroom. Just forget it's even there," he said.

I remembered that from the contract. I imagined them breaking down the door in the middle of the night because my microphone came off in my sleep. I imagined them suing me if I looked at the camera. I thought I might have an anxiety attack. "Now, I need you to wait in here," said the production girl. She gestured to a door leading into a glass-enclosed conference room. A third girl, this one in a simple green dress, smiled warmly. "Hi, Faith. I'm Polly, Sybil's assistant." She opened the door for me.

I walked into a very brightly lit room. There were already three other contestants sitting around a conference table. They all looked at me: a woman with jet-black hair cut into severe bangs and a bob who had been talking loudly but stopped in midsentence when she saw me; a neat, impeccably dressed, somewhat balding man with wire glasses, a perfectly tailored hounds-tooth jacket, a bow tie, and a matching pocket square; and a tall, stunning blonde woman with long wavy hair and a vacant expression. She looked familiar, but I couldn't quite place her.

Polly put her hand on my arm. "And please remember, you are *not* allowed to speak to anyone."

"But that woman in there was talking," I said.

"It's been noted," she said. What was she, the Domestic Goddess Gestapo? Were they taking off points? Docking her paycheck?

The elevator dinged and she turned and walked away. I entered the room and sat down next to the black-haired woman. "You've already been written up for talking," I said sarcastically, out of the side of my mouth.

She looked delighted. "Really? Wonderful." She had the classic Brooklyn accent. "I've already been noticed. Shari Jacobs," she said.

I took her hand and shook it firmly. "Faith Brightstone."

In an exaggerated whisper from across the conference table, the well-dressed, bespectacled man said, "If you're caught breaking the rules, Sybil plucks out your toenails. She's almost got enough to mosaic a café table."

I laughed, then remembered the camera, then looked through the glass door to see if I was being written up, too. Oh, what the hell. "What are you doing here?" I whispered back. "Isn't this *Domestic Goddess?*"

"Honey, I can outgoddess any woman," he said. He held out his hand. "Chaz Murphy."

"I'm Faith. Has anyone seen *her* yet? Is she really a hard-ass?"

"You *guys,*" hissed the blonde woman. "We aren't supposed to *talk.*" She looked both terrified and irritated. "We're being . . . *recorded.*" I looked at her closely. She looked familiar. I knew I had met her before, somewhere long ago. Maybe in L.A., but I still couldn't place her. She didn't seem to recognize me at all.

"You better get used to being recorded, honey," Chaz said. Just then, the door opened and a tall, regal-looking woman with neat dark hair and a stunning antique bib necklace walked in and sat down. She had perfect posture and looked down her nose at us. Something about her kept us all from talking anymore.

Over the next hour, six more people came in, each looking scared or nervous or excited or some combination. Nine women and three men. I recognized the chef from my audition. The other one—the one with the knockoff Chanel bag—wasn't there. Maybe she'd already been axed, or they'd replaced her with me.

Twelve contestants. Nobody spoke but we were all eyeing one

another carefully, competitively. I wished they would bring us some coffee or even water. So much for the famous Sybil hospitality.

Finally, Polly came back. "Sybil will see you now," she said. "Follow me."

We all looked at one another nervously. This was it. We were all about to see the woman we'd come to see. I realized Sybil Hunter wasn't just my idol. She was the idol of every person in this room—and of millions of others all around the country, which is why Ovation Network had given the show the big thumbs-up. *Come on, Faith. You can do this. Use your instincts. Separate from the pack.*

We all filed out of the room behind another production person. We were told we weren't allowed to go anywhere without them. Down a long hallway, around a corner, and into another conference room. Within minutes, the door opened . . . and there she was.

Sybil Hunter, flanked by a huge fluffy black Newfoundland, who stuck to her side like a bodyguard. My eyes widened. She was larger than life. She must have been over six feet tall, with broad shoulders and a hard jawline, wavy auburn hair cut into a chin-length bob, and steely eyes. She wore an expensive-looking cashmere sweater the color of buttercream, ivory-colored slacks, and camel-colored heels—the clothes of a tasteful and very rich woman. The expression on her face dared anyone to question anything she wore, or said, or did. She radiated power. She turned her intimidating gaze toward us. I was mesmerized.

"Welcome, everyone," she said. Her voice was deep, no-nonsense, almost masculine—the voice of a matriarch. She looked each one of us in the eyes in turn. When her eyes fell on me, it felt electric. I stared right back at her, trying to match her confidence. Her eyes narrowed slightly, and then she looked at the woman next to me.

"I'm so glad to welcome you here to my show," she said. "Sybil Hunter Enterprises has grown over the past fifteen years from a local corporate event-planning business to a billion-dollar empire. As you may know if you've followed my career, after my first cookbook, *Domestic Goddess,* I developed a product line, and then a magazine, and then a television show, along with four more cookbooks, all best sellers. Today, I have over one thousand employees who work in all the different divisions of Sybil Hunter Enterprises, including over five hundred employees already working on my new network, which will launch next year: Sybil Hunter Enterprises Television, or SHE TV." All the cameras were locked on her.

She continued. "My brand is known worldwide for its quality, beauty, and supreme functionality. Everything we do here at SHE must meet my very high standards, and I personally oversee everything this company produces—products, recipes, all media. If it comes from SHE, you can count on it."

That was her slogan. She was known for it. She'd tell you how to make Halloween cookies or install a shelf or refinish a wood floor or arrange flowers, and then she'd say, "You can count on it."

"Now, let me explain what's at stake for all of you." She gave us another sweeping, withering stare. "The winner of this contest will receive a prize we haven't yet revealed. You may know about the $100,000 cash prize. However, that's just a small part of what the last remaining contestant will receive." She paused dramatically, and the cameras moved to catch all of our reactions—*what could it be?* I realized it was all part of the game. Finally, she told us: "With the launch of SHE TV, the winner of *Domestic Goddess* will get his or her own television show, to be broadcast on my new network. Our network executives will work with you to develop a show around your personal talents."

A few people gasped. We all gawked at one another. My own television show? My own *cooking show?* This was *everything.* There was no way I could possibly do anything else but win. I'd been right to put my relationships on hold, to leave L.A., not to get married. Everything I'd done had led to this.

"We have a unique group of people here," Sybil continued. "We have an interior designer, an event planner, two chefs, a baker, an antiques dealer, an accessories designer, a concierge, a lifestyle coach, an organic farmer, a headhunter, and even a housewife—of course, the housewife is the *original* domestic goddess," she said, smiling at my new friend, Shari, who looked around to make sure everyone noticed Sybil was talking to *her*. We all looked at one another, wondering who was who. "You will be paid a generous salary of two hundred and fifty thousand per year as long as you host your own show. On top of that, you will receive the cash prize of $100,000, a new Toyota Prius, and your own corner executive office right here at Sybil Hunter Enterprises, fully equipped with the Domestic Goddess Technology Suite."

She paused and looked at our shocked expressions proudly.

"Now, I'd like to introduce you to my team."

The door opened again and we all turned to look. In walked a tall young woman with a strawberry blonde ponytail and an older man. I did a double take. I knew that man! It was Ian McGinnis, the sweet older magazine editor I'd casually dated back in L.A., the one who liked to buy me things but who'd never once made a real pass at me. The last time I'd seen him had been at Carol Kameron's party. I experienced a surge of fear. Would this be a conflict of interest? Would I be disqualified? Would he say something? Would he even remember me? At least we'd never slept together—God, that would have been a nightmare. I hoped and prayed it would go unnoticed.

As soon as he came in, Ian looked right at me. I could tell he already knew I would be in the room, but of course it would make better TV if nobody told *me*. Did Sybil know?

So far, she gave no indication. "Everyone, this is my sister, Alice Hunter. As you may know, Alice is on the board of directors of Sybil Hunter Enterprises, and she is one of my top advisers." Everyone knew about the love-hate relationship between Sybil Hunter and her younger sister, Alice. Some people said Alice was the brains behind the whole operation at Sybil Hunter Enterprises. Others said it was nepotism, and that Alice didn't do anything except cash her paychecks and sleep around with men—or women, depending on who was talking. I was fascinated to see them together.

"I can't cook, decorate, or arrange flowers," Alice joked. "But I know how to make money." Everyone laughed dutifully. She looked like Sybil, but softer around the edges. Was the softness an illusion? Alice looked directly at me, as if she'd heard my thoughts, and smiled. I smiled back.

"She's right," Sybil Hunter confirmed. "Alice knows about business. She's got a real eye for what works and what doesn't, so she'll be key in judging your efforts during each challenge." Then she turned to Ian. "And this is Ian McGinnis, the west coast editor of my magazine."

"Hello everyone!" Ian said in his kind and jolly way. Then he looked at me. Here it comes. "And Sybil, you may not know this, but I actually know one of the contestants!"

Sybil froze, then turned to look at him, her eyes like daggers of ice. He hadn't told her! Either that, or she was a damned good actress, on top of all her other talents. I was mortified. The cameras swung around to catch Sybil's expression. Quickly, she composed herself.

"Oh really, Ian! And who might that be?"

She glared at us all, every one of us a traitor. Ian turned to me and pointed. "This young woman right here, Faith Brightstone. She's a friend of mine from back in my L.A. days. How are you, Faith?"

"I'm just fine, Ian. How have you been?" I tried to sound casual and unflappable, and not to let my voice shake. All the other contestants stared at me.

"Oh I'm fine, just fine, it's great to see you again," he said, merrily. He really was a sweet old man, but seemed totally oblivious to the implications of his big reveal.

Sybil cleared her throat. "Well, Ian . . . can you assure us you won't be biased in your assessments of the contestants? Because I'm sure that's what we're *all* wondering." She looked at the other contestants, suddenly in league with them against me. I had a bad feeling that this wasn't the way I wanted to start things off with Sybil Hunter.

"Oh yes!" he said jovially. "Of course, her work will have to stand on its own. No favoritism!" He wagged a friendly finger at me. This would actually be a disadvantage—if I won, everyone would say it was rigged. They might be even harder on me. Shit, shit, shit.

Sybil gave him a look. "Finally, this is Rasputin, my most trusted adviser." She snapped her fingers and the big black Newfoundland jumped to his feet. He was so large, he could rest his chin on the table. "Contestants, my assistant, Polly, will now take you to your living quarters, where you can unpack and get to know one another. Then, I would like you to meet me back here at seven p.m. You'll have to wait to find out why." She smiled coolly at us, then walked out of the room, a camera following her.

We all looked at one another, then some of us started to stand. "Hold up," said a man in a production T-shirt. Everyone sat.

One of the cameras rolled over to me and a producer pulled me aside. "Hi, Faith. I'm Mike. We need an OTF. Just answer my questions," he said.

"What's an OTF?" I said.

"On the fly," he said. "We want to get your thoughts. Just answer honestly."

"Sure," I said, sitting back down.

"Faith, how do you feel, being here? What does it mean to you?"

This was weird, to have the camera pointed right at me with everyone looking. "This is my dream. It's everything I've ever wanted," I said, sincerely. "I really, really need the money and the boost to my career, but having my own TV show would be the culmination of everything I've been working toward."

"So, you know Ian McGinnis," Mike said. "Was that a shock when he walked in the room? What did you think?"

"Holy shit balls, that's Ian McGinnis! That's what I thought," I said. When I said "holy shit balls," Mike smiled and wrote something down. I smiled, too. I love an environment where it's OK to curse. I was starting to get a headache from holding it in.

"Excellent, Faith. That's just the kind of attitude we're looking for. Tell me how you know Ian McGinnis?" I thought for a moment. How to portray our relationship sympathetically, without making me look like a gold digger. I laughed to myself. Suddenly it was a *good* thing that I'd been such a failure at sleeping with guys for money.

"When I was trying to make it as an actress in L.A., Ian was a supportive friend. We worked out at the same gym, when I was just a lowly actress and he was an editor for an entertainment magazine. He gave me good advice over cocktails a few times." And that was true. I left out the part about sleeping at his house.

"And what do you think about the other contestants so far?"

"I don't think they can beat me," I said. "And I can guarantee nobody wants it more than I do."

"Perfect, thanks, Faith," Mike said. Then he went over to the other side of the room to talk to some of the other contestants. I heard him ask one of the other girls, "So what do you think of Faith knowing one of the judges?"

"Girl, you're already the standout," Chaz whispered to me.

"Hopefully not in a bad way," I said.

"Good, bad, who cares? It's television."

"I guess so," I said. "But this could come back to bite me in the ass."

"True," he said. "I hope Ian giving it to you in the ass back then was worth it."

"Very funny," I said.

"It's a nice ass at that," he said. I liked his style.

Finally, a production person stepped forward. "OK, we're ready. Everyone, this way," she said. The place was a maze and I wasn't sure I could find my way back on my own. Three long hallways, and then we came to a door with a brass plate on it that said, "The Loft." Here we are," she said. "This is where you'll be living." She opened the door with a key, and we all filed into the room that would be our home—our prison—for the next two months.

chapter twenty-one

The space was incredible—a huge apartment with a beautiful living room filled with couches and comfy chairs and a long dining room table covered in buckets filled with ice and champagne bottles. "Three in a bedroom," Polly said before closing the door, leaving the camera crew in the room with us. One of them directed the blonde whom I was still trying to place toward a card on the dining room table.

She picked it up. "Hey everybody, listen to this!" she said. She read it out loud: "Welcome everyone to the Loft. I hope the accommodations are suitable. Please enjoy a glass of champagne, but not too much. You'll be receiving your first challenge in the conference room tonight at seven p.m., and I expect you to be prompt. Do not be late. Cordially, Sybil Hunter."

"Are we supposed to remember how to get back there ourselves?" said an anxious, dizzy-looking girl with wispy, feathered hair. "I would get completely lost. Hey, is that rosé champagne? I could really use some bubbly." She sounded like she'd already had a few glasses.

"I'm sure they'll send someone to show us where to go," I said. "From what I can tell, they run this thing like the military."

Chaz opened a bottle and the cork popped and flew across the table. "Oops, I got a little excited!" he said. We all took our glasses and I sat down between him and Shari.

Everyone looked nervous and stressed and pretty tired. I guess I wasn't the only one who hadn't slept the night before. Shari stood up as soon as I sat down. "So, I think we should all introduce ourselves," she said, taking the group in hand. "I'll start. I'm Shari Jacobs, and I'm the one Sybil referred to as 'the housewife.' I'm very proud of that title. I have a wonderful husband and two beautiful daughters, and my husband owns a floral design center in Manhattan. We're the largest flower importers in New York." She said "flowers" like "flowiz"—pure Brooklyn. "If you see flowers at the Plaza, Le Cirque, Balthazar, those are our flowers." She glanced at the camera, then addressed us, articulating carefully: "And if any of *you* ever need flowers, just go to flowersflowersflowers.com." She sat back down looking pleased with herself, then gestured to me.

I cleared my throat. "My name is Faith Brightstone, and I'm also from New York, although as you all know *now,* I did live in L.A. for a while. Now I own a vegan baking company called Have Faith Bakery. My signature muffin is banana oatmeal chocolate chip."

"Wait!" said the blonde girl. Suddenly, I realized where I'd seen her. She was Katie, the party girl I used to see at clubs in L.A., the one who liked to dance on the bar with her shirt off—the one who'd been at Carol Kameron's Hearst Castle party! "So . . . you and Ian McGinnis. That's not really fair, is it? You already have an advantage."

I sighed. "Really, we were just casual friends, I didn't even know him that well. It's no big deal." I wondered if I should mention that Katie and I had met before. I decided to wait.

"Don't you think he's too old for you?" said a man with strange spiked hair and little glasses. "I mean, look at you. You're a Ferrari. He's a . . . a . . ."

"A Model T?" said Chaz. "What I want to know is, did you sleep with him?"

"Yes," I said, wryly. "I was giving him a blow job while Sybil was introducing him in the meeting room, didn't you notice?" Chaz and Shari laughed, but nobody else did. Tough crowd. "Kidding! No, I didn't sleep with him!" I said, trying to lighten the mood. "He's old enough to be my father! He was just a nice man I met at a party and we socialized a few times. That's all."

Katie looked scandalized. What a faker. I remembered her swinging her shirt around over her head while dancing on the bar. I had a feeling she was no stranger to a blow job.

"You can't put that in the show," said Katie to one of the cameramen, pointing at me. "You can't put her talking about giving a blow job to one of the *judges*. That's not fair. The viewers will be biased!"

"Miss, you can't speak to us. Please just pretend we're not here," he said.

"The audience isn't voting, you idiot," I said. I was tired and irritable and suddenly didn't care if I was on camera or not.

"How do you know?" Katie said. "We don't know how the show works."

"Reality!" one of the cameramen said.

"What?" said Katie.

"Please don't refer to the show," he said. "When you refer to the show, we call 'Reality!'"

"*Anyway,* I'm Chaz," said Chaz, patting my knee supportively. "I'm an interior designer and right now I live in Philadelphia. I own my own firm and I specialize in gallery spaces, although I also do a lot of *fabulous* homes for a lot of *fabulous* artists."

He looked at Katie, who was sitting on an ottoman next to the couch Chaz shared with Shari and me. She rolled her eyes and looked annoyed. "I'm Katie Swindell," she said, shifting back and forth. "I live in L.A., where I own my own business." She seemed restless and a little hyperactive. "I love astrology, and I design headbands with astrological art on them. Movie stars go crazy for my headbands. My business is called 'Crown of Stars.'" She gave me a look, almost a sneer. I was so tempted to ask if she still liked to dance topless on bars, but I bit my tongue. She touched her temples so everyone would notice the wide headband painted with fish that she wore in her long blonde hair. "I designed this," she said. "I'm a Pisces."

"My name is Nadine La Charlotte," said the regal-looking woman who'd silenced us with her presence in the conference room earlier in the day. She had what almost sounded like a British accent, but it wasn't quite right—like the way Madonna talked after she moved to England. "I'm an antiques dealer living in London with my husband, Clark La Charlotte." She paused, meaningfully, so we all had a chance to recognize that of course she meant the heir to the La Charlotte steel fortune.

"La Charlotte, as in *the* La Charlotte family?" Chaz asked.

"I don't like to brag . . ." she said, smiling.

"I can tell," I said under my breath. She gave me a dirty look.

"Are you . . . from England?" Chaz asked. "I'm trying to place that accent."

She reddened slightly. "I've lived there for many years. And as I said . . . I travel."

"Where are you from originally?" Chaz asked.

She paused. "Queens," she said.

I almost spit out my champagne. Chaz smiled serenely, as if he'd just been handed a great gift. "Ah," he said. "I see."

A girl with very long hair braided down her back was next. "I'm Sadie Danielson, and I'm from Texas," she said. "I have to say, I'm feeling a little homesick, but I'm also very happy to be here." She had a calm, even voice and a blank expression. "I'm the organic farmer. I have a farm outside Dallas, and I also own a large and very successful market in Dallas."

"I'm Mikki Winn," said the next woman. She was tall and incredibly thin, almost skeletal, with a cloud of gold hair that seemed to hover around her face, and an unusual dress that looked very expensive. "I'm an event planner in New Jersey, with a bad shopping habit." She looked around shyly.

"I'm Jodi Sue Jerry," said the next woman, the one who had been in the simulation audition with me. She wore a tight scoop-necked blouse under a very closely fitted suit. The outfit showed her enormous cleavage and curvy figure to its greatest advantage. "I'm a celebrity chef in Beverly Hills," she said.

"Aren't you Ted Jerry's wife? The heavy metal rock star? My daughters have posters of him all over their room!" Shari said.

"I am," she said proudly. "But I have my *own* career."

Chaz then leaned into me and whispered in my ear, "We have some mutual friends. Her rock star husband finances her business and she just cooks for his celebrity friends because he makes them hire her."

I somehow resisted snickering.

Next up was a tall woman with broad shoulders, large chiseled features, long brown hair, and a Midwestern accent. "I'm Linda Pavlovski, and I just have to say that I don't like the way we're being treated, led around like children. I'm a professional headhunter in Chicago," she said. "I specialize in placing executives with Fortune 500 companies." She talked loudly and aggressively, and had a belligerent expression like she wanted to punch someone. "And I really don't even know why I'm here. My boyfriend made me try out, and of course, I got it."

"He was probably trying to get rid of her," Chaz whispered.

The dizzy girl with the wispy blonde hair spoke up next. "I'm Monica Reynolds, and I'm a lifestyle coach. I live in Santa Fe, New Mexico, and I help people manifest their dreams." She paused. "Is there more champagne?" She stood up and wandered over to the table and started peering into the bottles. "It wasn't rosé, but it was OK."

Chaz and I looked at each other and smiled. What a group.

The last two to introduce themselves were the remaining men, who had been pretty quiet. I suspected they weren't as comfortable as Chaz in out-goddessing the rest of us. The first one took a deep breath and seemed to launch himself into the center of the room. "I'm Andy Spencer, and I'm a chef at Jeux de Mots in Las Vegas, and I just have to say watch out, because this may be a show called *Domestic Goddess,* but when it comes to skill in the kitchen, I'm a *god.*" He gave all the women in the room a blatant once-over and a big salty smile, then sat down looking very satisfied with himself.

"Okaaay," Chaz whispered to me. "Make way for the Ego of Andy."

Finally, the tall, strange-looking man with the spiky hair, small black glasses, and expensive suit said with a tight smile, "I'm Christophe Valentine, and I own a concierge business in Miami. We supply all the major hotels. We're very successful." He said it directly to Mikki, whom he'd been eyeing since we were all in the conference room. She blushed.

"Oh my God, that was exhausting!" said Shari, standing up. "And I'm starving. But I'm not going to eat. I've been so bad today. My diet starts tomorrow! Is it seven yet?"

We had a few more minutes, so everybody explored the Loft and eyed one another suspiciously, trying to figure out who might be a potential ally, and who was a threat. Shari and I immediately gravitated toward each other, and asked Mikki if she wanted to share a room with us. I was interested that she was an event planner and told her I'd been one, too. "Then we'll have a lot in common," Mikki said, "because I love to bake!" She didn't look like she'd ever eaten a carb in her life.

Our room had three single beds, each on a wall, with one small window looking out over the river. As we unpacked, Shari entertained us with a running monologue of her opinions about the other contestants—who was too fat, too stupid, had potential, might be someone to watch out for, and which ones Sybil would probably favor.

She was funny, quick-witted, and gossipy, clearly a woman who liked to know everybody's business and who reveled in putting people together. Mikki seemed more reserved but smart with a good sense of humor. "I'm aligning myself with you two," Shari told us. "Faith, you're connected. And Mikki, you obviously have taste."

It looked like Katie, the astrology freak designer (and party girl who was obviously pretending not to remember me), had paired up with Monica, the ditzy blonde lifestyle coach from Santa Fe, and Queen Nadine, the antiques dealer with the rich husband. That left

Down-Home Sadie, the organic farmer, to share a room with Jodi Sue Big Boobs, the groupie, and Man-Eater Linda, the loudmouthed headhunter from Chicago.

"Are we already forming alliances?" I asked.

"Sure," said Shari. "Why not? That's what makes it fun." I was more comfortable competing on my own, but I supposed this was how it was bound to go.

At six forty-five, one of the production people knocked on the door. Jodi Sue let her in. "Is everybody ready? We need to go *now*."

We followed her back through the labyrinth to the conference room. Sybil Hunter was already there. She'd changed into evening attire—a sleeveless gray cashmere sweater dress and low heels.

"Good evening, everyone. I hope you like your living quarters." Everyone nodded enthusiastically, and muttered words like "Oh yes!" and "Gorgeous!" and "It's heaven!" Brownnosers.

She nodded. "I have a surprise for you," she said. "Someone wants to pay you a visit, and he just might have some advice for you."

We all looked at one another, then at Sybil. When she turned to the door at the back of the room, we all followed her gaze. The door opened, and in walked Hugh Pritzker, megabillionaire and the man almost solely responsible for making cell phones ubiquitous with the invention of the ePhone. We all knew exactly who he was. He was always on the covers of magazines. I'd actually met him briefly before, too. He was a friend of my former employers, the Kamerons, but I didn't dare say anything, and I prayed he wouldn't, either. I was beginning to feel like New York and L.A. were two tiny little towns where everybody knew everybody else.

"Welcome to Manhattan!" said Hugh Pritzker. "This is the city of dreams, where anyone can become a billionaire, whether you're building bridges or skyscrapers, inventing phones or baking cookies. All it takes is a good idea, and the guts to make it come true." He sounded bored, reading the cue cards in a monotone.

"But he's from California," I whispered to Chaz. He bit his lip, trying not to laugh.

"He looks like Jabba the Hutt," Chaz whispered to me.

"He's worth fifteen billion and he can't join a gym?"

Nadin was sitting on the other side of Shari. She slid a note for both Shari and me to see. She had a huge antique jade ring on her finger. The note said, "And I slept with *him*. That was a wild night. *Shhhhh.*" I looked up and stared at her, then stared at Hugh Pritzker. She winked at me, then put her manicured, red-polished finger to her lips. Was this when she was still in the market for a rich husband? I had a momentary fantasy of waving the note in the air, saying, *Ms. Hunter, Queen Nadine is passing notes; you'd better read this one out loud to the class!*

"I'm sure you all know entrepreneur and mobile phone technology trailblazer Hugh Pritzker," Sybil said. "He's a close personal friend of mine, and although he may not be the first person you think of when you think of *Domestic Goddess,* we all know every successful Domestic Goddess needs a reliable phone to coordinate her life. Mr. Pritzker is here to announce your first challenge, courtesy of the next generation ePhone," she said.

Suddenly, I got nervous, realizing this thing was actually about to start. The beautiful Loft, the champagne, meeting Sybil Hunter had all been great, but now it was time to get down to business. Hugh Pritzker stepped forward. "Home cooks have come into the future. One of the most popular apps on our e-Phones is our Recipes 2 Go app, which makes food preparation easy for Domestic Goddesses everywhere. You are about to have the chance to be part of that cutting-edge trend."

I looked around the group. Everyone was on the edge of their seats. "For your first challenge, you will be divided into groups of two." Ugh. I hated working in groups. I wanted to do it myself! I looked around, wondering if we would get to pick our own partners. I made eye contact with Shari and Chaz, just in case. I noticed a lot of other people trying to make eye contact with me, Jodi Sue, and Andy, the three people whose professions involved cooking. Andy grinned at everyone. Jodi Sue stared at her hands, looking petrified, not meeting anyone's gaze, probably because she didn't actually know how to cook.

Hugh continued: "Each group will develop a quick, easy recipe suited to an ePhone recipe app. The recipe must not be more than three hundred words in total, including ingredients list and directions. It must use commonly found ingredients, and you will have use of the Sybil Hunter test kitchen to create and test your recipe."

Sybil stepped forward. "In addition to creating the recipe, you will also execute the recipe, and serve it at an informal cocktail party I'll be hosting for a group of influential local businesspeople. Presentation counts, as does taste, the ease of preparing the recipe itself, and appropriateness for the Recipes 2 Go app. Each team will be ready to serve their recipes and turn in the written versions by three p.m. tomorrow afternoon. I will taste your results, and then my recipe testers will test each written recipe. One team will win, and one team will lose. One person from the losing team will be eliminated. Hugh, would you like to tell them about what the winning team will win?"

"Sure, Sybil!" he said, stepping forward again. I wondered if *they'd* ever slept together. Everybody knew Sybil Hunter was single, and I'd read in the gossip magazines that she'd been spotted socializing with Hugh Pritzker's business partner, George Branson, the billionaire computer operating system inventor. It gave me a little shiver to imagine both Sybil and Nadine sleeping with the large man talking at the front of the room. At the same time. They could probably be on either side of him in bed and not even know the other one was there. *Stop it, Faith! That's disgusting! Get your head in the game!*

"Both members of the winning team will receive a next-generation ePhone. Also, the name of the winning recipe along with a photo of the dish will be featured as the splash screen for Recipes 2 Go," Hugh continued.

"Now, it's time to form your teams. I'm going to draw your names, one at a time," Sybil said, holding up a dark blue velvet drawstring pouch. "When I call your name, I will give you a number, from one to six. Your partner will be the one with the same number as yours."

We all shifted in our seats and looked around nervously. Sybil reached into the bag and drew out a wood disk with a name written on it. "Nadine," she said. Queen Nadine looked proud to be called first, as if it were her royal privilege. "You're number one."

"Of course she is," I whispered to Shari.

"Christophe, you're number two. Katie, three. Shari, four."

"Pray you get four!" Shari whispered.

"Chaz, five." Chaz looked at me hopefully. "Andy, six. Monica, one." Monica, the ditzy lifestyle coach, looked at Nadine and waved. Queen Nadine looked annoyed. "Mikki, two." Mikki looked at Christophe, the concierge, and smiled—almost seductively, I thought. She was already on the make. Silent but deadly.

"Sadie, three." Sadie, the organic farmer, looked at party-girl Katie, the headband designer, suspiciously. "Jodi Sue, four." Shari pouted at me, then immediately offered a radiant smile to Jodi Sue and her over-exposed jugs. Maybe she thought she'd score more Ted Jerry tickets that way. *Any friend of Jodi Sue's breasts is a friend of Ted Jerry.*

"Faith, five," she said. I grinned at Chaz and he silently clapped his hands. Thank God. "And that leaves Linda, six." Linda, the mouthy headhunter from Chicago, glared at Andy, the equally mouthy chef from Vegas. I thought they made a pretty good pair. They could see which one could out-obnoxious the other.

"At least you got Chaz," Shari whispered. "I'm stuck with the groupie bimbo!"

"Tomorrow," Sybil said, "you will have some time to experiment with the Recipes 2 Go app, to get an idea of how it works and what kind of recipes are most successful. Then you will purchase your supplies and come back to the test kitchen to work. Now remember, I handpicked each one of you to compete on this show, so I have very high hopes for the results of this first challenge. I can't wait to see what you all create. Good luck, everyone. Hugh, are you ready for dinner?" She gathered up her things and walked out the door.

We sat in the conference room for a few minutes after they left, as the camera crew ran around doing more OTFs. I was considering all the possibilities for recipes. Decadent? Healthy? Fast? Fun? So many options. I hoped Chaz would be open to letting me choose.

The longer we all sat, waiting, the more I had to pee. And I had a terrible headache. I shouldn't have had so much champagne. A cocktail wouldn't have given me a headache. That's when the lightbulb went off: a cocktail! That's what our recipe should be. I should do what I'm passionate about! I couldn't wait to tell Chaz.

But in the meantime, I really had to pee. I wondered if we would get to go back to the Loft soon, but the producers looked busy. They were getting a long-winded reaction from Andy. I couldn't wait anymore. Finally I leaned over to Shari. "I seriously have to find the bathroom. Cover for me!"

"Sure sweetie," she said. "When you gotta go, you gotta go."

I alerted a producer, who sent a cameraman to follow me. I opened the conference room door and looked around. I went down one hallway but didn't see anything. I went back the other way, turned a corner, and finally found a bathroom. On my way back out, I heard a voice down the hall. It sounded like Sybil Hunter. Glancing at the cameraman, I quietly crept toward the sound, not wanting to get too far away from what I was supposed to be doing, but wanting to hear what she was saying. I was just hoping and praying it wasn't about me.

It was.

"I want that girl off the show," she said, her voice tense and angry.

I peeked around the corner and saw Sybil towering over Mike, the producer who had asked me questions. Polly, Sybil's assistant, stood by Sybil's side.

"No, Faith is great," he said. "We need her on the show. The viewers are going to love her. You should have heard her OTF. She's a natural."

"I don't care. Next challenge, she's out. She knows Ian McGinnis, and Hugh Pritzker tells me he knows who she is, too. That's simply unacceptable. I don't need someone who's running in my circles on this show, do you understand me? This is a show for up-and-comers."

"She is an up-and-comer, Sybil. Check her background. She used to be Carol Kameron's assistant, that's the only reason she knows people. She's got a failing muffin business. She's nobody."

Sybil looked doubtful. "And who knew about this?" she said. "You never, *never* hide something like that from me again. This show is about surprising *them,* not *me.*"

Polly cleared her throat. "I think Faith's going to be a positive . . ."

"Nobody told you to think, Polly. You're a prop on this show, and don't you ever forget it." She turned back to Mike. "I suppose you can use that footage if you think it's necessary—it wasn't a disaster. But I want to know exactly who found out Ian McGinnis *knew her* and told him he should *bring this up on camera.* I don't care if the show is on your network. I'm in charge. One more mistake like that and you are fired."

"Sybil, you can't fire me. I don't work for you," Mike said, sounding fed up.

"Oh, don't underestimate me, Mike," she said, spitting venom. "I can get anybody in this city fired."

"OK, Sybil," he said, his voice tired. "I'll see what I can find out." Then she turned. Our eyes met.

Mortified, I sprinted back down the hall and ducked back into the conference room, leaving the cameraman trailing behind me.

One day in and I'm already on Sybil Hunter's hit list.

chapter twenty-two

At seven a.m., we all sat at tables in a large workroom, already agitated about getting our recipes created and formatted and inputted and tested and served on time. Chaz and I had discussed the cocktail idea the night before, but we hadn't chosen the perfect one yet.

I could hear the other teams murmuring to one another, nobody wanting to give away their ideas. I was already bone tired, and it was just the first challenge. I hadn't slept all night, thinking about what I'd heard Sybil say in the hallway. I had to change her opinion of me, and fast.

"Are you sure you don't want to do a muffin recipe? Isn't that your specialty?" Chaz said.

"No, I want to show I'm versatile. I don't necessarily want to be typecast as a baker."

"But we should go with our strengths."

"This is my strength. I love making cocktails! And I went to bartending school."

"OK, then . . . what about a Manhattan?" Chaz suggested.

"No, too old school. And too brown. Women use ePhone recipe apps. It has to be pretty and sparkly and girly."

"Something with chocolate?" he suggested.

"No, that's too heavy. Something lighter. More original. Fun. *Sexy.*" I flashed back to the night in L.A. where I'd created the pink lemonade cocktail at the afterparty. Hey, that was it! "I've got it. A pink lemonade mojito."

"All right. What the hell is in it?" said Chaz.

I had tweaked the recipe slightly over the years, but it was basically the same as the night I had crashed my dad's car. "White rum, pink lemonade made with freshly squeezed lemons, raw sugar, and a splash of cranberry juice, fresh mint, and club soda, with a lemon and a lime wedge," I said. "Glasses rimmed with lemon and raw sugar."

"You have to let *me* rim the glasses," he said. "I like the sound of it."

"The job is yours. Rim away."

Sybil had provided everybody with tablets of recycled paper and natural wood pencils. One wall of the workroom was lined with supplies—jars of pencils, pens, and Sharpies arranged by color and stacks of notebooks in all sizes. I thought about taking some to use at home, but realized I probably shouldn't steal Sybil's office supplies, considering I was being filmed—and already on her bad side.

Finally, I decided I had to tell someone. I lowered my voice. "Chaz, she wants me off the show."

"What?"

"I overheard her in the hallway last night. She wants me off the show. Don't tell anyone."

He looked around, then looked at me. "You mean . . . Sybil?"

"Yes!" I hissed. "Because I know Ian."

"She can't do that."

"Maybe she can." I tapped the eraser against the table nervously. Chaz put his hand on top of it to stop the annoying noise.

"You realize of course that you just said 'Don't tell anyone' into your microphone?" he said.

"Oh God! I get so flustered."

"Quit worrying. Just be so good that they can't kick you off. Be too good to fire."

"You're right," I said, looking around me. "I just need to be the best one." If I could just be the best, the only real choice, then Sybil Hunter would have to choose me. Plus, I had a feeling the network really was on my side. I couldn't imagine any of the other contestants hosting their own television show. "It has to be me," I told Chaz. "Not that I'm saying you shouldn't win. I'm just saying, look around us . . . how much competition do we really have?"

"Honey, not much," he said. "I don't know where they came up with this group. What a bunch of freaks. And *I* don't even want to be here. I'm already so stressed, I'm about to have a heart attack."

"Calm down, we'll be fine," I said. "We can do this. I know I have what it takes to go all the way, as long as the contest is fair. They told me they wanted a ballbuster who had the guts to stand up to Sybil."

"Who told you that?" said Chaz, surprised.

"Roxanne Howard herself," I said.

"Well there you go," he said. "Start busting some balls and Sybil's not going to get the OK to kick you off. She's just the talent. Roxanne Howard is the producer. That's where the power is." He paused. "But don't make the mistake of thinking this contest is fair."

"We're not going to lose this one," I said. "Let's get to work."

At nine, one of the tech guys from ePhone was coming by to consult with everyone about formatting their recipes for the ePhone. Then we had to go to the art department to meet with photographers and layout artists. We needed sketches and design ideas. At eleven, we were going to the store to buy supplies. Then it would be back to the test kitchen to make our recipes, in time to serve them artfully at Sybil's party. While Chaz looked up ePhone recipes for ideas, I sketched out design concepts. When we thought we had some good ideas, we paused long enough to look around.

Everyone was frantically scribbling, erasing, arguing. I gave Chaz a knowing look. "I think we've got this one in the bag. Ours is clean. Simple. I think everyone else is overcomplicating it."

"I hope so," he said.

At nine-fifteen, it was our turn to meet with the ePhone guy, then we planned a fun pink and green layout with the art department. I was moving on high speed, but I could tell Chaz was stressed. Occasionally, the cameramen caught various contestants for OTFs and I heard a few of them mention my name, but I couldn't hear what they were saying. I didn't care. I just knew we were going to win. Finally, one of the production people came into the room and directed everyone to gather their things and head downstairs to the vans. On the way to the market, everyone sat in stony silence, afraid to give anything away, too stressed to talk.

Finally, I tried to break the silence. "So, Monica," I said to the blonde lifestyle coach who obviously loved champagne. "You're the . . . what do you do in your line of work again?" I said.

She looked offended. "I'm a lifestyle coach, if that's what you mean by 'line of work,' " she said, flipping her feathered hair and rolling her big eyes. "But it's not work to me, it's a calling. I'm really good, especially at past-life regression. I have this talent for manipulating energy."

"You have a talent for manipulating champagne bottles," muttered Nadine in her fake English accent.

"Just because you're married to an ATM machine doesn't make you better than us, *Queen Nadine,*" Monica said, defensively. I couldn't help laughing. I hadn't heard anybody call her Queen Nadine to her face yet.

"Just because you spew a load of self-help crap doesn't mean you're better than *us,*" said amnesiac-party-girl Katie.

Everyone was silent for a while, but after catching Katie staring at me with a disgusted look on her face, I'd had enough.

"What is your deal?" I said, looking her in the eye.

She just looked away. I felt like I was back in high school.

At the market, Chaz and I bought bags of fresh organic lemons, raw sugar, club soda, a bottle of cranberry juice, and white rum at a liquor store. Then I saw a display of retro frilly aprons. "Chaz! We have to get these! They are *so* Domestic Goddess."

"She didn't say we were supposed to wear costumes," Chaz said.

"So what? We're supposed to serve to businesspeople at a cocktail party, like a 1960s housewife, right? So we should wear these. Or . . . I should. You should wear a suit or something. Or a hat."

"I've got a fedora," Chaz said.

"You would," I said. I bought an apron for myself.

When the wrangler blew the whistle ("Did she really just blow a whistle at us?" Chaz asked me), we got in line to buy our purchases with our allotted money.

The test kitchen was fabulous, as expected, and inspired by Sybil's actual kitchen. It had low, wide stainless-steel counters, a bank of double ovens, and twelve burners along a middle island. I memorized every detail, obsessed with the perfection. Each of us chose a work-station, then ran to grab the supplies we needed. Chaz found some antique martini glasses and filled a silver ice bucket with ice. I collected a classic silver shaker and a big, old manual metal citrus juicer. Others were grabbing mixers and blenders, bowls and wooden spoons, cake pans and loaf pans and soup pots.

I squeezed all the lemons, pressing down the handle of the manual juicer over and over, until my arm ached. We made simple syrup from the raw sugar, then mixed the sugar syrup and cranberry juice into the lemon juice until the proportions were right. I adjusted the recipe draft—a little less sugar, a little more cranberry. "We'd better make the actual drink, to be sure it's right," he said.

I smiled. "Now that's using your head," I said. I muddled the mint and ice in the shaker, poured in the rum and lemonade, and shook. Chaz rimmed two glasses with raw sugar, then I poured in the drinks. We tasted.

"These are amazing," Chaz said. "Sybil's going to love them."

"Let's hope so," I said, downing my drink in one gulp. "But I think we'd better make a couple more, just to be sure."

When a production person came into the room and told us we had fifteen minutes, Chaz had just come back from retrieving his fedora and putting on a tie. He looked like he was ready to investigate the Kennedy assassination—or at least investigate a martini and a cigarette. Suddenly I had an idea. "I'm going to do my hair," I said.

"Now? It's almost time!" Chaz said nervously.

"I have time," I said.

"Sure, it's not like the pressure's on or anything." His voice dripped with sarcasm.

"We don't have anything left to do," I said. "We're good to go."

I looked around the workroom, but I couldn't find anything resembling bobby pins. Then I noticed Mikki was wearing a few. I begged her to lend them to me, and being the nice and nondramatic person she was, she slid them out of her cloud of hair and handed them to me. I ran to the bathroom, a cameraman following me, and piled all my hair up onto my head in my best imitation of a beehive hairdo, teasing my hair with my fingers to give it volume. Then I ran back to the workroom. I twirled around for Chaz, my frilly apron billowing out. "How do I look?"

Chaz stared at my hair. "Like you're from Jersey?" he said. I slapped him on the arm.

"I was going for Audrey Hepburn in *Breakfast at Tiffany's.*"

"Oh sure, that, too," he said, rolling his eyes.

The reception area was tastefully decorated with flowers and six cocktail tables. As we brought in our food and set it up at our designated table, the other teams were making fun of my costume, but it didn't even faze me. I wanted to stand out. I realized how far I'd come since my insecure days in L.A., when Donna Shannon's snub put me in a tailspin. This group was even worse than the cast of *Hollywood & Highland,* but they weren't going to intimidate me. *Look at you,* I thought to myself. *Maybe you've actually grown up a little.*

We set up our station, and then I noticed that our ice was almost completely melted. "Chaz!" I hissed. "Chaz, the ice is melted! We need ice!"

"Oh crap," he said, looking around. "Does anybody else have some?"

"Nobody's going to help us!" I said. "We've got to get more."

"You can't do it, you have to present," he said. "I'll go."

"For God's sake, hurry up!" He dashed out of the room.

We waited, everyone nervously buzzing with anticipation.

A few minutes later, the door opened and Sybil walked in, followed by Rasputin, looking particularly fluffy, and then Alice and a tall Indian woman. But where was Chaz? We would lose for sure if we were missing half our team! How long could it take to fill a bucket of ice?

"Hello everyone," Sybil said, stiffly. "Are you all ready to present your dishes to our guests?"

We all nodded, obediently, and I felt a little thrill that I didn't have a dish, I had a *glass*. But any of us might be going home tonight. My pulse was racing and I felt a little unsteady on my feet. I looked around. Nadine smiled calmly at me. Shari waved. I couldn't even focus on what other dishes everyone else had made. *Where was Chaz?*

"Excellent. But first, let me introduce you to someone very important here at Sybil Hunter Enterprises. You all know my sister Alice, but you may not know Ruby Prasad." The Indian woman with impossibly long legs nodded. "Ruby is the executive food editor for *Domestic Goddess Magazine,* and an experienced cook as well as recipe tester and recipe *taster.* Ian had to be away on business today, so we brought Ruby in to help evaluate your creations."

"Hello everyone," the woman said, her voice low and sexy.

"And now," said Sybil, "let's welcome our guests."

She waved her arm at the door, and it opened, as if by magic. Eight men and eight women walked in, all of them wearing suits and looking very serious. At the same time, Chaz slid in the door behind them, clutching the ice bucket, and quickly walked along the edge of the room, back around to our table. Sybil watched his every move, but didn't say anything. Instead, she said, "These are some of my friends, influential local businesspeople who have contributed in one way or another to Sybil Hunter Enterprises." None of them looked very friendly to me, but maybe that was to be expected. *Any friend of Sybil is . . . probably not a friend of mine,* I thought, morosely. "And now, everyone, please enjoy yourselves," she said to the businesspeople.

"Thank God you're back!" I said. "I thought we would lose for sure!"

"Here," he said, putting a fresh bucket of ice on the table. "Let's hope she comes to our table before this one melts!"

It was do or die. Our glasses weren't chilled anymore and my hair was falling down, but they'd love our cocktail, or they'd hate it. We'd done everything we could do. Chaz wouldn't stop shifting back and forth and rocking forward and back on his heels and toes.

"Stand still!" I whispered.

"I think I'm going to have a panic attack!" he whispered back.

"You'll be fine," I hissed, but I wasn't sure I wasn't about to have one, too.

The first person to come to our table was a tired-looking woman in a gray suit with hair pulled back into a tight and unflattering bun on top of her head. "What do you have?" she said, looking hopefully at the cocktail shaker and the bottle of rum.

"Pink lemonade mojitos," I said. "Would you like one?"

"God, yes," she said. I muddled, shook, and poured as Chaz began rimming glasses. I poured her drink, finished it with club soda, and Chaz garnished it with a thin slice of lemon and a thin slice of lime.

"This is excellent," she said, after taking a long drink. She was actually starting to look human. "I like your hair."

As soon as the guests realized we had liquor, we had a line. We made drinks one at a time—muddle, shake, rim, pour, garnish. Meanwhile, I watched Sybil making her way around to the other tables. She didn't seem to be saying much, just tasting and moving on.

Finally, Sybil approached our table, with Alice, Ruby Prasad, and, of course, the dog. She looked very tall, and she looked down upon us like a god on judgment day. A Domestic Goddess on judgment day. A disgruntled one.

"So, what do you have for me today?" she said. "This doesn't look like muffins."

I had butterflies, and I was suddenly more aware of the cameras than I had been for the last few days. I just had to impress her. I had to make amends. I had to repair whatever damage had already occurred, so the contest would be fair and I could be judged on my performance, not on my past, or on whatever else it was about me that obviously irritated Sybil Hunter.

"Well, it's true I'm a baker, but I also went to bartending school, and this is a little drink I created a while back that's always a big hit at parties. I call it the Have Faith Pink Lemonade Mojito."

"What did you do to your hair?"

I could feel my cheeks burning, but I played it cavalier. "We were going for a theme—the 1960s Domestic Goddess serving drinks for her husband's colleagues after work." I twirled around in my apron again. Chaz tipped his hat.

"I see," Sybil said. "That was . . . probably not necessary."

"Let's just make you a drink then," I said.

"Interesting," Sybil said after taking a sip. "Did you use simple syrup?"

"We made our own with raw sugar," I said. She paused. I could tell she liked the drink.

"It's nice," Ruby said, nodding.

"This is great," Alice said. "Can I have another one?"

"Why not? I've already had three," I said.

"You've been drinking these?" Sybil asked. "Are you drunk?"

"Um . . ." Suddenly I regretted saying anything. "Well, we had to taste . . . and be sure they were right."

"I see," Sybil said. "And that required drinking three of them. Well, that explains your judgment about the costumes."

"It's been a very stressful day," I said, apologetically.

"A Domestic Goddess always has herself under control," Sybil said. She turned to Chaz. "The drink is named after your teammate. What did you do to help in this team effort?" she asked. "Did you have three drinks as well?"

"I . . . I did the . . ."

I jumped in to save him. "Presentation is key in a cocktail, and Chaz was in charge of rimming the glasses with raw sugar and garnishing with the lemon-lime wheels."

"Really?" she said, raising her eyebrows.

I realized I'd pretty much taken over our team. I hadn't listened to any of his suggestions, so I felt like I had to give him credit for something. I hoped I hadn't unintentionally sabotaged him.

"It looks to me," Sybil said thoughtfully, "like Faith took the lead on this one. Is that correct?"

"The drink was definitely her invention, and I would say she was in the role of team leader, but we worked on it together," Chaz said.

"OK," Sybil said. "I do like the drink, even if I think your outfits are tacky. Your recipe, please."

Finally Sybil and her entourage continued to the next table and I could breathe again. Before Alice moved on, she leaned in and whispered to us, "I think your outfits are cute."

"Oh, my God," I whispered to Chaz, when they were out of earshot. "That was so stressful, I wanted to die."

"You and me both, honey," he said. "I don't know how much more of this I can take. Just between us, I wouldn't mind if she cut me. I'm happy to take the blame for anything and everything, if it means I don't have to go through this again."

"Don't say that!" I said. "She's not going to cut you." I glared at him. "You did more than help, Chaz. We were a team."

Suddenly, a cameraman jumped in front of me and Mike appeared. "Faith, how do you feel after that challenge? Talk us through it."

"I think she liked our drink," I said. "I think she really would have liked to have three or four of them. In fact, I strongly suspect Sybil's a secret party animal. I think we'll probably win this challenge, after she swings back for another one." Mike gave me the thumbs-up, then the camera swung away toward Team Six.

"Do you really believe we're going to win?" Chaz said.

"Sure!" I said cheerfully, not feeling sure at all.

chapter twenty-three

Back in the Loft, we all ate dinner and waited, although for most of the contestants, dinner meant an energy bar and a diet soda. Nobody had an appetite. We were too tired and wired and ready to blow. We all knew that Sybil's testers were having their way with our recipes. I gazed, glassy eyed and exhausted, out the windows at the panoramic view of the sun setting over the Hudson River, but I hardly saw it.

"Is there any of that champagne left?" Monica said, pacing back and forth in front of the couch.

Katie looked disgusted. She put her long legs up on one of the white ottomans and crossed her arms, slumping back into the cushions. "You people are so bizarre," she said.

"Honey, we're all in this together, so why don't you just cut the diva act?" Shari said.

"Excuse the hell out of me!" Katie said. "At least I'm not trying to sell my flowers to everybody I meet like I'm some dirty street vendor."

Chaz raised his eyebrows at me, and mouthed the words "dirty street vendor?" I giggled.

"Have you guys thought about how much money they are making off of us?" said Andy, the chef, bouncing up and down on the balls of his feet like he was on springs. "The question is, how do *we* cash in on this whole reality show concept?"

"Reality!" yelled one of the cameramen. I thought how ironic it was that we couldn't talk about this one major aspect of reality on a reality TV show. They called it "breaking the fourth wall," between the action and the audience.

"I just want to prove myself, so Sybil doesn't hold this whole Ian thing against me," I said.

"Too bad you can't give Sybil a blow job," Katie said. "Then you'd be just fine."

"If I had, I'd own her company by now," I shot back. I rubbed my eyes. They wanted so badly to close.

"Sybil loved your cocktail," Shari said.

"Probably not as much as she loved your beautiful cupcakes," I said. Shari and Jodi Sue had made pink cupcakes with real flowers on top.

"They were beautiful," Shari agreed. "I'm so glad I thought of them."

"It was my recipe," said Jodi Sue, crossing her arms over her overexposed cleavage and pouting.

"Whatever," said Shari. "The flowers made the recipe. How can you not love cupcakes with fresh flowers on them?"

"I think our meat loaf rocked it," Andy said, bouncing back up again and pacing in front of the window.

"I think our meat loaf is going to win," said Linda. "But will you sit the fuck down, Andy? You're driving everybody crazy."

"Hey, I'm a mover and a shaker," he said. "I'm a wild man." He made a pelvic-thrusting motion.

"You're manic," I said. "Get off your high horse."

He started moving like he was riding a bucking bronco. "Yee ha!" he said. "You can ride me anytime."

"Yeah, I'll get right on that," I said.

"That's what she said," Andy said.

"I know one recipe that isn't going to win. A stupid salad," said Katie, sulking.

"Hey, I resent that," said Sadie, tossing her long braid behind her back. "The only thing she didn't like about our salad was your horrible dressing."

"Bitch," Katie muttered.

"You know, Katie, you seem to have an anger problem," I said. The lack of sleep was stripping away what little subtlety I had.

"A what?" she said, jumping up, like she wanted to take it outside.

"Do you even remember that we've met before?" I said, getting more and more irritated.

"No," Katie said, scrunching up her nose. "I don't know you. Thank God. I hardly think I would have hung around with your type."

"What do you mean my 'type'?" I said.

"I mean, there's me, and then there's you. The two don't mix."

"Well they're mixing now," I said. "We'll see who's who when this is all over."

"Whatever," she said. "Bitch."

"You're just mad because I wouldn't let you dance on the bar at Hearst Castle," I said.

"I have no idea what you're talking about," she said, reddening.

Chaz put his hand on my knee. I took a deep, calming breath. Katie looked wildly around at everyone. Suddenly, she seemed to deflate. "I need some licorice," she said, and stormed off to the kitchen, where she kept a huge stash of candy.

Shari raised her eyebrows. "Can you say 'blood sugar issues'?" she said.

"Why don't you just leave her alone," said Nadine directly to me.

"You want *me* to leave *her* alone, Queen Nadine?" I said. Ever since she'd passed me the note about sleeping with Hugh Pritzker, I wasn't sure what to make of her. Was she trying to befriend me, or get me in trouble? Now that she was roomies with Katie, who obviously hated me, I could tell I was no longer on her good side, if I ever was.

The front door opened and one of the producers walked in. "It's decision time," he said. "Let's go, everyone."

We all stood up and a new wave of nerves swept over me. Shari came up and squeezed my hand. "It's between you and me," she whispered. "I'll be happy if it's either one of us!"

"Me, too," I said. "I'm glad you're here." I felt supported with Shari around. She was confident and less nervous than the others, and that calmed me. But I also knew we were both in it to win.

"Some of you did very well on this challenge. And some of you did not," said Sybil, as she came into the meeting room, where we all sat, nervous and on edge, waiting for the verdict. She walked brusquely to the table. "You all remember Hugh Pritzker." She motioned to the door as he came bursting in, followed by Alice and Ruby. "And of course, you remember my sister and colleague Alice Hunter and *Domestic Goddess Magazine*'s executive food editor, Ruby Prasad."

Ruby and Alice nodded.

"We've been very busy this afternoon in the Sybil Hunter Test Kitchen," Sybil said. "We've tested every single one of your recipes. In many cases, I have to say, the results varied from what I saw and tasted when you created your own recipes. But there were a few standouts . . . and one winner."

My heart beat faster. It had to be me. It just had to be me. I shot Chaz a look. He smiled nervously.

Sybil continued, "Your recipes were judged not just on results, but on ease of preparation, simplicity of ingredients, and on how well the final product could be photographed for the Recipes 2 Go splash page on the ePhone. We also took into account input from the guests at our reception. A few of you did *not* measure up."

"First of all, I didn't like Team Three's salad," said Ruby. "There was nothing to it. It wasn't really a recipe at all. It was raw vegetables in a bowl," she said. "And the dressing was just terrible."

"The dressing was indeed terrible," Sybil agreed. "Inedible. Whose idea was that dressing?"

"Katie made that dressing," said farmer Sadie. "I had nothing to do with it. And I have to say that while I understand a salad may not exactly be a recipe, the point was to feature and celebrate the most vibrant organic produce that New York has to offer—"

Sybil interrupted her. "Nobody is going to look to an ePhone to choose the best tomato," she said, dismissively.

"Team Two's cookies were vile," said Alice. "They tasted like cardboard."

"One of your bellboys could come up with something better than those cookies," Sybil said to Christophe, the concierge, who looked humiliated. "And Mikki, as an event planner, didn't you taste the cookies before you served them?"

"Yes," Mikki said, quietly. "I thought they were"—she glanced at Christophe—"I thought they were OK."

"They most certainly were not OK," said Sybil.

"I had to spit mine out," said Ruby.

"In the test kitchen, the recipe didn't even work," said Alice. "The cookies fell apart."

"And I'm afraid I wasn't a big fan of Team Five," Sybil said, finally.

"What?" I couldn't help saying out loud. "How can you say that? Everyone loved my mojitos! *You* loved them!"

Sybil looked annoyed that I was arguing with her.

"The drink itself was acceptable," she said. "But I wasn't a fan of the presentation, and I don't think it's reasonable to expect the average ePhone user to squeeze all those lemons by hand."

"*You* would squeeze all those lemons by hand," I countered. "You know you would."

"Yes, but this particular challenge was not about what I would do; it was about creating an appropriate ePhone app. The taste was fine, but the implementation of the idea was lacking, and you can't make up for an impractical idea with a beehive hairdo and a silly apron." Ouch.

Alice gave me a sympathetic look, but I was burning up inside. I couldn't believe it. We were going to lose because Sybil wanted to get rid of me, and she was using any excuse she could. I gave Chaz a "this is totally unfair!" look. He shrugged, helplessly.

"Now for the good news," Sybil said. "Team Six's meat loaf was quite good and easy to make." Linda jabbed Andy with her elbow and gave him a "told-ya-so" look. "However, it came out in the test kitchen much differently than what was served at the reception, so I'm not sure where the disconnect was. Even so, we think it would be quite a popular recipe on the ePhone."

"The three-layer coconut cake was another standout from Team One," said Ruby. "It was quite attractive, moist, and had an excellent texture. I suspect one of you is a closet baker," she said to Monica, who looked sober for once, and a nodding Nadine. I couldn't imagine Nadine had ever baked anything. She probably had servants for that.

"Finally," Sybil said, "Team Four's flower cupcakes were absolutely charming, and I particularly liked the way you worked as a team, using Jodi Sue's recipe and Shari's knowledge of flowers. Just lovely."

Shari beamed, and I smiled at her, but it felt false. I was crushed. I couldn't believe we weren't going to win, and I was even more astounded that we were considered one of the three worst teams, when our recipe was obviously the most popular.

"And now, to announce the winner. Hugh?" said Sybil.

"Of course," he said, rubbing his hands together as if he was about to engage in a hostile takeover. "The winner of this challenge is . . . Team Four, for their photogenic cupcakes. Congratulations."

Shari leapt to her feet with glee, then quickly sat back down. "Thank you, thank you so much," she said.

"Thank you so much," echoed Jodi Sue, her cheeks flushing and her chest heaving with embarrassed pleasure. Celebrity chef my ass. I knew a groupie when I saw one. But apparently she did know how to bake.

"Teams One, Four, and Six, you may leave the room," said Sybil. The top three teams all stood up.

"I won! I won!" Shari chanted.

"I think you mean *we* won!" Jodi Sue said.

"Yes, yes, that's what I meant, of course!" she said, and hugged Jodi Sue, to make up for it. Then she ran around the table to give me a hug, too. "Can you believe it? My recipe"—she paused and looked over at Jodi Sue—"*our* recipe," she corrected herself, "is going to be featured on an ePhone app!"

I smiled. "You deserve it," I said. And she did, even if I didn't like it. I tried to be gracious.

"Thanks, honey," she said. "That's so true." Then she whispered in my ear, "There's no way they're going to fire you. You're great. And your cocktail was gorgeous. It's you and me." She kissed my cheek, then skipped out the door.

The rest of us sat tensely waiting for the verdict. Sybil looked at us for a long moment in stony silence. Then she spoke. "Teams Two, Three, and Five, your recipes were *very* disappointing." She turned to Mikki and Christophe. "Team Two. Your cookies were stale tasting, even though they were freshly baked. Some of us couldn't even swallow them." Ruby nodded. "Your recipe was not up to the Recipes 2 Go standards, nor up to my standards."

Mikki lowered her head.

"Team Three," she continued. "Your salad left much to be desired. People don't look to an ePhone app for how to make a tossed salad. The dressing was too tart and salty, and frankly, offensive. This recipe was a total failure." Sadie looked like she might cry. Katie rolled her eyes and sighed with irritation. "Katie, do you have something to say?" Sybil asked.

The cameras swung around.

"Actually, I do," Katie said, flipping her long blonde hair back to reveal little silver fish earrings. "This woman," she said, pointing to Sadie, "is a freaking hillbilly who thinks people like vegetables." Sadie's mouth dropped open and she stared at Katie, her face turning red. "And that dressing is served at one of the most high-end restaurants in Manhattan, and anyone who thinks it isn't good is just . . . just . . ."

"Let me stop you right there," said Sybil, calmly, her mouth sliding into a smile. She reminded me of a hungry snake who's just eyed a rat. "First of all, if you used a recipe from a Manhattan restaurant, you are clearly in violation of the rules. And second, if you did use such a recipe, you obviously didn't follow it precisely, because that dressing was truly horrific, and no respectable Manhattan restaurant would ever serve it." Katie scowled and didn't say anything else.

Then she turned to us. Oh my God, it was our turn. Would it be me? Would I go home first? I couldn't imagine a worse fate. I clenched my teeth to keep them from chattering. "Faith, Chaz, your pink lemonade mojito was tasty enough, but we weren't fans of your silly costumes. Also, the typical Recipes 2 Go user is a busy woman in her midthirties to midfifties, and we don't believe people in this age group would take the time to prepare a cocktail like this. Mixologists, they are not. Remember, the recipes were judged for simplicity and ease of preparation. This might sell well in a bar, but we don't think it's right for an ePhone app."

"But you're in that age group, and you liked it, didn't you?" I couldn't help bursting out.

Sybil looked uncomfortable. "As I said, it was tasty enough," she said.

"No, you loved it, I could tell. This is a damn good cocktail."

Chaz kicked me under the table.

"Furthermore," Sybil said, ignoring my outburst, "your team obviously suffered from a problem we didn't see on the other teams. Faith, we believe that you took over the challenge and the spotlight, and Chaz did very little. This challenge was not about one contestant being the star and the other being the assistant. It was about teamwork, and I don't believe you worked together as a team. From what I've seen, I'm not sure you're capable of being a team player."

I couldn't believe what I was hearing. She was saying we didn't have teamwork, after Katie just called her teammate a crazy hick?

"It's not true, we were a team!" I protested.

"Chaz," Sybil said, continuing to ignore me. "I hold you largely responsible. When you are on a team, you need to work as a team. Even a Domestic Goddess—or God, as the case may be—has to work with family and colleagues to get the job done. You need to stand up for yourself and not let somebody else bully you and take over."

I gave Chaz a helpless look. He shook his head just slightly, telling me silently, I hoped, that I wasn't a bully. "To work at Sybil Hunter Enterprises, and to have your own television show, it is extremely important to be a team player, even when you are the star, and it is just as important to assert yourself in the presence of stronger person- alities," she said, giving me a sidelong glance. "Chaz . . ." she paused for a long, torturous minute. "I'm sorry, but I'm afraid you're just not necessary here at Sybil Hunter Enterprises."

Chaz blanched. I felt like someone had just punched me in the stomach. How could she call him "not necessary"? Was this how she was punishing me for knowing Ian? Making my friend the victim? Sybil reached out to shake Chaz's hand, then she said, "Good-bye, Chaz, and good luck."

Chaz stood up, a strange look of disappointment mixed with relief on his face. "Thank you, Sybil, Alice, Ruby," he said, shaking their hands. "It was an honor."

Suddenly, a cameraman was in my face again. And there was Mike. "What's your reaction, Faith?" he said.

I just stared at the camera. "I . . . I . . . I . . ." I shook my head. "All I can say is . . ." My mouth was wide open, but nothing came out. For once, I was speechless.

chapter twenty-four

There are eleven of you left, and today, I have a special treat for you," said Sybil.

Really, Sybil? It was seven a.m. and we all stood, bleary eyed, in the Sybil Hunter Craft Studio, practically vibrating from stress and lack of sleep, and the only "special treat" I could imagine wanting from Sybil Hunter right now was the use of one of her glue guns, to seal my eyelids shut. This whole experience was turning into some warped sleep-deprivation experiment. We all stayed up all night, sick with worry, bickering and talking about one another, and I was grumpy and irritable and I wanted to blame everybody around me for how rotten I felt. From the looks of everyone else, they all felt the same. So Sybil has a treat for us? Ha. I didn't even want to know.

Alice looked fresh faced and well rested. Ian looked hung over, and from what I remembered about him, that was no surprise. His red nose practically glowed.

The crew had filled the studio space with baskets labeled with every craft item under the sun—scissors, pipe cleaners, Popsicle sticks, artificial flowers grouped by color, lace, yarn, buttons, sequins, doilies, glitter, bells, glass balls, jars of markers, paintbrushes, and drawing pencils—and a line of sewing machines against the back wall.

It was like a Michael's craft store had exploded and then been even more fastidiously put back together. Not a sequin on the floor, not a single scrap of paper or speck of dust.

I stood between Shari the yenta and Mikki the wallflower. Shari whispered to me, "I used to do crafts with my daughter. Whatever this is, I'm going to be good at it."

Mikki looked nervous and pale. "Are we going to have to sew?" she whispered. "Or paint?" She looked like she might faint.

"As you know, the holiday season approaches," Sybil said. We all knew it was July, but we'd already been instructed that magazines had a big lead time and the show itself wouldn't begin airing until October, so in our warped reality, it *was* almost holiday time. "And nothing welcomes guests to the holiday table like a gracious and beautiful table setting."

I looked at Mikki eagerly. As a fellow event planner, surely she, too, was used to designing an impressive table. She looked at me, relieved, some of the color coming back into her gaunt face. I thought about Chaz. He would have loved this challenge.

"You will be divided into two teams. Each of you will be assigned a table to design for a holiday dinner for twelve. The table may be decorated in any way your team decides, as long as it is a festive and appropriate table for the holidays. You will also plan an entire twelve-course menu, although you will not actually be preparing it. Instead, you will have it printed on a menu card for display. You will also each have an entire room to decorate. Your table should be the showpiece, and the rest of the room should support its design in a unique and beautiful way. Your holiday dining room designs will be judged on attractiveness, creativity, and elegance. You will also choose a team theme for this challenge.

"You may use anything in this room," she continued. "You may also choose from my collection of antique china and silver. You have a two-thousand-dollar budget to spend on supplies from Affair to Remember, a beautiful party supply shop on Madison Avenue, run by a dear friend of our family. Each team will receive one of these." Sybil held up a heavy binder. "This is the Rulebook. It details what you can and can't do for this challenge. Shari, since you were the winner of the last challenge, you get to choose the two team leaders. Whom do you choose?"

Everyone stared at Shari. We all knew that to be the team leader was to be the most vulnerable, especially in a challenge where there were only two teams. If a team crashed and burned, the team leader was likely at fault. Thank God Shari and I were such good friends. I knew she wouldn't put me in such a vulnerable position.

Shari looked pleased. "Well. Let's see," she said. "Being team leader is an important responsibility." She surveyed all of us. "I choose Andy," she said, with a sweet smile, "and Christophe."

It was a good strategy—Andy was a wild card, who could easily go in the wrong direction and create a complete disaster. Then again, he could create something brilliant, so it was a gamble. Christophe seemed like he would be easy to manipulate, so I could only assume she was hoping to be on his team. She gave me a knowing look.

Andy leapt out of his seat and started rubbing his hands together. "OK, if I'm going to be a team leader, then I'm going to *lead,* damn it."

"The two men. Interesting choices," said Sybil. "Andy and Christophe, come up here. Andy, your last challenge was more successful than Christophe's, so you get to choose your first team member."

"Awesome. I'm going to have the team that *rocks* this challenge," Andy said. He always looked like he was being run by a motor. He seemed at first to focus on the most obvious cleavage. "I choose Jodi Sue." Jodi Sue stood up and went to stand beside Andy, keeping her distance. She made a pouty face at Shari.

"I choose Mikki," said Christophe. Big surprise. Mikki flushed, then went over to stand next to Christophe. They looked like two grade school kids afraid to admit their crushes on each other.

"OK, let's see," said Andy. "I think I'll go with Linda. We were an awesome team in the last challenge."

"Damn right," said Linda, hoisting herself up and striding over to stand beside Andy. She looked down on Jodi Sue and her cleavage with obvious disdain.

"Shari," said Christophe. Of course, the two winners from the last challenge would go at the beginning, but I was having gym-class anxiety—would I be picked last?

"Nadine," said Andy. I couldn't believe he'd choose Queen Nadine over me. Not that I wanted to be on his team.

"Faith," said Christophe. Shari winked at me. I was relieved. It might be fun to be on a team with Shari.

"Katie," said Andy. Katie stood beside Nadine and they began to whisper.

"Monica," said Christophe. Monica bounced over to us, looking excited.

"And that leaves Sadie," said Andy. Farmer Sadie, looking embarrassed to be chosen last, went to stand with Katie, Nadine, Linda, Jodi Sue, and Andy. I looked around at our team—Shari, Mikki, and I already knew one another pretty well from sharing a room. Then we had Monica, the lifestyle coach, and eccentric Christophe, the concierge. All the really difficult personalities, it seemed to me, were on the other team—Andy, Katie, Linda, Nadine—and I could definitely do without any of them. This could work. I was already thinking of ideas for the most gorgeous holiday table Sybil had ever seen.

"Now, to tell you about the prize," Sybil said. Everyone stopped whispering at once to hear. "The winning table will be featured in a photo spread for the holiday issue of *Domestic Goddess Magazine,* with do-it-yourself instructions for how our readers can replicate the look at home, so keep that in mind when planning your designs. But that's not all. Your table and room design will also be featured at a very special event." She paused dramatically. "My own family Thanksgiving dinner."

We all gasped. Her family Thanksgiving was practically a national holiday in and of itself. Even if this was actually happening in July.

"As such, your design will also be photographed for the magazine *and* filmed for my show. And that brings me to your special treat,"

Sybil said, smiling. She turned toward the door. "We have a very special guest judge, who is the perfect person to help decide which table will be featured at my family Thanksgiving. That's because he's a most cherished member of my very own family. I would like to introduce you all to my dear son, Harry."

The famous and reclusive Harry Jansen? Everyone knew about Sybil's only son from her first marriage to Reginald Jansen, the media tycoon who shot himself a decade ago. Harry Jansen had retreated from the press after that, and was known for refusing the trappings of his billionaire mother's lifestyle. He was rarely seen—one of Sybil's cookbooks had a picture of him as a child, but I remembered hearing from my old friend Jeannie Klein back in L.A. that he was an exceptionally handsome eligible bachelor with quite a reputation. We all looked at one another, amazed that we were actually going to see him. This was like getting to see JFK, Jr.!

The door opened, and in he walked. Harris.

I gasped. Harris! The man from Spring Seven. The man whose kiss was a lightning storm. He was Sybil Hunter's *son*? He was *Harry Jansen*? I realized my mouth was hanging open. I closed it.

I looked at Shari and Mikki and grabbed both their arms. What was up with this show? It was like being on some bizarre, sadistic, roller-coaster version of *This Is Your Life*.

"What? What?" Shari whispered. I couldn't speak. I just shook my head. *Stay calm, Faith. Stay calm. Whatever you do, don't act like you care. You don't care. You barely remember him. He doesn't matter. Don't let this throw you. Don't let her know. Don't let Sybil know! Don't let anyone know!*

Suddenly, I realized that not only was I about to face Harris again but if Sybil found out I'd been making out with her son at a nightclub, that might be the final straw. I was amazed she hadn't eliminated me already, but three strikes, and I was likely to be out, no matter what Chaz thought about Sybil being "just the talent." *Stay calm. Act cool. You'll be fine. It'll all be fine,* I told myself, frantically.

Sybil was still talking, oblivious to my inner turmoil. "Thanksgiving is *very* important to my family, especially now that my son is engaged to be married." Everyone smiled and clapped politely . . . except me. *He's getting married?* To that bimbo in the microscopic skirt? The one he told me he'd just met that night? Oh yeah. All right. Game on. He really was a player. I fumed. I hated him. It was all I could do not to leap forward and throttle him. How could he have led me on like he did? *Engaged?* I cast him an evil glare, but he wasn't looking at me. I didn't think he'd even noticed me yet. He was watching his mother. I noticed that he didn't look particularly happy. Then he spoke.

"I'm not engaged, Mother," he said.

"Well . . . we'll see about that," Sybil replied curtly. "In any case, Harry will be a special guest judge during this challenge. He doesn't normally like to be involved in my shows," she said, putting a hand on his back, "but he's agreed to fill in, just this once. He'll help choose the winning table."

All I could think was *What did he mean by "Not engaged, Mother"?* Was he or wasn't he? In any case, clearly he couldn't be trusted. Like mother, like son. He was probably as heartless and power hungry as she was. *Calm down, Faith. You don't hate anybody. Keep your eye on the prize . . . and the prize is* not *Harris. Or Harry Jansen. Or whatever his name really is.*

"Harry, why don't you tell the contestants what you would like to see in this challenge."

"I think you or Aunt Alice will be better suited to do that, Mother," he said, looking around at us. And then our eyes locked. I tried to look calm and cool, but I got that weak-in-the-knees feeling again. His eyes widened and his face turned red.

"But Harry, you agreed to offer your input."

He just kept staring at me. Uh-oh. "What's wrong, Harry? Cat got your tongue?" Sybil said, smiling. Then she looked at him, to see what he was looking at. In a low voice, she growled, "Don't tell me you know her, too."

I gave him a panicky look, a tiny shake of my head. *Please don't sell me out,* I tried to tell him, telepathically. *If I ever meant anything to you at all, even for five minutes, please don't sell me out.*

He turned to her, and smiled calmly, completely composing himself. "Who, Mother?"

She narrowed her eyes. I noticed that Alice was catching everything, a little smile on her face, like she was watching something very amusing.

"And yes, you're right, I did agree to offer my input," he said, suddenly the model son. He turned to us, not looking at me. "Our family likes a table that's both traditional and original. My mother also prides herself on maintaining a beautiful home. So try to combine those three elements," he said.

"Thank you, Harry," Sybil said, looking satisfied. "And yes, my son is right. Tradition, originality, and beauty. That's what we'll be looking for. You have thirty minutes to plan. Then you'll have the rest of the afternoon and evening and tomorrow morning to gather supplies elsewhere or to work in the craft room. You'll each have a mock room to decorate, right here in the studio. Harry, Alice, and I will be here at noon tomorrow to judge your creations."

Sybil turned to leave.

"Harry and I will stay here to monitor the progress and report back," Alice told Sybil.

"Excellent," said Sybil. She and Ian left the room. Harris shifted back and forth, watching his mother walk out. As soon as she was gone, he started to walk toward me.

"Just hold on," Alice whispered and grabbed his arm.

He stepped back. I looked away, quickly. *Stop watching him,* I commanded myself.

Our team gathered around the table, and Shari started talking about who was going to do what. No matter that Christophe was the team leader, he was happy to let Shari take over. She already had a theme: "Authentic Holidays." I tried to listen, but I was still reeling. My Harris was Sybil Hunter's son? But he wasn't my Harris. I had to get over it. I had to get in the mood. I had to pretend he wasn't stand-ing *right over there.*

Think, Faith. You can do this. You know how to do this.

I sat down at the table, as if I was a dinner guest—in part because I'd snuck another glance at Harris, and it had made me practically swoon. "Let's all sit down for a minute," I said to my team. "Let's think about what would impress us the most if we were sitting at this table." Everyone sat. I pushed Harris completely out of my mind and thought of nothing but that table. Holidays. Thanksgiving. What was I thank-ful for?

I realized how thankful I was to be right there, at that moment. To be on a television show. To have this amazing opportunity to work with Sybil Hunter. She was a difficult person, but that's probably why she was so successful. And here I was, learning from the best. What kind of Thanksgiving table would be good enough for the best?

"Red," I said. "Let's start with red. We need a rich red brocade tablecloth set with sprays of evergreen under silver chargers with simple, snow-white plates, and a long, low, lavish centerpiece of natu-ral materials—evergreen boughs, pinecones, and red roses with white candles. Extravagant, but not so tall that people can't see each other across the table."

"I love it," said Shari. "Red, white, and silver, with natural greens. Gorgeous."

"Let's do place cards," said Mikki. "We could paint pinecones with silver paint and put place cards in them, one at each place. Maybe put them on little wire stands so they stand up straight."

"That's a great idea," Christophe said.

"And finger bowls with rose petals," Shari added.

I could hear the other group arguing. Katie was yelling that they should have a fish theme, and Andy was telling her she was an idiot. I smiled, but tried not to get distracted. *Stay in your own lane, Faith,* I reminded myself.

"We need something else, too," I said. "Something big, something that will make us stand out." I looked at the table for a moment. Then it came to me. I lowered my voice and gestured for everyone to lean in. "How about a champagne fountain, on a sideboard that matches the table. That's what I would want to see if I came to someone's Thanksgiving dinner. That would make my day."

"That would make my day, too," said Monica.

Shari agreed. "We'll put roses on the top." With Shari around, we'd never be lacking in flowers.

"Faith, when we get to the store, you handle the fountain rental. Monica, can you and Faith also plan the menu and make the menu cards?" Shari said.

"Sure we can," Monica said.

"I've got an idea for where to find the perfect white carpet for under the table, and let's paint the walls a deep evergreen. Christophe and Mikki, can you handle the paint and constructing the sideboard?" Shari said.

"Of course," said Christophe. "We'll handle it. Good job everyone." As if he hadn't already ceded entire control to Shari.

Then I looked up, and there were Harris and Alice, standing right behind me.

"So, how is this team doing?" Harris said, nonchalantly, acting like he didn't recognize me. But I knew better.

"Harry, it is such an *honor* to meet you," Shari gushed, pumping his hand up and down. "You're just as handsome as they say. If you're not actually engaged, we should talk. I have a lot of gorgeous single friends!" she said. "In fact, here's one now." She nudged me. *Shut up, Shari,* I thought, *Shut up right now!* I tried to smile. Harris's ears reddened just a bit, in an adorable way.

"Well . . . thanks," he said.

"We're pulling our ideas together pretty well, I'd say," said Christophe, trying to act the part of the team leader in front of the judges.

"Does everyone know who is doing what?" Alice asked.

"Yes," I said, looking directly at Harris. "In fact, we do. Some of us are going to stay here, and some of us are going to leave. I just hope the ones who leave are considerate enough to tell their team members before they just walk out." I smiled sweetly.

"What?" said Shari. "What are you talking about?"

"Well," said Harris, obviously catching my drift. "Maybe some of you should make sure you're not in the bathroom when your teammates leave, so they have a chance to *tell* you where they're going and why they're going and who they're going with. Because things aren't always what they seem to be."

"Why would we all be in the bathroom?" said Shari, totally confused. "What are you . . ."

"I think what Harris means," said Alice, jumping in, "is that if you all know what everyone else is doing, you'll be more efficient and minimize the chance for a communication breakdown."

"That's exactly what I meant," said Harris.

"He's not very articulate, is he?" Shari whispered to me.

"Up-front communication and honesty are very important to avoid misunderstandings," I said to Alice. "People should make it clear where they're going *before* they leave."

The producers motioned to Alice. "We've got to go, but stay focused," she said, giving me a look. "You want to win, right? So act like it."

Harris gave me a little smile, and then he turned and walked out the door. I couldn't help smiling back. I loved that he was clever.

"What the hell was that all about?" Shari said.

I watched him leave. "I'll tell you later," I said.

At Affair to Remember, everyone dashed around looking for the things on their list. I saw Katie grabbing painted wooden fish and a bolt of fishscale sequin fabric, and felt even more confident in our idea. While Shari and Monica found white votive candles and red velvet ribbons, I asked for the manager. The girl at the counter brought back an older woman with white hair and half glasses.

"Hello," I said, extending my hand. "My name is Faith, and I'm hosting a very special event. I am in need of a beautiful champagne fountain. Can you show me what you have? What's your price range?"

She looked at me, then looked at the camera. She'd obviously been fully debriefed.

"Our fountain rentals are typically between four and five hundred," she said. I knew that would really squeeze us on budget for other items.

"Can you give us any sort of deal?" I asked, with my most charming smile. I knew that she knew what this kind of exposure could mean for her business.

"Of course!" she said. "I'm sure we can find something in your price range. Why don't you come over and see what we have."

We arranged to have the fountain delivered. "I can't believe you got that for two hundred," said Shari. I'd even convinced the store owner to throw in some champagne for the setup. Before we left, she handed me a case. "Give Sybil my regards," she said.

"Gladly," I said.

We still had to pay for the flowers and greenery and the menu printing, and have some money in reserve in case of emergencies. We'd have to be creative and use what we had in the workroom for the rest of it.

Shari went over to the Rulebook to see if she was allowed to call her husband's flower shop. "I can't do it," she said. "It says right here, no help from family members."

"What if you called one of your suppliers?" I suggested. "They all know who you are, right?"

Her face lit up. "Yes, they do!" she said. She picked up the phone and dialed. "Hello, Carl? This is Shari," she said. "I need eight dozen red roses and a big box of the winter greenery, delivered to the Sybil Hunter Enterprises offices first thing in the morning."

Late morning, woodworkers came by to build the two separate rooms we would be decorating. We each got three walls, a floor, and a ceiling, so our holiday tables would be displayed like enormous shadow boxes. I cajoled two of the carpenters into building us a sideboard to match our table out of wood from Sybil's lumber room.

Ditzy Monica had ditched her New Agey lifestyle coach persona for this challenge and taken on the part of artist with surprising competence. She designed beautiful menu cards that described the twelve-course meal I'd come up with: pumpkin bisque, goat cheese and walnut salad, shrimp cocktail, beef satay skewers, roasted Brussels sprouts, green beans with bacon, turkey, beef tenderloin, sweet potato cups, cloverleaf rolls, baked apples with ice cream and caramel sauce, and a cheese tray to finish. "I'm really, really glad we don't actually have to cook all this by noon," I said.

"I wish we could eat it now," said Christophe. "I don't remember the last time I had a decent meal."

Monica and I took the mock-up to the printer, while Shari went out to find art for the walls, hardware, chair covers, and other room décor. She came back with an upholstered chair, a painting of a pretty winter scene, two antique framed photographs that looked like family portraits, and some antique glass vases for flowers.

When she got back, Shari launched into a micromanaging frenzy. "Monica, those snowflakes need to be smaller," she lectured.

"I'm the creative one," Monica whined. "I know how big they should be."

"Christophe and Mikki, quit flirting and get back to painting!" Shari commanded.

"We're just discussing what to do next," Mikki said, defensively.

Shari even ordered the woodworkers around, claiming they were building our sideboard the wrong way.

We worked all day and into the night. When Christophe was staining our new sideboard, Andy noticed it. Before he was done, the other team was building one, too. The woodworkers had already left, so they were trying to do it themselves.

"They're copying our idea!" said Monica. It was almost midnight, and we were all so bleary-eyed and sleep-deprived that productivity had virtually ceased.

"Calm down," I said, noticing that Linda had the hammer. I don't think I would have given that large angry woman a hammer. "Ours will be better. They don't know what they're doing." For the first time, I stepped back and glanced over to the other side of the huge room, at the other team's table. It was decorated in aquatic colors—greens, blues, and bronzes—with an ugly centerpiece of wicker cornucopia forms filled with gourds. It was schizophrenic. I was dead tired and jittery and running on fumes, but seeing their hideous table made me feel a lot better. When the clock struck two, it was time to head back to the Loft.

"Would it be horrible if we took a bottle of champagne with us?" Monica asked.

"Not in my opinion," I said. "I think we deserve it."

chapter twenty-five

The champagne fountain was spectacular—four levels of gleaming silver bowls in graduated sizes, with a vase at the top for flowers and a clear center column glowing soft pink, lit from within. The champagne flowed down over the bowls, bubbly and festive. We all stepped back and surveyed our creation.

The other team stared, and I could tell they were intimidated. They started arguing with one another. "They're going down," I whispered to Shari.

"I know," she said. "And our room looks amazing."

It really did. "We got our shit together for this one," I said.

"Do you think it's too Christmas-y?" Monica asked.

"No way," I said. "It's Sybil Hunter. She starts getting ready for Christmas in August."

Monica eyed the remaining bottles of champagne. "Can we open another one of those?"

I looked at Shari and shrugged. "I don't see why not," I said.

"It's eight in the morning," Shari said.

"So?" I said. "I bet Monica has champagne for breakfast all the time."

Monica sprinted into the storeroom and came out with five tumblers. The sound of the champagne popping gave her a second wind. Suddenly, she was jolly and rosy cheeked again, and talking at top speed as she downed a glass and then quickly refilled it. "I just know we're going to win," she said. "There's no way that other team with their silly fish table is even in the running against our beautiful, elegant table."

"It's spectacular," Shari said, sipping her champagne and compulsively rearranging rosebuds and evergreen boughs. "Oh my God, I'm so tired, this is going to go straight to my head." She held up her glass. "How many calories do you think this is?"

"I think they cheated," I heard Queen Nadine say to the camera on the other side of the room, mid-OTF. "There is no way they could get all of that for two thousand dollars. If they are using unfair influences, then they should be disqualified."

Shari snorted. "Look who's talking about unfair influences," she said, rolling her eyes. "From what I've heard, Mrs. Earl-of-Snob-shire hand-jobbed her way right into the family, and her husband's so-called fortune doesn't even exist anymore."

I thought of the note Nadine had slipped me about Hugh Pritzker. "I believe it," I said.

Monica clapped her hands over her mouth. "I knew her hoity-toity act was a big fake." She stood up and started dancing around, a champagne glass sloshing precariously in one hand. "I'm Miss Superior. I'm better than you because my husband is the King of England, and I'm from Queens!" she said in a sing-songy voice. Then she burst into a fit of giggling. It was like hanging out in the loony bin, drinking with this girl.

"I think Monica is sleep deprived," I said in her defense.

"Plus she's had three glasses of champagne to our one," Shari said.

"I think we're all sleep deprived," Mikki said, rubbing her eyes. "I don't know how much more of this I can take." Christophe rubbed her back, protectively. I wondered if they were sleeping together yet. Not that they would have had the opportunity in this pseudomilitary compound, but we could all see it was imminent.

"Here's to us, the winning team!" I said, optimistically, even though

I was teetering on the edge of a nervous breakdown. Our table was the best. No question. But what other secret factors would influence the decision? I knew we *should* win, but obviously, that didn't mean we would win.

"Five minutes!" As we all ran around making last minute changes, Shari ordering everyone around, Christophe meekly obeying, Mikki starting to get annoyed at Shari, we could hear the other team biting one another's heads off. "You idiot!" Andy screamed. I couldn't tell who it was directed at, but at this point, it could have been anyone.

When Sybil Hunter came into the room at noon, the other team was still moving things around on their table. Sybil was flanked by her dog, Alice, and Ian, with Harris lagging behind, looking nervous. I got shaky suddenly. I'd almost forgotten about him, but there was no denying his presence now. Sybil stood back, crossed her arms, and looked at Andy's table for a long time. Nobody spoke. Andy looked like he might vibrate right through the floor. Katie looked disgusted, her arms crossed defiantly. Finally, Sybil cleared her throat.

Andy jumped in. "We decided on a . . . a harvest theme," he said. Sybil raised her eyebrows. "As you can see, we created an impressive and dramatic centerpiece out of gourds and cornucopias and . . . and . . . fish." He looked humiliated. "We chose the burnt-orange-and-gold china, and over here on this sideboard, we built a crystal tower to display desserts." A stack of empty platters wobbled on the rickety sideboard, next to an old lamp. Andy stepped nervously in front of them, probably hoping Sybil wouldn't notice the bad craftsmanship. As if. He held up the menu cards. "The dessert buffet items are listed right here."

She looked down her nose at him. "Hmm," Sybil said. "I see. And tell me, what did each person do?"

"Well," Andy stuttered, talking too fast, "Katie, Sadie, and Nadine created the centerpiece."

"I wanted to do a fish theme," Katie chimed in, "but some people on the team weren't in the mood to get along."

"What do you mean?" asked Sybil.

"I mean, *some* people wanted to do a stereotypical cornucopia that doesn't match the fish theme at all," she said, glaring at Sadie, who was apparently obsessed with all things vegetable.

"This is a Thanksgiving theme," Sadie said, pulling nervously on her long braid. "I wanted the centerpiece to reflect the abundant harvest with a display of organic vegetables and local flowers, and I didn't see where stupid gold fishscale fabric and fake seaweed fit into that theme at all."

"It sounds like you had some disagreements," Sybil said.

"I tried to get everyone to see the other's point of view," said Nadine, haughtily, her faux English accent on full display. "But I found our team to be sorely lacking in basic manners."

"That's a laugh," said Linda, towering above her teammates, her Chicago voice booming. She stood almost as tall as Sybil herself. "Talk about everybody behind their backs and then lecture us on etiquette. That's a good one. Nadine didn't do any of the manual labor. I was painting and building and sanding and staining, and she just stood around and criticized us. She really dragged our team down."

"I have no idea what you're talking about," said Nadine, standing up very straight as if she were trying to match Linda's height. "I arranged everything in this room, including the centerpiece."

"I arranged the centerpiece!" said Katie.

"I was responsible for that centerpiece, neither of you did anything," said Sadie.

"I don't know if I would claim credit for that centerpiece," said Alice, from behind Sybil.

"What did you do in this challenge, Nadine?" Sybil asked.

"Not only did I arrange everything tastefully but I was able to borrow this beautiful antique stained-glass lamp," she said.

"Hmm," Sybil said. "We don't believe in replicas here at Sybil Hunter Enterprises."

Nadine blushed and didn't respond.

"And Linda, what was your part?"

"I helped Andy build the sideboard, and I made the chair cushions." Sybil picked one up and looked at it. It was blue and green with gold thread. I couldn't quite imagine Linda at a sewing machine.

"Hmm," Sybil said again. Alice looked like she wanted to say something, but pursed her lips and remained silent.

"Jodi Sue?"

Jodi Sue looked down. "I . . . helped with the centerpiece, too," she said.

"It took four people to make *that* centerpiece?" Sybil said.

"Jodi Sue also planned the menu," said Andy. "Because she's a *chef.*" He said it with disdain.

"And what about this menu?" said Sybil. "This isn't a holiday dinner menu. I only see desserts."

"I . . . didn't quite understand the assignment," Jodi Sue said.

Sybil shook her head. "It's all in the Rulebook," she said. "How would you all say Andy did as a team leader?"

They all began to argue about what Andy should or shouldn't have done. "I painted the whole goddamn thing and built everything, I practically did the whole challenge myself," Andy yelled over the din. "When obviously I should have been the one planning the menu."

"Just because you work in a restaurant doesn't mean you're more of a chef than I am," said Jodi Sue.

"Andy, do you think your team should win this challenge?" Sybil asked.

"I definitely do," he said. He began a long list of reasons why he thought their table was the best, but I wasn't listening. I was trying not to look at Harris, who stood back from his mother and wasn't even looking at the table. He was looking at me. Finally, I stole a glance, and our eyes met. His were questioning. I could feel the heat rising in my face. I shook my head. *Focus, Faith. Don't get distracted.*

Sybil finally came over to our table. Her face brightened when she got a closer look. "Ahh," she said. This gave us all hope.

"Welcome to our Thanksgiving table," Shari said. "Our theme was Authentic Holidays."

Sybil nodded. "Tell me about what you've done here," she said.

"The centerpiece is made from fresh greens, pinecones we painted ourselves, these beautiful white votive candles, and of course, fresh roses," Shari said. "We wanted something lavish, a centerpiece that extends to become almost a table runner. We painted these silver charger plates and added the snowflake details," she said.

Sybil picked one up. "Is this balsa wood?" she said.

"It is," said Shari.

"You wouldn't know it from looking," she said. "Very nice."

"I painted the snowflakes and did the calligraphy!" Monica burst out. "I think it's the prettiest part!"

"But Shari, you aren't the team leader," Sybil said, looking at Shari, as if even she'd forgotten until now who was supposed to be in charge. "Didn't you choose Christophe to be your team leader?"

Shari looked embarrassed. "Well, yes, that's true," she admitted.

"I am the team leader, but I know talent when I see it and I delegated tasks to Shari that I knew she would be best at, including our table demonstration," Christophe said, surprising everyone.

"I see," said Sybil. "That is definitely the sign of a competent leader."

Shari gave Christophe a grateful look. I couldn't help being a little annoyed. When Shari took over the team, it was the sign of a competent leader? When I took over the team, I'd almost been axed for it, and Chaz was the casualty.

Sybil walked around the table, looking at all the placecards. Then she smiled. "I see you included the members of your team at the table. Very . . . optimistic," she said. I couldn't help looking at Harris with pride. He smiled at me and I quickly looked away.

"We're going to take some photographs and make some notes, and then Alice, Ian, Harry, and I are going back to the conference room to have a discussion. When we have made our decision, we'll call you in."

We all stepped back to let the photographers shoot the tables. Then Sybil, Alice, Ian, and Harris left the room. I refused to watch him leave. If he gave me a backward glance on his way out, I didn't see it.

For nearly an hour, we sat, in chairs or on the floor, waiting to be called into the Decision Room, arguing about who had screwed up, who had done the most work, who had slacked off. I sat by Andy for a while. "This sucks," he said. "I picked the worst people."

"But you were a strong leader," I said. "At least, from what I could tell."

"I am so sick of Sadie and her farmer crap. She's a complete idiot. The worst part is, she actually thinks she knows what she's doing. At least Jodi Sue stays out of the way. She *knows* she's an idiot."

I didn't want to put down any of my team members, although it was tempting to crack a joke about Monica mainlining the champagne, or how Mikki and Christophe should get a room. "Shari's a contender," I said. "She pretty much took over Christophe's job."

"Christophe is an easy target," Andy said. "I'd like to keep him around for a while because he's easy to beat. And you're right—Shari won't be as easy."

I thought about that. What if it came down to Shari and me? We were friends. But I couldn't even think about how that might go. I was so tired, I could hardly see straight, but I was also so full of nervous energy that I could hardly sit still.

Katie couldn't either. She began to pace, and finally came over to stand near me. I had to say something. "Hey, why do you hate me so much?" I said.

She looked away, her arms crossed. But finally she answered. "You know why."

"No, I really don't," I said.

Finally she turned in exasperation and looked at me. "You made a fool out of me in front of Peter Jarrell that night at the Hearst Castle. I'd seen you around, but frankly, you didn't interest me. I thought you were nobody. But then you pulled your strings with Josh Kameron to get me kicked out. I've never been kicked out of a party before or since. And it was because of you."

"What? They kicked you out? I swear, I didn't tell them to do that. I just told Peter to . . . well . . ." I paused. "I told him to just take care of you."

"Well, he did," she said.

"Hey, I'm really sorry, I didn't know that happened," I said.

"Whatever," she said, and walked away. Well, at least that explained her attitude. I felt a little guilty—but not so guilty that I was going to lose my focus.

When Andy started pacing, I knew he was about to blow. Finally, he turned on Katie and Sadie. "You guys are morons, you know. You blew this for us. You destroyed our team unity."

"What team unity?" said Sadie. "You people don't even understand the point of Thanksgiving."

"Sure I do," Andy said. "The point of Thanksgiving is to *win*. And I can already tell who in this room is oriented toward winning, and who isn't. And if you're not in this game to play hard, I say you should just go home."

"Don't look at me," Sadie said. "Nadine's the one making everybody paranoid, with her fake two-faced manners, so we all start suspecting one another."

"I'm not paranoid," Andy said. "If you're paranoid, that's your problem, and that makes you a drain on all of us."

"You're the drain," Katie said, playing with a scrap of fish scale fabric. "You're so hyper, you can't even calm down long enough to look anybody in the eye."

"Look who's talking," Andy said to Katie, his voice getting higher pitched. "If it was up to you, we'd cover our Thanksgiving table with dead fish."

"Lunatic," Katie muttered.

"Long-legged freak," Andy shot back.

"Enough, now can't we all get along? This is unacceptable behavior," Nadine said. "This isn't how civilized people behave."

"I hardly think we're civilized at this point," I threw in.

Shari raised her eyebrows at me. "They're going *down*," she whispered.

Finally, Polly came back in the room. "Sybil will see you now," she said.

"Today's contest showed your creativity, your style, and your ability to work with others," Sybil said to us as we all sat around the table. "Each table had its strong points and its weak points, but we've decided there was a clear winner."

She looked at Alice, who nodded. Harris kept his gaze down, obviously not enjoying being a part of the show at all.

"Tonight, I'd like the other judges to speak," Sybil said. "Alice, let's begin with the first team. Tell me your thoughts."

"This table was terrible," Alice said. "I don't know what else to say. The centerpiece was ugly, the colors were ugly, the fish theme was absurd, the sideboard looked like it was about to topple over, and I wouldn't dare put any desserts on that dessert stand."

"I agree," said Harris, suddenly volunteering to speak. "I didn't understand this design at all. It was just bad, and I think it was pretty obvious that the team didn't get along."

"I think the internal conflicts on your team showed glaringly in the final product," agreed Sybil. "The themes clashed, and so did the team members. I like the *idea* of a fish theme, but the execution just wasn't there."

"And what about Christophe's team?" Sybil asked Alice.

"I thought the color scheme was much more successful. It was very Christmas-y, more a table for Christmas Eve dinner or a holiday party than Thanksgiving perhaps," she said. "However, it was really beautiful, and I loved the champagne fountain. A very nice touch."

"I agree," said Harris. "Christophe's team's table was coherent, and the team worked together. Everyone's ideas complemented everyone else's. I'd be proud to have our family Thanksgiving at that table."

"Anything else?" Sybil asked her son.

"Only that Christophe's table was more beautiful," he said. He looked directly at me. "Beautiful," he said again. I blushed furiously and looked down.

"I agree with all of you," Sybil said, seeming not to notice to whom her son had directed his comments. "But there is much to consider." She clasped her hands and put them in front of her on the table.

This is it, I thought. Are we going to win, or is she going to surprise us all and choose the other team? I wouldn't put it past her. I held my breath. I couldn't stand the suspense. We couldn't rely on anything anymore. Reality? Common sense? The sun coming up tomorrow? At this point, who knew?

We waited. And waited. For what seemed like long, crawling, torturous minutes, the clock ticking in slow motion. Finally, she spoke.

"Christophe, although you seemed to be a weak leader who let Shari take over, a good leader does know how to delegate effectively, and your team created a spectacular table. I have chosen it to be featured in our magazine, on our show, and most important, for our family Thanksgiving dinner. And as a special surprise, your team will be joining my family for Thanksgiving dinner, so I will see you all tomorrow in Larchmont."

Everyone on our team let out a collective sigh. Shari looked delighted. "Thank you, Sybil!" she said. "I'm so honored to win again. And so honored to be invited to your home." Monica and Mikki looked at each other and rolled their eyes. I could tell Shari was wearing on their nerves.

"Andy, your team loses this challenge," Sybil continued. "And one of you will be eliminated. Shari, you and your team may leave the room."

Ten minutes later, the door opened. Andy strutted into the room, followed by Linda, Jodi Sue, Nadine, and Katie. "Old McDonald had a farm . . . and she just went back there. See ya!" Andy said brazenly. I couldn't help being disappointed that it wasn't Katie. Sadie didn't have anything against me. Katie seemed ready to hire a hit man to take me out, for whatever reason.

"So it's Sadie. The farmer's gone," Shari said, nodding. "I had a feeling."

"Thank God. I couldn't stand another minute of her organic local seasonal blah blah blah," Andy said, adjusting his tie.

"She was boring," Monica said. "And she needs to cut off that crazy long hair. And she was like . . . a nothing. She had no personality."

"As opposed to your excess of personality?" Andy said.

"My personality is sparkling, like champagne!" said Monica. "Can we go back to the Loft now? I need a drink."

Back at the Loft, Monica poured herself a glass of wine. Linda and Andy took energy bars from the cupboard and supercharged caffeine drinks from the refrigerator. "You're drinking that now? That's the last thing *you* need," Katie said to Andy, as she opened another bag of black licorice.

I was dead tired, but I knew I needed some kind of nourishment, so I went into the kitchen and cooked myself some scrambled eggs. "That smells great," said Mikki. "Will you make me some?" It was the first time I'd ever seen her eat anything.

"Don't make me any!" said Shari. "I'm just going to enjoy the smell. I can't spare another calorie today." She grabbed a bottle of club soda from the refrigerator. "So it was interesting to have Harry Jansen involved today, don't you all think?" she addressed the room generally, and carefully did not look at me, but I could tell she suspected something.

"I heard he really was engaged," said Monica. "I read it in a gossip magazine. This Christine person is a supermodel, and they were photographed together at a club."

Knife to my heart! A supermodel? I sighed. I wasn't really holding out any hope about Harris. But it still bothered me a little. A supermodel. Fantastic. I ate the eggs slowly, chewing carefully, and thinking, thinking. I couldn't turn off my brain. *Let it go, Faith,* I told myself. *Let him go. He's not the one for you.*

I had to seduce Sybil, not her son, and today had given me a little hope. If I could just keep going, if I could keep from getting distracted, making any mistakes, falling asleep on my feet, fainting from starvation, or additionally offending Sybil, then maybe, just maybe, I could come out on top.

chapter twenty-six

As the limousine pulled into the long, tree-lined driveway that led up to Sybil Hunter's waterfront estate in Larchmont, Shari, Mikki, Christophe, Monica, and I—the winning team—stared out the window at the gardens and orchards and the acres of lawn, gorgeous in summer, even though we were pretending it was Thanksgiving. I couldn't believe I was going to her house! And then I saw it: a four-story storm-gray Victorian with white gingerbread trim.

It was even more incredible on the inside: gleaming oak floors, ivory-painted crown moldings, big windows, a marble fireplace, chandeliers everywhere, along with more rustic elements—a willow chair, natural wood beams, big vases of cut flowers and tropical trees in pots, sun pouring into the windows.

"Why does she have animal heads on the walls?" whispered Shari.

"It's weird!" Monica whispered. "I feel like that moose head is *looking* at me!"

Rasputin, Sybil's Newfie, trotted into the entryway to meet us, his big fluffy tail wagging agreeably. Then Polly came down the stairs. "Welcome," she said. "Sybil would like you to put your things on this table, and then I'll give you a tour. I'm sure you want to see the house." Everyone nodded eagerly.

"Come this way," Polly said. "Now, we'll start in the great room. As you can see, Sybil collects taxidermy."

"So fascinating!" said Shari. "What an idea!" She cast me a look. The more Shari relaxed, the more she criticized Sybil behind her back, telling everyone how Sybil's style was too WASP-y, how everybody really knew that Sybil was born a Jew but pretended not to be, and how this dilution of her natural heritage had leached out all her character. Of course, in front of Sybil, Shari was as ingratiating and tractable as a well-trained Labrador retriever.

Polly took us from room to room, each more beautiful and fabulous than the next, and finally made it to Sybil's country kitchen. I felt like I had already been there from reading all her cookbooks, but it was still a highlight of my life to actually be in it.

It was a dream kitchen to beat all dream kitchens. Floor-to-ceiling cabinets set with antique glass, infinite marble countertops, a huge butcher-block island, and the biggest pot rack I'd ever seen, hung with stainless-steel and copper pots and pans and bakeware of every shape and size and era, from sleek and modern pieces to rare antiques that probably came from Europe. One counter was devoted to a massive Italian espresso maker, and the cabinet above was stocked with every possible cup and plate related to serving coffee or tea. Another area was set up just for baking, with double ovens under a massive cast-iron gas stove. The refrigerator was actually a restaurant-style walk-in. There was enough room in there for an entire side of beef.

"This is incredible," Mikki said, peering over my shoulder. "Is anybody ever even here to use this kitchen?"

"Wow." It was all I could say.

"Does she have a wine cellar?" Monica asked hopefully.

"Yes, but we won't be going down there today," Polly said.

"Does she have a butler?" Mikki asked.

"No," Polly said. "But she does have a gardening staff, two housekeepers, and a chef."

I was dying with envy, and with respect for what Sybil Hunter had amassed. So she had a bitchy side. After seeing her house, I felt more inclined to excuse it. If it were my house and my money, I probably would have had a lot less stuff. The antiques, supplies, furniture were overwhelming. I would have been more minimalist. Still, I was overwhelmed with what she had accomplished. You had to be aggressive to get the kind of success that could buy resources like this, unless you were born into them. Sybil was self-made. I understood why so many women wanted to be her. It was the domestic dream. The woman had an entire room devoted to wrapping gifts!

But at the same time, all the provincialities of domesticity were absent. Sybil was no old-fashioned, subservient, doting housewife at the mercy of her husband's money and power. She wasn't making martinis for her man at the end of the day. She was making them for herself. She was the homemaker, not the house*wife*. There was no room for *wife* in her life. She embraced domesticity on her own terms. She was an independent, wealthy, powerful businesswoman marketing the *My Three Sons* concept, the *Donna Reed* lifestyle, even though she was anything *but* Donna Reed. I admired it—worshipped it, even. I also wondered if it was lonely.

"I think they're done shooting the table," Polly said, after answering her cell phone. "We can go back into the dining room now."

"I didn't realize we were being kept out of the way," Shari said, offended that they hadn't asked her to consult on the photo shoot.

"It's time for cocktails," Polly said. "Just as a reminder, please keep in mind that you are in Sybil Hunter's *home*." She said it like she would tell us we were in the Vatican. Shari raised her eyebrows at me.

"What does that mean?" I said.

"It just means that it's important to behave with a certain . . . decorum," she said, glancing at Monica.

Suddenly I got nervous. Harris would be in there. I was about to see him. And the mysterious Christine—fiancée, supermodel, whatever she was.

I was irritated at myself for feeling so obsessed. Harris was just another guy in just another club. I could meet another guy like him in a minute. So what if he was engaged, in quotation marks or not in quotation marks? Who cares? Not me, I told myself, striding boldly into the dining room.

Our table really did look beautiful. It was the first thing I noticed. Then I saw Sybil, Alice, Harris, and a pale, thin, pretty young woman with long blonde curls. Across the room was an older woman who had to be Judith, Sybil's mother, laughing at something Ian was saying. The rest of them were standing around the table, drinking champagne from crystal champagne flutes and talking in low voices. As we entered, Sybil turned to us. "Here they are," she said. "Everyone, let's welcome the winning team!"

Alice and Ian put down their glasses to clap for us. Judith, who could have been an aged copy of Sybil herself, but with short-cropped white hair and large round eyeglasses with dark red frames, surveyed us critically. "Help yourselves to a well-deserved glass of champagne," Sybil said, almost warmly. As we moved past the table to the champagne fountain, I noticed Sybil had made some alterations to our design.

Shari noticed, too, and since she'd taken credit for the whole thing, she took the edits as a personal affront. "She changed the flower arrangement," she said. "And those roses aren't as nice as ours. Who supplies her roses? My husband needs to supply her roses."

"She grows her own roses, Shari," I whispered back.

"Oh, right." Clearly, Shari didn't approve.

Monica and Shari picked at the appetizers, but I wasn't hungry at all. I was too nervous. I looked back to where Harris was standing, looking uncomfortable, while the pretty pale girl chattered to him. She appeared luminescent in the dim light of the dining room, her long curls like a mermaid's. She had a strange, otherworldly beauty. I, on the other hand, looked like I'd been hit by a train. Gray hairs were growing in, and I had black circles under my eyes that made them look like empty sockets. She looked fresh as a daisy. She was also wearing an incredibly short skirt—even shorter than the girl in the club that Harris had left with. He must like short skirts. I looked down at my own modest-for-the-show hemline. Then I noticed Sybil watching the two of them fondly. But Harris seemed uninterested. Maybe even unhappy. And then he looked at me.

Our eyes locked again—I wished he would stop doing that to me! It felt like an electric shock. Then his whole face softened. He smiled just slightly, almost apologetically. I smiled back. I didn't know what it meant—were we agreeing that he was unavailable? Was he saying he was sorry for all the misunderstandings? Was he telling me that no, she was not the one for him—that maybe he was trying to untangle himself from something, and he wanted me to understand?

"Shall we sit down?" Sybil said suddenly. I wondered if she'd seen me making eyes at her son. I looked down at the place cards. They weren't the same ones Monica had drawn, but they were written in silver on card stock, tucked into Christophe's white-painted pine-cones. I was seated between Shari and Christophe, as far from Harris as possible. Had he told his mother about me? Now I was paranoid.

Sybil raised her glass. "Thank you, everyone, for joining us this Thanksgiving. I'm so happy to have you all here, to share in this very special holiday with me." The cameras hovered. "I want to welcome the winning team from my show, to share in this dinner at this beauti-ful table, which they so creatively designed. I want to welcome my mother, who taught me everything I know," Sybil said, raising her glass.

I'd seen her mother only once, on Sybil Hunter's show, and she'd always seemed tough, or at least not very nurturing. In person, she looked energetic and feisty. She raised her glass, too. "You're still learning, my dear," she said. Alice smirked.

Sybil smiled stiffly and continued. "And to my sister, Alice, an asset to my business. And to my son, Harry, my pride and joy." Harris looked uncomfortable, but raised his glass civilly. "I also want to welcome my good friend and colleague, Ian, and my late best friend's daughter, Christine. I've always considered her part of the family." She raised her glass and we toasted.

Then the kitchen staff began to bring out the food.

We had course after course—not the menu from the challenge I'd designed, of course, but certainly one that Sybil had decided on her-self. As each dish came out, Sybil regaled us with the details of what it was and how she had prepared it, and Judith added her commentary about what was done well or not quite right.

"Alice makes the cranberries better," Sybil's mother griped.

"Unofficially," said Alice, smiling at her sister. "Officially, I can't cook at all."

I was astounded by how good everything tasted, and by the sheer amount of food. I didn't want to miss a single dish, so I was careful to taste everything but never eat more than a few bites of anything.

As we ate, Christine, "the fiancée," kept looking at us, the contes-tants. Finally, she addressed us, her voice soft and musical, like a lul-laby. "What's it like to be on Sybil's show?" The question was a general one, so Shari jumped in to answer.

"It's such an honor," she said, glancing at Sybil. "It's the rarest of opportunities. We're all *soo thankful*." Leave it to Shari to go for the extra brownnose points.

"It's the hardest thing I've ever done," Monica said, her cheeks flushed from the champagne, already a little tipsy. "I can't believe how hard it is. Such long hours and so much stress. I really think it's asking too much. No offense, Sybil," she said.

"It's only going to get harder, my dear," Sybil assured her.

Mikki nodded shyly. "It's intense, but it's thrilling, too," she said in her quiet voice. She took another bite of turkey. "This food is so deli-cious, Sybil."

Sybil nodded approvingly. "Excuse me while I check on the des-sert," she said. She got up and left the table.

That's when Christine turned her gaze to me, her fork poised just over the peas on her plate. "And what about you? Faith, is it?" she said. I sensed a sudden chilliness in her tone. Her eyes were drilling into me. Had she seen Harris looking at me? Had he said something to her? "This must be quite a step up from selling your little muffins?"

I looked right at her. "Definitely a step up," I said. "My baking business has really taught me a lot. I owe my place on this show to those little muffins."

"That's so sweet," she said, dismissively.

I paused. *Don't say it, Faith.* But I couldn't help myself. "I hope you don't plan to step up in that skirt, or we'll all be able to see *your* muffin," I added.

Shari almost spit out her drink. Mikki's eyes went wide. Christine opened her mouth to respond, but nothing came out. She just stared at me. Harris looked like he might burst out laughing.

Of course, this now meant war. I remembered that Polly had told us to act with decorum. But Christine started it. And Sybil was, at least temporarily, out of the room.

"Aren't you funny," Christine said.

"That's what they tell me," I said, smiling at her.

"The flower business taught me a lot about the world, too," Shari chimed in, uncomfortable that the attention had shifted off of her. "You know, flowers are what won us this very challenge. We wouldn't be here in this beautiful house if it weren't for flowers!"

"What do you do?" Mikki asked Christine. "I think I've heard you're a model? I've always wanted to try modeling."

"Christine is the daughter of my dear friend Pamela Claiborne," Sybil said, coming back into the room with a tray of mini cream puffs and a silver pot of coffee. "God rest her soul."

Shari and I stared at each other. Pamela Claiborne! We both knew who Pamela Claiborne was—former founder and CEO of Claiborne Cosmetics, and one of the richest women in the United States, until her death last year. Maybe even richer than Sybil Hunter herself. If her daughter was heir to the Claiborne fortune . . . I looked at Harris hopelessly. Why would he ever choose someone like me over someone like her? She had an angelic face, perfect skin, glorious hair, and one of those bodies that looked like it had never once dared to put on an unnecessary pound. Plus, millions of dollars. And she adored Harris, that was clear. Besides, he'd been so silent, so compliant through the whole meal, I was beginning to suspect he was just some mama's boy who was going to do whatever his mother told him. He could cast me all the longing looks he wanted. I was more interested in action. Was he a man or wasn't he?

"I model on the side sometimes, just for fun," she said.

Now that was a kick in the balls, I thought. Just for fun? She occasionally poses in pictures looking flawless and beautiful just for fun?

Suddenly, I couldn't eat another bite. I downed the rest of my champagne in one gulp, and the server immediately stepped forward to refill my glass. I didn't look at Harris again for the rest of the meal, pretending instead to be fascinated with Shari's endless story about her husband's long list of celebrity clientele and which kind of flower each celebrity preferred.

And why should I feel bad? So what if he was going to marry an heiress? It had nothing to do with me. *There will always be heiresses out there, Faith,* I told myself. *It doesn't make you any less worthy. It's more important to work to achieve something, rather than have it handed to you.*

As we got up from the table and went into the sitting room, Monica and I both foregoing the coffee for yet another glass of champagne, I began to feel angry, and that felt better than feeling inferior. Who did she think she was? Just because she had money didn't mean she could control everybody around her.

I looked at Harris, finally, brazenly. He obviously wasn't enjoying her company. And why should he? Christine was obviously an asshole, even if she looked like an angel. When she sat down, he'd chosen a seat across the room, and then she had the gall to get up and go sit next to him.

"Shall we play a game of Scrabble?" Sybil proposed. "I'll fetch the board." She got up to leave again, giving Christine another shot at me.

"You know," Christine said, settling into a velvet-upholstered love seat, "Harris and I saw the most interesting movie the other day."

"Christine . . ." Harris said, his voice a warning.

She ignored him. "It was this cheesy B-movie with these girls who meet their boyfriends at an old house and they all play truth or dare."

I froze. My mind shot back to L.A., to that movie I'd played a part in, just before leaving town. I couldn't believe they'd actually made it. I'd almost forgotten all about it, or at least put it out of my mind. Christine went on. "It has the most pathetic plot. The girls just sit around taking their shirts off and kissing each other. It is so bad. We laughed through the whole movie, didn't we, honey?" she said, putting her hand on Harris's knee.

No. No no no no no! People were seeing it? That stupid movie, where I'd been topless, and worried about the implications for about thirty seconds? This woman had seen it? *Harris had seen it, too?* Shit shit shit. If Sybil had seen it, I was literally going to drop dead right there in her sitting room.

I stood up. I wanted to leave the room, but I realized I had no-where to go. I was a slave to the cameras and to the producers. A camera zeroed in on my face, and I knew this was one of those moments that was sure to be on the television show. How could they resist a moment like this? I sat back down.

But wait a minute. How had she found it? *Had she Googled me?* Why would she do that? Harris must have said something to her. I was dying to know what he said that would have inspired her to go to the trouble of Internet stalking me, finding out about that movie, and actually renting it and watching it.

"What's she talking about?" Shari whispered to me. I had to say something. *Say something, Faith. Say something. Blow it off. Make it funny. Prove to her it doesn't matter!*

"One of those topless girls looked an awful lot like you. But much younger," she said, driving it home.

Ouch.

I swallowed and tossed my hair back. "Actually, it wasn't a B-movie, it was a double-D movie," I said. "I bet you'd love to be in one of those, but . . ." I shook my head, looking apologetically at her small breasts.

That's it, Faith. Don't complain, don't explain. Own it.

Christine reddened.

"What's this now?" Shari said. She hated not knowing what was going on.

"She's talking about a movie I was in back in L.A.," I said to Shari. "I consider it part of my journey. Everything I've done in the past has brought me here, and here I am, having this amazing experience. Who knows, I might not be here today if I hadn't kissed that girl and taken my shirt off all those years ago." I smiled sweetly.

Harris grinned. He obviously found it amusing. "I've certainly done some things I regret," he said. "I suppose we all do. I think it's pretty interesting that you had that experience."

"Well, I can't imagine doing something like that," Christine said. "I think it's a sign of poor breeding."

"What's it a sign of, if you initiate a conversation about topless actresses at a dinner party?" I asked politely.

"I . . . I just thought I'd mention it since it was relevant to one of the guests," she said.

I leaned in toward Christine. "You think you can outbitch me, bitch?" I whispered. "Well, think again. While you were riding horses and getting manicures with your boarding school friends, I was betting trifectas at Aqueduct Racetrack. I wouldn't play with knives if I were you. You might get hurt."

Monica gasped. Harris laughed out loud.

Just then, Sybil entered the room. "Who's up for a game?" She began to lay out the board and letter trays.

"I think I'll excuse myself from the Scrabble game," said Christine, standing up. "I've got an appointment. Harry, walk me to the door."

"I think you know where it is," Harris said. She looked at him with disgust, then turned and left in a huff. Sybil cast her son a dirty look, but didn't say anything. Harris and I looked at each other, and there was some kind of change—some mutual understanding.

After the token game of Scrabble was over—I got the impression it had been more for the sake of the cameras, to show everyone how civilized Sybil's parties were—Sybil (who won) stood up. "Well, this has been very nice," she said. "Thank you for joining my family Thanksgiving. But you need to get back to the city because I'll be seeing you in three hours to give you your next challenge."

We all groaned and sighed, exhausted. We really had to do more tonight, after all this? I knew this whole dinner party was supposed to be our reward, but it had felt more like work—and a few more hours where my eyes couldn't be closed.

"And Faith?" Sybil said.

"Yes?" I cringed.

"I expect a certain level of sophistication in my employees."

Crap. Had she overheard some of our volley of insults? Had Christine blown it for me?

"Of course, Sybil," I said. Surely Christine had told her about my movie career, such as it was, but I refrained from trying to justify anything. It happened. I did it. Now I was going to have to live with it. If there were consequences, so be it. But I was damn sure going to make up for it by being better than anybody else in this contest, checkered past or no checkered past.

We all thanked Sybil, then went outside to wait for the limo to take us back into the city. Sybil came out the door and got into her Town Car with Ian and Alice. She opened the window and called to Harris. "Are you coming, dear?"

"No," he said, waving to her. "No, I'm going to hang out here for a few days. If you don't mind."

"Of course, honey, that's fine," said Sybil. "You've done a good job. Thank you for all your help!" She rolled up her window and the car pulled out of the gravel drive and headed down the tree-lined road back to the highway. As soon as she was out of sight, Harris came over.

"Faith." I turned to look at him, still standing there in the doorway. "Can I talk to you? Alone?"

I glanced at the cameras. "I'm not sure if you're aware, but that big black thing following you around is actually recording everything you say."

He smiled. "I'm not sure if *you're* aware that my mother runs this fucking show, and I can get any tape removed that I want to get removed."

"My bad Scorsese," I said, following him into the house, the camera in tow.

"OK. Look, Christine is gone, and I just had to talk to you," he said, as soon as we were inside the house with the door closed.

"About what?" I said. "Your girlfriend isn't my business."

"Come in here," he said. He took my hand and led me back into the sitting room. "Sit down," he said, indicating the couch where he had been sitting after dinner. Next to *her*.

I sat.

"I've been thinking and thinking about why you did what you did, and I finally realized how it all must have looked from your point of view."

"What do you mean 'why I did what I did'?" I said.

"Why you walked out on me at that club that night," he said.

"I walked out? Are you crazy? We had this great time together, and then you left with another woman. I saw you."

"No, that's the thing. I didn't. After I put that girl in a cab, I came back and looked everywhere for you. You were gone. After all that time we spent together, you left. I thought we really had something, and I just couldn't believe you would disappear like that."

"Of course I just left, you asshole," I said. "I turned around, and you were gone. Then I went to the restroom, and I came back and see you all chummy with that blonde bimbo, and then I saw you leaving together. And she wasn't even your fiancée. So I have to wonder, how many other girls in this city are pining away for you because you made them think you actually connected with them?"

He looked angry. "First of all, I don't have a fiancée," he said. "My mother . . . it's complicated with my mother. And second, I didn't leave. You did. I mean, I did, but just for a minute. I was coming right back.

When your friends pulled you away, she came stumbling up to me and started hanging all over me, begging me to take her home. I knew she was drunk, so I went outside with her to get her safely into a cab. But you didn't wait around for an explanation. You just bolted. So I assumed you were looking for an excuse to run. You seem like a runner to me."

That was a low blow. If an accurate one. "Well, that's just great," I said. "Meanwhile, I saw what I saw." I knew it sounded irrational. His explanation actually made sense, but I wasn't sure I could believe him, and I certainly couldn't let him seduce me right now. "It's fine," I said. "You don't owe me anything. You barely even know me. We spent one evening together. And in case you didn't notice, I'm pretty busy here, trying to win this damn thing, trying to make sure your mother isn't unfairly biased against me for whatever stupid reason she might have on any given day, so I can be judged on my actual skills. If you're just wanting to clear up what happened that night so you can get back to planning your wedding . . ."

"Oh for God's sake, I'm not getting married!" he said, turning even redder. "You're as bad as my mother! What's the point in trying to explain? You've already decided to believe the worst about me. I guess I misjudged you. I thought you were different."

"Are you insane?" I said. "*You* misjudged *me*? You kissed me, and then you left with another girl, and you misjudged *me*? *You* walked out on *me,* just in time for me to come here and spend a month getting abused by your mother, and then by your fiancée. Did you guys plan this? Did you all get together and say, 'Hey, I know, let's pick a girl off the street and torture her for a couple of months! It'll be a hoot!' " I was aware I was shouting, that the cameras were rolling, but I couldn't stop myself.

"You're crazy. You're not even listening to me. I don't know why I'm even having this conversation with you." He stood up and started pacing. "I have enough crazy women in my life!"

"I'm not in your life. So walk away."

"That's just it!" he shouted. Then he lowered his voice. "I can't walk away. I can't walk away from you."

I bit my lip. Why did he have to be so fucking charming? I was trying to hate him.

"OK, look," he said, calming down. "We're not understanding each
other, and I just know we're both intelligent people who are capable of
straightening this out." He took my hand. "Please, just listen to me for
a minute. Can you do that?"

"I suppose I can," I said, taking a few deep, calming breaths.

"First, this whole fiancée fiasco. My mother is very attached to
Christine, especially since Christine's mom died. She was my mother's best friend. She always imagined us together, and our families
have always been friends, since we were kids. I dated Christine a
few years ago, but it wasn't right, and I broke it off after a couple of
months. I don't connect with her. But ever since, my mom has been
pushing me, even though I've told her many times that it's never going
to happen. She invites Christine over all the time, whenever I'm going
to be around. You know her now. She thinks what she wants to think,
and you can't tell her anything different."

"I do get that impression," I admitted. "But Christine seems to
have the impression you're together, too. I just . . . I just don't know if
I can believe you."

"I don't know how to prove it to you, but all I can say is this." He
took both my hands in his and looked me in the eyes. "I promise you,
right here, right now, even though I don't know you very well, that
I will *never* lie to you."

This surprised me. His eyes were pleading and sincere. And sexy.
But my guard was up. "Then who was that girl in the club?"

"That really was a girl I just met, like I told you. She was drunk
and high and she'd been harassing me all night. I just felt responsible
for her in some way, even though I didn't know her at all. As soon as
I got back into the club, I looked everywhere for you. Listen." He held
my hand up against his heart. "Everything I said to you that night was
true. And everything I'm saying now to you is true. If you believe nothing else about today, please believe that."

The cameras moved closer. I wanted to cry. I looked at him, blinking back tears. "All right," I said. "All right. I believe you." I paused. As long as he was truth telling . . . "Why did you tell me your name is Harris?"

"My name *is* Harris," he said. "My mother started calling me Harry when I was a kid, and then, so did everyone else. But my father called me Harris. It's my real name."

I nodded. But did any of it matter? "OK, look," I said, "I'm going to be totally honest with you, too. I really like you. A lot. I've been thinking about you ever since that night. But I don't know where we can go from here. I'm in this contest to win. I need this. I have nothing else in my life but this. I can't tell you how much I need it. It's everything to me. And if being involved with you is going to put that at risk, well . . . I've gone through too much at this point to throw it all away for a big 'maybe.' Do you understand?"

"Sure I do," he said. "I get it. It's OK." He handed me a handkerchief, and I dabbed my eyes with it. "Even if this never goes any further, I just wanted you to know I didn't lie to you."

He lifted my hand up to his lips and kissed the back of it, without taking his eyes off me. "Good luck," he said.

Shari stepped into the room. I wondered how long she'd been standing there. "The limo's here, sweetie," she said. "We have to go."

On the ride back to Manhattan in the dark, Mikki fell asleep with her head on Christophe's shoulder and Monica was strangely quiet, melancholy and staring out the window. Shari was the only one who seemed to be in the mood for chatting.

"So what is going on? Tell me! Tell me *everything*," she said. "What was this movie you were in? That Christine was such a bitch. How dare she talk to you like that."

I sighed. "We're friends, right?"

"Of course, honey! You can tell me *anything*."

I leaned in close, glancing at Monica. Her eyes were closing. Christophe was staring out the window. I knew the cameras were on me. But so what? They'd caught the rest of it. I could hardly be in any more trouble. I just didn't want any of the other contestants to hear.

I whispered, "Harry Jansen and I spent a whole evening together at a club a few days before the contest started. At the time, I didn't know who he was. He told me his name was Harris."

"Are you kidding me? Does Sybil know?" Shari whispered back. "This could be a serious conflict of interest, way worse than Ian McGinnis."

"I know," I said, miserably. "But that's not the worst part. The worst part is that I liked him. I mean I *really, really* liked him. I know it sounds crazy, but for a little while there, I was thinking he was the one."

"Well that explains a *lot,*" she said. She glanced back at our team members. They all seemed to be sleeping. "You can't tell *anyone* about this, do you understand?" she whispered. "If you want to have any shot at winning, you have to play it completely straight, like it never happened."

"You're right," I said. "And you can't tell anyone."

"Of course not, honey," she said maternally. "My lips are sealed. Besides, you're my new best friend." It seemed like a strange thing for her to say, but I brushed it off because I really needed at least one other person to understand.

Back at Sybil Hunter Enterprises, we all sat yawning at the conference table. It was only seven p.m., but it felt like three a.m. The losing team wanted to know everything they'd missed, and Shari was happy to tell them. "Nadine, you should have seen the antiques," Shari bragged. "Fantastic. Gorgeous. And the food was absolutely unbelievable. I must have gained ten pounds. I'm starving myself tomorrow. Totally starving myself."

"Faith's champagne fountain was a big hit," Monica said. "Sybil was dipping into it all night."

"Oh, that's a good one," Andy said, rolling his eyes. "*Sybil* was dipping into the champagne."

"She was!" Monica said. "I think she could use some life coaching."

"I think Sybil Hunter is doing just fine," Andy said.

"She is indeed," said Ruby Prasad, coming into the room in a form-fitting dress that skimmed her narrow curves, and glittery diamond earrings. She looked like she was on her way out to dinner. We had been expecting Sybil—but then again, why would she bother to come back to the office in the evening if she didn't have to? We all knew Ruby's presence meant we had another food challenge coming. "Sybil has a message for you," Ruby said. She pushed a button on the wall and a screen lowered. Ruby pointed a remote control at the screen and pushed a button. Sybil's face appeared. She looked at us from the screen with the satisfied look of a cheetah who had just feasted on a gazelle she'd taken down herself.

"Some of us have just enjoyed an excellent dinner, in good company. And the rest of you ought to try a little harder next time," she said, as if she were in the room with us.

"You all remember Ruby Prasad, executive food editor for *Domestic Goddess Magazine*. She's back, and she's going to tell you about your next challenge. Ruby?"

Ruby pushed the pause button, freezing Sybil's face into a sly, somewhat crooked expression. "Any Domestic Goddess knows that cooking for a big family isn't much different than running a small restaurant. One of the latest trends on the culinary scene is the food truck. We want you to prove you can feed a family—a family of hungry New Yorkers during lunch hour in Times Square."

We all gasped. "For your next challenge, you will be divided into two teams of five. Each team will develop a concept for a food truck, plan a limited menu, design the advertising, buy enough food and supplies to stay open for four hours, from eleven a.m. to three p.m., and then, man your food truck for the designated time. The team that brings in the most money by three p.m. wins the challenge. The money you earn will be donated to the local food bank." Ruby pointed the remote at the screen again, and pressed a button. Sybil's frozen image moved again, and she spoke:

"The winning team will be richly rewarded. You'll get to dine at

Le Bernardin with SHE network executives, who want to get to know you better. Then, you'll get a night on the town. One person from the losing team will be eliminated."

The prize was brilliant, but what really excited me was this challenge. It had my name written all over it. I vowed to forget everything else. My team would win, no matter the cost.

"Tomorrow morning, meet me in the conference room at eight a.m. sharp. Sleep well—you're going to need it!"

The screen went blank. Ruby left the room without another word. We were dismissed. One of the production assistants led us back to the Loft, and although we were all more exhausted than we'd ever been, nobody was ready to go to sleep. We were too wired. Shari hovered protectively near me for most of the evening, and kept casting me meaningful glances. I began to regret telling her about Harris. Was it a mistake? Would she use it against me? I got nervous when I saw her in the kitchen, whispering with Nadine. I swear that Nadine looked over. But nobody said a word to me about Harris, so I hoped I really could trust Shari to keep her mouth shut.

Monica opened a bottle of wine and began dancing to some private music in front of the window, while Shari, Mikki, and I discussed what might be coming.

"I hope we're all on a team together," Mikki said. "It makes me nervous to be around some of those *other* people. Especially Linda. She looks like a man. I'm always afraid she's going to hit me."

"Jodi Sue is the weak link," Shari whispered. "She's always trying to get away with not doing anything. She's so afraid of making a mistake that it's going to be the death of her."

"I'm always wondering what Andy's going to do next," I said. "But at least he has energy. I could see being on a team with him."

"Not me," said Mikki. "He's way too intense for me. And too loud." Her pale skin seemed to go a shade paler at the very thought of Andy. She glanced nervously across the room at him.

"Who do you think is going to be cut next?" Shari whispered, leaning in. "Because I think it's Jodi Sue. She's got her rock-star husband to go home to, and I don't think she has what it takes to win. Not the way we do," she said, patting my knee.

"I think it's Andy. I *hope* it's Andy," Mikki said.

"I hope it's not Monica," I said. "She cracks me up." I looked at her across the room. She was trying to get Christophe to dance with her. "I think it should be Katie. She's got a serious attitude problem, and she hates me. I don't understand what her talent is."

"Eating candy?" said Shari. "Making headbands? Telling fortunes?"

"Taking off her shirt," I said. "That's what I remember from L.A."

"Apparently you did some of that yourself," said Mikki, blushing.

"Touché," I said.

chapter twenty-seven

Now, to decide the team captains, I'm going to give you all a little quiz. The first one to call out the correct answer will get to choose the first team captain. Is everyone ready?" Sybil looked at us all with amusement. It was eight a.m. sharp, and we were all falling apart from anxiety and exhaustion, but she looked well rested and perfect in her lavender cashmere sweater and cream-colored slacks.

We all nodded. My senses switched into high alert, despite the extreme fatigue and approaching armageddon.

"I was wearing something yesterday that I am still wearing today. What is it?"

I scanned her from head to toe at top speed. What was it? What had she been wearing yesterday? I'd been so nervous about Harris, I'd hardly noticed her. Suddenly Katie shouted, "Cartier emerald earrings!" Weird as she was, the girl did know her accessories.

"Excellent," she said. "You are correct. Katie, whom do you choose to be the first team captain?"

Katie looked around at all of us. Then she smiled. "Faith," she said. Oh, she was out to get me, all right. Everybody knew that the team captain was at the greatest risk for elimination. She still hadn't gotten her revenge on me, for what I knew about her in her L.A. days.

"Very good," said Sybil. "Now, the next question. Is everyone ready?"

We all nodded.

"What is the first recipe in my first cookbook, *Domestic Godd—*"

"Almond-stuffed dates wrapped in bacon!" The words shot out of me without my even having to think. I knew that cookbook inside and out. I'd practically memorized it. "Right after the . . . chapter on . . ." Everyone was staring at me. "Entertaining with flair," I said, a little embarrassed.

"Very good!" Sybil said, pleased. "Faith, you are our first team captain. Who do you choose to captain the opposing team?"

Who would I want to compete against? I looked at everyone, as Katie had. Then I smiled. "Katie," I said.

Katie rolled her eyes in annoyance.

"All's fair in love and war," Sybil said. "Faith, Katie, please come up here and stand next to me."

OK, this was just as it should be. I was ready to be a team captain, especially on a challenge like this. I knew how to cook, and I knew how to open a business. I was happy to go head-to-head with Katie, too. I'd had just about enough of her condescending attitude.

"Katie, who do you choose for your first team member?"

Without hesitation, Katie said, "Shari." Then she sneered at me. So she thought she would steal my alliances? Fine. Little did she know, Shari was likely to take over her team. Katie wouldn't be team leader for long.

"I choose . . ." I paused. I wanted to win. Andy was unpredictable and impulsive, but I knew he would kill for me and hustle on the task, lunatic or not. "Andy," I said.

"Nadine," Katie said. They'd obviously become friends. Nadine looked gratified, and cast me a dirty look. What did she have against me? Probably just the fact that I was a threat. Or whatever Katie had told her about me.

"Jodi Sue," I said. Even if her celebrity chef title was a joke, she made those winning cupcakes.

"Linda," Katie said. I was surprised she wanted pushy, loud-mouthed Linda on her side, but they seemed to have formed an alliance—Loudmouthed Linda, Crazy Katie, and Queen Nadine.

"Mikki," I said. I knew Mikki would work hard for me, too. She was shy, but sensible, and she would be quiet and not annoy me.

"Christophe," Katie said. Separating the lovebirds, Mikki and Christophe, was just mean.

"Monica," I said. If I could keep her sober, she would probably be good at helping promote the food truck. She could flirt with anyone.

"And those are your teams," Sybil said. "You will have all day to develop your concept, buy your supplies, prepare food, advertise, sur-vey your location, and do anything else you think needs to be done to ensure your success. Tomorrow at eleven a.m., your truck will open for business."

The day was a blur of activity. By seven, we were all in the workroom, poring over the new Rulebook. We had to submit a concept by nine, and so far, our team couldn't agree.

"I think we have to go with your specialty, Faith," said Andy. "I think we need to do a muffin truck."

"I really don't want to do that," I said. "I want to stretch beyond what's safe. Our team has to stand out. And it's a lunch truck. Muffins aren't for lunch."

"What about cupcakes? Everybody loves cupcakes," said Jodi Sue.

"You and Shari won the first challenge with those flower cup-cakes," Andy said. "We'd look unoriginal. And cupcakes aren't lunch, either."

"I agree," I said. "We want something that's not labor-intensive to make, but that we can do a lot with in terms of serving. Hey . . . what about hot dogs? It's classic New York. Sybil will love it."

"Hot dogs are disgusting," said Jodi Sue. "We want something classier, like healthy smoothies, made to order."

"Smoothies are cliché," said Andy. "Just like you."

"Shut up, you asshole," she said.

"OK, seriously, you guys, I know we're all dead tired and irritable but we've got to make this happen," I said.

"What about falafel?" said Monica. "I love falafel."

"We have no credibility selling falafel," Andy said. "None of us are Middle Eastern. What do we know about falafel? That's an idiotic idea."

"All right, Jodi Sue makes a good point that we should have a healthy option," I said. "How about we do gourmet hot dogs. We can have Kobe beef and veggie as well as turkey and maybe duck if we can find it. Regular or whole wheat buns, and . . . what if we made our own flavored mustards?"

"That's a great idea," said Andy. "Just the sound of it makes me hungry."

"We can call it What Up, Dog?" I said. Everybody laughed.

"That's great," said Monica.

Jodi Sue shrugged. "Whatever," she said. "I think it's kind of a disgusting idea, but I guess I could get into the assorted mustard thing."

"I know all about hot dogs," Andy said, jumping out of his chair. He started gyrating his hips. "I've got a twelve-inch one right here, baby."

"Oh really?" I said. "I knew you looked familiar."

Andy cackled. "Right here, baby. Right here."

Across the room, we could hear the other team arguing, too. Words floated across the room: *ice cream, tacos, barbecue, candy by the pound*. Katie kept yelling, "Why do you all hate candy?"

"We don't hate candy, darling, we just think it's juvenile," Nadine said.

"Don't listen to them," I said to my team. "We have to focus on what we're doing."

"She's a lunatic anyway," Andy said, looking in Katie's direction.

"And you aren't?" Monica said.

"And *you* aren't?" Andy said back to her.

"OK, OK, we're all bat-shit crazy; no normal person would partici-pate in this insane sleep deprivation experiment. Now can we get this done?" I said.

Andy, Mikki, and I went to the location to scout it out, on 41st Street between 6th and 7th Avenues. Then we called around to find the best sources for hot dogs. I found a great price on bulk veggie dogs, and Andy tracked down a good deal on Kobe beef dogs. After a lot of searching, I found uncured duck dogs. Turkey dogs were easy. Andy and I went out to pick up everything, including yellow and brown mustards at the grocery store that we would use for the bases for our gourmet mustard flavors: cranberry mustard, spicy brown mus-tard, barbecue mustard, maple mustard, chipotle mustard, classic yel-low mustard, and relish mustard. We weren't making the hot dogs, but I hoped our effort on the condiments would impress Sybil.

I sent off Monica and Jodi Sue to make flyers with the advertise-ment we'd designed for a One-Day Times Square Gourmet Hot Dog Extravaganza. "Hand them out in Times Square, to everyone you see," I said. "Dress up before you do it. Look cute." I was glad it was them out there, and not me. I'd never felt less cute in my life.

"Why do I have to do this?" Jodi Sue complained. "I want to make the mustard."

"Because you and Monica are the most flashy. People will notice you. You can work on the mustard when you get back," I snapped. She sighed and rolled her eyes but agreed.

Back at the workroom we mixed the ingredients into the mustards and sampled and tweaked until the flavors were just right. We all had our second wind and were moving at warp speed, talking fast and laughing at stupid things and snapping at one another, like we were all about to lose it. I kept asking for Jodi Sue's input, but every time I talked to her, she just shrugged. Finally I just gave up and called the shots. I won-dered how a personal chef could be so lacking in opinions.

"I just know we're going to win," said Monica. "These are so good. We're definitely going to win."

At six, I went to the T-shirt store to pick up our "*What Up, Dog?*" shirts, then I met everyone back at the studio. Andy practically pounced on me when I walked in the door. "Katie's team is doing a taco truck," he said. He looked panicky. "It sounds really good. They've got a whole menu; it's way more complex than ours." He was wild-eyed and practically vibrating.

"Calm down," I said, not feeling calm at all. "It's fine. We just have to make ours better; that's all. Don't focus on them, it will kill us."

"What do they know about tacos anyway?" said Mikki. "People are not going to want to buy tacos from Nadine with her fake British accent or Shari, who's straight out of Bensonhurst. Nobody on that team knows anything about Mexican cooking."

"How do you know?" said Andy. "Maybe they do. Maybe somebody lived in Mexico or has a Mexican grandmother or something. We should have done muffins. Or even cupcakes, so ours would be harder to compare to theirs. That was a big mistake. A *big* mistake. We're going down. This is your fault, Faith."

"It's going to be fine," I said, starting to panic myself. Were we really going down? This could be it for me. I had to get everybody back on track. "Our idea is better. How often can you find a duck dog with a whole-grain bun and gourmet mustard?" I said.

"We all just have to 'Have Faith,'" Monica said, using air quotes.

"Shut up, you ditz," Andy said. "Let the grown-ups talk."

"Hey!" said Monica. "That's mean."

"You're insane, Andy," Jodi Sue said, her hands on her full hips, her cleavage jiggling.

"No, Jodi Sue, you're the drag on this team." He turned on her. "You're not pulling your weight. You fly under the radar and everybody else has to pick up the slack, and it's going to be your downfall. If I decide you should go next, then you'll go next, I guarantee it."

"You can't do that, you jerk," Monica said. "You're not even the team leader! *God* I need a drink."

"All it takes is the right kind of comment in front of Sybil," Andy said smugly. "And any of you are gone. Believe me, I know what I'm doing. She listens to me, and you don't want to get on my bad side."

"Delusions of grandeur," Monica muttered.

"Do you know who I am? Do you know who I know?" Jodi Sue sputtered. "My husband has connections. He's a *rock star*. I can make sure you not only lose this show but that you never work again!"

"I'd like to see you try," Andy said.

"Everybody, stop!" said Mikki, looking like she might faint. "Sybil doesn't listen to any of you. Just stop! There's enough pressure, we don't need to add more!" Christophe hurried over from across the room, where the other team was working, and put his arm around her.

"Are you all right, darling?" he said.

"Get back over here, Christophe!" Katie said. "No sharing team secrets!"

"I'm just checking on my friend, if you don't mind!" he yelled, his voice quavering. He was almost as pale as Mikki, and his skin looked bad—definitely the worse for wear from lack of sleep.

"We do mind!" Queen Nadine said. "No fraternizing with the enemy."

"Mikki is not the enemy!" he shouted.

"It's all right, honey, just go back," Mikki said faintly, patting him on the arm. "I'm all right." We all stared at Mikki. Darling? Honey?

"What?" she said. "So . . . we're together now."

Monica wrinkled her nose. "Eww."

"OK, this is getting us nowhere," I said. "Andy, just shut up. Jodi Sue, stop letting him get to you. All of you, forget the other team, and focus on us. If we aren't unified, we'll definitely lose this challenge. Now let's all go downstairs and work on decorating the truck."

The night before, the other team's truck hadn't been on the lot. Now it was back, and they'd obviously paid to have it professionally wrapped—it was covered in a blue-and-orange Aztec-style design with a big orange sun and cacti, and they'd hung real piñatas from brackets on the roof. The whole thing fluttered with multicolored pennant flags.

"Look how tacky that is," Mikki said, her voice shrill. I was becoming more and more freaked out and it wasn't just because I had volunteered to drive our truck through New York City traffic.

"How did they afford to do that on the budget we had?" Andy said.

"Somebody must know somebody," I said. "But this isn't about who can decorate the best truck. It's about revenue!" I was talking too loud, but I couldn't help it. I felt like my head might explode.

"Ours is classier," Mikki said. But nobody really believed it.

"We're so screwed," Andy said. "They're going to win."

"Shut up, Andy," Jodi Sue said. "Don't even say that. We're going to make the most money. Ours is the best. Just shut up!"

We all sat in tense silence as I drove the big truck down 43rd Street to Seventh Avenue, then back around to 41st, inching along surrounded by cabs and delivery trucks and a few terrified-looking tourists in their sedans. They're not as terrified as I am, I thought. What's driving through Manhattan compared to the insane experience of being on this show? We pulled over where the producers had marked off our spot with orange cones. They were already there, moving the cones out of the way as I maneuvered the truck into place. It was ten thirty; we had half an hour until we opened.

Jodi Sue and Mikki immediately started passing out flyers. Mikki made coffee and checked that the drinks were cold. Her hands were shaking. I arranged the stacks of napkins and paper plates, and took the lids off the steam trays filled with dogs and sauerkraut, which we'd heated in the test kitchen. Everything looked good. Andy set up the mustard station and straightened the signage. Then I pulled out the first bag of hot dog buns.

Oh shit. They were soaking wet. "How the hell did this happen?" I shrieked. "The buns are wet!"

Andy ran over to look. "Fuck," he said. "You can't serve those. This is a disaster!"

"Did somebody sabotage us?" Mikki said, her eyes wild with paranoia.

"No, look," said Andy. We'd stashed the buns in a cabinet under the steam trays for the drive over, and water was dripping down from where the hot dogs were warming, right on top of the bags of buns. "Somehow, the water got into the bags," Andy said, opening up another bag. "These are wet, too."

Mikki grabbed the rest of the bags, and we all opened them up. Two bags were still dry—one bag of white and one bag of wheat. I thought fast.

"Andy," I said. "You have to find a toaster with as many slots as possible. We can toast the buns to dry them. Most of them are just damp."

Andy looked wildly around. "Go!" I screamed. He ran out the door.

"Let's lay these all out in the corner and open them up so they can start to dry," I said. "I just hope the dry ones last until he gets back. We don't want to lose because of soggy buns."

"At least it's better than losing for saggy buns," Mikki said.

We looked at each other, then burst out laughing.

"We've already got a line!" Monica said, peeking in the door, her wispy blonde hair glinting in the sun, her cheeks and nose rosy. "They're hungry! Are we ready? Is everything ready?"

"Do you need any help in there?" Jodi Sue said, coming up to the window. She looked good in that tight T-shirt, I had to admit.

"No, get out there and shake it," I said. "We need customers."

"Whatever," she said, giving me a dirty look. But she tucked her T-shirt in and went bouncing back outside. This time, she could be *our* groupie. Mikki came in and took her place at the cash register next to the window. I peered out. I could see Monica and Jodi Sue handing out more flyers and directing people to the line. "Get them while you can, one day only!" Monica shrieked.

At eleven I went outside, rolled open the windows, and rang the bell hanging over the window. No sign of Andy yet. I was getting more and more nervous. What if we ran out of buns before he got back?

Why didn't I tell him to buy more buns? Why the toaster? That was stupid! What was I thinking? I was too tired to think clearly. I ran back inside as Mikki took our first customer. "What up, dog?" she said, awkwardly.

"I'd like a Kobe beef dog with chipotle mustard and a lemonade," said a young woman, handing Mikki a five-dollar bill.

"White or wheat bun?" Mikki asked.

After a while, I took over for Mikki at the counter because she was just too shy for the job. She was happy to take the money while I took the orders. "You're better with interfacing," she said. "I've had enough talking."

"That's fine," I said. "I'm on a roll. Or . . . a soggy bun."Nobody laughed.

But the customer experience is what would earn us a win. We had to make the most money, so I sucked it up. "What up, dog?" I said, trying to look more cheerful than I felt to each new customer. Every time I said it, the customer smiled. That was a good sign. After an hour, we still had a line, and everyone outside the stand seemed to love the hot dogs.

But we were almost to the end of the dry buns, and Andy still wasn't back.

And then I looked up, and Harris was at the window.

"Hi," he said.

I blushed. "What up, dog?" I said. He laughed.

"I'm here to check in on your team," he said.

"Oh, really?" I said. "Because you're just so into being involved with your mother's media ventures?"

"Yep, that's me. I'm just a fame whore," he said.

"I suspected as much," I said. "What can I get you?"

"I'll take a Kobe beef with spicy brown mustard and sauerkraut on white, and a duck dog with relish mustard on whole wheat," he said. "How's business?" he asked, while Mikki scrambled to get his order.

"Pretty steady," I said. "Who doesn't love a hot dog?"

"I like your cheerleaders out front," he said, gesturing to Monica and Jodi Sue.

"I know. Hot, right?" I said.

"They drew me right in," he said, with a twinkle in his eye.

Then Mikki elbowed me. "We're out of buns," she whispered.

Shit.

"Um . . . Harris?" I said, trying to look sweet and winning. "It seems we have a little technical difficulty. We're . . . temporarily out of buns."

He looked worried. "You'd better get some more before my mother gets here," he said. "She'll frown on that."

"Can I give you your order without a bun?" I said, apologetically.

"Sure," he said. "I'm easy."

"So I've heard."

I handed him his plate. "Thanks," he said, picking up the hot dog with his fingers. "I'll be critiquing these."

"Do you want a fork?" I said.

"Nope, I'm good," he said.

"I hope you enjoy."

"Oh, I'm already enjoying," he said, winking at me. "I'll see you later."

Just after Harris left, Andy showed up with a four-slice toaster in his arms. "This was all I could find. Don't ask how I got it," he said, bursting into the truck and plugging it in. "And I had to yell at slacker Jodi Sue out there to get off her ass and start bringing in customers. She was just sitting on a bench."

The toasting worked—the buns dried out just enough, and people seemed to appreciate the warm buns more than the untoasted ones. "We should toast them all," he said.

"Go for it," I said, wishing he'd arrived just a few minutes sooner, so I wouldn't have had to give Harris a second-rate product. No matter what positive thoughts he might be having about me now, he was still one of the judges, and if he was honest the way he claimed to be, he was going to have to be honest about this.

"I'm tired of this," Monica said, coming up to the window.

"Move off," said Andy. "Get out there and do your job. We're working our asses off in here. We've only got an hour left."

"My job's harder," Monica pouted, then went back to her post. "One more hour and we're gone forever!" she yelled hoarsely. "Gourmet hot dogs in Times Square!"

"Everyone's doing a really good job," I said to Andy. "Except Jodi Sue."

"She's lame," he said. "She has to go. If we go down, we have to make sure Sybil knows that she did the least work."

"If we go down, it's probably going to be my head on the block," I said. "I'm team captain." The idea terrified me. I *couldn't* go home now. I just couldn't. I'd given too much. I had nothing else left for my regular life. It was all riding on hot dogs.

Jodi Sue peeked in the side door. "You guys, I really need a bottle of water, my throat is dry from yelling," she said.

"You weren't even yelling," Andy said. "Monica's doing all the yelling."

"I'm yelling just as much!" she said. "Even though I should be in here doing the easy job."

"Screw you," said Andy. "This is a hard job. Here," he said, grabbing a bottle of water and handing it to her. "Just go away."

"Screw *you*," she said. She opened the bottle, tossed the cap in the trash, and turned to go back out. Then her shoe caught on the top rim of the step, she stumbled back, and the bottle of water went flying out of her hand. We all watched it make a perfect arc, then land spout down . . . right in the toaster. The toaster fizzled and sputtered and exploded with a tiny poof of flame, followed by a curl of black smoke.

"Oh shit, Jodi Sue, you broke the toaster," I said.

"Oh, that's rich," Andy said. "You don't do a damn thing to help us, and then you break the one thing that's keeping us going." He turned to me. "It's two thirty. I've got these buns I've already toasted, but I don't know if it's enough to last another half hour."

"I'm sorry. I'll get out of the way," Jodi Sue said meekly.

"We'll just have to make the best of it," I said. But inside, I was fuming. And horrified. Would I really go home? Was this the end? Because of a clumsy lazy groupie who didn't care whether we won or not?

Fifteen minutes later, Sybil Hunter and Ruby Prasad showed up at the window. Of course. We had three already toasted buns left.

"What up, dog?" I said, feeling silly saying it to Sybil Hunter, but putting on my best game face.

Sybil surveyed the menu. "I'll have a duck dog with maple mustard on wheat, and a Kobe beef dog with cranberry mustard on white," she said. "And another Kobe beef hot dog, for Rasputin here." She was holding his leash. "No mustard, no bun." The big Newfoundland wagged his bushy tail.

"Right away," I said.

"I'll have a veggie dog with chipotle mustard on white," said Ruby. "And a duck dog with relish mustard on wheat."

"Of course," I said weakly. Where the hell were we going to get the fourth bun?

I looked at Andy. He stared back at me. Did we give Ruby a soggy white bun, or Sybil? Or did we come clean and tell them we didn't have any buns left? "What do we do?" Mikki said in a panicky whisper.

"Is there a problem?" Sybil asked.

"Not at all," I said, smiling. "We did have a slight mishap with some of our buns getting a little damp, but we were toasting them. And of course"—I tried to laugh—"just before you came to see us, our toaster blew out." I wanted to die.

"I see," said Sybil. "So what are you going to do about it?"

I looked past Sybil. Our line had dwindled as the lunch hour had passed, but a group of people had already gathered, having recognized Sybil Hunter. They were whispering and pointing. I wondered what Sybil would do.

"May I suggest that Rasputin has excellent taste, in ordering without a bun, and we would love to offer you an alternative preparation for your Kobe beef dog?" I suggested. "The quality and flavor are so high that we actually prefer to serve it sliced and drizzled with mustard. Would you be interested in this? We can still offer you a bun for your duck dog."

Sybil smiled. "All right. Did you hear that, Rasputin? You have excellent taste. I'll try one, Rasputin-style," she said. I handed them their plates, and leaned out the window to offer Rasputin his Kobe beef dog. He gulped it happily and wagged his tail.

Sybil and Ruby began to eat, just as the clock struck three.

"Thank God," I said. "We're done."

I could see Sybil and Ruby conferring. Then Sybil approached the window again.

"The hot dogs were good, and the mustards were excellent," she said, smiling.

"I agree," said Ruby. I wanted to faint with relief.

Sybil looked at me. "I remember when I was first starting out in corporate event planning," she said. "I had to do a dessert buffet, and the caterer's truck crashed on the way, so we were left without any desserts."

"What did you do?" I said.

"The event wasn't too large, and it was being held in a local church. I panicked, of course, but only for a moment. Then I went to the kitchen, where I found eggs, milk, butter, sugar, a few spices—just the basics. But the freezer was full of bread that the church would cut into cubes for communion Sundays. So I made four trays of bread pudding. And it was good," she said. "It was a success."

"Wow," I said. I felt privileged. Sybil didn't often share personal stories.

"The food truck challenge was your most difficult test yet," said Sybil, standing up. "You were face-to-face with the public, and every detail mattered. Both teams rose to the occasion. However, one team emerged as the clear winner." We sat in the conference room in front of Sybil, Ruby, Harris, and Alice. Andy and I looked at each other nervously. We had no idea how the other team had done.

She looked around at us, making us wait, before she continued.

"I was impressed that Faith didn't get flustered by the mishap with the hot dog buns, and deftly served me a very nice platter without a bun. However, the one *with* the bun was uninspired," she said. "The bun was cheap and flavorless, and the duck dog wasn't as interesting as the Kobe beef. But I don't understand why you didn't just go out and buy more buns. Harris, what do you think? Did you get a bun?"

Harris turned red and looked at the table. "No, actually, I . . . they were out of buns just when I arrived. But the hot dog was very good!" he added quickly.

"Hmm," Sybil murmured, raising her eyebrows at me. Harris looked furious at himself, but at least he'd proved his point that he wasn't a liar. "It's unprofessional to keep getting caught unprepared like that. I think you could have done better," Sybil said, directly to me. "Also, your truck wasn't very appealing. It didn't command attention. You would have drawn a much bigger crowd had you put more thought into the truck's exterior."

"But we had a line the whole four hours," I said.

"If you would have had more customers, you would have raised more money for the charity," Sybil said.

"We also polled some of the people on the street," said Ruby, "and the consensus was that the Kobe beef hot dogs were excellent, but the other flavors were merely adequate," she said. "I was also mildly offended by the team members you set out on the street to jump around and yell."

"Yes, that was tawdry," Sybil agreed. "I would have preferred to see all the team members working inside the truck. This kind of advertising, yelling and bouncing around with signs, is just crass. In the end, What Up, Dog? made $1,102 in four hours. And now . . ."

That sounded like a lot of money to me. I looked at Andy hopefully. How could the taco truck have made any more than that? It was probably going to be neck and neck.

Shari and Katie both sat up very straight. I couldn't read their faces, but Katie looked angry, and I could only assume that Shari had taken over. Controlling every situation was her MO. But I didn't care about them. I was crushed. I'd thought we'd done so well, and now, here we were, getting reamed. When she visited our truck, Sybil had seemed so pleased, and so understanding. I should have known not to trust that.

"The other team's taco truck business was simply called Taco Truck, which I found unimaginative," Sybil continued, "but which the people we interviewed seemed to like, for its straightforward nature. And while Taco Truck had an interesting menu with many choices, many commented that a lot of the advertised choices weren't actually available. Can you explain this?"

"That was Linda's fault," said Katie. "She was supposed to get everything and she totally dropped the ball."

"Or she just didn't feel like exerting herself," muttered Shari.

Suddenly, the mouthy headhunter seemed to be the team's target. I couldn't believe they were taking her on. Had they decided she was a threat? Were they plotting? I looked at my team members. I wondered if any of them were plotting against me. I'd been too busy trying to get everything done to notice.

"That's a lie," Linda said. "The only things I couldn't find were chipotle peppers and the salsa verde."

"Chipotle peppers and salsa verde are available in any grocery store," said Ruby.

"And it's not my fault that we ran out of chicken," Linda said in her brusque voice. "I killed myself to get everything done, which is more than I can say for Queen Nadine."

"I took in all the money, and that was the most important part," Nadine said.

"The tacos themselves were not authentic at all," said Ruby. "They were Americanized versions of tacos, with premade shells and meat seasoned with a mix. I couldn't even finish mine. Harris, what did you think?"

Harris seemed more eager to offer his thoughts on the taco truck. "I didn't like them at all," he said. "The truck looked great, but the product itself was disappointing."

"Taco Truck's exterior was certainly impressive," Sybil said. "This is important because it draws a crowd, and Taco Truck apparently drew a much bigger crowd than What Up, Dog? While I also agree that the tacos themselves were mediocre, Taco Truck did an excellent job of advertising their taco stand and pleasing their clientele. This is not a cooking show. The goal was to give the public what they wanted, and to earn the most money for the local food bank. Authentic or not, the people we interviewed said they loved your tacos. Taco Truck also had an efficient assembly line system that worked."

"For the record," said Ruby, "the hot dogs were better than the tacos."

"And yet, Taco Truck brought in $2,205," said Sybil. "Significantly more money than What Up, Dog?"

"How?" Andy mouthed to me. It did seem impossible.

"However," said Sybil, "I heard there was some trouble with the team leader. Katie, can you explain?"

"Yes," she said, putting on her typical scowl. "My alarm didn't go off, and everybody left without waking me up."

Shari looked down, but I swear she was smiling.

"And thank God," said Nadine, "if Shari hadn't handled everything, it wouldn't have worked nearly as well." Nadine and Shari seemed to be in league. That worried me.

"We did it for the team, honey," Shari said, patting Katie's shoulder condescendingly.

Katie just crossed her arms and shook her head.

"Katie got there just before we opened," said Nadine. "Just in time to start taking the money."

"Which is just the way you wanted it," said Andy. "Pretty scheming, Shari. Devious even."

"I had nothing to do with it," said Shari, innocently. "But I saw a need for leadership, so I stepped up."

"That doesn't sound like good teamwork to me, but when the leader falls, it's good to have someone who can step in. Good job, Shari. Katie, perhaps you need a better alarm clock."

"Shari's the one who probably turned off my alarm!" said Katie. "And you're congratulating her?"

"I am," said Sybil. "I'm congratulating all of you, because Taco Truck is the winner of this challenge."

They all clapped. I wanted to be sick. Or murder someone. Sybil would do. But it was dollars and cents. It didn't matter if Ruby liked our hot dogs better or Sybil thought we made the best of a bad situation. And now, somebody had to go home. My heart began to race, knowing that the judgment was coming. How would I go back to my life now? I didn't even remember what it was. The show had consumed my entire consciousness. I didn't know how to do anything else anymore.

"Every member of your team will be joining the network producers at Le Bernardin in one hour, and then you'll be treated to a night on the town. Team Taco Truck, you may all go back to the Loft to get ready."

"Now," Sybil said, looking at our team, "even though you did a decent job on your product, and I thought your team name was clever, your team didn't really pull together and I question some of the management decisions. Someone from your team must go home. Faith, you were the team leader. Who do you think was most responsible for any failures your team encountered?"

I paused. This was going to get sticky. I'd been dreading this question. If I played it wrong, I'd get sent home. If I played it right, maybe I could save myself. I definitely wasn't going to take the blame for something that wasn't my fault. I'd done everything I could. The whole idea was mine. "I think . . . I think every team member played a role in our success. But some worked harder than others," I said hesitantly.

"Like whom?" Sybil asked.

"Well . . . Andy was my go-to guy. He worked very hard for the team. Mikki was determined and did a great job behind the counter, and she was right there getting everything ready. Monica was a real trooper out there on the street. Even if you didn't like our advertising plan, I think Monica did a lot to get people into our line."

"And Jodi Sue?" said Sybil.

"Jodi Sue . . . helped make the mustard, but she did break the toaster, and honestly, she slacked off. When Monica was out there getting customers, Jodi Sue was sitting on a bench doing nothing. She was the dead weight on this team. Whenever we gave her a job, she tried to get out of it. I don't think she really wants to be here." It was a fair assessment, but was it enough to save me?

"That's not true," Jodi Sue said, indignantly. "How dare you say that! I want to be here as much as anybody! *You're* the one who put the buns under the steam trays. *You're* the one who wouldn't let Monica and I come in to help. *You're* the one who had to take over and do everything and make the rest of us look bad. And I thought the street advertising was tacky, too—I totally agree with Sybil on that one."

"Faith did her best," said Monica, her voice almost gone from her What-Up-Dog yelling, "and you did nothing except jump around with your big boobs going everywhere. And I say it's Andy who causes all the discord. He's always trying to pit people against each other."

"All right, I've heard enough," said Sybil. "It seems to me that Faith failed to maintain team unity, although she exhibited creativity. Andy provided a lot of the drive and forward motion for the team." She looked back and forth between Mikki, Jodi Sue, and Monica, and conferred quietly with Alice, Harris, and Ruby. Then she turned back to us. "Mikki, Jodi Sue, Monica, none of you have particularly distinguished yourselves yet, but some of you have been less motivated to fulfill the role of Domestic Goddess." She paused. Was she really going to cut one of them? Was I saved? I was just waiting for her to swing back toward me and point a finger at me.

The cameras hovered. Finally, she delivered the verdict. "Jodi Sue,

I'm sorry, but you just aren't necessary here at Sybil Hunter Enterprises."

I couldn't believe it! She'd agreed with my assessment over Jodi Sue's! Was I really still here? Was I still part of the contest? I wanted to faint with relief.

Andy grinned at me and made a motion as if wiping sweat from his brow.

Jodi Sue looked thunderstruck, but didn't say a word. She just smiled weakly, nodded, stood up, shook Sybil's hand, then left the room. "What's her rock-star husband gonna do about *that*?" Andy said under his breath, looking self-righteous. He was going to be even more impossible now that he was feeling totally vindicated about his claim that he could influence Sybil to drop Jodi Sue. At least I was still safe, against all odds. And I was even more determined never to lose another challenge.

But I did lose another challenge. Several more. And I won some, too. As the next few weeks rolled on, Sybil cut us off at the knees, one by one. The challenges got more and more brutal. We had to run a bed and breakfast for forty-eight hours, and Christophe, the concierge, was sent home, leaving poor heartbroken Mikki to weep alone in her bed for the next three nights until she was sent packing, after a challenge in which we had to decorate a condominium for a wealthy socialite. She hugged me before she left. "I'm rooting for you," she said. Then she whispered, "Watch out for Shari. She knows you're her biggest competition. She's been trying to set the other people against you."

"Really?" I whispered. I found it hard to believe. Shari was my friend, but on the other hand, I couldn't help feeling suspicious.

After a corporate catering challenge, Linda, the mouthy headhunter, was given the axe. She was the only one to really freak out at Sybil, calling her "an egomaniac with a god complex." I suspected that bit wouldn't make it on to the show. And then, much to my relief, candy-crazy Katie and her astrology headbands, were let go after a challenge where we had to design a clothing collection and put on a fashion show. I was grateful I wouldn't have to see her scowling at me anymore. Boozy Monica left us after the Sweet Sixteen Party challenge, when she got too drunk and started dancing with the guests.

Nadine the Queen of Queens left in a huff after she refused to play the role of server during the Supper Club challenge. And finally, there were only three: Andy, Shari, and me.

Shari had stood by me all along, never selling me out, whether she was on my team or on the opposing team, so despite what Mikki had told me, I still believed in our friendship, and it was important to me. I knew Shari was ambitious and wanted to win, but at night, we always spent at least an hour talking about the other contestants, the challenges, who was doing well, who was a threat, who would be easy to beat. We also talked about her family, about mine, about our plans, and what would come next. She defended me against anyone who said anything unkind to my face, and when we talked about our personal lives, she was always on my side. I even told her about my parents, and she railed against their treatment of me. "How could anyone treat their beautiful daughter that way?" she said. It was exactly what I needed to hear.

She said she wanted me to come visit her at the Jersey Shore for the summer and promised me a place to stay. "We'll sit around drinking coffee and reading the gossip pages," she said. "And then we'll lie in the sun all day and drink fruity drinks and watch the cute boys walk by." In the midst of all the insanity, I was grateful to have her. She was my one comfort, although I knew at some point, one of us would have to go home.

Meanwhile, I was too thin, I was exhausted, and I felt disgusting. Nobody looked good—everyone who was still there looked like they'd lost at least ten pounds. I wondered how the eliminated contestants were doing, sequestered at their undisclosed location. They weren't getting paid, but they were getting to sleep and eat and probably talk to one another, and they *weren't* having to endure any more challenges, or any more of Sybil Hunter. But I was also riding high on my success, so I didn't envy them. I'd really hit my stride and my teams were winning challenge after challenge.

But now, for the rest of the contest, it would be cutthroat. Shari, Andy, and me. And I was ready to go balls to the wall to win it. I was focused and driven and winning was my priority, even if a small part of me was still thinking about Harris.

Every so often, I'd see him in the hall or he'd show up to help judge a challenge, but the security on the show was so tight, and we were so closely monitored, that we never got a chance to really speak beyond the casual. Still, our conversations were fraught with double meanings and the looks we gave each other went from shy and suspicious to increasingly steamy. It was like we were having a whole relationship without ever touching or saying anything directly. I wondered what would happen when it was all over. Would we go our separate ways? Would he marry Christine, after all? I didn't think so. But would I ever see him again? Of that, I wasn't sure.

We had just completed the latest challenge producing a makeover segment on a new mom, filming "before" pictures, buying her new clothes, getting her hair and makeup done, and filming the "after" segment. We wouldn't get the results until the next morning. There was no clear winner, no clear loser. We were all good at what we did.

The three of us sat together in the now mostly empty Loft. Nobody said it, but we were all thinking the same thing: one of us was about to go home, and Sybil was going to start asking us who should stay and who should go.

"May the best one win," I said, raising my glass.

"To the one with the biggest balls," Andy said.

"You don't want to put your balls up against mine," I said.

"Our last night as a threesome," Andy said. "Maybe we should *have* one."

"One what?" Shari said.

"A threesome!" he said, hopefully.

I threw a plastic cup at his head.

"Hey, you can't blame a guy for asking."

"Sure we can," said Shari.

"I can't believe we get to go home next week," I said. "God, I miss my dog and even my shitty apartment."

"I miss my kids," Shari said.

"I'm going to miss this," said Andy. "It's been a rush."

We all nodded silently. If nothing else, it had certainly been a rush. Tomorrow, we'd find out the final two, and then, one more challenge before everyone went home for six months, to our real lives, or what was left of them. And then we'd be back, for the results and the finale. Whatever happened after that would surely be different than anything I'd ever known before.

chapter twenty-eight

We sat along one side of the conference table: Shari, Andy, and I. Sybil sat facing us, between Ian and Alice. Rasputin sat on the floor under my feet. Ever since I'd given him that Kobe beef hot dog, he always came over to me when we were all in the room. I patted his giant, fluffy head under the table—his head alone was bigger than my whole dog. His big tail thumped against the carpet.

Sybil surveyed us and we all looked back at her with confidence, with hope, and with desperate ambition. Each one of us *knew* we would win, felt we absolutely *had to win*. Nobody was giving up or backing down.

"This final challenge revealed many things about each of you," Sybil said. "Although you were not informed, during this last challenge, some of the most influential people here at Sybil Hunter Enterprises were behind the scenes, watching you and evaluating your performance. I trust and highly value my colleagues' opinions, and I've brought three of them here today to ask you a few questions."

This was unexpected, but I'd been so involved in the New Mom Makeover challenge that it probably wouldn't have mattered even if I'd known. Shari looked startled but confident. Andy had a confrontational look on his face, like he dared anyone to question his methods. I knew he'd been uncomfortable with the final task. Makeovers weren't exactly his thing, but he'd barreled right through in his usual over-the-top way and his new mom had actually looked pretty good at the end of the challenge. I guessed he'd probably tried to sleep with her, or at least flirted enough to give her the radiant glow of sexual flattery.

The door opened and in walked an older bald man with little wire glasses and two older women, one with a brunette wedge haircut and tortoiseshell reading glasses, the other with gray-blonde bangs and blunt-cut, shoulder-length hair. "Let me introduce you to Phillip Wagner, Marcelle Eklund, and Ruth Richardson," she said. She turned to her colleagues. "Please sit down. I'm so happy to have you here, as I truly value your opinions."

The three sat on Sybil's side of the table. Now we were outnumbered, and it was intimidating. To compensate, I sat up straighter.

"Let's begin with Shari," said Sybil. She turned to her colleagues. "What did all of you think about her, and what you witnessed as you observed her during this last challenge?"

"I was impressed with Shari," said the brunette, Marcelle. "She was polished and professional, and she knew how to put people at ease by drawing them into the conversation. My only concern was a sense I had that she wasn't always sincere, that her friendly manner was put on. But on the surface, she seemed approachable and warm."

"Shari, I was surprised to learn you are a housewife. You exude the ambition and competitiveness of a businesswoman," said Phillip. "Tell me, what would you bring to Sybil Hunter Enterprises?"

"I believe I can bring the stay-at-home mom's perspective, combined with my interest in all the things Sybil Hunter does," Shari said. "I've always been a great admirer of Sybil's brand, and with my social connections and my aesthetic sense, I believe I would be a great asset to the company."

"You do strike me as a woman who can get things done and I have a good mental picture of how your show would look on our network," said Phillip. "But I agree with Marcelle that you seem to be a very calculated person and we may not be seeing the true Shari yet."

Shari looked startled. "I have to disagree," she said. "What you see is exactly what you get. I'm a good friend, a hard worker, a devoted homemaker, but I'm ready to enter the working world. I'm perfectly poised for it."

"I disagree about Shari being a good fit on the network," said the gray-blonde woman, Ruth. "To me, Shari wasn't surprising. She's a cliché, really. The rich housewife with the successful husband. She says what people want to hear, but who *is* she? To me, she seemed grabby and braggy and a little bit pushy. She's also a bit of a know-it-all. We need someone with a unique personality, not someone who will rub viewers the wrong way. The only one in this group that I could imagine carrying a television show is this young woman, Faith. To me she has the kind of passion and creativity we associate with our network."

"Then let's talk about Faith," said Sybil. "What did you all think of her?"

"I thought she was a bit manic," said Marcelle, "and I got a sense that she is the kind of person who will bite off more than she can chew, but that she'll do her very best to chew it anyway." They all laughed. I blushed but I had to agree with them.

"You're right, I do that a lot," I admitted. "But I would kill or die for this job. I'm Sybil's biggest fan. I can cook, I can bake, I'm very creative with decorating, I love beautiful clothes, I love dogs, and I've got that entrepreneurial spirit." I reached down to pat Rasputin's massive head, partly to help calm me and partly to dry my sweaty hands.

"My impression of Faith is that she seems to want to have very high standards—but perhaps hasn't quite managed to achieve this the way you yourself have, Sybil," said Phillip. "With time, perhaps, she will. She certainly has the energy, and I like her scrappiness."

"I also get a sense that she is all over the place, like maybe she's experimenting with a lot of different approaches or styles, and she hasn't quite discovered her own yet," said Marcelle.

"Like you yourself did, Sybil," said Ruth. "I see a lot of similarities between you and Faith. You're both entrepreneurs at heart, and I see a similar outside-the-box creativity that I think our viewers would respond to. I am worried, though, about Faith's inability to self-edit. She can sometimes come across as perhaps too honest."

"And what about Andy?" Sybil said.

They were all silent for a moment. Finally, Phillip spoke: "Andy is . . . well, let's just say I get the impression that he is a strategist."

"What do you think about that, Andy?" Sybil asked.

"Well, sure I am," he said. "This is a contest, and I want to win. It's all a game. Life is a game."

"I was concerned when I heard him talking to his makeover client about 'playing the game,' and how it would benefit him most if one or the other of these young ladies," Phillip said, gesturing to Shari and me, "were eliminated. I found this unprofessional and highly inappropriate, not to mention indicative of a character I don't think we necessarily want associated with our network."

"I agree," said Ruth. "I hardly think you can call Faith manic next to Andy, who makes her look like a Zen master." They all laughed again. She turned to Shari and me. "How did you both work with Andy?"

"I liked working with Andy," I said. "And I figure if I can work with Andy, I can work with anybody. I know it's important to be able to work with all kinds of creative types, even the ones with difficult personalities."

"I liked working with Andy, too!" Shari echoed, looking annoyed that she hadn't spoken first.

"I often couldn't even understand what he was saying—and I'm not sure I would have wanted to," said Marcelle. "Wait, I wrote this down." She looked at a pad of paper in front of her. "He said, 'I represent the paragon of the coming millennium for personal development in domestic marketing.' What does that mean? I don't even know what that means."

"He talks quite a lot, so we got quite a lot of information about him, but when he said things like, 'Someday, I'm going to be running this company,' well frankly, Sybil, I have to say I don't think I would trust him to be a team player," said Ruth. "And I certainly wouldn't want to give him any power."

"Can I just say something in my defense," Andy said, frantically. "I'm completely trustworthy. I don't know what you heard, but you must have misunderstood. I wasn't plotting against anyone." Shari made a little snorting sound. Andy turned on her. "If anybody is a plotter, it's Shari," Andy said. "She's the one you can't trust. She's nice to your face, but she'll cause major friction on a team because as soon as your back is turned, she'll exploit all your vulnerabilities for her own gain. She's been doing it throughout this entire experience—especially to Faith, her supposed best friend. She's been telling people not to speak to her, to try to get her eliminated. At the very beginning, she told Nadine never to get on a team with Faith because Faith would screw her over. She told Katie that Faith was spreading rumors about her party-girl past. She told Jodi Sue that Faith thought she was a moron, and maybe Faith did think Jodi Sue was a moron, I know I certainly did, but this is all while Faith's thinking Shari is her BFF."

I stared at Shari. Could it be true?

"I think you're projecting," said Shari calmly, not looking at me. "Because you're describing yourself, not me." But she looked rattled, like she'd been caught off guard and had lost control of the situation. Shari hated to lose control of any situation. If it was all true, she'd certainly been a master at hiding it. But not from Mikki. I remembered Mikki's whispered warning before she left: *Watch out for Shari.*

"At least I'm not a liar," Andy said.

"I'm not a liar," Shari said. "I'm a good friend."

"Yeah, if by good friend you mean backstabber," Andy said.

"Andy, who do you think should be sent home?" Sybil asked.

"Obviously Shari," he said without hesitation. "Faith has integrity. Shari just wants this for the power and the social prestige. She has no real interest in your company, or anyone but herself. And you can't trust her."

"Look who's talking," Shari said. "You're the power-hungriest of us all. You'll throw anybody under the bus to keep yourself safe. And you have no message."

"I work hard," he said. "That's my message."

"Faith, what about you?" Sybil asked. "Who do you think should be sent home?"

I was feeling a little stunned and conflicted. Could what Andy was saying really be true? I felt loyal to them both, even though it wasn't in my best interest at this moment. I had to be objective! The only thing I could do was speak the truth, as far as I knew it. What Andy said was hearsay. Shari was good. She'd never fallen down on a challenge. She was consistent and competent. I had no personal proof that she'd been backstabbing me all along.

And Andy? I really had thought he should be the one to go home, but suddenly I was questioning myself. But I had to be true to what I believed.

"I love Andy. I think he's got a very unique personality," I said. "He's incredibly creative and ambitious. But I also think he's a loose cannon. I don't know how consistent or dependable he is. I think . . . I think . . ." I almost didn't say it, but then I did: "I think Shari and I would make for a far more equitable and interesting face-off." I turned to Andy. "I'm sorry—don't take it personally."

He shrugged, looking offended. "It's all good. I'm your biggest defender, but whatever." I was sick to my stomach, especially seeing the look of hurt and disappointment on his face.

"Shari, who do you think should be sent home?" said Sybil. Shari was quiet for a moment. What would she say? Would she redeem herself, prove Andy wrong? Prove that she really was my friend?

She looked directly at Sybil and said, "Well, I wouldn't trust Andy farther than I could throw him, and believe me, I couldn't throw him very far." She laughed. "But . . ." She paused, looking at me for just a split second. "I think Faith is the one who should go home at this point."

What?

I stared at her. I couldn't believe what I was hearing. Or could I? Was she naming me because she thought I was her biggest threat? Because she knew she could beat Andy? Maybe she really had been the game player, the backstabber, the fake friend. Shari continued: "At least Andy has the kind of experience a network like this requires. He's got a dynamic personality and as a chef with an established reputation and clientele, I could envision him as the exciting, controversial star of his own show."

What was she doing? I was dumbfounded. But she wasn't finished.

"And honestly, I don't think Faith can be trusted. She's got weaknesses that haven't even been revealed on this show yet, and I believe she's hiding important information from you, Sybil. Important *personal* information."

My blood ran cold. She wasn't . . . she wouldn't . . . "Frankly," Shari went on, "Faith put me in a very awkward position by confiding personal information to me that I felt should be revealed to you, Sybil."

I couldn't believe she was saying it. *Don't say it, Shari, please don't say it,* I prayed silently.

"What kind of information?" said Sybil, raising her eyebrows at me.

Shari shook her head. "I'm not the kind of person to betray a secret, I'm a good friend, but I'm just saying, she isn't what she seems, in ways that directly impact *you,* Sybil." She wasn't looking at me. "In ways that impact . . . your son. If only you knew what went on between them . . ."

Sybil looked at me with narrow eyes, then glanced at the camera. "Faith, is there anything you would like to say to this?"

I stared at Shari. She stared back at me. Her face was completely cold, completely devoid of emotion or empathy. She gave me the tiniest smile—an evil smile. I didn't even recognize her. I looked at Sybil.

"I . . ." I swallowed. "I happened to meet Harris . . . I mean Harry . . . a few days before I was cast on the show," I said. "It was a total coincidence. I didn't have any idea who he was, and we didn't part on good terms. It's not like we're in a relationship or anything . . ." I realized as I said it that I wished we were. But that didn't seem likely now.

Sybil sighed. "I see," she said. "Well, I don't think that really has anything to do with the business at hand, and wasn't a particularly appropriate subject to bring up in this setting."

I looked up. Really? She wasn't going to hold that against me? It didn't seem possible.

Shari looked disconcerted, like her ace in the hole had failed her. She continued on at rapid-fire pace, trying another approach. "Well, in any case, Faith doesn't really have anything you could build a show around. I mean, muffins?" She chuckled nervously. "Please. Nobody wants to watch a show about muffins. And she doesn't fit in here. Frankly, she's a bit lowbrow for your network. I, on the other hand, understand what's appropriate, what's beautiful, what people want."

Finally I had my voice back. "Lowbrow? Did you just call me lowbrow?" I said. "With Andy over here talking about threesomes and his twelve-inch cock for the past two months?"

Andy grinned, proud of himself even after everything we'd said about him. Sybil cleared her throat. I'd said too much.

"See?" Shari said to Sybil. I'd just proved her point. "Lowbrow. And now she's going to sell out Andy."

"Excuse me, but you're selling *me* out." I turned to Sybil, trying to stay rational and not sound like I was pleading. "I think I've proved many times over during the challenges that I have the kind of ambition and spirit to make a show into anything. Sybil, I've always envisioned myself as your protégé, someone who could take your message to a whole new generation of women who might not know about it yet—young women who crave meaning and quality and validation in their lives." I was fighting for my life now. I'd never imagined it would come down to begging. "I understand you," I said. "And I understand what you try to do with your company. And I understand exactly what the next generation of women wants. I would be the most valuable employee you could imagine. *Please.*"

Sybil looked at me, but didn't say anything. Marcelle was nodding and smiling. The camera operators looked riveted. *At least we're making good TV*, I thought cynically.

I turned on Shari. "I always thought you deserved to be here because you're good at these challenges, and I do think you deserve to be in the final two. We've been through a lot together, you've been such a good friend to me, and I won't pretend to understand why you're saying these things about me now, except to say that I was warned about you, and I didn't listen because I trusted you."

Shari looked genuinely surprised. How could she not suspect that at least some people might notice her treachery and report it? I sent up a little prayer of thanks for Mikki's heads-up. "But you're not the right person to win," I said.

"Oh, I'm the right person alright," she said, smugly.

"No, Shari, you're not. What do you have to say? What's your expertise? You don't need the money, you can wipe your ass with hundred-dollar bills if you want to. Are you just bored? Are you just looking for something else to brag about?"

"I would be perfect for a show on Sybil's network," Shari said. "How dare you imply I don't need or deserve to win this show. I'm the best one here."

"What's your show going to be about?" I shot back. "Being a housewife? Who would ever want to watch a show about being a housewife?"

Sybil looked at the three of us and smiled. "Never underestimate the power of a housewife," she said.

I was really panicking now. I thought I was going to be sick right there in the room. Had I blown it? Was she going to cut me? I just couldn't believe Sybil would send me home after keeping me here for so long. But we'd all been here just as long. And somebody had to go.

"Shari, Faith, Andy, you've come a long way in this contest, and each one of you has distinguished yourselves. You've outlasted everyone else, but one of you has to go home today." She paused for what seemed like five full minutes, although it was probably only twenty seconds.

Finally, she spoke. "Andy, you've been unpredictable from the start. Your volatile behavior and uninhibited style have been the source of a lot of creativity throughout these challenges. You're a hard worker, and there are a lot of successful, passionate, volatile people out there. I'm sure you'll be successful in whatever you do. However, I'm afraid you aren't right for us here at Sybil Hunter Enterprises. I'm sorry, Andy, but you're just not necessary. Good-bye."

Wave after wave of emotion passed over Andy's face. He nodded and stood up. "Thank you, it's been an incredible opportunity," he said. He reached out his hand, and Sybil shook it firmly, looking him directly in the eye. "Good luck to you. I'm sure you'll do well." He didn't look at Shari or me, just turned and walked out of the room. And then he was gone.

I looked over at Shari with new eyes. I saw her now for what she really was: cunning and mean, and solely out to win the game. Well, I could be cunning, too. She smiled innocently at me, a "can you believe we did it?" expression, but it was too late for that. She had probably been sure it would come down to Andy and her, and now it was me. That wasn't what she'd planned. That was my advantage. Because now I knew who she really was—a snake. Someone I could never trust again, no matter what else happened, whether or not she ever apologized. I was through with her.

"Congratulations, Shari and Faith," said Sybil. "You are the final two. There is one last challenge to complete, and you will each get to choose three of the eliminated contestants to work for you. Choose carefully, as the employees we all hire can make or break us."

She looked at me. "Faith, your challenge will be to produce an indoor charity carnival, in conjunction with the Rainbow Ice Cream Company, to raise money for one of my favorite organizations, the Dreams Come True Foundation. The event must include a private reception for celebrity guests but will be open to the public. You must use all your skills and resources to create a memorable and profitable event."

She turned to Shari. "Shari, your challenge will be to produce a star-studded baby shower for my cousin, the film actress Natasha Darius, which will also raise money for another one of my favorite charities, the Babes in Arms Foundation. The shower will include guests Natasha selects as well as celebrities you recruit, who will be willing to donate money to the charity. You will each have a budget of five thousand dollars. You will have two days to complete your challenge. Now, I suggest you go back to the Loft and get some rest."

She stood and walked out of the room, followed by Alice and Ian. "Good luck," Alice said to us. "Chins up!" She winked at me. She of all people must know what it's like to be under Sybil's thumb.

Shari and I walked back to the Loft together without saying a word. Finally, when we got back inside, I turned on her. "Really?" I said.

"What?" she said.

"I thought you were my friend. I guess I was really dense to think that."

"Oh, Faith, stop," she said lightly. "You would have done the same thing."

"No, Shari. I wouldn't have, and didn't, because they asked me who should go home first, and I knew it should be Andy."

"You sold out Andy," she said. "I didn't do anything different than you did. You just don't like it because I chose you to go home first."

"It's not the same. I didn't say a single thing to Sybil Hunter that I hadn't already said to Andy to his face at one time or another. But you . . . you stabbed me in the back. You turned into somebody I've never even met. What happened to 'It's you and me'? Do you really think I'm the one who should go home?"

"Yes," she said, "I do. I want to win, and you're the one standing in my way."

"So it is a game to you. It's a strategy."

"Don't even pretend it's not just as much of a game to you," she said. "I see how you play the game. You're always plotting how to win. You just have a different strategy than I do."

"I don't worry about anyone else," I said. "That's my strategy. I always want to compete against the best. I said Andy should go home because he's not as good as you. You're the strongest opponent."

"At least we can agree on that," Shari said.

I could see that things had changed between us forever. "Who are you going to pick for your team?" I asked.

She shrugged. "Pick whomever you want. It doesn't matter. I can guarantee you, I'm going to win, no matter whom I choose. They all love *me,* and that's more than you can say. There are consequences, my friend, to being so *truthful* all the time." She slammed the bedroom door behind her.

I sat down on the couch, feeling completely alone in the huge Loft that once held twelve hopeful contestants. And now I had to choose three of the people who probably hated me to come back and help me. Chaz was my first friend, but he hadn't wanted to be there, so I didn't think he would want to come back, and he was so easily stressed that I couldn't imagine he would provide the kind of help I needed. Sadie had been cut too early to understand the pressure of what had to be done. Katie and Nadine definitely hated me, probably because of Shari, and Linda was too bossy and volatile for me. Christophe and Mikki were useless unless they were together. And even then, they weren't particularly helpful. Nice isn't the same as helpful. And they were probably on their honeymoon by now.

Although I was hesitant to turn around and hire him after saying he should be sent home, I wondered if I should choose Andy. What better environment for him than a carnival? He was big and over the top. Monica was a boozehound, but we'd parted on good terms, so she might actually be willing to try to help me. Or at least, not to stab me in the back. And . . . I hated to admit it, but the only other person I could really think of that knew me and knew how to work with me and hadn't totally despised me from the start was Jodi Sue. Andy was right, I did think she was a moron, and I knew she was pissed off at me for what I'd said about her after the food truck challenge, but she had more experience than Chaz or Sadie, and she understood the pressure and the rhythm this task would require. And she was the only other one I'd really worked with before. I'd never been on a team with Linda, Nadine, or Katie. At least Jodi Sue was a known quantity.

I wasn't remotely sure it would work, but they were the only choices I really felt I had. Andy, Monica, and Jodi Sue, a team of lesser evils. After a few minutes, Shari came back out of the bedroom in her robe to make some tea. She didn't offer to make me a cup. We didn't speak until the phone rang. I answered it.

"Hello, this is Polly. I need to know the team members you've chosen. I'll have them in the conference room to meet with you at nine tomorrow morning."

"Hi, Polly," I said. "I've decided on Andy, Monica, and Jodi Sue."

"Really?" said Polly. "Are you sure?"

"As sure as I'm ever going to be," I said.

"And who has Shari chosen?"

I handed Shari the phone. She murmured a few words, then I heard her say, "Katie, Nadine, and Linda." She hung up the phone and took her tea back into the bedroom.

I sighed and lay back on the couch. I didn't want to go into that bedroom, where Shari was sleeping. I didn't want to sleep where any of the others had slept, either. I could sleep out here. It was only for a few more nights. I shifted so I wasn't lying on the microphone pack on my back. I couldn't wait to take that thing off. I couldn't help but wonder where Harris was right at that moment. Was he in bed with Christine? Was he out at a club looking for the next girl, or was he home thinking about me?

And what would happen if Sybil saw the footage of Harris and me, from that day at her home? I was pretty sure she couldn't have seen it yet. She'd acted surprised tonight when she heard about Harris and me. If she knew or even suspected that there might still be something between us, I was sure I'd lose all her respect, and any chance of winning.

Would I be disqualified, after all of this? Would she make sure we never saw each other again? I couldn't bear the idea. I hadn't felt like this about anyone since Vince Beck. I was suddenly overwhelmed with sadness. Soon, very soon, I would at least get to go home and see my friends, especially Victoria and Bronwyn. Most of all, I wanted to hold sweet little Muffin in my arms. At least I had that to look forward to.

I woke up the next morning at five a.m. and went into the kitchen. I made brown rice with cinnamon, almond milk, and blueberries. I sat at the table and ate it in silence.

When Shari came out of her room an hour later, I was already dressed and working on a long list of ideas for the carnival.

chapter twenty-nine

Andy was surprisingly positive about being back, but also clearly resentful about our last encounter. He felt betrayed, which I totally understood. Monica seemed perfectly happy to help, but the way she babbled on about how much she missed us, and how she never really expected to win, and how she was just happy to be part of the finale, I wondered how much serious work I was really going to get out of her. Jodi Sue was still nursing a major grudge and pouted through our first meeting, but I ignored her attitude and pretended she was on board.

We jumped right into work. First we had to meet the Rainbow Ice Cream Company representatives at the venue, a warehouse-style nightclub on Bleecker Street. It was a warm and sunny August day and the Rainbow Ice Cream team all wore shorts and polo shirts with rainbows on the fronts. They looked out of place in the dark club, but they were all business when it came to how the carnival would feature their product.

Then we met with the club manager, who asked us what we needed. I had all my notes on a clipboard and a pen behind my ear. "We're going to need a lot more lighting in here, so we'll be installing spotlights and stand-up gels. I'll also need all the furniture cleared out. We need open spaces on all levels, except for a café area. We also need your largest private room for the VIP reception," I said.

After the meeting, I called the best event-planning company I knew—the one I used to work for, Event-ually. I was able to get my former boss, Leslie Brauer, on the line. "Leslie, this is Faith Bright-stone."

"Faith! It's great to hear from you, how are you?"

"Leslie, I need a huge favor. I need to hire you, and I need to hire you now. I have to produce a charity carnival in two days. It has to raise money, it has to be fantastic, and I need resources. Please tell me you can drop whatever you are doing and send everyone possible my way to help me. I can guarantee you it will be worth any inconvenience."

"What's this for? We're pretty booked . . ." she said, hesitantly.

"Can we meet? I'll be able to explain better when we meet, but believe me, if you will do this, it will be very good for your business. Big, big exposure." I knew she'd understand more once she saw the cameras following me, but I wasn't allowed to mention them on the phone.

"I have some time at lunch," Leslie said. "Do you want to meet at the usual place?"

"Lunch is perfect. I'll see you there at twelve."

Twenty-seven hours to go. I sent Jodi Sue to a vendor I knew back from my event-production days that rented cotton candy and popcorn machines. "I'm putting you in charge of all the concessions, can you handle that?" She scowled at me. "Look, don't take it personally," I said. "I'm sorry if I hurt your feelings, but we all need to pull together now and make this work. I chose you because you're good." I figured a little flattery couldn't hurt. "And frankly, you're getting more airtime, which can only help you, right?"

She shrugged, still sulking but mildly placated. "Whatever," she said. "I'll help you but I'm not endorsing you."

"That's fine!" I said. "I don't need your endorsement, I just need your two hands and your brain. Now Andy, I need you to wrangle the performers. Get with the Rainbow people. They've booked the characters who will be walking around the carnival, dressed like giant ice cream cones. They also said they could get some stilt walkers and jugglers who can walk around the carnival. Kids will love that. Find out who they all are and what else they need."

"Yes, boss," he said, saluting me.

"And Monica, I need you to work with the charity. Find out their expectations and what they need? Remember, it's a children's charity, so be G rated, OK?"

"Sure, Faith," she said. "I'll take care of it."

"Now I've got to run to a meeting. Everybody go! Let's meet back at the workroom at two."

I spent the rest of the morning making arrangements with Leslie, my event planner, who thankfully agreed to put all her available people on the job to help me. Leslie said she could get a brass band, and she knew a company that rented carnival staging and rides. But how were we going to make money? We would charge admission and sell concessions, of course, but we needed something more. Back at the workroom, Monica told me the charity was expecting to make a sizable amount of money from our event.

"What about a silent auction?" she said.

"Monica, that's brilliant," I said. She looked proud of herself. "Find people to donate items. Can you organize it?"

She looked unsure. "I'll help her," said Jodi Sue.

"Now Andy—this is crucial—I need you to find people to operate the carnival rides—people that don't look like they slept under a bridge. OK?"

"I'm all over it," he said.

I spent the rest of the afternoon running around and making calls. I was wired . . . the kind of wired you get when you've got to perform and be brilliant on no sleep and very little food. It was the last push, and I knew after it was over, I could go home—and maybe even sleep through a night. But not yet.

Twenty hours to go. In the bathroom outside the workroom,

I stared at myself in the mirror in a daze. Polly walked in. "You're doing great, but you don't look so good," she said.

"I know, but what am I going to do? I can sleep when I'm dead."

She washed her hands, looking at me. "From the way you look, that might be sooner than you think. It's just a show; it's not your life."

"It is my life right now," I said.

"Your life shouldn't kill you."

"I know," I said. "But it's all I've got. It's all I want."

She crossed her arms. "You're really smart," she said. "And I can tell you're going places. Just be sure this is where you want to go. Sybil's no picnic."

I laughed. "Are you allowed to say that? Doesn't she have you wired?"

"Of course she does," Polly said. "That's my point. It's working for an overlord. She doesn't appreciate what people do for her. She's forgotten what it's like to struggle, to be coming up from the bottom. She used to remember, but she can't afford to look too far back anymore."

"Why do you keep working for her?" I asked.

"I've learned more than I ever would have dreamed from Sybil Hunter. She's brilliant. But I don't plan to work here forever."

"If I ever get to where she is," I told her, "I'll hire you."

"I wouldn't be at all surprised if that happens," she said. She turned to leave the bathroom, but paused by the door. "And Faith, if you do ever get to that level?"

"Yes?" I said.

"Remember where you came from," she said.

Fifteen hours to go. We'd gotten the programs to the printer just before they closed. Monica and Jodi Sue had rounded up a huge list of sponsors. The carnival rides were all under control. The venue was ready. But I still had a checklist a mile long, and we kept going, kept pushing, kept checking off items one by one, until we were all exhausted.

We passed out in the Loft on the living room couches, while Shari's team holed up in the bedroom. We hardly spoke to them. They were now the enemy. It was official. No more secrecy.

Two hours to go. Everything was falling apart. I'd just screamed at Jodi Sue. It was all going to hell. And here I was standing outside, knowing Sybil Hunter was in the building behind me, registering every mistake: the popcorn machine dripping oil, the signs that fell down and tore, the spotlight that didn't work, the audio system that popped in and out, and worst of all, the missing performers. We had no ice-cream-cone mascots, no jugglers, and no stilt walkers. The rides weren't fully assembled yet, and a crowd was already gathered outside. We still had balloons to tie, streamers to hang, the brass band to organize. I hoped Monica was handling the VIP reception until I got there. I prayed Jodi Sue had the food carts ready to go and had finished up the details on the silent auction before I'd pissed her off with my ill-timed request that she go sit in the corner and keep her mouth shut.

But where was Andy? I felt like I'd spent the last two months frantically waiting for someone to show up right before a challenge, but this was the most important one of all, and I was in full panic mode.

Then I saw him—Andy, driving the van. He pulled up in front of the building, and the stilt walkers and jugglers and people in their ice-cream-cone costumes, holding their giant ice-cream heads in their hands, piled out.

"This way!" I said, directing them into the building. "Please get set up and ready to go in thirty." Andy jumped out. "Where the hell have you been?" I practically shrieked at him. "You about gave me a heart attack!"

"One of the jugglers was late, so we had to wait. But we're here, it's OK," he said. "Andy saves the day." He flexed his muscles.

"Yes, you're a paragon of testosterone, now get inside and help me! I've already burned my last bridge with Jodi Sue, and Monica's busy in the VIP room—I hope."

Together, we ran back in, down the hallway, and into the main carnival area, practically running into Jodi Sue. "I'm leaving," she said.

"You're leaving?" Andy said. "You can't leave."

"Just watch me." Cameras hovered behind her. "You've insulted me one too many times, Faith. Your programs are by the door and the food carts are all ready. I've done my job." She walked out the door.

"What was that all about?" Andy said.

"Oh, I made a rude comment about her cleavage when she told me she was bailing," I said.

"If you didn't, I would have," he said. "That was some tight shirt."

"She was heading straight toward sabotage mode. Whatever, we don't have time to dwell on it. We're better off with her gone. Go check on the status of the lights and sound and just be down on the floor to direct anybody who needs to know what they should be doing, OK? And get the band started!" I said.

Thirty minutes to go. I ran upstairs to check on the VIP reception. Monica was chatting up all the celebrities and I prayed she wasn't drinking. From this vantage, looking down on the carnival, it looked like a big mess. My exhaustion was making me almost hysterical, as I saw how many things were going wrong. Then the jugglers and the stilt walkers all came out at once, in their vibrant costumes. The lights popped on and the whole carnival was lit with color and swirling spotlights. It was impressive. It really was. I might just pull this off.

It was almost noon, so I went back downstairs, grabbed my megaphone and the stack of programs, signaled the sound guy to start the carnival-music loop, and stepped outside. The entrance looked fantastic. I only hoped Sybil would agree.

And then it was go time. "Welcome everyone," I said through the megaphone, my voice just slightly quivering with nerves. "Welcome to the Rainbow Carnival! All proceeds benefit the Dreams Come True Foundation! Have a Rainbow Ice Cream and ride the rides!"

Over the next four hours, the carnival had its highs and lows. A sign fell down, a bank of lights blew out, and the band wasn't very good. The kiddie roller coaster broke and we had to close it and lift seven kids out of their seats and carry them down a ladder. But when Sybil, Alice, and Ian showed up at the ticket booth, I ushered them inside and showed them around, and at that moment, everything seemed to be working exactly as it should. Sybil seemed particularly impressed when a stilt walker loped by us in his eight-foot-long silk harlequin pants and called out to her: "Have a Rainbow Day, Ms. Hunter!"

At the Rainbow Ice Cream booth, the representative gave them each an ice cream cone, and although she didn't actually ride any of the rides, Sybil spent a long time walking through, followed by her dog, commenting quietly to Alice and Ian. The VIP reception was over by the time she arrived, but a few celebrities still wandered the crowd with their children, causing a stir wherever they went. Sybil seemed impressed. She actually looked like she was having fun.

I watched her like a hawk. What would she decide? I wanted it so badly, I couldn't even fully comprehend it myself. I'd never wanted anything more.

When we finally closed our doors and counted our money, we'd raised almost $80,000, most of it from the silent auction. Was it finally over? Was that it? Now what?

I felt like I was in limbo. We still had to meet with Sybil one more time, but I knew we wouldn't find out the winner yet—not for six more months. I couldn't even begin to imagine how I would be able to wait that long. But of course, I had no choice.

Back at Sybil's conference room, I was riding high from our success. Andy and I kept high-fiving each other. Monica was tired but smiling. Jodi Sue had returned, but looked petulant. "You guys all did great," I said. "Really great. I think we did the best we could have possibly done."

"Do you think we'll win?" Andy said to the team.

"You mean do you think *she'll* win?" Jodi Sue said. "*We've* already lost."

I could see that Shari was flushed with excitement, too. Her challenge had obviously gone well. I wished I could have gotten a peek at it. A celebrity baby shower was exactly her element. Nadine, Katie, and Linda looked elated, too. But none of us could possibly know who would be the winner.

"I was very pleased with the results of this final challenge," Sybil told us. Nobody dared to speak. "These challenges were the most difficult yet. You had very little time to make these complex events happen."

She turned to me. "Faith, your carnival was fun. It was exciting and dramatic, and had all the elements of a successful event. It wasn't without flaws, however. There were some raised eyebrows in the VIP event, and I don't believe you properly managed Monica, whom I'm afraid to say might have been enjoying the wine a bit too much. Some inappropriate things were said."

Monica blushed but didn't say anything. I kicked myself for not checking up on her more often during the event, but I'd had my hands full at the door and on the floor.

"I also noticed some shoddy workmanship on the banners, and there were some technical glitches with the lighting and music. Also, I understand one of your team members walked out on you, which speaks to your management skills."

I nodded, mutely. What could I say? She was probably right. A good manager wouldn't insult her employees.

"However," Sybil went on, "the programs were beautiful, the food was quite good for carnival food, the crowd really seemed to enjoy the rides and games, and perhaps most important, you raised $80,000 for the Dreams Come True Foundation, a truly impressive amount. Rainbow Ice Cream was also quite pleased with the publicity they received from this event. They said, and I quote, 'The Rainbow Carnival was up to our high standards.' Congratulations, Faith, on a job well done."

"Thank you," I said, beaming. "It wasn't easy, but I feel like we really pulled it off."

"Shari," Sybil said, turning to her. "The baby shower for Natasha Darius was spectacular. You managed to compile quite an impressive list of celebrity attendees, along with all of Natasha's friends, and everyone raved about the beautiful décor, the delicious food, and of course, the centerpiece of the event, the stunning four-tiered pink champagne cake, covered in fresh flowers. The photographer doing guest photos was a lovely touch, and the baby fashion show was brilliant. Your team appeared to work well together, with no internal squabbling, which speaks to your superior management abilities. Also, many celebrities donated large sums, and your event brought in $43,000 for the Babes in Arms Foundation. Very good job, Shari."

I could tell Shari was annoyed that my event had brought in more money, but she looked haughtily proud nevertheless, probably still coming off her celebrity-contact high.

"Of course, while the charity component was important, it was not the sole determinant of the winner. That will be up to me. You won't find out who has won the competition until we come back for the live finale in January," Sybil continued. "I wish you safe travels on your journey home, and I'll see you in January."

She stood up and walked out, followed by her dog. As the cameras followed her, I realized that it was finally over. I could go back to my actual life now. Unimaginable. Back to Muffin, whom I missed more than I could express.

It was oddly easy to leave. I took off the microphone pack, picked up my already packed bag, and after a few quick good-byes, walked out of the building and climbed into the car the production company had arranged to take me home. Alone in the backseat, with nothing but my suitcase, I suddenly broke down into tears. The emotions had been so intense, and after white-knuckling everything for the past two months, it was finally miraculously over. I sobbed from exhaustion, from emotion, from feeling so frayed that there was barely any of me left. The car ride was so quiet, peaceful . . . lonely.

I watched the city go by the window, the streets full of people. I knew my apartment would be empty until I went back out to pick up Muffin, but I was tempted to just crawl into bed and sleep for a week, not talk to anyone, just try to forget, try to pass the next six months in solitude. When the driver pulled up at my building, I wiped the tears from my face, thanked him, and went inside, up the elevator, and then I wheeled my suitcase down the hall toward my apartment door. And, there he was, holding a bouquet of roses.

"Hi," he said.

My heart stopped. I smiled, in spite of myself. "Hi."

chapter thirty

Harris was a hand holder, a hugger, and an amazing kisser, and he made me feel safe. Muffin actually liked him, which was definitely in his favor. We became inseparable.

I saw Harris several times a week at first, and then almost every day, but our relationship was a secret. We couldn't imagine what Sybil might do to me if she knew. I worried about the footage from Sybil's home, but so far, I'd heard nothing, so I hoped for the best. We were careful. My friends weren't allowed to meet him, or even know who he was, no matter how much they begged. I felt like he was my secret. We lived in our own private little world. It was beautiful.

I was ecstatic to be free from the confines of that horrible reality show, and being out of that Loft made me realize exactly how awful it really had been. At the time, I'd handled it, because I had no choice. Now I appreciated my freedom like I never had before—the fact that I could go to the bathroom without a camera waiting outside, sleep without a microphone pack, was a miracle. I could go out for coffee with my friends, I could walk down the street alone, I could spend a quiet morning doing absolutely nothing. Sometimes I felt like I was still in shock, like I had post-traumatic stress disorder, or like my life wasn't quite real.

During my sixty-day absence, my bakery business hadn't done so well. Alanna had fulfilled all the orders from the trade show, but the business had become too expensive to keep going, so after talking with my business partner, Stefan, I temporarily shuttered it, since neither of us knew whether I'd be free to continue with it. It all depended on whether I won the show. It wasn't time to try to grow the business anymore. My whole life was in wait-and-see mode.

But that was OK with me. It gave me more time, and my favorite way to spend the evening was with Muffin on my lap and Harris's arm around my shoulders. I was rapidly falling for the son of the Domestic Goddess herself. Life was pretty good, even with all the uncertainty.

I was still obsessing almost constantly about the finale, and who would win, and how it would go, and what Sybil had decided, and what Shari might be up to, but I was happy, too. I hadn't been really happy in a long time. My life was finding its rhythm again.

Harris and I spent the last week in August at the beach together, in a house his mother owned but rarely visited. "She's not really a beach person," he told me. "She'll never even know we were here." One night, after a bottle of wine, Harris took my hand and led me out to the ocean's edge. The moon was out and the dark water shimmered. We dipped our toes in. The water was cold, but the August heat was oppressive. Then Harris gently lifted my dress over my head, peeled off his own clothes, and dove into the surf. I didn't need an invitation to follow. That night, we made love for the first time, under the moon, covered in saltwater and sand.

We shared everything, in long rambling conversations. The show, our strange relationship and how it had developed, and our parents—such as they were. He told me all about growing up with Sybil, and how hard he'd tried to stay out of the spotlight, and how she'd bribed him to help her with the show by promising she would never ask him to appear on television again.

He told me how close he had been with his father, and how hard it had been when his father died. Harris had been just fourteen. "Someday, when I have children, I'm going to make up for what I missed," he said.

Life in his house was always about his mother, her fame, and her brand. After his father died, he felt sorry for his mother because she had no husband, but he said she used that against him, guilting him into things he didn't want to do. And then there were her boyfriends. "I never knew if the next man to come into our lives wanted her because of her, or because of her fame and money," he said. "After a while, I didn't care. I had to get away from all that to figure out who I was, apart from 'Sybil Hunter's son.'"

I told him about my parents, too—my painful relationship with my father, how he'd been absent through most of my childhood and how I was never able to connect with him, and my dysfunctional relationship with my mother, her drinking, her wild tantrums, her constant money issues, her condescending attitude. I told him how they had both disappointed and hurt me over and over again until I'd finally decided to break off communication, for my own sanity. I was so relieved that he didn't encourage me to reconnect with them, as so many others had. "If they hurt you, you don't need them in your life," he said. "Family is about love, not blood." I smiled to myself, and let myself daydream, for just a moment: What if Harris was my family? Could that ever happen?

As we were lying in bed on the morning right before we had to leave the beach house, he said, "I think I fell in love with you when you told Christine you could see her muffin." He laughed. "That still cracks me up. I've never heard anybody talk to her like that."

I snuggled up against him and he held me tighter.

"I love you, you know," he said, kissing the top of my head.

I closed my eyes. For the first time in my life, I felt like the person saying those words to me was actually telling the truth. I wasn't quite ready to say it back . . . but I thought I might actually love him. If I said it out loud, would I jinx it? Could I really trust him with my heart? Would he hurt me, the way Vince Beck had? Would I hurt *him*? Would I leave him, like I left the others? I decided to wait. Better to be completely sure, without a doubt. And until the *Domestic Goddess* finale, I couldn't really trust myself to be sure about anything.

Crisp fall air outside, and the leaves in Central Park just starting to turn. It was the middle of October, and I felt more deeply content than I had in years, as Harris and Muffin and I sat together in my warm apartment to watch the premiere of *Domestic Goddess* with baked ziti in the oven and a bottle of wine on the coffee table.

None of my friends could believe I hadn't been allowed to see the show yet, but I hadn't even had a sneak preview, and I was dying to see it! The week before it aired, it was all I thought about. Harris and I discussed it endlessly: Did I want to invite people over? Was it premature for them to meet him? Should I invite the girls over and not watch it with him? But no, we had to watch it together! Finally, I decided I would be so incredibly nervous and wound up, I was better off just watching it with Harris and Muffin and a bottle of wine.

I couldn't wait to see what the producers had made out of the thousands of hours of footage they must have had from our sixty-day imprisonment—and I hoped they didn't make me look bad! The network had bombarded the television with ads promoting the show for the last few weeks, with tantalizing clips, but not enough to really tell anything. There was one clip of Shari and me whispering, another of Andy and me acting silly in the Loft, and one of me leaning out the hot dog truck window yelling, "What up, dog?" but everything was so brief, it was hard to discern what the show would be like.

And Harris and I couldn't help asking each other, again and again: Had Sybil seen it yet? Did she know about us? She hadn't said a word to him, but that didn't mean she didn't know. It was all a waiting game, but finally, the evening arrived.

Harris sat down next to me, wine glass in hand. "Are you ready?" he said.

"I hope so!" I said, feeling both eager and terrified.

My phone vibrated. It was a text from Perry, watching the show in L.A.: *It's really happening! I can't wait to see you on TV!*

The music started. "Look!" I said to Harris. "There's your house!"

As dramatic music swelled, the camera panned over Sybil's property: inside shots of the magnificent kitchen, the charming sitting rooms, the butler's pantry, the orchard, the gardens, and tree-lined drive. And then there was Sybil, standing in her kitchen.

"They say home is where the heart is, but running a home with skill and proficiency isn't something you do in your spare time. It's a full-time job," she said, in her curt and sensible way. "That is, if you want to be . . ."—quick pulsing shots of Sybil stirring something in a soup pot, arranging flowers, picking a tomato, brushing her dog, and standing at the head of a conference room table in a suit—"a Domestic Goddess." A pulsing beat kicked in then . . . shots of New York, of Sybil's building, of her offices.

My phone vibrated again, this time from Victoria: *Sybil's so full of it!*

"There you are!" said Harris, as they showed me getting out of the car.

"They didn't use the part where I stared directly at the camera like a moron," I said.

You look so powerful! And nervous! said a text from Bronwyn.

They showed other contestants arriving, and all of us sitting in the conference room, as Sybil's voiceover explained how the competition would work. Shari and I were whispering together and giggling. It made me sad. Harris took my hand and squeezed.

That bitch, said a text from Perry. I'd told her all about Shari during a long catch-up phone conversation.

They showed the moment when Ian McGinnis revealed that he knew me, and Sybil's angry glare. "She did *not* like that," Harris said.

Oh my God, I remember him! A text from Jeannie, also watching from L.A. *Thank God you didn't sleep with him!*

"She didn't like that I knew him, or that she didn't know about it first?" I said.

"That you knew him at all," Harris said. "She was ready to cut you right from the start. I remember her talking about it, before I knew it was you. You're supposed to be below her, not hanging with her peeps."

"Or sleeping with her son."

"Yeah . . . let's hope she doesn't find out about that one for a while," he said.

"Because you're ashamed of me?" I said, half serious.

"Because we want you to *win*," he said.

"There's Chaz!" I said. "I miss him. But he hated it there."

They showed a long segment of Chaz and me making the pink lemonade mojito, then shamelessly swilling it.

I remember that drink!!! A text from Brooke. I wondered if she was watching the show with my father.

"They're using a lot of clips of you," he said. "Probably because you're so cute and funny."

"You just notice my clips because you love me," I said.

"That must be it," he agreed.

And there I was again, in one of the interview clips: "So, everybody's still working on their tasks, and Chaz and I are boozing it up," I said to the camera. It was strange to watch myself on television. "I'm sure Sybil would be so impressed with our behavior. Hey, Shybil," I slurred from the TV screen, pretending to be drunk, "Why don't you come have a little drinky with us!"

Harris laughed. "That's my girl," he said.

They showed a clip of Shari ordering around Jodi Sue, demanding she place the flowers on the cupcakes in a certain way.

We hate Shari! said a text from Victoria.

"They're making Shari look horrible," I said. "Was she that obnoxious?"

"I thought she was pretty obnoxious," said Harris. "But not as insufferable as that crazy Katie woman with her astrology fetish."

"She was just certifiably insane," I said.

"Or Nadine."

"You mean, Your Excellency, Queen Nadine?"

Finally, the closing credits rolled. "It's weird to see how they put it together and how it looks compared to how it really was," I said. "It was so much more stressful and grueling. They make it look almost fun."

"I wonder how my mother thinks it went," Harris mused. "She comes across as pretty cold."

"In person, too," I said. "No offense to your mother."

"None taken," Harris said. "She's not exactly the warm-and-fuzzy type."

The next day, my world turned upside down. First, the phone rang at eight a.m.

"Faith Brightstone? This is Cathy Tower from Ovation Network. How are you this morning?"

"Fine," I said, suspiciously. What did they want from me now? I was in the kitchen making coffee, holding the phone against my ear with my shoulder.

"Great," she said. "Hey, I'm just giving you a call because our website has been flooded with requests for the pink lemonade mojito recipe. We would like to offer you the chance to write a note to your fans along with the recipe, which we will post on our website."

It took a minute for this to sink in. "Fans?" I said.

"Yes, fans. You've got a lot of them, and they want your recipe."

"I could do that," I said.

"Do you think you could have it to me by this afternoon? We want to take advantage of the momentum."

"Of course," I said. It was another challenge.

I sat down at my computer and thought for a minute. Then I checked my e-mail.

I had more than three hundred messages.

Dear Faith: You don't know me, but I just wanted to tell you how much I enjoyed you on the show last night.

Dear Faith Brightstone: You are hilarious! My fave on the show. Is this really your e-mail?

Dear Ms. Brightstone: You were wonderful on Domestic Goddess. I hope you win!

Dear Faith: I love you! I can totally relate to you. You remind me of me.

Dear Faith Brightstone: Your pink lemonade mojito looked so delicious. Can you please send me the recipe?

Dear Faith: Watch out, I think Sybil's got it in for you! You totally should have won that challenge.

And it went on and on like this. Some were long, people sending me their whole life stories. Others were more bursts of encouragement, but they all said some version of the same thing: We liked you!

"Harris, quick, come look at this!" He came out of the bedroom in his pajama bottoms and peered at the computer over my shoulder, rubbing his eyes. "How did all these people find my e-mail address?"

"Wow!" he said. "It looks like you have fans."

"Ovation wants my Have Faith Pink Lemonade Mojito recipe."

"Do you own the rights to it?" he said.

"I think so," I said.

"Let's be sure," he said, always the lawyer. "Before you hand it over."

It was a strange feeling. People all over the country knew who I was, and not only that, they were motivated to reach out to me. I decided to check Facebook. I had hundreds of posts!

Faith, you're the best!

Love u on Domestic Goddess!

Rooting for u!

You crack me up—LMFAO during all your scenes!

Your drink was the best! Wish I had the recipe on my ePhone right now!

Who needs cupcakes? We want cocktails!

Having a mojito in your honor, wish it was pink!

You and that geezer Ian? Seriously? Girl, you can do better.

If we could vote I would vote for u!

Holy shit balls, this was crazy! And just the beginning. The e-mails and Facebook messages doubled with each passing episode, and the network began to send me huge packets of fan mail. The reports were that the ratings were high, and polls about each character showed me running as extremely popular. The fan mail confirmed it. "America loves you!" as Harris put it.

It was all too strange to comprehend. I began to get calls to appear on morning shows, news programs, afternoon talk shows, radio interviews.

After the second episode, where Harris and I had our exchange in the craft room, the letters and e-mails and phone calls exploded, and I had to unlist my phone number. Victoria, who called me the minute every episode was over, was practically screaming at me over the phone. "Is it Harry Jansen? Tell me the guy you've been seeing is Harry Jansen. You guys have *chemistry*!"

"You'll know soon enough," I said.

"Damn it, Faith! I'm not a patient woman!" she said.

The entertainment shows kept bringing up the amazing reappearance of Harry Jansen, and speculating on his relationship with *Domestic Goddess* fan favorite Faith Brightstone: "Are they or aren't they?" they all asked.

"We are now," Harris said, with a laugh. I laughed, too, but I was worried. Surely, Sybil was aware of all this. I felt I'd finally earned her respect during the show, but what did she think of me, now that the whole world was speculating about my relationship with her son, whom she was so sure belonged to someone else?

And sure enough, the network was savvy enough to run everything they had taped at Sybil Hunter's house. It was a ratings bonanza. The viewers thought I was hilarious, and they were rapt by the now not-so-private heart-to-heart I'd had with Harris there.

"Shit, Harris, what are we going to do?"

"She doesn't know we're involved now," he said. "She asked me about it . . ."

"What? She asked you? What did she say?"

"She asked me if I was still in touch with you."

"What did you say?"

"I kind of implied we weren't."

I wasn't sure whether to be offended or relieved.

"Am I off the show?"

"Are you kidding?" Harris said. "The network isn't going to allow that, no matter how powerful my mother thinks she is. You're making them millions."

Watching the episodes, I saw things I never knew about during the filming, like what other people said about me when I wasn't in the room. And I began to see that I'd been duped by Shari all along. In her OTFs and interviews, or when interacting with the other contestants, she said things like "I don't think Faith is going to make it much further," or "If someone has to go, it should probably be Faith," or "If they ask you, I would advise you to say what you really think about Faith," or "I only wish I could tell you what Faith Brightstone just told *me*!" How could I have been so blind?

"She just went for your weak spot, like a jackal," Harris said. "She could tell you needed someone to talk to. Forget her. Forget them all."

"I'm going to have to face them all in a few weeks," I said. "So I can't exactly forget them. And at some point, they're going to find out that you and I are actually together."

"Let's worry about that when the time comes," Harris said, pulling me into his chest and hugging me.

The finale was three weeks away, and I was getting more and more anxious. Every day, I played over the last challenge in my mind—everything that happened at my benefit carnival, and everything that might have happened at Shari's baby shower. What had Sybil said about me behind closed doors, to Ian and Alice and Ruby Prasad? I imagined Alice defending me, Ian defending me. I imagined Ruby arguing that I should be cut, and Sybil nodding and smiling with that little devious knowing smile she had. If she had even an inkling that I was with her son, all the respect I'd earned from her would most certainly become a thing of the past. I would become her enemy. Would she really want me to host a show on her network, even if she secretly thought I was the best choice? No way. Even without the Harris factor, the more I knew her and watched her and heard about her from Harris, the more I suspected we would clash too much. I was no Sybil Hunter clone, and if that's what she wanted . . .

And then, there was the question that was beginning to bother me more and more: if I did win, would I really *want* to work for her? I tried to imagine what life would be like, hosting my own show on Sybil Hunter's network. Would she actually let me do what I wanted to do? It was hard to imagine that I'd have much creative control. If I'd learned one thing from my experience on *Domestic Goddess,* it was that anybody who threatens Sybil's control better watch her back.

Harris agreed. "I'm not sure you'd like working for my mother," he said, cautiously. "She likes people who worship her, not people who could actually compete with her. I know you want to win. I know how competitive you are. But do you really want to have that kind of life? In my mother's shadow?"

"I have a pretty big shadow myself," I said. But I couldn't help remembering what Polly had told me. *Sybil's no picnic.*

"I know," he said. "That's the problem. You're too much alike. I think she would make life . . . difficult for you."

The finale was two weeks away when Harris and I went to a little bar near my apartment, and I started to explain to a bartender how to make me a pink lemonade mojito. He surprised me when he said he already knew. "People order that all the time in here," he said.

"What?" I said.

"Sure, they heard about it from some reality show. Everybody loves it. Here you go," he said. "We make up the pink lemonade in batches now, to meet the demand."

"Maybe you should market that drink," Harris said.

"I was just thinking the same thing," I said. "I wonder if any liquor companies would be interested."

"Obviously, people want to drink it, so why wouldn't they want to buy it in a bottle?"

"I would," I said. "If I would, other women would."

"And men," Harris said. "I love this stuff." He grinned at me. "Even though it's pink."

"I like a guy who's not afraid to admit to his girly side," I said. "Let's design a logo!" I took a pen from my purse and began drawing on a cocktail napkin.

The next day, Harris and I looked up the numbers of some of the big liquor companies, and I made some quick calls to see if anyone would be interested in meeting with me. I told them who I was, what kind of publicity the drink was already getting, and my vision for it: a bottled mojito with the alcohol already in it. I got almost the same responses from everyone:

"We don't market to women."

"Ready-to-drink cocktails are a tiny market."

"It's not the kind of thing we do."

But then, a few days later, the phone rang. "Faith Brightstone?"

"Yes?"

"This is Myra Eastman with Bacchus Global Liquors. I'd like to talk to you about your Have Faith pink lemonade mojito. Do you have time to meet with me this week?"

"I think I can find some time for that," I said. I hung up the phone. "Harris!" I yelled. "We got a bite!"

I met with Myra Eastman the next day, and I brought along Harris.

I didn't think there would be a risk of us being seen together because nobody else knew about the meeting, and I knew he was good with contracts. It's one thing to say you'll show something to your lawyer. It's another thing to have your handsome young lawyer at your side.

"You would have to produce the drink according to my recipe," I said.

"Of course," Myra Eastman said, "as long as it works for mass production."

"We need it in writing," Harris said. "And you'll be a partner, you won't own the brand."

"I can talk to our lawyers about that," Myra said.

"You don't have the power to negotiate?" Harris asked.

"Well . . . I do, but . . ."

"I need to be able to approve all marketing of the drink," I said. "I don't want you misrepresenting me."

"And Faith will be the primary spokesperson," Harris added.

"Now, is there any issue with Ovation TV or Sybil Hunter having any ownership over the drink, since it was first publicized on the show?"

Fortunately, the one thing I'd managed to wrangle out of my contract was an agreement that anything I thought of on my own, before or after the show, would belong exclusively to me. I'd been protecting my muffin business at the time, but I realized now this could apply to anything I invented or any business I decided to start. "No, I was making this drink before I was on the show," I said.

Myra Eastman agreed to talk with her supervisors and draft a contract we could look over. She said she'd be back in touch with me after the finale. Harris and I walked out of the building hand in hand. "I think this calls for a drink!" I said.

And then, I met my first paparazzo. "Miss Brightstone! Faith! Hey, Faith is that Harry?"

chapter thirty-one

There we were, on the front page of the gossip section in the *New York Sentinel,* holding hands for the world to see. Harris looked startled (and superhot), and I looked, well . . . if not superhot, at least respectable in the business suit I'd worn to the meeting. The headline: *"Domesticating with Sybil Hunter's Son?"*

I grabbed the paper off the newsstand and read it frantically:

> *One week before the live finale of the popular reality show* Domestic Goddess, *finalist Faith Brightstone is seen exiting the Bacchus Global Liquors offices, hand in hand with host Sybil Hunter's son, Harry Jansen, from Hunter's first marriage to the late media tycoon Reginald Jansen. Friends and colleagues speculate that Brightstone and Jansen were involved throughout the filming of* Domestic Goddess, *and that Brightstone may also be in talks to sell her trendy pink lemonade mojito to Bacchus Global for an undisclosed sum. Will Brightstone's off-camera antics seal her win, or destroy her chances for real stardom? Sybil Hunter did not immediately return our calls.*

Shit. This was bad. The timing couldn't be worse. Why couldn't this have happened *after* the finale? And what "friends and colleagues" had dared to comment? Had they questioned the other contestants? Had Shari Jacobs tipped them off? Had they interrogated Victoria? Bronwyn? Were they following me? Furious, I bought the paper and immediately called Harris, but he didn't answer his phone. "Answer, Harris. Answer the phone!" I said to myself, dialing him again, and then again. I hoped he was in a meeting and that he'd call me back as soon as he saw I'd called. Then my phone beeped and I clicked over.

"Did you see the *Sentinel?*" Victoria screamed in my ear.

"I'm looking at it right now! What am I going to do?" I said.

"You're just going to have to play it cool," she said. "Just pretend you didn't do anything wrong."

"But I didn't do anything wrong!" I protested.

"Right! That's good!" she said.

The phone beeped again.

"Victoria, I have to go," I said. I clicked over again.

"Faith, this is Cathy Tower from Ovation Network. We need to talk. Today."

I felt like I was being called into the principal's office. "OK," I said.

"Can you be here at two?" she said, sternly.

"OK," I said again, guiltily. I hung up and tried to call Harris again. Nothing. This was a disaster. Had I thrown it all away? Why now? And where the hell was Harris? I had visions of Sybil and Christine, nefariously plotting to imprison him in Sybil's Larchmont wine cellar, bound and gagged. *You will never see that woman again as long as I have breath in my body! And she will never work in this town again!* "Come on, Harris, pick up, pick up," I said, calling him again. I ran home as fast as I could, clutching the paper, watching out for paparazzi, suddenly paranoid that everyone was watching me.

I took a cab to Rockefeller Center to meet with the Ovation Network people. I was feeling queasy, and I hoped it was from nerves, not the flu. This was no time to get sick. I was mostly terrified that I would be fired . . . but for what, I wasn't sure. For fraternizing with the host's offspring? For considering a business opportunity?

When I walked into the conference room, everyone was smiling.

"Faith, I'm Cathy Tower," said one of the women, standing up. "We spoke on the phone a few months ago about your mojito recipe?" She had long red hair and a lot of freckles. She shook my hand. "Please have a seat, and I'll explain why you're here." I sat down.

"Faith, as you may be aware, your picture was in the *New York Sentinel* with Sybil's son, Harry."

"Yes . . ." I said. "Was that . . . not allowed?"

"On the contrary," she said. "It's great publicity so close to the finale, but we just want to make clear some ground rules."

"Like what? Like no more sleeping with Sybil's family members? Because Alice and I have a date tonight . . ."

Cathy Tower blushed. "Well . . ."

Several people around the table chuckled. "I love her," said one of the women.

Cathy Tower pushed a paper across the table to me. I didn't look at it. "What is it?" I said.

"This simply states that you have not had any contact with Sybil herself during the period between the last challenge and the finale, and that you have in no way attempted to influence her decision, nor will you at any time. We would also like you to agree not to see Harris again until after the finale." *That shouldn't be a problem, seeing as I can't even find him,* I thought, morosely. "This is for our protection and yours, in case of any controversy about who wins and who does not win *Domestic Goddess.*"

"Did Harris sign one of these?" I said.

Cathy Tower paused. "Yes," she said. "He did."

So they'd gotten to him, too. He wasn't imprisoned. Or dead. Or any of the other horrible things I'd imagined. He'd just promised not to see me.

"Also, there is the matter of the Have Faith mojito," said a dark-haired, bushy-eyebrowed man at the end of the table. "We would like to be involved in any negotiations to sell that formula."

"No," I said firmly. "It's in my contract that you don't have rights to that. I have proof that I invented it before the show."

The room was silent. Finally, Cathy Tower spoke up. "Well, we'll have our lawyers iron out all the details with your lawyers," she said. She must not realize that I was about to sign away the right to *see* my lawyer. "In the meantime, I assume you haven't actually had dealings with Sybil herself, nor tried to influence her, and that you'll sign this form."

I read it over to be sure they hadn't snuck in some cocktail-recipe-stealing clause. It looked straightforward, but I wished Harris was there to read it. I noticed that Sybil had already signed it. But she wasn't in the room, thank God. I signed.

"Is Sybil . . . angry about this?" I asked.

"She was unhappy with your efforts to sell the mojito," said Cathy Tower. "I'm not aware of her feelings about . . . the rest of it," she said.

"But I'm not disqualified?" I asked.

"No," said Cathy Tower. Some of the group exchanged glances. I wondered if that meant some had wanted to disqualify me. Maybe Sybil had wanted to disqualify me. "Now, during the finale, there will be a question-and-answer session. If this whole business with Harry comes up, or questions about your liquor deal, can you tell us what you plan to say?"

"Look, you people controlled every aspect of my existence for two months. From now on, I'm going to live my life the way I want to live it." *Unless you start working for Sybil Hunter,* I thought. "I haven't had any contact with Sybil, and I will not be trying to influence anybody about anything. But all's fair in love and reality TV." I stood up. "Is that all?"

"For now," Cathy Tower said. "Thank you. And we'll see you at the finale next week. Good luck!"

No. No no no no no. This can't be happening.

The finale was just days away, and I sat on the bathroom floor, the pregnancy test in my hand, its little pink plus sign innocently mocking me. So I thought I was going to get my own TV show, did I? So I thought I was going to be the next big liquor mogul, did I? So I thought I could live happily ever after with the man of my dreams, did I? That pink plus sign was like a giant X over my career, my plans, my partnerless life.

Harris had said he loved me, and I'd believed him. But maybe none of that mattered now. They'd finally succeeded in separating us. Was I stupid? Naive? Would I soon see a wedding announcement in the paper, with a picture of Harris and Christine? And now I was *pregnant with his child*?

I held my head in my hands and whispered the words: "No no no no no."

And yet, some small, glowing, radiant part of me was saying . . . *yes.*

The cold bathroom tile felt good, helping to quell my nausea.

I imagined a future on my own. No man to depend on, just me and a baby and my career. I would have to do everything myself. I was completely broke and alone. I was kind of famous at the moment, but if I didn't win, that fame would be all too temporary. I put my hand on my soon-to-be-expanding stomach. "Are you in there?" I whispered. "Are you really in there? We can get through this. We can do this together. It's going to be OK. Even if it's just you and me. I promise, it's going to be OK."

The phone rang. I jumped up. Could it finally be him?

"Faith Brightstone?" It was a man's voice, but it wasn't Harris. "This is Bill, the therapist from *Domestic Goddess*. I'm checking in with all the contestants to see how you're doing. How is everything going? Is there anything I can do?"

I laughed. "Bill, how much time do you have?"

chapter thirty-two

I had to look better than this! I stared at myself in the mirror. My breasts were swollen and tender, a symptom of pregnancy I guessed, and although I'd been too queasy to eat, I was obviously retaining water, which had softened some of my sharper edges and given me a fuller, more curvaceous look. Or bloated look, if I was going to be realistic about it. I put on the cute red dress I'd picked out, but my boobs looked even more gigantic than usual, and the skirt felt too tight. What a disaster. The morning of the *Domestic Goddess* finale, and I had to completely rethink my wardrobe. I ransacked my closet looking for something less fitted and revealing. I finally settled on a red silk blouse and a white suit with a pleated skirt and a blazer buttoned over my slightly swollen midsection. It wasn't what I'd pictured myself wearing, but it would have to do.

It was a frigid January day, and I had to be at the studio for Sybil's morning show, along with the other contestants, for a prefinale Q&A. On the way out the door, I grabbed my warmest down parka, said good-bye to Muffin, and at the last minute, put the pregnancy test in my coat pocket. I wasn't sure why. In case I needed to show Harris? In case I collapsed onstage and the EMTs needed to know I was pregnant? So I wouldn't feel so alone? This time, no cameras followed me into the studio or hovered over me when I saw all my old cast mates again. Sybil's morning show was popular, but nothing like the pressure we'd experience tonight at the live finale. *It's the warm-up,* I told myself. *Don't be nervous. It's just the morning show.*

As soon as I arrived at the studio, I hugged Monica, Mikki, and Christophe. I gave Chaz a huge hug—I was so glad to see him again. I smiled at Katie but she looked away. I didn't even try to approach Shari or Nadine, and although Jodi Sue was on my team, she was giving me the cold shoulder. Linda and Sadie nodded to me, and then Andy walked in the room and squeezed me from behind. "Wow, baby, what's up with the bodacious tatas?" he said. "What have you been doing right?"

"Eating and sleeping again?" I said. Although it wasn't true. When Sybil's staff brought crab puffs and crudités to the green room, where we were all waiting to go on camera, all I could do was nibble on a piece of celery.

Sybil came in a few moments later. She walked by me, then stopped and looked me up and down, as if she was registering that something was different. She didn't say anything. A momentary pause, and then she moved on. Self-consciously, I buttoned another button on my blazer. The way she looked at me made me paranoid. "It's so good to see all of you again," she said in a voice that implied she didn't think it was good to see us at all.

The show went as smoothly as could be expected. Sybil spent a long time talking up the finale and telling the audience how lucky they were to get a sneak preview. The morning show audience was cheerful and liked to applaud. Sybil interviewed us as we all sat together on the tasteful couches. Sybil didn't bring up Harris and didn't look at me at all. There was also plenty of tension between Shari and me. I didn't look at or speak to her, but our falling-out was the elephant in the room. It had been broadcast for the world to see on the final episode, yet Shari chatted cheerfully to Sybil and the cameras about the extreme challenges of her celebrity baby shower, how much work it was, how much Nadine and Katie and Linda did to help her.

But everybody in the audience wanted to know about our fight. When an audience member asked me if Shari and I were still friends, I paused, then said, "I wish Shari all the best. We've had an . . . interesting and sentimental journey together, and tonight will be the next step in that journey."

When someone stood up and asked, "Shari, you were so mean to turn on Faith like that, why did you do it?" Shari said something about the pressures of the final challenge and how the whole thing got blown out of proportion and about how the editing made it look worse than it really was. She ended with something about how she knew we'd be friends again someday. I hardly heard her. I tried to smile, but I felt dizzy and sick. I knew it wasn't true that we would ever be friends again. I was surprised how invested the audience seemed to be in our friendship. I suppose it's a timeless theme—the betrayal of a friend.

Nobody asked me about Harris. It was clear from the questions that they had been screened. Sybil surely wouldn't have allowed a question about her son. My fight with Shari was the perfect distraction.

Finally, at the end of the segment, we all gathered on Sybil's couches and she passed us each a glass of champagne. Even as it was happening, my mind was on tonight—on the finale.

"I would like to propose a toast, to all of you, and especially to Shari and Faith, for making it all the way through the contest. May the best Domestic Goddess win!" Everyone raised their glasses, but I didn't drink, I put my glass down.

Sybil looked at me, then at my untouched glass. "Are you feeling all right, Faith?" she asked, coldly. "I'd hate to see you get sick right before the live finale."

"No, I'm fine, just a little . . . under the weather," I said. *Calm down, Faith. There's no way she could know you're pregnant.* But then I thought: *Doesn't the devil know all?*

After Sybil's morning show, I walked around the city with Chaz to clear my head and try to quell my nausea before the next piece. He was nice and didn't ask too much about Harris. We spent the time trying to get into Sybil's head. "It's not about who's the best," Chaz said. "It's about the numbers and the bottom line. Sybil will choose whomever Sybil wants to choose—with the approval of the network. But Faith," he said, taking my hand, "seriously, you don't want to win. You want to come in second. You don't want to work for that bitch."

"I don't like to come in second," I said. "In horse racing, you can lose by a nose and it counts for nothing. Sybil and I don't get along, but what else am I going to do? I can learn from her. She's truly committed to perfection. I admire her."

"Still?" Chaz said. "Oh, honey, she's a twenty-four-carat twat."

I couldn't help laughing. "Maybe you're right, but what else do I have? I need this." I was tempted to tell him why, since my reasons had completely changed, but I held my tongue.

Roxanne Howard came up to me while I was in the makeup chair and asked me how I was doing. I hardly knew what to say to her—she was the mastermind behind the whole torturous amazing experience, and I was intimidated. Did I despise her, or admire her? Maybe both. I couldn't even focus on her words. All I could do was obsess. "I'm fine . . . I think," I said.

"You'll be great, honey," she said. "They love you out there." I hoped she was right, but would it matter? Sybil's verdict was the only verdict.

And then I was waiting backstage, and it was surreal. I knew my friends were out there, and I even thought I heard Victoria cheering my name. I saw signs in the audience, "Team Faith" and "Team Shari" and "Faith + Harry," people shaking them up and down. The lights were so bright, I couldn't see anything very well—no faces, no Harris. Was he out there? I squinted toward the audience. I couldn't see them all from where I was standing. My face felt stiff with the thick makeup, my hair perfectly arranged and sprayed. My outfit felt tight and I was beginning to sweat. *Breathe, Faith. Breathe slowly. Calm down. Think about your answers, don't just blurt out any shit that comes into your head. Everyone's watching. It all hangs in the balance. Months of torture have all come down to this. Be smart. Think about what you say.* Then Shari was standing next to me. We didn't speak or look at each other. We just waited there together for the cue to come onstage.

I was dizzy with the intensity of it. And then the little sign lit up: ON AIR. And the show began.

The audience's cheering was deafening as Sybil came onstage, followed by Alice and Ian and Rasputin, wagging his tail. He obviously wasn't intimidated by the audience, but even Sybil looked overwhelmed. She smiled her chilly smile at the camera and the world, and even stumbled over her opening words, made nervous, perhaps, by the whole "primetime live" aspect of this show. None of us were used to that. It felt like a sports event. The audience thundered and the lights glared, so that I could hardly see. I was nervous, and excited, and terrified, all at once—because of the contest, and because he was out there in the audience, somewhere. I knew it. I could feel it.

First, they brought out our teams—Andy, Monica, and Jodi Sue, and then Katie, Linda, and Nadine. The rest of the contestants sat in the front row of the audience, looking well rested and excited. Sybil asked them about their experiences with the final challenges, and what they thought of us. I couldn't even listen to what they said, although I heard some bickering and shouting and the audience laughing. Andy was grinning, obviously the center of attention.

Be careful how you act, Faith, I told myself. *Be careful what you say. The cameras are relentless. They don't care if you look good or bad, smart or idiotic, whether you win or lose. It's all about the best shot, the most scandalous comment, the best possible entertainment.* I felt like I was about to enter Rome's Colosseum, where people were slaughtered by lions. Our slaughter would be metaphorical—cleaner—but just as devastating . . . and entertaining. I glanced at Shari. She looked as nervous as I felt. Then I heard Sybil asking each former contestant who should win. Predictably, all of Shari's team said Shari. I heard Andy say "Faith!" and Monica say "Faith!" and then I heard Sybil ask Jodi Sue. She paused, then said, "Shari." The audience made the "ooh" sound they make when someone says something scandalous.

"Let's bring them out!" Sybil said. Backstage, one of the wranglers pushed us forward and the cameras followed Shari and me as we walked onstage together, smiling for the cameras. *It all matters, how you look, how you stand, how you sit, how you speak. Do it right! She could still change her mind at the last minute. Whatever she's decided, she could still change her mind!*

The crowd went crazy, shrieking and screaming and applauding. I felt like I was in a dream. Shari and I waved and smiled with our perfect faces and perfect hair and perfect clothes, and then we each sat down on opposite ends of the long couches, next to our respective teams.

Sybil introduced clips of the final challenges, and I watched with interest, eager to focus on something I knew, something other than this strange, alien experience of live television.

I'd seen the challenges on the last episode, but these clips went into more detail, and it looked like Shari did well, but I was astounded at how much less she had to do than me. The baby shower was charming and the celebrity guests were polished and lovely . . . but I would have liked to see Shari try to pull off half of what I'd had to do. I couldn't believe we'd had the same budget and the same amount of time. Could Sybil see how much harder I'd worked?

I squinted toward the audience again. I saw Ruby Prasad, and then . . . I saw him, just as Sybil asked me a question.

"Faith, how do you think you and your team did during this challenge?"

Had he seen me looking at him? "I . . . well." *Don't get distracted, Faith. You'll never get another opportunity like this.* I smiled at Sybil. *Remember, Faith, this is live. Think before you speak.* "I think we did a fantastic job pulling off an extremely complicated and difficult challenge," I said carefully.

"Faith, you lost one of your team members before your event was over. Can you talk about why there was dissension on your team? What went wrong?"

I thought about that for a moment. I had to answer in just the right way, because I didn't want to look like I was trashing my teammates, and yet I had to stand up for myself so Sybil could be reassured that I wasn't weak, that I was strong and capable and could handle anything. Suddenly I felt very calm and rational.

"Doing a challenge on this show isn't exactly like managing a team to produce an event," I said. "I have a lot of event-planning experience, but I've never had to hire people who were already angry at me."

"That was your fault, wasn't it?" Sybil said, slyly.

"Oooh," said the audience.

"I don't think so," I said, smiling. I wanted to add the word *bitch,* but edited myself. "Everyone in this contest who got eliminated is likely to be angry about it. We're all very 'type A,' very sure of ourselves, sure we all should have won. So by choosing three people who had made it pretty far in the competition, I was giving them a chance to prove to the world that *they* should have won, and I knew they would jump at that. I was counting on that motivation, their competitive spirit, even their egos, so that even if they didn't like me, they would do their best to pull off the challenge."

"Interesting strategy," Sybil said. "What about you, Shari? Did you feel your team was angry at you?"

"Not at *all,*" she said loudly. I could tell by her voice that she'd been back in Brooklyn for a while. "I appreciated every single member of my team for their unique skills, and they know exactly how much I appreciate them because I know how to show it." She gave me a sidelong glance.

"I may be straightforward and not the best at small talk and false praise," I said, "but I know how to get a job done right."

"Let's talk to our judges. Alice, what do you think?"

"I think"—Alice looked at both of us—"I think that Shari has a distinct personality that might not necessarily translate well to the network. While she might bring in a different segment, I'm not sure it's the most relevant segment. I think Faith is more tapped into the audience your network is seeking. She's passionate and creative, even if she's not always the most sensible person. I think she'd be a great host of her own show. I would vote for Faith."

The audience applauded. I gave Alice a grateful look and she smiled at me. Shari looked offended.

"And Ian? What about you?" Sybil said. "We all know you knew Faith from before this show, but who do you think is best suited to win *Domestic Goddess*?"

Ian shifted in his chair, his white hair gleaming in the bright light. His red nose could lead a sleigh. "Well, well, let me see," he said. "I do think Faith is a very nice woman. But a Domestic Goddess? Maybe not. I see Shari in that role, more than I see Faith. I think Shari has a lot of spunk and she seems more like a housewife to me. She's clearly skilled in the domestic arts. Yes, I think I'd have to go with Shari. No offense, my dear," he said, gesturing to me.

I nodded and smiled—none taken. The audience applauded again. Somebody yelled, "Team Shari!"

"Well," Sybil said, clapping her hands together. "It's time to make a decision, and here we go." She looked around at Alice and Ian. Alice looked hopeful. Ian looked bored. I held my breath. Sybil cast her eyes out over the audience. She seemed to be looking at Harris. Then she looked at me.

"Faith," she said, "you are ambitious, driven, and passionate about what you do. You are creative, but I also feel that your sense of humor is sometimes inappropriate, in ways that don't really fit in with the Sybil Hunter brand. You seem compelled to call attention to yourself, to dress and act in ways that demand people notice you, but then, as soon as you get noticed, you can be offensive. That's really not the Sybil Hunter way. Also, your team members aren't loyal to you. I know you appreciate what my company represents, and you are, I must admit, a competent cook, but I'm not sure you're Domestic Goddess material. I believe you may be too much of a show-off."

I heard a few people in the audience gasp. My stomach flip-flopped and I felt myself breaking out in a cold sweat. Inappropriate? Compelled to call attention to myself? Offensive? A *show-off*? I went from pale to flushed with embarrassment and anger. How could she say those things to me on live television? *Smile, Faith. Don't make a scene. Smile.* I wanted to drop dead right there on the stage, just to escape the humiliation.

After all I'd given up, the months of torture and effort, the sacrifice of my business, putting my whole life on hold, not being able to speak to my friends, being away from my dog, and I don't get so much as a thank-you, just a dig, just a humiliating insult? *Come on, Faith. Suck it up. You are inappropriate sometimes, and you know it. It doesn't mean you're a bad person. It doesn't mean she won't hire you. Maybe she'll be even worse to Shari.* I took a deep, shaky breath, gave the camera my best modest, appropriate, non-show-off smile, and waited.

Sybil looked at Shari. "Shari, you have consistently proven yourself competent and tasteful. Although I believe you could stretch yourself a little beyond your comfort zone, and you can be pushy, I believe your personal style and method are more in line with the Sybil Hunter brand. You are in touch with the women who embrace my lifestyle, and you are not just our target audience here at SHE, but you have a lot to offer us in terms of your perspective and your ideas."

That's it? All she gets is a "stretch yourself a bit more, dear"? I began to get a sinking feeling, one I hadn't let myself really indulge in until this moment, right there on live television. I began to suspect that maybe I wasn't going to win this thing.

"Faith, Shari," Sybil said, her eyes glittering with what looked to me like malice, "you've both done very well, but only one of you can be the next *Domestic Goddess*." Silence. The long pause. The torturous pause. My eyes met Shari's, and she smiled nervously at me. I tried to smile back, but I couldn't. And then Sybil turned to Shari.

"Shari, congratulations. You are the next *Domestic Goddess*."

Everything began to move in slow motion. Sybil stood up, then Shari stood up, beaming for the cameras, and Sybil shook Shari's hand, and then Alice stood up and walked right off the stage without acknowledging anyone, and then Ian stood up, gave me a sympathetic look, and went over to congratulate Shari.

I turned, the lights and crowd a moving blur, and walked over to Shari and shook her hand and hugged her and said "Congratulations," and my voice sounded hollow and the crowd noises echoed around me and Shari beamed at me and said, in a voice that sounded strange and slow, "I'm sorry for everything, I hope we can still be friends." I couldn't answer, I just turned away, and then I saw Harris, right there in the front row, standing up, his face red with anger. He looked at his mother, and then he looked at me, and then his whole face changed, flooded with an emotion I couldn't read, and then he turned and stormed out of the studio.

I stood there onstage, the cameras closing in to catch the emotions of the loser, trying to smile, as people patted my back and shook my hand and offered their condolences and whispered that I should have won. I tried to keep a smile on my face, but my whole body had gone cold. Chaz hugged me. "You'll see someday soon how lucky you are," he whispered, and then he was gone.

The only thing I knew how to do was go home, but as I turned toward the green room, I almost collided with the woman from Bacchus Global. "I'm so sorry!" she said. "I didn't mean to run into you like that."

"That's all right," I said, trying to pull myself together. "What are you doing here?"

"The board wanted me to come and see how you did. And to bring you some news . . . not good news, I'm afraid. You see, I haven't been able to convince them to invest in your pink lemonade mojito. I tried, I really did, and if you had won the show, well, maybe it would have been different, but . . . well, I'm sorry," she said. "But it was very nice to meet you." She held out her hand. I looked down at it, then turned and walked away.

I found my coat and purse, and then I went outside, and without looking back, I began the long, long walk home.

It took me almost an hour to walk back to my apartment from the studio, but I needed the cold night air to clear my head. I'd crashed and burned. I'd been so high for so long, going through it all, and then so anxious and obsessed waiting, waiting for that moment, and now I felt a crushing emptiness. I was going back to my old life of scraping by, being broke. I was so disappointed in myself. I needed to forget I'd ever heard of a woman named Sybil Hunter. I considered the best ways to burn those cookbooks. Finally, I saw my apartment building in the distance.

And then I saw him in front of it.

I stopped. He hadn't seen me yet. He was pacing, his hands in his pockets, his cheeks red from the January cold. His breath came out in clouds of frost and his brow was furrowed. I couldn't believe he was here. What did he want? Was he angry at me? Was he coming to say good-bye? Or . . .

I walked quickly toward him, trying not to run, and then he saw me. He looked so relieved, and I felt like I was coming home to something I'd desperately missed, that I'd been without for too long. I walked up to him and stopped.

"Hi," he said.

"Hi." I paused. "I lost," I said, not knowing what else to say.

"I know," he said. He looked miserable. "I . . . need to explain."

"Damn right you do," I said. I crossed my arms, protecting myself, protecting my heart.

"I don't know how to say this," he said, looking at the ground. "So I guess I'll just say it."

"OK," I said. "I'm waiting." The air was cold but I was burning up inside, with anger and grief and despair and desire.

"After that picture of us appeared in the paper, my mother, as you can imagine, was angry. She ordered me never to see you again."

"And you're such a mama's boy that you agreed? After everything? After . . ." I swallowed. I wanted to say, *after saying you loved me,* but I couldn't get the words out. I was too afraid.

"Wait, hold on," he said. "I didn't agree. I told her it was none of her business. I told her to go screw herself."

I couldn't help laughing a little. "You told your mother to go screw herself?"

"Well . . . maybe not in those exact words," he said. "But still, I absolutely refused to stop seeing you. And then . . ."

"And then what?" I said. "What could she possibly have said to keep you away?"

I thought he might start crying. *Oh God, Harris, don't start crying,* I silently begged him. "She said . . . she told me that if I agreed to stop seeing you, then . . . then she would choose you to win."

"What?" I said. "What?"

"I know. It was stupid. And probably illegal. But she was so angry about the footage of us on the show, and then after our picture was in the paper, she was absolutely determined to keep us apart. It was a bribe. But . . ."

"But what?"

"Look, Faith, I knew how much this meant to you. I knew how much you wanted it, how much you *needed it.* I thought it was the most important thing to you."

I didn't say anything for a moment. He was right, in a way. I'd spent the last six months obsessing to him about winning the show. It was all I ever said I really wanted.

"I did want it. I thought I wanted it," I said. "But don't you see that I never wanted it the way I wanted you? Even from that first night we met." I tried to swallow the lump in my throat threatening to make me burst into tears. It was so hard for me to admit, but being without him had made me realize how much I never wanted to be without him again. "Don't you know I'd rather have you than that stupid show?"

"No," he said, shaking his head. "I don't know that. When I said I loved you, you didn't say anything back. And I know how important your career is to you. It was never about doing what my mother wanted. I wanted to give you what you wanted the most—even if it meant giving you up."

I started to cry.

"But when she chose Shari over you anyway, when she went back on our agreement, after swearing to me that she would pick you to win, I realized that there are no certainties in life. You can't manipulate fate. When I look at myself, and my own life, I realize it doesn't mean anything without you. When I couldn't call you, I was so miserable that I realized I can't be with anyone else. When she went back on her word and named Shari the winner, I was set free."

Then he did something that blew me away. He knelt down on one knee in front of me, right there in front of my building. The doorman leaned out to watch. A woman walking her dog slowed down as she passed us. Then Harris reached into his pocket and pulled out a little velvet box. He opened it and held it up to me. It was a large sparkling diamond solitaire on a platinum band set with tiny diamonds. It was the most beautiful ring I'd ever seen. Was this really happening?

I reached into my pocket and pulled out the pregnancy test. "I'll trade you," I said.

He stared at the little plastic stick in my hand for a moment, and then a look of recognition came over his face. Then, it was as if a great weight was lifted from his brow. He leapt to his feet and pulled me into his arms. "Oh my God," he said, his face pressed against my neck. "I can't believe it."

Then he pulled back and looked at me. "Is it mine?"

"No, it's the doorman's. I was just coming to tell him." The doorman was still watching us. "Hey, buddy, guess what?" I yelled to him. "I'm having your baby!"

The doorman ducked back inside the building. Harris laughed. "You're crazy," he said.

"And you already have too many crazy women in your life?"

"I think I could use one more." He pulled me back against his chest. He felt so warm.

"I could do this alone," I whispered in his ear, wrapping my arms around his neck. "But I'd rather do it with you."

"We're going to be a family," he whispered back, pressing his cheek to mine. "Faith, Faith, I love you."

I pulled back from him and looked him straight in the eye. I took a deep breath, and then I said it: "Harris, I love you, too."

We heard about it first on television. Harris was getting ready for work, and I was still lying in bed, trying to figure out what to do with my life next, when I flipped past the Entertainment News channel.

"Domestic Devil?" the host said. "Author, entrepreneur, and television personality Sybil Hunter just wrapped her *Domestic Goddess* reality show finale, but she may also have inadvertently wrapped her career." The screen flashed an unflattering picture of Sybil with her mouth open. "This morning, anonymous sources leaked this recording of Hunter, talking about the contestants on her popular reality show."

"Harris, get in here!" I yelled. He came out of the bathroom in his boxers with shaving cream on his face, to the sound of his mother's voice. The words showed up on the screen, as she spoke:

"They're all a disaster. Every one of them. I don't want to hire any of them. They're all ridiculous."

A muffled voice responded, saying something like "Contractually, I think you have to hire one of them."

Sybil answered: "I don't care about a fucking piece of paper, I can do whatever I want to do. I'm Sybil Hunter."

The barely audible voice said something about how she had handpicked the contestants.

Sybil answered: "Handpicked? I disown any responsibility for that. I don't even know where they got these people. Faith should probably win. She'd be great on her own show, which is exactly why I'm not going to choose her. I can't stand that girl, and I can't wait until the day I never have to see her again. I suppose I'll just choose that whiny, simpering, ass-kissing Shari to win, but I can guarantee that as soon as she's hired, she's fired, so my business can go on operating at the standard I expect."

The anchorwoman came back onscreen. "Sources at Ovation Network claim that Hunter may be fired, for violating her contract. No word on whether plans for Hunter's new SHE network will be influenced by these events, or whether the winner of *Domestic Goddess* will actually receive the promised prize."

Harris and I stared at each other. "No fucking way," I said.

I slumped back into the pillows. She couldn't stand me? She couldn't wait until she never had to see me again? I laughed out loud. The woman was about to become my mother-in-law! And Shari . . . poor Shari. I almost felt sorry for her. What an awful thing to come out on national television—Sybil Hunter calling her a simpering ass-kisser.

But it all made sense now. She chose Shari because she never intended to give her a show at all. Had she chosen me, I wouldn't have gone down without a fight, and she probably knew it. Especially if I was with her own son. And she couldn't stand me! I smiled. In a way, it was a huge relief just to hear her say it.

I wondered who hated Sybil enough to secretly record her, then leak something like that to the press. I thought momentarily about Polly. Could it be? Or Alice? Whoever it was . . . well, I was impressed.

Harris ran back into the bathroom, wiped the shaving cream off of his face, then came back out and grabbed his phone. "I need to call her," he said.

"I thought she wasn't speaking to you," I said.

"She's not, but if she needs legal advice, I have to at least offer it. If she doesn't want it, then that's her call," he said. "But she may really be in some serious trouble here."

"Will her new network be in jeopardy?" I said.

"Maybe. Although who knows what will happen. She's always been a fighter. Just like you," he said.

"I always knew we had a lot in common," I said. "Although that scares me." And then the phone rang.

"Faith Brightstone?" the voice said.

"Yes?"

"This is Roxanne Howard."

"Wow," I said. "Hi, Roxanne." I turned down the sound on the television.

"Look, Faith, I wouldn't normally be calling you directly, but I called around and you don't seem to have an agent."

"No," I said. An agent? Why would I need an agent?

"I'd like to talk to you about a little proposition. Can you come into the office?"

"Can you tell me what it's about first?" I said.

"Sure, I suppose I can," she said. "You may have heard about recent events involving Sybil Hunter."

"I just heard, actually," I said.

"Yes, well. It looks like great changes are afoot. We've canceled *Domestic Goddess*. There won't be a second season. We've also canceled Sybil's daytime show."

I gave Harris a look. "What?" he mouthed to me. I shushed him.

"Faith, we're in the process of considering replacements for those slots, and I have an idea for a show that I'd like you to consider. We want to call it *Have Faith*. It would be a completely new kind of reality show. We would follow you around in your normal life, and make a show out of *you*."

"Make a show out of *me*?" I said. "Who would want to watch that?"

"I have no doubt it would be extremely popular. You were the fan favorite on *Domestic Goddess*, so you've already got a fan base. People want to know what happens next, with you, with your career, and with Harry. Are you two getting married?"

"I . . . I think so," I said. I'd said yes, but I still couldn't quite believe I would be able to go through with a wedding.

"Excellent, TV gold," she said. "And don't take this the wrong way, but I heard from Sybil that you're pregnant. Is that true?"

"It is," I said.

"Platinum!" she said. "There's nothing more engaging on a show for women than a pregnancy. If you can come down to the studio to-morrow, I can talk to you about all the details." The sound of her voice gave me a creepy feeling. My baby was a profit opportunity?

"Look, Roxanne . . . I don't know," I said. "I think I'm kind of done with reality television."

"Honey, you don't want to miss this opportunity," she said. "You've gotta strike while the iron is hot. It's happening for you right now. Don't lose your momentum."

"Let me think about it," I said.

"That's all I ask," she said. "Of course, Harry would have to agree to be part of the show. And that adorable little baby you're going to have, too. It will be all about your family. Call me when you're ready to schedule a meeting. And I'm quite confident that you'll be calling."

I hung up the phone. "Harris?" I said. He came back into the bed-room. He'd put his suit on and was tying his tie. He looked adorable. Roxanne's words echoed in my ears: *Your family.* I had no doubt Harris would be extremely telegenic. The world would fall in love with him. But did I really want to put him through all that?

"Yes, my irresistible wife-to-be?" he said, kneeling on the bed and wrapping his arms around me.

epilogue

I peeked out from behind the white curtains that separated my dressing area at the Waldorf Hotel from the rest of the ballroom. I was six months pregnant, it was a gorgeous June day, and I was in the most beautiful white wedding dress I'd ever seen.

I saw all my friends gathered there, in chairs facing the altar—Victoria, Jennifer, and Samantha, Bronwyn and her husband, Chaz and Monica, Mikki and Christophe, and my bakery assistant, Alanna. My old friends Perry and Jeannie had both flown in from L.A., and at the last minute, Larry Todd, my old boss, had decided to fly in, too. "It will be like going to my own daughter's wedding," he'd said over the phone.

Sybil Hunter was there, of course—she couldn't miss her son's wedding, even if he was marrying me. She sat in the front row, on the groom's side. She was going to be my mother-in-law, for better or for worse, and we'd both have to get used to that prospect.

My own mother sat primly on the other side, trying not to stare at Sybil Hunter, looking like she had a bad taste in her mouth. And then I gasped—my father was there, standing uncomfortably against the back wall, with a bouncy and smiling Brooke on his arm.

Nobody saw me peeking through the curtains, but I saw them all, and it was perfect, no matter what had happened in the past, no matter who had said or done what. They were all here, all come together to usher me into my happily ever after, and whatever happened after this moment would be up to me. I was done blaming other people for my unhappiness. I was done being unhappy. And if my life was not about to be perfect, it was about to change in ways I'd only dreamed.

After much discussion, Harris and I had turned down Roxanne Howard's offer to do a reality show about our lives, but had made her a counteroffer: I would do a show more like the show Sybil Hunter had done—a talk show with guests and cooking and tips for making life easier and better, but for a younger generation of women. It would be funnier, lighter, more irreverent, like talking to your girlfriends. I might even throw in a mixology segment now and again. We agreed the show could still be called *Have Faith*, and Harris could come onto the show only when and if he wanted to. And as for our daughter—the sonogram had revealed last month that we were having a baby girl—well, we would keep her off screen, at least for now.

After Bacchus Global had turned down our deal for the Have Faith Pink Lemonade Mojito, one of the other companies I'd called, Summit Liquors, changed their minds after hearing I'd scored my own show. They made me an offer I couldn't refuse. I was going to bottle my signature cocktail and sell it after all. And I had a million other ideas, all waiting to happen. My future was wide open. No limits. Just space—and love.

Then I saw Harris. He was at the front of the room, in his tuxedo, looking nervous and handsome and beautiful. He was waiting for me. He turned, feeling my gaze, and our eyes met. His face relaxed. He smiled.

Then the music started, and I stepped out from behind the curtain, on no one's arm, on my own two feet, to begin my next great adventure.

acknowledgments

Thank you to my fans. I would never be anywhere close to where I am without your support. You have accepted me, embraced my flaws, and taken such an incredible journey with me. This next stop on that journey is filled with so much passion and joy that I know you will love it as much as if not more than anywhere I have taken you before.

Thank you to Jeremy Katz. You were the first book agent who believed in me, and I will never forget beginning this incredible journey with you. Thank you to Zachary Schisgal. You gave me my first break in this industry and believed in what I had to say. Without that faith, I wouldn't have succeeded enough to take this remarkable leap in my writing career. Thank you to Julie Plake. You have been so excited and passionate about this book. I would love the excitement in your eyes after you read each chapter. Thank you, Jacqueline Lagratta. You were there when the idea of fiction was first introduced, and were so enthusiastic about this being the best next step in my literary journey.

Thank you so much to Touchstone, the only publisher that I will ever know. We've had three great successes together, and it has been a thrilling ride together. In particular, thank you to Stacy Creamer. You are such a courageous and creative woman, and it was you, with the help of Matthew Benjamin, who brought up the crazy idea of my writing a novel. At that moment it seemed insane, and it became the most inspiring, thrilling journey of my entire career. Writing this book filled me with so much joy that it felt like it was writing itself. Thank you to Matthew Benjamin. You have been so wonderful to work with. I appreciate your love and passion for the process. Thank you to Marcia Burch. It has been an honor to collaborate with you to make all of my books a success.

Thank you to my BlackBerry. You make it possible for me to be anywhere in the world and still write. Try not to break down and give me any more aggravation going forward.

Thank you to Eve Adamson. You are a gift, a positive support system, and an incredible partner. You and I together define "A Place of Yes."

Thank you to Jason Hoppy, my husband. You are incredibly supportive and such a positive force in my endeavors. Thanks for believing in this idea. I love you. Thank you to my beloved dog, Cookie. You and I have been through everything together. Your fur at my feet is all a girl really needs. Thank you to my baby bumblebee, Bryn Casey Hoppy. You are the joy and love in my life and the spark to my imagination to just let the words flow.

Skinnydipping

Faith Brightstone moves to Los Angeles determined to have it all—a successful acting career, a Malibu beach house, and a gorgeous producer boyfriend. While she has no problem finding her way in the party scene, her career and soulmate hopes are promptly dashed when her job turns out to be as a glorified servant to a sadist and her sleaze meter fails her miserably on the man front. Fast-forward five years and Faith has returned to New York and is finally finding her groove as an entrepreneur. When she lands a spot on a new reality TV show hosted by her idol—the legendary Sybil Hunter—her life is completely turned upside down. In the bizarre world of reality TV, Faith's loud mouth makes her both an instant star in front of the camera and also labeled a troublemaker by Sybil. When the show comes to a dramatic close, Faith discovers that the man of her dreams may have just walked into her life. Will she choose fame or love? Or can she have it all?

For Discussion

1. Faith says, "All I'd ever really wanted out of life was success in my chosen career, and perfect, passionate, eternal love with a hot and preferably independently wealthy soulmate." How do these dual objectives propel the plot of *Skinnydipping?* To what extent does one goal seem to take priority over the other? How would you characterize Faith's sense of irony?

2. How does Faith's brief stay with her estranged father impact her? How do her father's Hollywood connections help Faith? What do you think accounts for Faith's resourcefulness and drive?

3. On the set of *Hollywood & Highland,* Faith surveys the scene before her and thinks, "They were living the dream. Chic, beautiful, rich. And here I was—making photocopies and getting coffee. I had to catch up—I felt a sense of urgency, my career clock ticking." What motivates Faith? Have you ever felt a similar feeling that your "clock" was ticking?

4. How does Faith's on-the-spot creation of a pink lemonade mojito at a party anticipate her success as a reality television star? What does her inventiveness and knack for improvisation reveal about her as a character?

5. Consider the similarities Faith Brightsone's character shares with Bethenny Frankel. How does "life imitate art" in *Skinnydipping?* How did these parallels affect your reading experience?

6. How much of Faith's attraction to Australian producer Vince Beck is grounded in her desire for professional advancement? How much of her interest in him is physical? Emotional?

7. What aspects of Faith's job as personal assistant to Carol Kameron prepare her for the competition that she faces on the reality TV show *Domestic Goddess*? How are Carol's expectations similar to those of Sibyl Hunter? Would you watch *Domestic Goddess* if it were on television?

8. "My heart was torn in two, but I also felt cool and calm. I'd been released—from my obsession, from this path I was one, from Los Angeles itself." Discuss Faith's time in Los Angeles—the friends she made, the challenges she encountered, and the lessons she learned. How did this experience shape her? Did she have to first fail in order to succeed?

9. Of the many hilarious scenes in *Skinnydipping*, which did you find most memorable? Why?

10. How does Faith's move from Los Angeles to New York signal a return to her "true" identity? How does her encounter at the Fancy Food show propel her in a new direction? To what extent does Faith's experience in show business make her a more successful small business owner?

11. What about Faith's personality attracts the producers of *Domestic Goddess*? Why would a celebrity entrepreneur like Sibyl Hunter feel threatened by Faith's charisma? Were you surprised when Sibyl's true intentions were revealed?

12. A series of coincidences unfold when Faith accepts a spot on *Domestic Goddess*. Given the many unusual circumstances that could potentially disqualify Faith from the competition, why is she allowed to continue? Do you think this is a true-to-life ac-

count of what it is like to be on a reality television show? Why or why not?

13. Discuss Faith and Harris's relationship. How does he compare to the other men in her life? What makes him different? What challenges must they overcome in order to be with one another?

14. "My future was wide open. No limits. Just space—and love." Discuss the conclusion of the *Skinnydipping*. How has Faith grown as a character? Were you surprised that she and Harris turned down Roxanne Howard's initial offer? Do you have an lingering questions?

A Conversation with Bethenny Frankel

Skinnydipping is your debut novel. What inspired you to tell Faith Brightstone's story? How was the experience of writing fiction different from your previous experience writing *A Place of Yes: 10 Rules for Getting Everything You Want Out of Life?*

Truthfully, I never even dreamed of writing a novel. I'm such a literal person, and I had so much about my personal journey to communicate that I initially wasn't drawn to fiction. My publisher was the one who proposed the idea to me. It took me a few minutes to warm up to it. Then my imagination ran wild. I have found this to be the most creative, liberating process of my career. The book was writing itself. The reader will devour it.

Your fictional protagonist, Faith Brightstone, shares more than a few parallels with you. Was it cathartic to "write what you know"? What do you hope readers take away after reading *Skinnydipping?*

Everything I do is largely inspired by my experiences. I definitely know Faith Brightstone through and through. We have many parallels and many differences. I think she is a great and inspiring character.

You are a mother, a beloved television personality, and a business mogul. How did you find the time to write *Skinnydipping?* Is it true that you wrote it in installments on your Blackberry?

I do all of my writing on my Blackberry. I'm always on the go. I'm not that person who holes up in a room for two weeks to write. I have spurts of creative energy and I need to purge it immediately and later piece it together. That's how I've written every book, blog, or article in my career.

As the creator of the Skinnygirl brand and a mother, how do you hope to influence your daughter's body image and relationship with food?

I no longer have any noise about food or body image, so we don't worry at all about Bryn. These issues begin in the home. "Diet" isn't even in our vocabulary, and there is no emphasis in these areas at all. Skinnygirl is one word. It isn't about being skinny any more than "Apple" computers are about a fruit.

To what extent did your experience in the world of reality television influence *Skinnydipping*? Do you have a favorite reality show?

I don't have a favorite reality TV show. I flip around. Unfortunately, it has become very redundant. I'm not sure how much is "reality." Of course I have been influenced by being on reality television for more seasons than I care to admit. Don't hate the player. Hate the game.

You've said that you're not the type of person who has regrets. Can the same be said of Faith Brightstone?

Faith is at the beginning of her journey. I'm not sure that she knows yet if she regrets some of her decisions. That remains to be seen. Maybe in the next book we'll find out if it was worth the price.

What is on your nightstand? What was the last great book you read?

Live Wire by Harlan Coben, a Chelsea Handler book, and my therapist's book *I'm Right. You're Wrong. Now What?* Basically I read whatever someone sends or gives me and what is next to me. There isn't a method whatsoever. I'm just happy to be reading anything with my crazy schedule.

If you were planning a book club meeting for *Skinnydipping*, what would be on the menu? What would you serve?

Mini crab cakes, pigs in blankets with spicy mustard, caramelized onion, and smoked cheese quesadillas, and lots of Skinnygirl cocktails.

Faith lives by the maxim "Have Faith." What is your personal motto?

"Come from a place of yes" or "Go big or go home."

Can you envision a sequel to *Skinnydipping*? Will readers ever find out what happens at Faith's first family Thanksgiving with her new mother-in-law, Sybil Hunter?

I very strongly believe that there will be a sequel. Faith is just at the beginning.

Enhance Your Book Club

1. In *Skinnydipping*, Faith Brightstone makes her way from relative unknown to celebrity. Along the way, she takes a series of jobs that are far from glamorous. Can you relate to her experience in any way? What jobs have you taken in your career that lead you to unexpected places? Have you ever accepted situations that were less than ideal in order to get closer to your goal? Share and discuss your responses with your book club members.

2. Faith's "Have Faith" brand launches her into stardom and success. Tap into your entrepreneurial side with your book club members! If you started your own company or small business, what would you call it? What would you produce or sell?

3. Host a Skinnygirl book club party for your discussion of *Skinnydipping*! Visit www.skinnydippingbybethenny.com for great recipes like Bethenny's Mock-a-Mole, and pair your menu with Skinnygirl cocktails or Faith Brightstone's Pink Lemonade Mojito. Cheers!

DON'T MISS ANY OF
BETHENNY'S
NEW YORK TIMES BESTSELLERS!

In *A Place of Yes*, Bethenny takes us on an empowering journey and provides more of her no-nonsense advice for getting the most out of life.

Naturally Thin started readers on the Skinnygirl journey—then Bethenny served up the next step in learning how to cook fearlessly and make the foods you love in *The Skinnygirl Dish*.

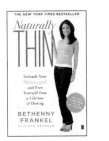

Available wherever books are sold or at www.simonandschuster.com

TOUCHSTONE
A Division of Simon & Schuster
A CBS COMPANY